Daniel Church

THE RAVENING

ANGRY
ROBOT

ANGRY ROBOT
An imprint of Watkins Media Ltd

Unit 11, Shepperton House
89 Shepperton Road
London N1 3DF
UK

angryrobotbooks.com
twitter.com/angryrobotbooks
In the deep dark wood.

An Angry Robot paperback original, 2024

Cover by Sarah O'Flaherty
Edited by Simon Spanton Walker and Andrew Hook
Set in Meridien

ISBN 978 1 91599 838 5
Ebook ISBN 978 1 91599 839 2

Printed and bound in the United Kingdom by CPI Group (UK) Ltd, Croydon CR0 4YY.

9 8 7 6 5 4 3 2 1

For Emma Bunn,
Beta-reader Extraordinaire.
MASHT!

THE LOST KNIGHT OF RUAD

In 1302 Christendom's last remaining possession in the Holy Land, the tiny coastal island of Ruad, fell to a Mamluk army under the command of Sayf al-Din Salar. Its garrison of Templar Knights surrendered following a promise of safe conduct, only to be massacred. The few survivors were taken to Cairo, where those who refused to convert to Islam died of starvation and ill-treatment.

Those are the facts. This is the legend:

After the slaughter, one of the Templars, Robert de Lavoie, could be found among neither the prisoners nor the dead. At first he was believed to have hidden in a room in the fortress, which had been locked from the inside. But when the door was forced, it was empty. No trace of de Lavoie was ever found.

Three Mamluk soldiers, however, claimed to have seen a figure flying away from the castle, although their stories were considered doubtful, the product of sunstroke or exhaustion. One insisted it was an angel, the second a demon or jinn; the third believed that it had been clutching a man in its arms, bearing him away.

Where the forest takes over
Where the forest gives birth
Lisa Baird

SKELETON SONG: TALLSTONE HILL, 2007

1.

The road through the forest didn't end. It unrolled in the headlights, the centre line flickering past like little white sparks. It was almost hypnotic; Elaine had to blink every few seconds to retain her focus.

There was a loud knocking sound and the car shuddered as if from a blow, then swerved. Elaine shouted in alarm; beside her, Jenna jumped and dropped her phone. Another knock sounded, and another, each one louder than the last.

The car swerved again, the steering wheel spinning out of Elaine's hands. "Shit," she said, and immediately bit her lip – she was forever chiding Jenna about her language and she wouldn't live down a slip like that – but then all that mattered was grabbing the wheel and steadying the car as it slewed across the road towards the ditch beside the tree-topped embankment.

With a final effort Elaine got the car into the left-hand lane and pumped the brakes. It juddered to a halt; there was a thump and the motor cut out, dead.

The only sounds were the hot engine ticking in the cold night air, and the tinny yammering of Kate Nash from Jenna's earbuds. She yanked them out, glaring at Elaine. "What the *fuck*, Mum?"

That kind of language would have earned Elaine a slap across the face at Jenna's age, but nowadays they'd call that child abuse. Political correctness gone mad, in Elaine's opinion, but this wasn't the time or place. It was pretty understandable anyway, given the shock; she'd be better letting it slide.

"I don't know," said Elaine, quite truthfully. She tried in vain to restart the engine, but it only made a faint, rattling groan. "God, I just had it *serviced*."

"Did we hit something?" said Jenna. "Deer or a rabbit?" She looked genuinely stricken at the thought: at fifteen, she already knew everything, despised her parents and humanity in general, but any hint of cruelty to animals reduced her to tearful anguish, unfocused rage, or both at once. She unfastened her seatbelt and opened the door.

"Jenna–" Elaine began, but might as well have tried to command the wind. Not for the first time, she thought she knew how King Canute had felt. Maybe he'd had teenage daughters too.

Jenna moved into the glare of the car headlights – the only source of illumination in the darkness and a decidedly limited one, as Elaine was uncomfortably aware. They reached a hundred or so yards ahead, beyond which the road might as well have ceased to exist. Likewise, the black trees looming atop the embankments could have extended beyond them for yards or miles. Impossible to tell.

"Can't see any blood," said Jenna.

"We didn't hit anything," said Elaine, hoping that was true. She'd been struggling to concentrate, had been wondering if she should pull over for a rest stop before carrying on; maybe her attention *had* wandered and something had run out in front of the car. Deer were tough: she remembered from working in the Claims Department how many vehicles ended up written off after cannoning into one, while the animal trotted away, seemingly none the worse for wear.

But surely a deer would have done far more damage. Unless it had been a baby one – and oh God, the fuss Jenna would make then! Some other woodland creature, maybe, like a badger.

Something moved outside Elaine's window. She choked back a cry of alarm, but not enough: Jenna – because that was who it was – shook her head in disgust, then walked on to inspect the back of the car.

Elaine put a hand to her mouth. So distracted she hadn't realised her daughter was next to her, and she was trying to convince herself she couldn't have run an animal over out of sheer inattention. *Or a person. Oh God, not that.* She threw the driver's door open and climbed out. "Jenna, don't."

"Get back in the car, Mum." Jenna scowled: the taillights' red glare made her look even more baleful, and the dark behind her more menacing. They didn't reach as far as the headlights, so there was even less of a clue as to what might be behind the car than what might lie ahead.

Elaine shook her head. They were in Cornwall; there were no wolves or bears or lions here. She shook her head again; Jenna snorted irritably, then turned and crouched behind the vehicle. "Nope," she said. "Doesn't look like you hit anything." She straightened up again. "Suppose we should be thankful for small mercies."

Without waiting for a reply, she walked back round to the passenger side and climbed into her seat. "Well?" Jenna said. "What now?"

Elaine returned to her seat and shut the door. "Not a problem. Just give the AA a call."

But, when she picked up her phone, there was no signal, not even for the emergency services. "Shit," she said again, but this time managed to do so under her breath.

Jenna rolled her eyes. "Told you that phone was crap."

"Jenna."

"You just said *shit*." Jenna rummaged in the passenger footwell, where she'd dropped her phone earlier as if it was so much rubbish – her brand-new BlackBerry, after she'd whined and pestered for the wretched, costly thing – then punched a button, finally shutting the racket from her earphones off. "Here. Try using a decent phone." Then her smug look faded. "Oh, bollocks."

"Isn't that working either?" Despite the circumstances Elaine felt a small, mean thrill of triumph, but it was short-lived: they were alone on a deserted road, in the dead of night and the middle of the woods, with no way to call for aid.

They could try and find help, but which way should they go? Elaine tried to remember the last road signs she'd seen, how far the next village was. She knew they were somewhere on a road called Tallstone Hill, but that was all: it was several miles long, and she wasn't sure how long they'd been on it. Elaine reached into the car, shouldering Jenna aside.

"Mum!"

"Sorry," Elaine mumbled, though even if Jenna heard her, it probably sounded more like an insult than an apology. She opened the glove compartment, found the atlas and studied it without enthusiasm: she was terrible at map-reading, normally leaving long journeys like this to Martyn.

This road was the final stretch of their journey, leading directly to the coastal village where they were staying, but it was still twenty or thirty miles in all. The question was how far along it they were.

She found the forest on the map, but the road passed through three other woodlands of various size too, and for all she knew the trees on either side of the road were just a narrow scrim beyond which was a farmhouse or even a village, if she only dared venture a little further.

The trees looked uncomfortably thick, but that was easy enough to settle. She leant past Jenna again, ignoring her snort of annoyance, got the torch out of the glove compartment and climbed out of the car.

Elaine crossed to the edge of the road and shone the torch into the trees. The light probed between trunks and branches, but only found more of the same.

Of course, the trees were atop an embankment – hard to see what was beyond them unless you were on the high ground yourself. Elaine stepped over the ditch onto the soft loam, glad she was wearing trainers rather than her usual heels.

"Mum?" Jenna's voice cracked slightly. "What are you doing?"

"It's all right, love," said Elaine, softening a little towards her. The fear in Jenna's voice had made her sound, just for a moment, like the little girl Elaine had read bedtime stories to, who'd clung to her arm when she heard about the witch in the gingerbread house or the Big Bad Wolf, her huge wide eyes full of fear but also trust, knowing her mother wouldn't let any harm come to her.

Everything was different now, of course. Elaine's friends had gone through the same with their teenage daughters, but she'd always told herself Jenna was different, special, because Jenna was *hers*.

Well, that had proven false, much like Martyn's belief that he'd never fall prey to male pattern baldness. Her daughter was full of an anger Elaine neither understood nor recognised; she might have chafed against her own mother's values sometimes, but never with this level of hostility. Unless she'd been as bad as Jenna in her own way, without even realising. Maybe a perpetual state of undeclared war was the norm for all daughters and mothers.

"I just want to see."

"See *what*?" A whine crept into Jenna's voice. Elaine didn't answer: apart from anything else, she was trying to keep her balance on the embankment's soft, crumbly earth. She grabbed a branch for stability as she neared the top. It shifted in her grip: Elaine gasped, afraid it was about to snap, but it held. Thank God for WeightWatchers; if she'd still been carrying that extra stone, things might have gone differently.

She made it up onto level ground and shone her torch ahead, but for all that effort there was no reward. The light reached further, but all it revealed was yet more trees.

She might see something if she went a little further in. Elaine picked her way forward. Brambles and undergrowth snagged her shins and ankles; her feet sank into soft, damp earth, then mud. Cold and wetness seeped through the thin material of the trainers. They might be better suited to this than her heels, but that was all she could say for them.

"Mum?" called Jenna again, the fear sharper in her voice. She wouldn't be able to see Elaine at all now, only the backwash of light through the trees.

"I'm all right," said Elaine, then yelped as the beam flashed across something that moved. She glimpsed its eyes, palely reflecting the torchlight, before it retreated into the darkness. She wasn't sure what it was. A deer, maybe. Yes, that was it; it must have been. She thought she'd seen antlers. Whatever it was, it was large and in motion: she heard the crackle of splintering twigs and undergrowth. Thankfully it wasn't coming at her. It was moving away, to her left, up the road from where the car had stopped.

If they managed to get the car running again, it would be up ahead of them, waiting. But that was silly. Deer didn't attack people, not that Elaine had heard of. If she'd literally fallen on top of one it might have lashed out at her in its panic, but it was hardly going to wait on the bank for them to drive by and launch a kamikaze attack. She shook her head. Silly.

If it was *a deer.*

What else could it be? Britain had no large land predators, unless you believed the urban legends of escaped big cats living wild on the moors. Although those stories didn't seem quite as ridiculous as usual, out among the trees in the darkness.

No; it had been a deer. Elaine had glimpsed the antlers. At least, she thought she had. All she could really swear to was the eyes and a vague, bulky shape. She *thought* she'd seen antlers; then again, she also had a vague, lingering impression of having seen a face of some kind. A face – or, more accurately, a skull. And that made no sense at all.

It didn't matter. What mattered was that they were in the middle of the woods, even if she wasn't sure which ones. Even if she could identify where they were, whichever way she went might take them further from help, instead of closer to it.

Unless, of course, she got the car started again: a solution so simple she hadn't even considered it. Elaine had to laugh.

"Mum?" Jenna sounded genuinely frightened now. If there was a struggle for dominance between them, Elaine had won this round.

"I'm all right," she said. "Coming back now."

Stealthy movement sounded in the undergrowth behind her as she retraced her steps to the car, but Elaine perceived no threat from it. And she was right. They were only the sounds of small woodland creatures that had gone utterly still when something huge and terrible had come near them, resuming their normal activities after it had moved away through the trees.

2.

Jenna breathed out as Mum climbed back down the embankment, half angry and half relieved. What'd she been going to do, hack her way through the woods in search of help? Maybe she was having a brainstorm – have to be mad or stupid to think *that* was a good idea. Either was possible with Mum.

Well, Jenna wasn't mad, or stupid. She'd been reading on the internet earlier about big cats living wild in Britain, usually out on the moors. And even if those weren't real, any animal would go for you if you startled it. Foxes, badgers; even deer. She'd seen a video of a hunter, out with his rifle, who'd been caught off-guard by a stag; the animal had reared up on its back legs and pummelled the fuck out of him with its front hooves. And serve the dickhead right, frankly.

The sensible thing to do was follow the road. With nothing better to do she'd been listening to *Made of Bricks* by Kate Nash, staring out of the window as Mum drove. Before they'd gone into the woods she'd seen a village, then a sign – five miles to somewhere, straight ahead. But she wasn't sure how long before: one minute, two or three. Maybe longer. Nor could she remember how long after they'd entered the woods the engine had conked out. By then she'd been half-hypnotised by the flickering trees, the unwinding road, the moon and stars flashing through the branches overhead to the rhythm of "Skeleton Song".

Jenna didn't like the idea of walking, which was crap, but she wasn't waiting on her own in the car. Could be anything out there. Paedos. Rapists. Serial killers.

Anyway, she couldn't let Mum go on her own. Mum did her head in, but Jenna didn't want her to *die* or anything. They'd have to go along the road together, for safety. It'd be all right with the torch, long as Mum hadn't worn the batteries out dicking around in the woods. What'd she been trying to do there? She could've fallen and broken something; what'd Jenna have done then?

She braced herself for the order to get out and start walking, but instead, Mum went round the front of the car, tucking the torch between her neck and shoulder and fumbling at the hood.

Jenna got out. "What you doing?"

"What does it look like?" A pop, and with a triumphant grunt Mum lifted the hood, fumbling underneath till she unfolded the metal rod that propped it open. "I'm going to try and get the bloody car going again."

"*What?* What do you know about fixing cars, Mum?"

"A sight more than you, young lady. Now get back in the car and wait."

"Mum, the torch'll run out."

"No it won't."

"Mum, we've got to *walk* and get help." Mum was about as mechanically minded as a rabbit, but she'd faff around with the engine for ages before admitting defeat. And then what? Even when they'd decided which way to go – probably end up tossing a coin for it, unless Mum had a better idea – the torch'd end up dying on them halfway there and then they'd be alone. In the dark. On the road.

When the car'd first stopped, it'd been more an inconvenience than anything else. But when Mum vanished into the woods and left Jenna all alone – not knowing what to do, only able to sit and wait – she'd started to feel the cold, and to remember every ghost story and urban legend she'd ever heard. Werewolves, vampires, escaped killers from Dartmoor, and, of course, those big cats.

She really didn't want to believe in the big cats right now; right now, she wanted to believe they were all faked photos and drunken nightmares. In the daylight it would've been easy to believe that, but she never wanted to in daylight, or even in a car at night as long as it was moving. Under those circumstances the big cats were just an exciting story – and, beyond that, the hope the world was a bigger, more enthralling place than the respectable semidetached suburbs where all anyone cared about were house prices and what the neighbours would think and where everyone read *The Telegraph* and the *Daily Mail*. Jenna would never – at the mature and cynical age of fifteen – have described it as the hope there might still be magic in the world, but that was what it boiled down to.

But when the car broke down at night, deep in the woods and far from anywhere, you remembered magic could be black as well as white. Boring they might be, but semidetached houses, neighbours and even the *Daily Mail* were also normal, predictable and above all, *safe*.

"Mum–"

"Jenna," said Mum, a real edge to her voice now, "get back in the car and wait."

Jenna obeyed. She hadn't heard that edge in Mum's voice before but knew what it was. Mum was afraid. Of the dark, of paedos, of rapists, of big wild cats.

Or, maybe, of something she'd seen in the trees.

Jenna tried to peer up between the raised hood and the top of the windscreen, but the trees' branches meshed too tightly for the moon or stars to be visible. There was only the car, this narrow piece of road, the trees and the embankments. Beyond that, thick, heavy blackness. The light from the car was like a fragile Perspex bubble; Jenna could feel the darkness pressing down on it, could almost hear it start to crack.

She pulled her seatbelt across and fastened it. Behind the upraised hood, Mum was muttering. Jenna could hear the odd thump and clunk. She'd no idea if Mum had a clue what she was doing but hoped so now because Mum was afraid and so was Jenna, even though she was probably being silly and panicking and they'd laugh about it later. She took deep breaths and gripped her knees, clenching her fists.

Mum made a short, startled noise, a little muffled cry, and Jenna yelped, startled too. She thought she heard Mum say "Fuck", which frightened her even more because Mum never used *that* word. "Mum?" she said.

"It's all right," came the reply at last. "Thought I heard something."

"Like what?"

Mum didn't answer. Jenna wondered if she wanted to know – but she did, of course: better to know than to imagine. "Like what, Mum? Another car?"

"No. Not a car. Up the road somewhere, but…" Mum trailed off.

"Mum?"

"Nothing."

"*Mum.*"

"Oh stop whinging and just sit tight, Jenna. Should have this sorted in a–"

Jenna wondered afterwards what had actually been wrong with the car and if Mum really could have fixed it; if, given two more minutes, she'd have folded down the hood and they'd have driven the rest of the way to the holiday cottage to wait for Dad. They'd have had another desultory sullen family holiday and Jenna would have been bored to death, but at least she'd have been safe, would still have had a family and would've grown up halfway normal, whatever that was. Or maybe something would have come creeping round the cottage even if they'd made it there, forcing the door or cracking the windows. In any case it didn't matter:

the engine never started again, and the hood never came down, because that was when Mum screamed.

Just once, but it was enough: it was the worst thing Jenna had ever heard, and there was no warning, no chance to cover her ears. It only lasted seconds, but they seemed interminable: there was something primal about it, as if all the monsters Mum had dreaded as a child at night had become real and come for her. Years later, deep in Jenna's skull, that scream would still be echoing.

Something slammed hard into the front of the vehicle, jolting the car. Now Jenna screamed too, and if she hadn't been wearing her seatbelt she'd have been flung headfirst into the dash by the impact. She rocked back in her seat, bruised and gasping.

The car didn't move again. No further impact. No sound.

She was afraid to make a noise, in case something that wasn't Mum heard her. She was afraid of the silence, because of what it meant. "Mum?" she said at last, keeping her voice as firm and clear as she could.

There was no answer.

Yet in a way, there was. No sound, but a sudden wave of the foulest odour she'd ever encountered, a compound of spoiled meat, halitosis, body odour, vomit, excrement and animal piss that made her gag and clap a hand over her mouth. And something else: a sudden, piercing cold, as if she'd been exposed to the bitterest wind in creation, though the air didn't even stir. It wasn't her imagination, either, because she could see her breath in front of her. Something on the other side of the upraised hood watched and waited and knew she was there. Knew, too, that the only question now was what it would do next.

No, that wasn't right. She didn't know what it had done to Mum and probably wouldn't want to, but she'd no doubt it would do the same to her. The only question wasn't *what*, but *if*.

The chill and the helplessness, the hopelessness, seeped deeper into Jenna, tainting the very marrow of her bones, and she realised the question wasn't even *if*, but *when*. Would it take her now, or wait? Leave her to ripen, then come back? Because it would. And it could always find her, because its home was anywhere in the dark.

At last, the chill receded; Jenna could no longer see her breath, but her teeth continued chattering. She knew the danger hadn't gone, only retreated, be it for minutes, days, weeks or years. Long enough, maybe, that she'd think she was safe, that whatever had happened to Mum had been a nightmare, so her terror on its return would be all the sweeter, all the worse.

"Mum?" She didn't even expect an answer by now, but waited for one anyway: whenever she'd been this frightened as a little girl, unable to sleep for nightmares about the Gingerbread Witch or the Big Bad Wolf, Mum had been there with a soothing touch and a warm hug to make the world feel safe again. It had been Jenna's last hope, really, that it might summon Mum back again somehow.

But it didn't.

A passing tractor found Elaine McKnight's Volkswagen Passat on Tallstone Hill shortly after daybreak, its hood still raised. Jenna was inside, physically unharmed but unresponsive. At some point in the night, she'd wet herself. They called an ambulance, laid her out in it and drove her to the hospital; on the journey there, at last, the girl closed her eyes and slept.

Of Elaine there was no sign. No evidence of a struggle, not even a drop of blood: just the empty car, the raised hood, the seemingly catatonic girl.

The police fingertip-searched the woods and surrounding moors, dragged rivers and ditches, questioned anyone on the Sex Offenders' Register in a twenty-mile radius and searched their cars and homes. Nothing was found.

* * *

There were doctors, nurses, the police with their questions, when Jenna woke; Dad sat beside her throughout, alternately sobbing or unresponsive.

Mum was gone. Dad told Jenna, over and over, that she might still be alive, that the police would find her and bring her home. He might even have believed it himself for a while, but Jenna knew better. Jenna knew Mum was never coming back. Jenna remembered that scream.

THE IDOL OF THE TEMPLARS

By the turn of the fourteenth century, the Knights Templar were one of the richest, most powerful organizations in the medieval world, with vast reserves of wealth and land. Pope Clement V feared their power and influence; so did his kinsman, Philip IV of France. Philip was heavily in debt to the Templars for his wars against the English, and now that the Order no longer held territory in the Holy Land, he was afraid they meant to carve out a state of their own in France.

And so the pope and the king conspired, and at dawn on Friday, 13 October 1307, five years after the fall of Ruad, mass arrests were carried out across France. Further arrests and suppression took place throughout Catholic Europe, on the pope's orders.

The Templars were initially charged with fraud and corruption, along with sodomy, idolatry, defiling the Cross and devil-worship, which were almost standard accusations for anyone the Church wished to persecute and rob of their wealth. However, one detail of the charges was unique to them.

The Templars were accused of worshipping the dismembered remains of a creature called Baphomet. The name itself was probably a corruption of Mahomet, i.e. the Muslim Prophet Mohammed: just part of the campaign to blacken the Order's reputation. Countless Templars were tortured into false confessions and burned at the stake; finally the Order was dissolved, and its properties seized.

During the reign of Edward III of England, an old hermit known as Henry of Tewkesbury claimed, on his deathbed, to have been Henri de Poictiers, a Templar Knight. The king's father, Edward II, had shown leniency to the Templars in his kingdom, at least at the beginning, so it wasn't impossible some had escaped into hiding, living in obscurity.

Henry, or Henri, claimed to have seen the idol known as Baphomet. Its remains had been contained in seven reliquaries, each with glass panels set in brass frameworks inlaid with gold, and each containing part of a blackened, mummified human body. Two arms, two legs; the trunk had been split lengthways, though not quite symmetrically, the genitals being attached wholly to the right-hand portion. And, of course, the head.

It was as blackened as the rest – skin hard as bark, taut as parchment – with thin dry hair clinging to the crown, brows, upper lip and chin. Discolouration aside, it was remarkably well-preserved: even the eyelids and eyelashes were still attached, though the eyes themselves were shrivelled up and flattened like a frog dried out in the sun. There were times, he said, when one almost thought it had changed expression. All who saw it felt dread or at least unease, and few wished to be left alone with it.

Such, said Henry of Tewkesbury (or Henri de Poictiers), was the so-called "idol" Baphomet. And yes, it was true that it was an unchristian thing, malefic and perhaps even demonic in nature. However, he insisted, it was a wicked lie that the Templars worshipped or venerated this idol in any way. Nothing could be further from the truth.

Instead, the hermit vowed with his dying breath, they contained *it.*

PART ONE: 2022
Day of The Wren

3.

Jenna had been dating Holly Finn for a month, and it was going well. So well, in fact, she'd let Holly talk her into camping in Wales.

Which was saying a lot. Jenna's ideal holiday was a city break. Paris, Budapest, Prague: bright busy places with clubs and bars and crowds. Holly's, apparently, involved tents, as few people as possible and long walks in the countryside. Such differences didn't usually augur well for a relationship, but Jenna genuinely liked Holly. More than anyone she'd dated in years, if not ever.

The trouble was that when you felt something for someone – Jenna refused to say *loved*, even to herself – they changed you. For a time, she'd wanted that: the night on Tallstone Hill itself and its after-effects had been bad enough, without the thought of it defining her for the rest of her life. But if you took it away, Jenna wasn't sure what would be left, which had made her vulnerable to entirely the wrong sort of partner; there was never any shortage of manipulative or outright abusive bastards out there, of whatever gender.

And so barriers had become a habit, along with a hatred of being pushed into doing anything she didn't want to. It made her exciting company in the short term, and an all-out fucking nightmare (to quote one of her exes) in the long run.

Jenna knew that, at least in her more thoughtful moments, but if there was an answer to the problem, she hadn't found it yet. She'd begun to suspect there was no fixing what Tallstone Hill had done to her, any more than there was growing back a severed limb, and that she'd have to learn to live with the damage as best she could.

Which wasn't particularly appealing either. In any case, it said a lot about this relationship that she'd been persuaded to try a Holly-style vacation in the first place, and even more that she was actually enjoying it.

Holly was certainly the best of this year's crop. Back in February, there'd been Kayla, a statuesque and decidedly athletic African American tourist from Atlanta. Jenna had basically been her holiday romance: fun, companionship and a more or less pain-free parting when it came time to fly home. Pleasant, but nothing else.

In March she'd met Brad, an Australian barman with – as it had turned out – fairly adventurous sexual tastes. Jenna had been just as wild herself, once upon a time, but at almost thirty years of age found that sort of thing more trouble than it was worth. So Brad went off in search of a more obliging partner, leaving Jenna to rediscover the joys of singlehood.

And then, in May, there'd been James – *Sir* James, if you please, newly succeeded to the title. His late father had been Sir Alec Frobisher, whom Jenna had never heard of, but who'd been, apparently, very rich. Neither the money nor the title had impressed her, which had only seemed to heighten James's interest. He'd been good-looking and persistent; she'd been bored. So they'd gone out, which had proved a huge mistake on her part: he'd been talking marriage and children within a fortnight, and Jenna wanted neither. Ever.

Worse, he'd been a control freak into the bargain; the only real surprise was that they'd lasted an entire month. Maybe the money *had* impressed Jenna a little, after all.

Well, people always left, one way or the other – like Mum, like Dad – and relationships always ended. Sooner rather than later, in Jenna's case. Three months was her all-time record.

Annoyingly, people always assumed it was related to her sexuality, but at least that spared her having to explain the real reasons.

The whole business with James had been enough of a car-crash that she'd fully intended staying single, for the rest of the year at least. But then, halfway through July, a week before her birthday, she'd met Holly at the gym where she practiced Muay Thai. She was a nurse, had a wicked sense of humour, a fondness for poetry – which Jenna shared – and was warm and tactile without being clingy.

They were an odd couple to look at: with her short red hair, strong jawline, lack of makeup and lean figure, Jenna had the kind of rather androgynous good looks that drew men's and women's attention in equal measure. Holly was short and plump, with a heart-shaped face and a wing of black, red-tinted hair hanging perpetually over one dark, long-lashed, gold-flecked eye. Nonetheless they'd clicked immediately, gone out for dinner that first evening, and now, here they were.

They'd spent four nights under canvas in a field near Criccieth, with daytrips along the Gwynedd coast in Holly's olive-green Suzuki Jimny: Shell Island, Harlech, Porthmadog and now, on the last day, Barmouth. Walking along beaches, clambering over hills and sand dunes; lunch in quayside cafés. Exercise and sea air.

There was a lot of woodland in Wales, but they'd largely avoided it, except on the drive from Manchester, which as far as Jenna was concerned had been more than bad enough. Shell Island had been all dunes and beach; Harlech, a castle atop a hill accessed by the steepest road in the world (according to Holly, anyway; after huffing and puffing her way up it, Jenna didn't doubt it for a second), and Porthmadog a pleasant seaside town full of pubs, cafés and charity shops. Barmouth was a beach, a selection of even nicer cafés, and a gorse-covered hillside called Dinas Oleu that rose high above the town.

Jenna was sweating hard as they crossed Dinas: it was a bright, hot August day, and Holly set a fairly punishing pace. She was far fitter than she looked and Jenna struggled to keep up. But she managed in the end, and despite the effort, found she was smiling. She had, to her own surprise, enjoyed herself, not just today but the whole trip.

The air was fresh, smelling of blossom, grass and sheep shit, and the only sound was the wind and the occasional bleat from the flocks that grazed the hills. On their travels they saw old manganese mines bored into the hillside, water dripping from the ceilings to form pools on the floors. Holly said her grandfather had caught newts in them as a boy, although there were none to be found today. They'd passed a tumbledown farmhouse surrounded with rusting old farm equipment too, and a Welsh flag blowing from a cairn on one peak.

And now they sat down, drank bottled water and nibbled bars of mint cake, resting their backs against rocks and letting the sweat dry. From the hill they could see out over the town, up the coast in both directions and out to sea. It was an impressive spectacle: the name Dinas Oleu, Holly had told Jenna, meant *the Citadel of Light* in Welsh, and now she could see why. After the exertion of getting up the hill, it was strangely soothing, too. Jenna remembered a poem she'd read: *"I don't think that we should have to earn beauty / it's just that / sweat sweetens it"*. It captured her mood perfectly.

All was well until they cut across Panorama Road, the steep track that led back down to the town.

Holly pointed across it, over the fields below – there was a farmhouse, and more grazing sheep – to another hillside, topped with trees like a pelt of brittle fur. "We just head up there," she said, and Jenna's stomach clenched.

"Up where?" she asked.

"Just up past the farm, then on through the woods. Takes us up to Panorama. You can see for miles. Up the coast, out to sea, inland–"

"No," said Jenna. "Thanks. Let's go down."

"Eh?"

Anger stirred. Hadn't she given way enough on this holiday? "I don't want to, Holly. Okay?"

"What?" Holly blinked at her, puzzled and maybe a little hurt. "What's the problem? We're nearly there, the view's brilliant–"

"Fucking hell, Holly, will you just leave it?"

It was more of a shout than Jenna had intended; Holly flinched as if slapped, and then her face tightened. Anger.

Typical. You let people in, and they took advantage: wouldn't take no for an answer, tried to override your every choice. Here came the big blow-up, Jenna thought, the one that turned everything sour and ended it all; they'd drive back home in sullen silence and by tomorrow morning Holly would be packing her bags. Once something like this started, once Jenna's back was up and the fur flying, it was no holds barred and she didn't know how to stop. Couldn't if she wanted to. And she wanted to already, even knowing it was too late. But nothing, nothing would make her go into the woods.

Holly stood, hands on hips, glaring, then breathed out. Her face softened. "Okay, babe," she said at last. "How about we go get our tea, then? That place near the quay, the Last Inn? Steak and chips looked good."

Jenna relaxed. "Yeah. I could go for that."

"All right, then." Holly squeezed her arm. "Come on, hun."

She started down the Panorama Road. Jenna stared after her; Holly's back didn't look stiff with anger, but she hadn't looked scared either. She'd almost looked *sorry* for Jenna. But that made no sense.

The important thing was that the fight hadn't happened. It might still be a matter of time before this ended, but it hadn't yet. Jenna drained the last of her bottled water and followed Holly down the road.

They went back into the town, and Holly didn't mention the topic again. And they went to the Last Inn for a meal before piling into the Jimny and driving back, and the steak and chips were very good indeed. They drove to the campsite and Holly opened a bottle of wine with the corkscrew on her Swiss Army knife; Jenna rubbed lotion into the angry red marks where Holly's clothes had chafed or dug in, and the two of them made love slowly and clumsily but ultimately very pleasurably on the air mattress in the tent.

But that night, Jenna found herself in the woods after all.

4.

Leaves fell from their branches, drifting down to the red-gold carpet in front of her. She stood between two rows of trees, laid out as tidily as if on either side of an avenue, but there was no road: no brick, no stonework, only the woods.

The trees were very, very tall, reaching up into a pale, twilight sky barely visible behind their interwoven branches. Roots as thick as arms and legs wormed through the soil, tripping Jenna as she tried to back away, almost sending her sprawling.

At the end of the avenue, the trees closed up, disappearing into a thick well of black shadow, like a cloud of fog or smoke. Jenna couldn't see what was inside it, but knew there was something. She didn't think it knew she was there, not yet, but it would if she lingered.

Run.

She turned and tried to, but at the other end of the grove, the trees closed in again. There had to be a path through them somewhere – how else could she have ended up here? – but she couldn't see it. Beyond the grove there was only rank on rank of trees, receding till they became blurs in the grey half-light; the ground was an unbroken expanse of fallen leaves, those snaking roots undulating endlessly beneath.

A cold, dank wind blew against her back and there was a stench of halitosis and rotten meat.

Wake up, she told herself. *You know this is a dream*. That was usually enough to bring her round, but not this time. And so instead she turned into the blast of that horrible wind, towards the end of the grove, a cold terror in her bowels. It was still all shadows, nothing she could make out in any detail, but something was there, and it saw her.

She took a step towards it.

No. No no no. The other way. Run.

But despite herself, she took another step towards the dark.

Wake up.

And then another.

Run, even if there's no path – force yourself between the trees if you have to, just get away.

But she wasn't in control. The end of the grove drew ever closer, and the blackness at the end began to disperse.

Wake me up! Somebody! Wake me up!

Something was squatting there. She couldn't see it clearly, only an impression of its huge, shadowy bulk. It had antlers. And eyes. Luminous, lamplike eyes.

This isn't a dream. You're not dreaming. Oh God, oh fuck, somebody, wake me up.

The lamp-eyes blazed; the thing was now looking directly at her, into her.

The dank wind blew; Jenna thought she'd vomit from the stench. Ice gripped her, crushing breath from her lungs; then there was a sound – a growl, or a laugh – and she was tumbling backwards, blown by that reeking wind.

She found herself gasping on the inflatable mattress in the tent, flailing at the air with her hands; beside her, Holly came awake with a cry.

"Fuck. Fuck." Jenna fought for breath; the dark around her was total. "What the fuck – what the fuck–"

"Jenn?" Holly's voice was thick with sleep. There was a click and the torch lit up the tent, playing over the ceiling before moving down towards the doors.

Jenna almost screamed aloud – thankfully she stopped herself – because the shadows at the far end of the tent looked thick enough to hide anything, like the shadows at the end of the grove, and she was certain the torch would reveal something huge squatting there, something with antlers and eyes like lamps.

But there was nothing but the inside of the tent, which only made sense as the thing in the grove had been huge, wouldn't have fitted in a tent Jenna herself could barely stand up in. Besides, with those glowing eyes she'd have known it was there, with or without the torch. And of course, both it and the grove had only existed in her nightmare. Neither were real.

However often she'd dreamt of them before.

"Jesus, Jenn. You all right? You're *soaking*."

She was, too; her t-shirt clung soddenly to her and when she wiped her forehead, her hand shone with sweat.

"Bad dream," she said.

"No shit." Holly stroked Jenna's back; her hands were small and soft, her touch delicate and light. "Never seen anything like that. You gonna be okay?"

"Yeah." Normally Jenna wouldn't have said any more, but it started pouring out. "I get these nightmares sometimes, just now and again, but really bad. Horrible. Since I was fifteen."

"That when your mum died?"

"Yeah," said Jenna, short and clipped. Holly didn't know what had happened to Mum, or Dad, just that they were gone.

"Same dream?"

"More or less." In it, she was always helpless, unable to flee and compelled to approach the end of the grove despite every impulse otherwise. Like a puppet. An empty vessel. A thing, controlled and manipulated by something else. Jenna didn't need Sigmund Freud to decipher that.

The last time, a couple of years ago, there'd been an added refinement that she still vividly remembered: the thing at the end of the grove had been no more clearly visible than usual, a blurred, antlered shadow with glowing eyes, but it had been gripping a human body: white, naked, streaked with blood. The gender had been unclear; its back was to her, the buttocks, the dangling legs, the right arm. No left arm, though, no left shoulder, and no head. Those were gone, sheared cleanly away in two overlapping, crescent-shaped cuts. *Bite marks.*

The image had seemed familiar, though Jenna didn't know where from. At least this latest dream hadn't included *that* detail. It was more than bad enough on its own.

She curled up against Holly, laying her head on her chest. "Hold me, yeah?"

"Okay," said Holly, sounding surprised. It was usually Jenna who did the comforting and Holly who received it. Jenna had established that early on. To be the giver of comfort was the stronger position; you weren't making yourself vulnerable to anyone else that way. But tonight, Holly's embrace was the only thing that made Jenna feel safe enough to sleep again.

5.

She didn't dream – of the grove or anything else – and when she woke the tent was warmer and brighter. Sunlight filtered through the canvas, and she could hear birdsong, counterpointed by the rumble of Holly's snores.

Jenna sat up, stretching. She was used to spreading out in bed, so the tent hadn't been ideal to begin with, and her back, hips and joints were complaining about it loudly. She needed to pee, and she needed fresh air. It was stale and close inside the tent, reeking of dried sweat and hot plastic weave, making her head ache.

She unzipped her sleeping bag, reaching for her boots, and then her stomach contracted violently. Jenna barely got her hand to her mouth in time and scrambled to the tent flap, fumbling at the zip.

The zipper was stiff and uncooperative, but she got it down in time to push her head outside the tent before heaving again. Bile spurted through her fingers and she crawled outside, moaning at the bright hot sun. She stumbled through prickly grass and rocky soil, treading in what she hoped wasn't sheep shit before throwing up in a patch of nettles, bent over in her t-shirt and cotton briefs. *Feast your eyes, boys and girls.* She wiped her mouth and straightened up, cleaning her hands on the shirt.

"Jenn?" Holly emerged from the tent, wearing vest-top and jogpants and looking equal parts worried and confused. "What's wrong now?"

"Felt sick." Jenna walked back to the tent, rubbing her foot as clean as possible on the grass. "Must've been something I ate."

But it hadn't been. She'd been sick the previous morning, too, and on several others in the past fortnight, most of which Holly hadn't even known about as she slept heavily and deeply.

Worse, her breasts were aching. Admittedly, so was the rest of her, but as Holly went back into the tent Jenna touched them, and found they were tender and sore. She wasn't stupid; she knew what that meant, however unlikely.

"Shit," she muttered.

They struck the tent, packed their gear into the back of the Suzuki, and drove away in silence.

Jenna's periods had never been regular; they were sometimes early, sometimes late, sometimes didn't come at all. So when last month's hadn't arrived, she hadn't been particularly worried. She'd been due this week, and had seen it as win-win either way: if it didn't come, that was one less inconvenience on a camping trip she'd already anticipated as being full of them; if it did, she'd at least know she wasn't pregnant.

But she hadn't bled, she was sick in the mornings, and her breasts were tender.

She didn't want to think about it. Especially not while driving through the Welsh countryside, which still had far too much woodland, far too many narrow winding roads overhung with branches for comfort. Besides, it was impossible: she'd dumped James two months ago, and they'd always used protection.

Nothing's 100%, Jenna. You know that.

She opened a book and read, silently, pretending not to notice Holly's worried glances. Holly had already asked twice if she was okay, and the second time Jenna had more or less snapped "I'm *fine*", which had apparently put Holly off asking again.

Maybe this was the end of it, after all. Jenna had hoped they'd last longer than this. Holly was warm and kind and open; none of those qualities were likely to last beyond her first serious collision with reality, but while they existed, Jenna was glad of them. As always, though, she'd no idea how to hang on to what she had. As if you ever could. Everyone left in the end; Holly was probably preparing to do that now.

When Jenna looked up it was a dim, twilit evening. Off to one side there was a city of tiny lights, full of long thin towers with flames on top. *A Goth princess's fairy palace*, she thought, and grinned, then realised it was the refinery at Stanlow.

She hadn't even noticed that they'd crossed back into England; more importantly, they were on a motorway, so if the car broke down they wouldn't be alone in the dark. She pushed herself upright in her seat.

"You okay?" Holly sounded almost scared. No, not scared. Jenna wasn't *that* frightening. Was she? Not scared: nervous, maybe. Worried Jenna would snap.

Vulnerability, weakness: Jenna wanted to comfort her and to snap at her, all at once. She managed a smile. "Yeah. Sorry. Bear with a sore head. Got any painkillers?"

"Soz. Ran out yesterday."

"Can we stop and pick up something?" She touched her belly. "Maybe some co-codamol?"

"Oh, hun." Holly's hand squeezed hers, then rested on Jenna's thigh. "You coming on?"

"Maybe." God, she wished. "Can we find a Boots or something?"

"Yeah, no problem. Just chill. Shut your eyes."

Jenna didn't, though, because it would be far too easy to fall asleep, and if she did that Holly would park up and quietly slip out to the chemist's on Jenna's behalf, so as not to wake her. And Jenna needed to do this herself. Holly didn't have to know. With any luck, this was a false alarm.

* * *

Jenna bought three pregnancy tests – *best of three*, she thought with grim amusement – plus a packet of co-codamol to keep up appearances, forcing herself to buy top-of-the-range items: this wasn't something to scrimp on.

They hadn't moved in together. Jenna had only ever done that twice, preferring to keep a little distance between her and her lovers, a place of safety to retreat to when everything went wrong. Holly's flat was in South Manchester, in Withington, while Jenna lived across the River Irwell in Walkden, a suburb of Salford. It was the Walkden flat they drove back to tonight; Holly knew Jenna would want to be back in her own lair after being away from it so long. Besides, Holly had been leaving more and more stuff here – changes of clothes, a spare toothbrush, a few books – as if moving in by stealth, a little at a time. Normally such encroachment on her territory would have annoyed Jenna, but once again – much to her own surprise – with Holly, she found she didn't really mind.

As soon as they were inside, Jenna put the kettle on, while Holly went to the bathroom. When she came back she slumped into an armchair, enabling Jenna to hand her a mug of tea and run to the toilet with no risk of being disturbed.

The advice was apparently to pee first thing in the morning, but she couldn't wait until then. Peeing on three separate sticks in rapid succession was something of a manoeuvre, but she'd performed more complicated ones in her time (notably at a sex party in Hanover in 2013 – ah, her misspent youth). She sat back, watching the pregnancy tests lined up along the edge of the bath, willing them to give her the all-clear.

Only to watch the blue lines come up, one by one.

6.

"Fuck," said Jenna, more loudly than she'd intended.

"You okay?" called Holly.

"Yeah." Jenna bundled the tests and packaging into the bin beside her, covering them with wadded-up toilet paper, then stood and flushed.

Holly frowned as Jenna sipped tea in her armchair, clearly sensing something awry but saying nothing. One thing that had given Jenna hope for the relationship, in the relative sense of it potentially outlasting her current record, was that Holly seemed good at sensing her moods. Jenna was self-aware enough to know that one reason she was a nightmare to live with was her assumption her partners should instinctively know if she wanted to talk or be quiet, to fuck or cuddle or be left alone. Or more accurately, her *hope* that they would, because if she had to tell them they'd want her to explain things, and she couldn't. Some parts of you needed to be sealed off from other people, like the bulkheads on a ship. You couldn't let anyone all the way in, however much you wanted to. That was how ships sank.

"Want another brew?" Holly said at last.

Jenna smiled at her. "Yeah. Ta, love."

Love. She saw Holly smile at the word, felt crap for lying to her, then angry with Holly again, for being so soft. Holly got up and put the kettle back on, then padded to the bathroom again while it boiled.

41

All of which reminded Jenna yet again of the blue lines and the question of what to do now – or more importantly, how to do it without Holly finding out. She'd be back at work next week, so if Jenna arranged an appointment during the day–

"What the fuck?" There was a clatter of cardboard and plastic from the bathroom. "What the *fuck*?"

Oh, crap.

"Jenn?" Holly's tone had initially been one of pure disbelief; now it was mingled with hurt, anger and bewilderment. *Oh for fuck's sake, Holly, please no fucking crying. Can't deal with that right now.*

"Jenn?" Holly came back into the room. "Jenn, what the fuck's this?" Her voice cracked.

Jenna took her hands from her face. Holly was holding up one of the tests. In the other hand was a much-folded typed sheet: the instructions. It must have fallen to the floor or into the bathtub when she'd opened the packet. Holly had seen it, hence the first WTF: the second had followed after rooting in the bin to find the test itself.

Holly's eyes were huge with hurt; they pulled at Jenna, made her want to say things, explain, share. Open the bulkhead doors and let the sea pour in. And she couldn't, wouldn't do that. "What does it look like, *Holl*?" she snapped.

Holly flinched; Jenna felt a moment's guilt and sympathy, followed by a fresh backwash of rage. She had to push the other woman away; she didn't know what she might have said next, but then Holly's mood turned too and she flung the used test, overarm and with considerable accuracy: if Jenna hadn't pulled back in time it would have ricocheted off her nose. "Don't you *fucking* talk to me like that." She stormed forward then halted, fists clenching and unclenching. "You're pregnant. How the–"

She broke off, but it was too late. "How do you think? Okay, Holly, I'll tell you – when a man and a woman love each other very much–"

"Oh fuck off, you bitch." Holly looked close to tears, but also as though she might throw something else at Jenna. Jenna stood, feeling another spasm of guilt that quickly became aggression.

But Holly stopped herself again; she wheeled around and stomped into the bathroom, slamming the door so hard the flat shuddered and the downstairs neighbour banged on the ceiling.

Jenna stamped on the floor in response, shouted "Fuck off" at it and looked towards the bathroom door; behind it, Holly was already sobbing. *Brilliant. Jenna strikes again.*

She wanted to knock on the bathroom door, but didn't: that would be lowering her guard, leaving herself open for the blow Holly would be fully entitled and amply motivated to deliver. No point anyway: Jenna knew she'd fucked it. They'd had a good run, she told herself again. Just not as good as she'd hoped.

As the adrenaline ebbed, she felt exhausted and miserable; she went to the bedroom, kicked off her boots and flopped down on the bed. She reeled off every obscenity she knew under her breath until she realised she was crying, then shoved the bedclothes into her mouth. Not that Holly was likely to hear; she was either skriking her eyes out in the bathroom still, or storming round the flat grabbing whatever items she planned on leaving with.

If the second, Holly would be in here shortly, so retreating to the bedroom might not have been the best move after all. Jenna's office would have been better: shut the doors, put music on, cry at her desk. But she'd felt so tired. Even so, it would have been better to leave the bedroom free – let Holly come in, take what she wanted and then just *go*. The break seemed inevitable; best to get it over with, quick and clean, and get back to being alone. In a way, it was almost a relief: she wasn't waiting for it to go wrong anymore.

But Jenna couldn't hear either Holly sobbing or the clatter of drawers that went with a post-breakup pillage session. And then someone knocked gently on the bedroom door. "Jenn?"

The floorboards creaked; Holly stepped into the room. "D'you wanna talk about it?"

"About what?"

The bed shifted as Holly sat on the edge. "Did–" Holly began, then broke off.

"What?"

Another pause. "Did something happen?"

"Well, *obviously*."

Another silence. Holly touched her hand, so suddenly Jenna pulled away. "Sorry," Holly said softly.

"S'all right," Jenna said at last.

"Do you need to – see someone? Like the police?"

"The fuck for?" Jenna realised what Holly had meant. "Oh."

"You mean you weren't – nobody–"

"I wasn't raped," Jenna said into the mattress. "Okay?"

"Okay." A silence. "Why'd you do it, then?"

"Do what?"

"Fucking hell, Jenna!" That bed juddered as Holly thumped it. "Why'd you shag around on me, then? The one thing – the *one* thing I–"

"I didn't shag around on you, you stupid cow." Jenna glared at Holly, wiping her eyes on her sleeve; Holly glared back. "It was James. Must've been."

"James? But I thought you and him–"

"Two months ago, and no, not seen him since. Just nonstop bloody texts, the annoying prick. But I've not come on since then, have I? And I was spewing up all morning, and my boobs were sore, so–"

"Oh, Jenn." Holly touched her hand again; this time Jenna took it. "I'm sorry. Thought you and him always used rubbers."

"One of them must've had a hole."

A breath. "You don't mean – not deliberately?"

Course not, she was about to say, but then stopped. Getting

Jenna pregnant so she'd stay with him would have been doomed to failure in every conceivable way, but that didn't mean James wouldn't have considered it a brilliant idea.

Holly stroked Jenna's knuckles with her thumb. "Oh, sweetheart."

Jenna didn't trust herself to speak. This wasn't right: Holly should have stormed out by now. Instead, she was the one apologising. Having braced herself for being dumped, Jenna almost felt disappointed.

"So what're you going to do?" Holly said.

"Think I'm gonna do?" The snap was back in Jenna's voice. Familiar ground. She pulled her hand free, sat up in bed and fumbled for her phone. "I'll book the dustbin now," she said, trying to sound as if it meant nothing. But her voice cracked, and she was shaking.

Holly squeezed her hand again. "We'll sort it, babe. Me and you. Eh?"

What's this we *shit?* Jenna almost said, but stopped herself. "Yeah," she said at last. She felt strangely warm. Almost *safe*. "Yeah. Thanks, love."

Holly held out her arms. Jenna curled into them, allowing herself, within the almost unheard-of span of twenty-four hours, to be comforted a second time.

Afterwards, Jenna made an appointment at the NUPAS clinic in Hazel Grove. Subject to the consultation, they could arrange a termination the same day, and the horrible intrusive thing James had inflicted on her – deliberately, she was almost certain now – would be gone.

They ordered a Chinese takeaway and watched Netflix, but neither could keep their eyes open. "Come on, babe," Holly said at last, bowing to the inevitable. "Beddy-byes."

Everything was hazy after that, till Jenna found herself suddenly awake, the bedroom black and searingly cold; her teeth were chattering. She was sprawled across the bed in her familiar claim-the-territory pose, with Holly moulded awkwardly against her and snoring obliviously away.

Despite the cold, the room was filled with an appalling smell of foul breath and rotten meat, which Jenna recognised from her dreams of the grove. She tried to roll over to see the source of the smell, yet she couldn't: she was paralysed.

Sleep paralysis. Night terrors. She'd dated a woman in Berlin, Hannelore, who'd suffered from those too. Felt presences were usually involved: you sensed someone, or something, standing over you, watching. Like she could now.

More than that: she could feel its breath on her, cold and rank. Which was impossible; it must be a night breeze, and yet this was rhythmic, a steady pulse of air that blew across her skin.

Now she sensed it move; in a moment it would touch her, and whatever the thing was she knew she wouldn't be able bear that. She wasn't sure she'd bear the sight of it either, but it couldn't be as bad, and if she saw it coming, she'd at least be able to try and avoid it.

But still she couldn't move, and she could feel it leaning over her, its cold lamp-like glare on her back. And then her muscles unlocked and she rolled over in bed with a cry, kicking at the shadows before scrabbling down the side of the bed for the baseball bat she kept there.

"What? Jesus! Jenn?"

She lunged for the bedside lamp and clicked the switch. The light came on and lit the bedroom, revealing–

Nothing.

Jenna slumped back and let the baseball bat drop. Her breathing was fast and ragged; she was close to hyperventilating and drenched in sweat, her t-shirt soaked and clinging to her. Just like before, in the tent.

"Fucking hell, Jenna." Holly squinted at her, face puffy from sleep, half annoyed and half concerned. "Fuck's going on?"

Jenna prodded the power button on her phone to light the screen. 00.32. Half past midnight. *Witching hour*. She took a long deep breath, then another. *Get it under control. Calm yourself.*

"Jenna?"

Holly's hand settled on her arm; Jenna almost pulled away, but squeezed the hand instead, forcing a smile. "Bad dream. Sorry."

"That's two nights running."

"Yeah."

"Babe?"

"What?"

"Mind if I say something?"

"What?"

"Being up the duff does *not* agree with you."

7.

She slept in late, vaguely aware of Holly calling out to her as she left for work, before plodding through to the bathroom to stand under the shower. She'd showered last night on returning from the camping trip, but felt no different this morning – still greasy and reeking of sweat. Probably because of the nightmares. And possibly being pregnant.

Being up the duff does not *agree with you.*

Jenna couldn't argue with Holly there. She didn't want children, never had: they changed you, physically and otherwise, and she'd been changed enough in ways she hadn't asked for, thank you very much. On top of that they were hostages to fortune, and on top of *that*, there were the circumstances of this particular pregnancy to consider: what James had done, if he'd deliberately impregnated her, was a step away from rape. She held onto the anger that thought engendered: the anger, along with Holly, kept her focused.

She dressed in sweats and trainers, made tea and toast and took them into her office, tried to draw but couldn't. She couldn't settle; she'd look at her notepad or laptop screen, consider some task, then choose instead the easier option of scrolling through her phone, looking out of the window, or thumbing through one of the crumpled paperbacks on her desk.

Jenna shut the laptop, stuffed it, her pad and pencils into a Hello Kitty backpack, let herself out and ran downstairs.

A morning in a coffee shop might help. Harder to avoid work in such a setting; besides, a change of scenery wouldn't hurt.

She got into her car – a Toyota Aygo in a shade of hot pink so vivid Holly had almost laughed herself into convulsions – and drove, aimlessly at first. On days like these she needed above all to get out of the house; where to was a secondary consideration. She had plenty of haunts where she could work quietly at a table for a few hours, as long as she bought enough tea and biscuits.

She mulled her options. Wilmslow Road in Didsbury had been a refuge of one kind or another for Jenna since her teens; the Canal Basin at Castlefield, all stone and steel and water, was another. The holiday had been fun, but Jenna had had more than enough of Nature's glory for now.

It would be lunch soon, and Wilmslow Road would be teeming. Castlefield first, she decided; she'd try Didsbury later, when it was quieter. She smiled, feeling better. She always did when she had a plan.

Jenna drove into Manchester, onto Deansgate, then turned down Castle Street and parked under the railway viaduct. She got out, shrugging her backpack on, and locked the doors.

She sensed someone behind her an instant before glimpsing a flicker of movement in the car window.

Jenna pivoted, one leg flicking out in a Muay Thai kick that Ron, her trainer at the gym, would have been truly proud of. It connected, and a man was flung backwards, caroming off a parked BMW and setting off the car alarm.

For a split-second Jenna was afraid she'd overreacted and assaulted some random passerby, then she saw the man wore a balaclava hood pulled down over his face, exposing only eyes and mouth, and knew her first instinct had been correct.

Something fell out of his gloved hand and clattered on the cobbled street: as he reached for it, Jenna saw it was a syringe.

That's not good.

She kicked out, sending it skittering away, then straightened to face her attacker again. As she did, she sensed movement behind her and turned again, glimpsing another balaclava-clad head, but this time she wasn't fast enough. Something sharp stabbed into her shoulder, and a coldness spread in it.

Bastards. How fucking dare they. The anger brightened within her and she lashed out at the second attacker, breaking away from them both.

A smooth plastic tube protruded from Jenna's shoulder; she pulled it free as she continued backing away across the cobbles. It was another hypodermic – already empty, its plunger depressed. It blurred, moving in and out of focus, and fell from her grasp.

She had to get away from them, and quickly, before the injection took effect. But she was already drowsy and slow. She couldn't run far. Had to hold on to the rage and use it. She stumbled towards the Aygo – if she could get inside, she could lock herself in, if nothing else – but her legs gave way and she fell against the car. Her eyes wouldn't focus; she pushed herself upright again, but hands grabbed her and she was dragged clear of the car.

Bastards. She kicked and thrashed, but her arms and legs were heavy and slow. Her attackers were talking. Jenna could tell one of them was a woman, but couldn't make out any words. When she tried to shout for help, only a slurred groan came out. Everything was too slow, and the sounds around her – her assailants' speech, the traffic on Deansgate – were echoey and distant, as if she was underwater.

Jenna made a last attempt to throw them off, but it was little more than a shrug. Then her legs gave way, and she went down into the dark.

8.

She was in a bed, soft and warm. Everything was faint and indistinct, sleep a cocoon that held her tightly, reluctant to let her go.

Jenna blinked and focused. The room was dim but hot; birds twittered, there was a faint breeze and the air smelt fresh. Faint shadows played across a pale, creamy white ceiling with a lampshade and dark wooden beams running across it and down the walls. There was a window open, but the curtains were drawn, and apart from the birdsong, the room was quiet.

Jenna's mouth was dry. When she licked them, her lips felt cracked. She swallowed and made a small, experimental sound: her voice was gravel, her throat scorched earth. A light duvet was pulled up to her chin; she moved her arms and legs under it. She felt weak, but otherwise everything seemed to be functional.

Propping herself up on her elbows, she looked around the room. The walls were the same cream colour as the ceiling, offset by the near-black of the wooden beams. There was a chair and desk, a dresser with a mirror on top, a nightstand and lamp each side of the bed, a door in the wall to her left, beyond which she could see a sink and toilet.

She was in a double bed. Had she been assaulted while unconscious? Her first reaction to the thought was shock, revulsion and fear, rather than rage: a testament to how out of it she still felt.

There were posters and charts on the wall. *Gestation*, said one. *Birth*, said another. There were diagrams on them, of embryos and foetuses in the womb.

She sat up, hugging herself. She was wearing a gown of some kind. No fastenings at the front, but open at the back: she could feel the pillows against her bare skin. A hospital gown, but this wasn't a hospital.

She wanted to get out of the bed, but when she tried, Jenna realised how weak she felt. She propped the pillows against the headboard and wriggled backwards so she could sit upright properly. By then she was trembling and breathless, heart hammering.

She realised she was also shaking with hunger. Thirsty, too: her throat felt scorched to ash. There was a carafe of water and a glass on the nightstand to her left. Jenna struggled towards it; as she reached for the carafe, the bedroom door opened.

"Wait wait wait," said a voice. "Let me. Might still be a bit shaky. Don't want you dropping it, eh?"

A thin, dark-haired woman entered and picked up the carafe. Over the birdsong from outside, Jenna heard the water trickle into the glass and her thirst became unbearable.

"Sit back." The woman had what Mum had used to call a "jolly-hockey-sticks" voice: clipped, cut-glass, no-nonsense. The kind of woman who said "gels" instead of "girls". Mum had once told Jenna she'd had a teacher like that, back in her schooldays, who'd introduced the sex education class with the announcement "Right, gels – this is the male *organ*", before drawing an outline on the blackboard resembling a lunar rocket. The girl next to Mum had fainted. "She's probably a nun now," Mum had laughed.

Jenna smiled despite everything; now and again she remembered Mum, however briefly, without being hit by the memory of her loss and all that had followed.

"That's right." The dark-haired woman took a paper straw from a jar beside the carafe. "A cheery countenance and all that. Now, here we are. Sip, don't gulp."

Patronising cow, thought Jenna, but for now did as she was told, not trusting her own strength. She was still slightly out of breath just from sitting up, and wondered how long she'd been asleep. She looked down at her arms. They didn't appear wasted, and still had the light tan she'd picked up in Wales. Not long, then.

The straw brushed her lips. She sucked gratefully. Cool water; when you were thirsty nothing tasted better. She swallowed and sucked harder. "Ah-ah." The dark-haired woman took the glass away. "Told you, don't gulp. Make yourself sick."

Jenna experienced an overwhelming urge to tell her to fuck off, but didn't. Her mind felt clearer now; after the water, she was properly awake, and could already tell getting sharp with the woman wouldn't help.

Bloody hell, you're actually thinking things through first. You must *be ill.*

This wasn't a hospital: it was a private home. So the Balaclava Twins hadn't been chased off in the nick of time. Jenna felt strangely calm, realising that. She wasn't looking over her shoulder for some vague, undefined threat. Maybe that was Holly's influence.

Holly. The girl must be climbing the walls wondering where Jenna was. Or maybe she'd already written Jenna off. Everyone left in the end, after all.

"More water?" said the dark-haired woman. Jenna nodded. The woman raised her eyebrows. "What do we say?"

Are you fucking kidding me? and *How old do I look to you, twelve?* were the first responses that sprang to mind; Jenna could think of several others too, but doubted they'd get the result she wanted. "Please," she said. Her voice was still a gravelly croak.

"There you go." The dark-haired woman put the straw to Jenna's lips. She was holding the glass left-handed. There was a plain gold wedding band on her ring finger, along with a diamond solitaire. "All right, Jenna. My name's Rose. I'm in charge of things here. So if there's anything you want – within reason – just say."

"I want to go home."

Rose sighed. "Within reason, I said."

Jenna managed to keep her voice level. "What's unreasonable about my going home?"

"You *will* go home, lovey. Just not yet."

"Why not?"

"It's for your own good."

"For my own good how?" If there was a chance, even a chance, she could pick up with Holly where they'd left off, Jenna wanted it. Her voice rose: it also cracked, because her throat was still dry. She started coughing.

"Now look what you've done. Overtaxing yourself." Again the straw was held to her lips. "Better?"

Jenna nodded, grudgingly.

"What do we say?"

I will fucking deck you before this is over. "Thank you."

"There. Wasn't hard, was it? Now, be a good girl–" Jenna managed not to grit her teeth "–do as you're told and we'll get along famously. Hungry?"

Jenna nodded at last.

"Right, well." Rose stood. "See what I can rustle up."

"How long?" said Jenna.

"Beg pardon?"

"How long was I–" *Unconscious? Asleep?* "–out for?"

"Not long, lovey. Just a day or two."

"Jesus."

Rose frowned. "Rather you didn't take the Good Lord's name in vain while you're here, Jenna. Just a preference." But her tone made it clear it wasn't.

"Fine," said Jenna, trying to make it sound as close to *fuck you* as possible without jeopardising her chances of being fed.

"Start you off with some porridge and see where we go from there," said Rose. "You're not an invalid, so, long as you haven't any problem keeping things down, could follow that up with some bacon and eggs. Sound good?"

"Yeah," Jenna admitted. Her stomach growled at the thought.

"Marvellous." Rose went to a corner and wheeled an overbed table across; Jenna remembered those all too well from hospital. Rose put the glass on it, topped it up and replaced the paper straw. "Have some more if you want."

The bedroom door closed; the key turned in the lock. Jenna sat for a moment, then reached for the water. Her throat was still parched. *Keep hydrated*; that mattered, if she wanted to get out of here and back to Holly, while there was still time.

She moved her legs slowly, as if pedalling a bike, then stretched her arms out and flexed them too. The kind of easy, low-intensity muscle warm-up older people did at the gym. Everything seemed in working order. Then again, she'd only been unconscious for a couple of days.

She studied her surroundings more closely. The chair by the desk was turned towards her: on it, neatly folded, was a soft grey sweatshirt, jogging pants and a balled pair of sports socks. There was a pair of trainers on the floor, too. So they were being civilised about it – up to a point, of course. She wasn't leaving till they had what they wanted. Assuming they let her leave then.

As for what they wanted, there was only one thing Jenna could think of. The charts on the wall were a pretty big clue, as well. And the person who'd be most interested in that, other than herself, had shown himself to be a creepy, controlling little shit, hadn't he? One who hadn't been happy taking *no*, or even *fuck off*, for an answer. Cloning a phone wasn't that hard: even Jenna knew that. James would have known about the abortion as soon as she'd booked it.

She slipped a hand under the bedsheets and palped her belly. She couldn't feel any swelling or movement. She doubted she would, this early on, but couldn't be sure, as it wasn't a subject she'd ever had any interest in. She'd known after Dad died that she didn't want kids, and had been fairly certain of it after Mum. She'd wanted to get her tubes tied for years – if she had, she mightn't be here now – but it was almost impossible to arrange. *What if you change your mind?* She doubted a man would have had his decisions questioned so relentlessly if he'd wanted a vasectomy.

The house looked pleasant enough. Old, too, if the beams and plasterwork were anything to go by; therefore, probably expensive. She listened closely – the bedroom window was open – but couldn't hear any traffic, so they were likely in the countryside. That would make sense. Less chance of her being seen, or attracting attention.

She was getting out, of course. She wasn't having anyone's child, least of all James's. And she had to find Holly, before the other girl gave up and left. But first Jenna needed to know where she was, and how many were watching her. It wouldn't just be Rose.

As if summoned by the thought, the lock clicked and the door opened. Rose re-entered, carrying a tray; the door was pulled shut behind her. At least one other person in the house, then.

Rose pulled up a chair. "I can feed you if–"

Irritation flared. "I can bloody manage."

Rose's face hardened. "No need for language like that, lovey. We don't want to have to chastise you, but you're expected to exercise some self-control."

"Right." Jenna shook her head, then turned her attention to the table. There was a bowl of porridge on the tray, a pot of jam and a tea service. She sprinkled sugar on the porridge.

"Good girl," said Rose. "Eat up before it gets cold."

"Don't call me girl."

Rose folded her arms. "You really need to think about your attitude, lovey," she said.

Jenna briefly visualised ramming the spoon into her eye, but used it to sprinkle more sugar instead. She reached for the sugar again, but Rose took it away. "Think that's probably enough," she said. "Mustn't overdo it, must we, lovey? Eating for two now, remember."

Jenna badly wanted to slap her – at the very least – but held back. She'd have to be careful, bide her time; that didn't come naturally to her, and she'd no idea how long she could do so. But she'd have to try. She forced a smile and asked Rose, as politely as she could manage, "Can I have a cup of tea, then?" When Rose's eyebrows went up again, she added: "Please?" She even managed not to grit her teeth.

Porridge was followed in short order by bacon, eggs, sausage and toast, as promised, with fried mushrooms on the side. Jenna wasn't overfond of those, but forced them down to keep Rose happy. At least there were no grilled tomatoes or baked beans; Jenna couldn't stand either. There was butter with the toast, and lime marmalade. Also a favourite of hers: someone knew her well.

With breakfast finished, Rose wheeled the overbed table back across the room. "Oh, lovey?" She went to the door, motioning to the toilet. "En-suite bathroom here. Loo, shower, even a tub if you feel up to it." She smiled, showing horsey yellow teeth. "All mod cons. If you want to use the facilities, just say the word."

Before Jenna could ask how, Rose picked up the tray and went to the bedroom door. This time when it opened, Jenna glimpsed someone just outside before it swung shut again. The lock clicked.

Two people, at least. And – she looked around the bedroom – there must be at least one camera here, because the man in the corridor hadn't needed a signal from Rose to unlock the door. Maybe Jenna was supposed to signal if she needed the toilet the same way. She wondered if they could listen in as well.

Assume they can until you know different.

She stretched again. Now she'd drunk and eaten, she felt better. Stronger. Clearer headed, more alert. But she'd felt that way before when ill, and it had only lasted until she'd actually tried doing anything.

Something small, first. She reached for the carafe on the bedside table: it was only half-full, but her arm still tremored from the weight. Nonetheless, she managed to refill the glass.

She put the carafe down and drank the water off. Time passed, and she waited. *What now?* Rose hadn't explained what came next; maybe she'd just assumed Jenna could fill in the blanks herself.

Didn't matter right now. She needed the bathroom, badly. Jenna threw back the covers, swung her legs over the side of the bed and sat waiting for Rose to come charging in. But the door stayed closed, so she lowered herself to the floor. She'd much rather manage for herself, anyway.

The carpet was thick and soft, caressing her feet. When she straightened up her legs wobbled, but only slightly. Jenna steadied herself on the bedside table, then crossed to the en-suite.

There was a frosted-glass window above the toilet, but it was securely locked with no key in sight. She doubted she could have squeezed through it anyway. She used the toilet, wondering if they were watching her here, too. She couldn't see any sign of a camera, but hadn't spied one in the bedroom, either.

Jenna flushed the toilet, went to the shower cubicle and fiddled with the controls. Hot water blasted from the showerhead and a loud whirring sound erupted above her, making her jump. It came from a grille just above the window; a fan, so the room wouldn't get too steamy even with the window closed. They thought of everything, this lot. Or believed they did.

Jenna stepped under the spray and let it pummel her, hanging onto the support rails on the shower wall. She didn't recognise the brand names on the shampoos and shower gels, probably because they were ridiculously expensive. What the hell. She used them all, leaving the caps off as a small gesture of defiance: a little extra mess for Rose to tidy up.

She emerged from the shower and wrapped herself in towels and a robe. There were slippers, too, but she ignored them and went back into the bedroom barefoot, leaving wet prints in the thick carpet pile: another little inconvenience for them. She'd see how much she could get away with.

You wild rebel, Jenna. Bet they're shaking.

She felt better already, though. She crossed to the chair by the desk and put on clean knickers and a sports bra, followed by the socks, jogpants and sweatshirt. Finally she laced the trainers up. Getting dressed helped as well. She felt a little less vulnerable now.

There were half a dozen books on the desk, all concerning pregnancy and childcare. No surprises there. Jenna shook her head and looked away, and saw one final detail she'd missed before. On the wall, above the bed, was a sign saying LIVE, LAUGH, LOVE.

Somehow that was the final insult. Jenna didn't want to spend another second in here; she had to get back. Had to find Holly again. She went to the bedroom door and tried it, but it didn't open. Jenna hadn't expected it to, but was astonished by how angry it made her. She was penned in, and the reality of it abruptly hit her full force.

She'd felt surprisingly calm till then, but now there was only rage. She began kicking the door, till wood splintered. She heard herself screaming: *"Let me out of here, let me the fuck out,"* and, *"James you piece of fucking shit."*

"Miss McKnight. *Miss McKnight.*"

Jenna stopped, breathing hard. The voice spoke again, overhead. "Have you quite finished?"

"Fuck you!" she shouted, and kicked the door again. A jolt of pain shot up her leg, and she realised her foot was throbbing.

"Miss McKnight." It was a male voice. "Please stop that."

"And if I don't?"

"Miss McKnight–"

"It's Ms."

"Miss McKnight, I'm asking you not to abuse our hospitality."

"Your hospitality?" The rage was still in the driver's seat; Jenna knew that, but all she could do was watch what happened next. "Your fucking *hospitality*?"

"*Miss McKnight.*" An edge in the voice now, a crack like a whip. Here it was at last: the naked threat, with all the bullshit stripped away.

Jenna folded her arms. "Go on."

"Miss McKnight, we're prepared to be reasonable about this."

"Are you now?" The anger was receding for the moment, like a wave. It wouldn't take much to make it wash in again, although. She stood up straight, despite her foot now throbbing agonisingly. If she was lucky, she'd just bruised the hell out of it: that would heal fast enough, but broken bones were another matter, and she had to be able to run if, *when*, her chance came. "Define 'reasonable', please. Kidnapping's reasonable now?"

"Preventing murder's reasonable, wouldn't you say?"

"What murder?"

"You've a right to your own life, Miss McKnight. No one disputes that–"

"Could've fucking fooled me."

"–but by the same token, so does your baby."

"It's not a baby."

A pause, and a faint release of breath. "As I said, we're prepared to be reasonable."

"And as I said, define fucking reasonable." Her voice rose to a shout.

"Miss McKnight." He spoke as if to a rebellious child. That *it's-your-own-time-you're-wasting* tone. Jenna dug her fingers into her arms to avoid shouting again. "Define reasonable? All right. We just want a little of your time. Seven months or so, no more. You'll be very well compensated, you won't even have to do anything other than relax and take care of yourself."

"And the precious fucking baby, right?"

"Financially," he went on, "it's a very handsome deal indeed. Just seven months, during which every – reasonable – need of yours will be addressed–"

"Again, your definition of reasonable–"

"At a little over fourteen thousand pounds per month. One hundred thousand pounds in total." A pause. "The rate is negotiable, if need be. We're open to suggestions."

"Not the ones I'll be giving you in a minute," Jenna muttered. They didn't get it. They had no idea how non-negotiable this point was. *No means no, you arseholes.*

The voice sounded faintly amused. "You'll be well looked-after, and paid a tidy sum for doing – well – nothing. Just for not killing your baby. I mean, the money aside, you wouldn't really want to be responsible for a murder, would you?"

"Depends whose we're talking about."

"Miss McKnight–" He broke off. Jenna heard a faint mutter. "–sure that's wise, sir? I can't guarantee – yes, sir." The voice returned to full strength. "Miss McKnight, please step back from the door."

"What if I don't?"

"We'll wait until you do."

She doubted they were really that patient, but shrugged. "Fine," said Jenna, and took two steps back.

The lock clicked. The buckled door shifted in its frame but didn't move, and Jenna almost chuckled. But finally it was forced open in dragging movements across the thick carpet, and James came in.

9.

He looked the same as ever. Tall and dark, a lean, saturnine face and curly black hair. She always half-expected to see horns poking out of it, though less those of a devil than of a pagan satyr. That had been part of his attraction for her: he resembled the kind of beautiful Mediterranean boy Pan might have assumed the form of, before revealing his true nature.

With his public-school accent, tailored suits and Rolex watch it made for an elegant enough package, but it was all surface. Under the polish, he'd just been a spoilt little boy who'd decided in advance what Jenna should want and how she should behave, and hadn't taken it at all well when she wouldn't do either. And despite his eagerness to hear about her experiences with other women, he'd been about as sexually adventurous as a goldfish.

Remembering that made Jenna smile. James's smirk faltered, if only for a moment. She squared her shoulders. Right now, he had the power, but in other respects he was still weak. She had to remember that, and find a way to use it.

He'd tried to control her, with money and with his rages, all of which had been guaranteed to bring out the worst in Jenna. He'd have ended up in hospital at one point, had he not had the sense to back off at the critical moment. She'd scared him, which was no doubt part of her fascination for him: unlike James, for all his wealth and privilege, she wasn't afraid to do as she pleased.

James put his hands in his pockets. He wore a white shirt, the collar open: a small gold crucifix sparkled at his throat. "Hello, darling," he said.

Jenna snorted.

"Going to behave yourself?"

She snorted again. "When have I ever done *that*?"

"Ha." With a small dry laugh, James leant back against the door, pushing it as nearly closed as it would go. Then he moved to one side, no doubt so his employees could ride to the rescue, before realising he was on the side the door opened and would be flattened into the wall if anyone burst through. He moved to the side opposite and finally settled into place. "Look, as they tried to tell you, I *am* prepared to be reasonable here."

"Yeah, you keep saying that. Having kidnapped me."

"Trying to prevent infanticide, love."

"You never seemed particularly devout before. Certainly didn't mind sex before marriage."

He shrugged and smiled. "Rather hoped one might lead to the other, old girl."

"Less of the 'girl', dipshit." Careful: she was slipping into the banter that had been one of the less toxic parts of their relationship. She mustn't forget he was the enemy. "I made it clear from the kick-off that wasn't going to happen."

Another smile, another shrug. "People change their minds."

"Well, I wouldn't have."

He spread his hands. "You *say* that…"

"And I *mean* it. Fucking hell, you wonder why I dumped you?"

"You're very unforgiving, Jenna. Anyone ever tell you that?"

"I wonder why?"

"I was willing to work at our relationship. How many people were you with before me – and how many after? Hasn't made you happy, has it?"

She didn't answer, not least because the first response she thought of was that nothing, probably, ever would. And he, of course, would think that he knew better than her, as always.

"Sometimes you have to stay and work at things," he said. "And sometimes you have to be open to change."

"Funny how *I* was always the one who had to change, though, wasn't it? Marry you, become a good little housewife, change my mind about having children. What planet do you live on?"

"Mine's a very interesting world," he smiled. "And you'd be surprised how many others I know. I know worlds you couldn't conceive of."

"Christ's sake. Listen to yourself. What part of 'you are dumped' were you too thick to understand, Jimbo?"

He'd always hated that nickname, and Jenna saw his face twitch. "I'd really prefer you didn't call me that."

"Well, I'd prefer you let me out of here right now and pointed me to the nearest train station, but I bet that's not gonna happen either."

He sighed and shook his head. "All right, Jenna. Have it your way. But let's just be clear, shall we? Two things are going to happen. One, you're going to have that child – after which I'll take care of it and you'll never have to think of it again – and two, you're staying here until you do. All right?"

"No, it's not."

"Well, that's just the way it is, baby." He smirked. "Cutty Wren Lodge is part of Daddy's Highland estate – sorry, *my* Highland estate, now. I keep forgetting. And the only people in ten, twenty square miles are in this house. On top of which–" his teeth glinted in an especially smug smile "–guess where this cottage is?"

"Scotland. You just said."

"The woods, Jenna. Miles of forest in all directions." That smirk was all she could see, hanging in limbo like a malign Cheshire Cat grin. "And we both know how you feel about *those*. So you see, there's really nowhere to go."

"Bastard."

"Sticks and stones may break my bones."

"You know, Jimbo, that's the best idea I've heard from you all day."

He stepped instinctively backwards, up against the wall behind him. "Remember, Jenna, I'm not alone. As I said, you're staying here and you're having the baby. That's non-negotiable. What *is* negotiable is how that time passes."

"You really love the sound of your own voice, don't you?"

"You must admit, I've a decent baritone. Seriously, though, look around you. This room's perfectly comfortable, and there's a lovely garden you can use if you behave yourself. I'll happily provide any creature comforts you like. Books, DVDs, video games? You name it."

It wouldn't include Holly, not that Jenna would suggest it; James might actually be stupid enough to kidnap her and bring her here if he thought it would seal the deal, and she'd no intention of subjecting Holly to this as well, much as she wanted to see her again. "How about porn?"

He rolled his eyes. "Whatever floats your boat, although bear in mind–" he gestured ceilingwards "–you might have company."

"Oh, you mean your little peeping toms?"

"My point, Jenna," some irritation was creeping back, "is you can have a very pleasant stay here. A nice long holiday, very well paid. It can be as simple, and as enjoyable, as that." His voice hardened. "*If* you let it."

"And if I don't?"

"We also have a cellar here. Clean and dry, but nowhere near as comfortable. Rather basic. And a lot of its features are optional. Like the lighting. Of course, it's got cameras, just like here, for your protection, including heat-sensitive ones. We'll always be able to see you, Jenna, but whether you can see us – or anything else – is quite another matter."

"Your mother must be so proud of you. Or did you eat her when you hatched out?"

James's mother had died when he was very little and he'd adored her, probably because she was the only person ever to have shown him real, unfeigned affection. The closest Jenna had ever come to feeling something for him had been when he'd told her that; for a moment there'd been a real human being there, a hint of the gentle, wounded boy he might once have been, expressing a pain that could have been her own. She'd occasionally wondered since if it had been something he'd made up to win her over, but from the way his face tightened now, she knew it hadn't.

"I can make things easy for you, Jenna," he said softly. "Or I can make things very, very hard."

"Promises, promises." She wiggled her little finger at him. "Heard that before, and it was bollocks then, too."

Any relationship's a source of ammunition, if you're only willing to use it; James had rarely opened up to Jenna in any meaningful sense, but she still knew how to hurt him. It was all she had the power to do right now. That last barb, like the one about his mother, went in deep and his jaw tightened. He straightened up, leant forward. "Maybe you need a spell down there, Jenna. Teach you some manners. Some gratitude and respect."

She laughed in his face. "Gratitude for fucking what?"

He motioned around. "Accommodation like this, for a start."

She needed to provoke him. Make him angry. She thought of Holly, trying to keep her own fury stoked and under control. "Don't do me any favours."

His fists clenched at his sides. "All right, then. Time for a little change of venue."

"Putting me down the cellar, are you, Jimbo?"

"You asked for it, you got it."

She spread her arms and beckoned him on. "Come on, then. Try."

He smirked. "No, darling. I have staff for that–"

But he'd let her get too close; Jenna seized the chance offered and punched him in the throat, hard. The blow might have been fatal had it landed full-force – it'd certainly have ruined that baritone of his for good – but his reflexes were quick. Even so, he staggered back, choking; Jenna followed up with a roundhouse kick to the stomach that sent him back against the wall.

So much for biding your time.

She stepped towards him, and he lashed out feebly. Perfect: she grabbed two of his fingers and bent them back till he screamed, twisted his arm behind his back and clamped her forearm across his throat.

"Keep fucking still," Jenna told him. Her blood hummed, and her head grew clear. She was in control now, and on familiar ground: give her an enemy, and she'd fight. She looked around for something sharp, but they hadn't been stupid enough to leave anything lying around. There was the carafe and waterglass, of course, but she'd have to smash one and hope to find a suitably knifelike shard. No: better to trust in her hands.

Jenna looked up at the ceiling. "All right," she said loudly. She didn't shout: that would sound as if she'd lost control. Calm sounded better. Calm made them take you seriously instead of thinking you were a hysterical woman who wouldn't do anything. "Now, here's what's going to happen."

10.

"You fucking bitch," James said, in a high, strangulated croak. "I will fucking–"

Jenna pressed harder on his throat and whispered in his ear: "Shut. The fuck. Up." She raised her voice again. "One, you're going to open the front door. Two, I want a car parked out front. Three, I want the door open, keys in the ignition. We all clear?"

"Very impressive," said James through his teeth. "But it won't work. They won't let you go."

"Yes, they will." Jenna raised her voice again. "Otherwise, I'll break your boss's neck."

"If you do, they'll kill you."

"Guess what, Jimbo, I don't give a shit. And you'll still be dead." She pressed on his throat again, making him gag and choke. "I will break his fucking neck, Rose. I promise you."

"All right, lovey," Rose called from the hallway. Her voice sounded considerably colder than before. Harder. Metallic. "All right. We'll sort everything out for you. Just don't do anything silly. All right, lovey? Don't want to do anything we'll all regret, eh?"

Jenna's arm muscles began to ache, but she consoled herself that James was far more uncomfortable. He was wheezing for breath, hoarse and painful, and his body was pulled back tight against hers: all the intimacy of lovers, but none of the fun. Not for him, at least. Sweat trickled down her spine.

A tremor developed in a thigh muscle; she straightened the offending leg, shifting position. James grunted in pain.

She hadn't been unconscious long enough for her muscles to atrophy. They still had all their normal strength. She could keep this up. At the same time, the power had passed from her now. This was the dangerous time: Rose and an unknown number of other "employees" were supposedly preparing the way for her escape, but she couldn't see what they were doing. "Talk to me, Rose. Where are we at?"

"We're getting everything sorted out for you."

Jenna frog-marched James to the door. "Pull it open. Slowly." She raised her voice. "I'm opening the bedroom door, so I can see what's going on myself, Rose. Don't try anything."

"All right, lovey. Again, just don't do anything silly."

James tugged at the handle with his free hand. The battered door inched open, catching and dragging on the carpet. Outside was a carpeted hallway, with the same cream-coloured walls and dark wood beams as the bedroom. It was dim and shadowy, doors set into the walls on either side.

Rose stood a couple of yards from the bedroom door, arms folded, face coldly calm. "You're just making things worse for yourself, lovey."

"Where's the car?" said Jenna.

"Hubby's bringing it round the front now," said Rose. Jenna heard an engine growling and tyres crackling on gravel; a fresh breeze blew along the corridor, presumably from the open front door. "But honestly, Jenna, this isn't a good idea."

"How do I find my way back to civilisation from here?"

Rose's jaw tightened; a muscle jumped in her cheek. "There's a dirt track. It's a few miles, but it'll get you to the nearest main road."

And from there Jenna could find her way home to Manchester. *Holly.* No, she mustn't let herself think of Holly yet. Mustn't distract herself. Couldn't let herself hope. "All right," she said. "Now, let's have the lights on, shall we? All of them, throughout the house. Don't want anyone hiding in the shadows. Do we, *lovey*?"

The muscle jumped in Rose's cheek again, but she moved back down the hallway and flicked a switch. Jenna narrowed her eyes against the light. Rose moved away; another switch clicked and the shadows at the end of the hall lightened. "Keep all the internal doors shut. Don't want anyone reaching out and grabbing me. Wouldn't end well for the lord and master here." She applied extra pressure to James's fingers, making him grunt in pain. "Rose?" There was no reply. "Rose?"

"I'm here, lovey." Rose stepped back into view. "Just putting all the lights on, as per your request." She glanced right. "Car's outside. Ready when you are."

"Stay where you are," Jenna said, "till I give the word. Okay?"

Rose nodded. "Whatever you say."

"And show me your hands."

"All right." Rose raised them to shoulder height, fingers spread. "All good, lovey?"

"Stop calling me that."

"Okay, lo– Sorry." Rose smiled. "Force of habit."

"Move, bitch boy," Jenna told James.

He grunted in pain and fury, but he didn't struggle and Jenna doubted he would. Like so many other privileged little boys who'd had things their way all their lives, he'd no tolerance for pain, or capacity to resist.

Rose stayed put as Jenna pushed James down the hallway. When they were about three feet apart, Jenna said, "Start walking backwards."

"Whatever you say." Rose's tone remained that of an adult addressing a petulant child, which annoyed and worried Jenna in equal measure. Still, she kept moving back and to Jenna's left, around the corner. Jenna glanced right automatically, to ensure no one was lying in wait, then followed, narrowing her eyes against the daylight coming in through the front door and silhouetting the other woman.

"Keep going," Jenna said. "Back. Back."

Of course, now she couldn't see behind her to check if anyone was trying to sneak up, and her palms were sweaty. If James tried a sudden move his fingers might slip from her grasp, although she'd have him round the throat even then.

Gravel crunched underfoot as Rose backed out of the porch. "Wait," said Jenna. "Where's the *hubby*?"

"He's here," said Rose, as a small, weedy-looking man whose bald head and glasses glinted in the sun moved to her side. Funny; Jenna had expected someone strapping and outdoorsy.

"All right. Now, the two of you keep moving back."

They obeyed, and Jenna moved out into the narrow, glass-fronted porch. The sides were glass too, so she could see all around. A Land Rover was parked on the gravelled apron outside the cottage, which had white rendered walls that seemed to almost glow against their dim surroundings. To the left, the gravel gave way to a rutted dirt track that wound away into the trees. There were more trees directly opposite the cottage, and a wall of them to her right; she was enclosed on all sides. Jenna fought to keep her breathing steady.

The drive up the track would be nightmarish – like the woods on Tallstone Hill, only worse. But it had been dark in those woods, and impossible to see what was out there. That wouldn't be an issue now. She'd just have to keep going until she was clear. She smiled to herself: *out of the woods.*

She stepped outside. "Over there," she said, motioning Rose and the bald man off to her right. "Now, hands behind your heads, and kneel down."

"Do we have to?" said the bald man in a thin, bleaty voice with a slight Scottish accent; he was pale and mealy-looking, and pot-bellied despite his scrawny build. A tweed jacket with patched elbows, a blue check linen shirt, a bowtie: no, not what Jenna had expected from Rose's husband at all. But it took all types. "The gravel – my knees–"

"Not my fucking problem," Jenna said. "Yes, you have to."

"Do as you're told," said Rose, impatiently and with what sounded like contempt.

"All right. All right. I'm sorry."

The last sentence seemed to be directed as much to Jenna as to Rose. Something wasn't right. Jenna looked around her, but couldn't see anyone else, in the house or out of it. The driveway was clear. No one in the trees.

Rose's lips tightened, barely perceptibly, as her knees made contact with the gravel. The bald man knelt stiffly and clumsily, gasping in pain, and almost lost his balance. He steadied himself with a smooth bare left hand, then straightened up when Rose glared at him and put his hands behind his head again.

Something niggled Jenna as she backed up to the Land Rover and the open passenger door. Something wasn't right. She looked over her shoulder, checking the keys were in the ignition, then sat back into the passenger seat. James moaned, bending his knees and arching his back as she pulled on his bent fingers. "All right, Jimbo," she said. "Crouch down and back up."

As she wriggled backwards across the seats, James manoeuvring himself after her awkwardly, she realised what had bothered her. Rose wore wedding and engagement rings, but when the bald man had put his left hand on the ground, it had been bare. No rings of any kind at all.

Not her husband.

Jenna sensed movement behind her; she started to turn, but wasn't fast enough. Something brushed the back of her neck and then there was a sharp, stinging prick, and a spreading coldness she'd felt before.

She lashed out, blindly. Something she was holding snapped, like a pair of brittle twigs, and James screamed. There was shouting; Rose and the bald man ran towards the car. James struggled; she still had her arm across his throat and tried to tighten her grip, but she couldn't hold on to him. She felt him being pulled away.

More shouting, and a weight landed on her; she struggled, but it pinned her down. She had to keep fighting; had to get free. But everything was slowing down and getting dark. Her eyes regained focus briefly; Rose's face appeared above her, lips pursed, looking coldly down. Jenna was going to spit at her, but suddenly she felt very, very tired, and that no longer seemed important.

Rose's face faded and distorted, as if seen through rippling water. All the sounds were distorted, too. And Jenna sank back into the welcoming dark.

11.

There was a pillow beneath her head and a blanket over her. She was on a mattress of some kind, but it was bare and lay on a concrete floor. She'd been stripped to her underwear. Light came from an unshaded bulb overhead: there were cobwebs around the fitting. The walls were bare brick.

Obviously, this was the famous cellar. Someone crouched beside her, but when she stirred they recoiled with a bleat of alarm and fell on their backside, knocking over a plastic bucket beside the mattress. It was the bald man; he pushed himself away from Jenna with his heels, then got up.

"Well?" said James.

Jenna rolled onto her back, squinting at the light. James stood to one side, nursing his throat, along with Rose and a big man with a slablike face.

"She'll be all right, as far as I can tell," said the bald man. "No issues with the pregnancy."

"Should bloody hope not." Even without Jenna's arm locked across his throat, James's voice still sounded strangulated and high-pitched. *No baritone singing for you for a while.* "Not with what we've been paying for your advice."

"Given under duress," said the bald man. "And if she's well, it's no thanks to you people. God almighty, what you've put the poor woman through–"

"I suggest you moderate your tone, doctor," said James sharply. "Just remember your situation here, yes?"

The doctor bowed his head. "Yes, Sir James." He glanced unhappily at Jenna.

James turned his attention to her now, and smirked. "How you feeling, sweetie?"

"Like a dog shat in my head. How about you? You sound like Kermit."

The smirk faded; James massaged his throat again. "I did warn you," he told her. "And I tried being nice. But here we are. Welcome to the cellar."

"How long you planning on keeping me down here?" Jenna sat up and the bald man retreated further; Rose and the big man moved forward. "All nine months?"

"Seven, lovey. You're already two months gone, remember?" Rose shook her head. "Not long, when you think. If you'd just been sensible, you could've had a lovely time here."

"A lovely time? Seriously?"

"Well, it's very nice out here, lovey. You could've treated it as a holiday and let us take care of you, but you had to make trouble. Now look at you. And you could've hurt your baby."

"It isn't a fucking baby, you silly cunt."

"Hey." The big man spoke for the first time. "Watch your language, Miss McKnight."

It was the voice she'd heard from the speakers in the bedroom. Rose put a hand on him. "You'll have to excuse Eric, lovey. He's a bit protective."

"Ah. This is the real *hubby*, then?"

Rose smiled and rubbed Eric's muscular arm. "All mine."

Jenna glanced at the bald man. "Didn't think this one was your type, somehow."

"This is Dr Reid," said James. "He'll take care of all your medical needs while you're here. He'll be delivering your baby, too, so you might want to be nice to him."

"What happens if I need a C-section on the day?" She regretted saying that immediately; it made her sound as though she'd accepted the situation. She wasn't having this child – *any* child, but this one least of all. She mustn't forget that. Had to hold firm. Couldn't give way to these bastards on anything, or they'd hollow her out.

"We'll have assistance brought in nearer the time," James said carelessly. "If need be. We're a long way from that being an issue just yet, I think you'll agree. And the cottage isn't *that* roomy. Don't want things getting too crowded. But don't worry. Dr Reid's fully kitted out a spare room for the delivery – it'll work as a surgery too, if necessary. You'll be fine."

"I'm fully qualified," said Reid. "Don't worry on that score, Miss. I'm sorry about all this, but–"

"Shut *up*, Reid," said Eric.

"Did Dr Reid recommend shooting me full of drugs too?" said Jenna.

James smirked. "Well, you wouldn't have come quietly, would you? Besides, you'd already decided to kill my baby. Desperate remedies and all that."

"The sedatives used posed minimal risk to the foetus," said Reid. "And the mother."

"Shut *up*, Reid," said James. "Anyway, Jenna, it's in your own interest to behave yourself and not put your pregnancy at risk. Sooner it's over, the sooner you go home."

Would he really just let her go? It wasn't impossible. She was one woman of no particular background, with a history of mental health problems and violent outbursts; he had money, influence, had been to all the right schools, and Rose, Reid and Eric would confirm whatever he said. If she *did* go to the police, she'd probably be one who got locked up.

For a moment, she almost considered acquiescing, though she was furious at herself for doing so. She couldn't let the bastards have an inch of ground. Had to hold on to who she was and what she wanted. In any case, there was no guarantee James would keep his word. He could pay her off and let her go, or once she'd served her purpose, decide that was too much of a risk to take. There'd be plenty of room in these woods for a shallow grave. Or a deep one.

Jenna doubted Rose or Eric would baulk at disposing of a body; Reid might, but once the baby came he'd be sent packing with whatever they'd promised him. Unless they considered him a weak link, in which case they'd just make that grave in the woods big enough for two.

"You're here for the duration," said James, "so the question's really what sort of a stay you want to have. Clean sheets, soft pillows, DVDs, video games, breakfast in bed – maybe even time outside in the garden if you're very good – or down here. A proper loo and a shower, or–" He gestured to the bucket Reid had knocked over, and shrugged. "All one to me."

Jenna clenched her teeth; James smiled. "You don't have to answer straight away."

"I can think of several answers," she said. "Just trying to decide which one best expresses what a cunt you are."

"Like I said," he told her, "this is really something you should think over before making a decision. You're not leaving here until you've had a baby, Jenna. Simple as that. That's reality. You can accept it, like we all have to accept things sometimes that aren't ideal–"

"Like me dumping you?"

"–or fight it. In which case, you *will* lose. And all you'll do is make life harder for yourself. Oh, and something else. It might not be as nice down here as the bedroom upstairs, but we can make it far, far worse. In fact, let's give you a little taster, shall we?"

Dr Reid looked alarmed. "Sir James, that isn't a good idea."

"When I want your opinion, doctor…"

Reid stiffened. "I've agreed to help under protest, but I can only do so much if you deliberately endanger the child's life."

"Hey," said Jenna, "how about mine?"

Reid flushed red. "Or the mother's," he said. "Solitary confinement of any kind is very damaging, both physically and mentally."

"She's got to be taught a *lesson*," James said, as if explaining to a child. "I won't stand for a repetition of this."

"Then kill me or let me go," Jenna shouted. Rose put a warning finger to her lips.

"You're putting your child's life in danger," said Reid.

James shrugged. "Calculated risk. If it comes to that, we can always start again from scratch."

"You fucking what?" Jenna said, at last. The statement had taken the others by surprise, too, she noticed; Reid looked appalled, and even Rose and Eric seemed taken aback.

James shrugged. "Means to an end, as I say."

"Try it," she said. "I'll fucking cut it off. Assuming I can find it."

"Don't flatter yourself." James inspected his fingernails, trying to look nonchalant, although his voice spoiled the effect. "If that became necessary, we'd go the artificial route. Nothing very high-tech. Got a perfectly good turkey baster in the kitchen." He glanced at Rose and smirked. "Don't worry, Rose – you'll get a new one to do the Christmas dinner with. I don't need that kind of extra flavouring."

"Sir James," said Reid, "I will not be a party to–"

"You don't have any choice, Dr Reid. I believe I've made your position here very clear."

"And if *she* dies? Or there are complications that leave her unable to bear children?"

"I have a name," Jenna said.

James ignored her, and Reid seemed to be pinned by his gaze. "The whole reason you're here, Dr Reid," James said, "is to ensure that doesn't happen."

"I'm trying to, but if you ignore my recommendations–"

"Shut *up*, Reid," said Eric heavily, and slipped his arm

around Rose. She squeezed his hand. Jenna had hoped James's willingness to risk the baby's life might cause a rift, given their pro-life inclinations, but apparently not.

"You," said James, "do not get to dictate terms to me, Dr Reid. You get to take my money and carry out my instructions. You know the consequences if you don't do as you're told."

Reid finally lowered his gaze, nodding miserably. "Good," said James. "That's settled then."

Reid gave Jenna a last wretched look. James turned towards the flight of steps at the end of the cellar, shooing the doctor ahead of him; the others followed. "Don't bother to get up," James told Jenna, as she started to rise; Eric watched her, arms folded, as the others left the cellar.

Jenna stayed put, fists clenched under the blanket. She wasn't going to break. She was going to get out of here. She was going to see Holly again. And she was going to get rid of what James had put inside her.

Eric moved backwards, turned, and went up the steps to the door at the top. It closed; Jenna heard the key turn, and bolts being drawn across. Then the light went out.

12.

She screamed herself hoarse with rage, hurling obscenities at the ceiling, but there was no response and the light didn't come back on. Why would it? He wouldn't reward her for bad behaviour.

Bad behaviour? She was angry all over again. That was how James saw the situation, and she could have killed him for his arrogance and entitlement alone. *No one* told her what to do, not like this.

Not much you can do about it now.

The darkness was cold and shapeless, a swirling black void. It was impossible to judge distances. She knew there were walls, but couldn't see them and was already struggling to remember the rough size of the cellar. Twenty feet square? A hundred? And that was only the part she'd seen.

Jenna sat up and hugged her knees to her chest. She closed her eyes – not that it made any difference – and breathed slowly in and out. *Calm. Calm.* She had to think now. They'd locked her up on her own, in darkness. Holly had told her once how solitary confinement was meant to work: you lost track of space and time, and hallucinations and madness followed. It was a way to break down difficult prisoners. But hardly ideal for a pregnant woman.

It made no sense, none of it. People got obsessed with having kids, an heir to pick up where they left off, but James seemed too young for that. Of course, that sort of thing might seem more important now he'd inherited the title – from what she remembered, his father had died quite suddenly – but if he was that desperate for a sprog, he could have found a volunteer easily enough, and one much more socially acceptable than Jenna. But apparently it had to be her. Simple entitlement on his part, maybe: he'd wanted her and she'd dared turn him down.

Jenna clenched her fists in rage. She'd had a comfortable enough start in life, but that had all been swept away after Mum's death. Everything since then had been gained by work and bloody-minded persistence. James, meanwhile, had had everything he'd wanted on a plate since birth, and it still wasn't enough. All Jenna had was her independence, and he even wanted that.

She breathed deep again. In this darkness she felt not just alone but untethered: drifting in a black void. She stood – still shaky on her legs – felt along the mattress to the end, then measured out its length and breadth in paces. Then she moved to the end of the mattress she'd been facing before the lights went out. She'd call this one the north wall.

She crossed the cellar floor, arms extended ahead of her. Gritty dust crunched underfoot. Her palms touched the north wall halfway through her fifth step. She eased her foot across the floor until her toes touched it too.

Slowly and methodically, she established the cellar's dimensions. The steps were in the north-west corner of the room, which was the furthest away from the mattress, so Jenna carried the plastic bucket over to them before making use of it for the first time, minimizing the inevitable stink.

It wasn't a pleasant experience, particularly in the dark, and she amused herself with fantasies of immersing James's head in the bucket – ideally once it was full – and holding him under until no more bubbles came up.

* * *

Three times a day – at least she assumed it was that often – the cellar door opened so Rose could put a plastic water bottle at the top of the steps, along with a cold, flavourless pasty on a paper plate and some vitamin pills. There was nothing on the plate Jenna couldn't eat with her hands – they clearly didn't trust her with anything sharp – and the plate and bottle had to be replaced on the step afterwards. She supposed she should be flattered they thought she could turn either one into a weapon.

The meals at least gave some structure to the day; to fill the black silent hours between them she developed a routine. On waking she warmed up, did push-ups and sit-ups and then paced the cellar, east to west and back again. Her stride was about two and a half feet, so she'd calculated that a hundred and thirty-six lengths of the cellar made a mile. She'd walk that distance – she couldn't feel the cellar floor now; the soles of her feet must be like boot leather – then lie down and rest before doing it again.

Sometimes, in the cellar, everything was black and it felt as though she was tumbling through emptiness. All she heard was her own breathing, fast and ragged, and the mattress felt like a raft on an angry sea. No anchor. No mooring. When she'd been a child, when it was dark and she couldn't sleep, Mum had told Jenna stories. Hansel and Gretel, Snow White, Red Riding Hood. So, at such times, Jenna began to recite the stories to herself.

She began with Hansel and Gretel: when she pictured the scene, the witch in the story bore a remarkable resemblance to Rose, and Jenna found herself devoting considerable time and descriptive energy when it came to visualising her death in the oven. Likewise, in Red Riding Hood, she imagined the Big Bad Wolf as James, who begged and whimpered for his life, shitting on the floor in terror, before Riding Hood – who saved herself in Jenna's version of the tale, no woodsman-to-the-rescue required – split him in two with an axe. Groin first.

Later, she moved on to novels, whispering her stories into the mattress. Sometimes she'd pretend the softness she lay on was Holly and imagine them together. Nothing erotic, just simple things like snuggling in bed of a morning, watching Netflix on the sofa, hiking over Dinas Oleu. She imagined that often: being confined to the cellar had made her yearn for sunlight and open air. She could smell the grass and flowers and sheep shit, feel the hot sun, see the sea stretch out to the horizon.

In a way it was almost better than the real thing: she could rewind and rewrite as she went so that they never fought. If it could only be like that in real life, she could stay with Holly for months, years. Maybe even forever.

That thought was so startling it snapped her out of her reverie. And then she was close to tears, because not only was real life not like that, but in real life, Holly would already be gone. She'd have assumed Jenna had left or given her up for dead, as people did: even if Jenna saw her again, what they'd had was finished.

She let herself cry. Couldn't really have stopped herself. When she was out of tears, she wiped her eyes, breathing deeply, then raised a middle finger for the benefit of any cameras.

Holly was something else James had taken from her; something that, unlike her liberty, Jenna could never get back. Something else she'd make James pay for.

I will not be forced to do what I don't want to. You never got that, James. I will get out of here. I will abort your bloody spawn. And if I've lost Holly because of you, I'll break your fucking neck.

Jenna closed her eyes and went to Dinas Oleu again, following Holly along the mountain path. Holly turned back, grinned: *Come on, slowcoach, move your arse,* she said.

And Jenna ran to meet her.

* * *

In the darkness, she recited:

My name is Jenna McKnight. I have been kidnapped. The cellar is fifteen and a half paces, west to east; twelve and a half, north to south. My mattress is three paces long by two paces wide and lies three and a half paces from the east wall, eleven from the west wall, six and a half from the north, three from the south. The shit-bucket is by the cellar steps, in the north-west corner.

I have been here three days.

Four days.

Five.

She changed the number after every third meal, as she assumed that marked the passing of another day. Everything else about her mantra stayed the same. Including the final sentence:

I will escape.

13.

The cellar was freezing, and the cold air stank of rotten meat and animal breath.

Jenna tried to sit up and assume a defensive crouch, but her body remained immobile. The paralysis was bad enough, but worse was the feeling of another presence in the cellar with her. She'd experienced that before in the cellar, but not the accompanying cold and stench. She'd encountered that only in her dreams of the forest grove, and only twice in real life: the summer of 2007, on Tallstone Hill, the night Mum had been taken away. And in her bedroom, the night before they'd kidnapped her.

Not real, she told herself. *Not real. Night terrors. Sleep paralysis, that's all this is. Hallucination. Nightmare. Not real. Not real—*

On its own, it was the faintest, most innocuous noise: something scratching the concrete floor. But it was sharp and clear and definite, and couldn't be anything but real.

It broke Jenna's paralysis at least, and she was finally able to roll into a fighting crouch, fists balled, glowering blindly into the dark. As if in reply an icy gust blew into her face, stinking so badly her eyes watered and she almost gagged.

Silence. She told herself there was nothing there: it *had* been sleep paralysis after all and the sound had been a rat or mouse – hardly unlikely down here, even if she'd seen no sign till now – but she could still feel the presence, sense its bulk: something that barely fitted into the cramped cellar, hunching so it didn't brush the ceiling. Her instincts insisted it was there, as fervently as her reason insisted it wasn't. And then she heard it scrape and rustle across the floor, and couldn't deceive herself any longer.

As it walked, the sound it made wasn't the scuff of leather, but a scrape like naked bone – claws, perhaps, or nails. The scraping came from overhead too, which made no sense. Perhaps it had raised its arms, so that its fingernails were trailing along the ceiling. Or perhaps something else. She could both hear and feel its breaths now, and the stench was even worse, as if it was growing realer by the second.

I know this dark. I know it.

A bizarre thought. Absurd. It didn't even mean anything.

I've been here before.

She'd have worked it out herself soon enough, no doubt, but as it moved closer, two faint, hazy, pale blotches appeared in the darkness. *Something white*, she thought – but there was no light to see anything by down here, unless it was luminous. And as if at that thought, the pale blurs brightened and grew more distinct, becoming two perfect discs of pale, ghostly light.

Eyes like lamps.

No: that had been a nightmare, a dream. Yet here they were, and as they glowed brighter still, the cold seeped further into her; her teeth chattered, and she could see her breath.

Jenna looked down at herself, but the glow from the thing's eyes didn't shine on her, or even over itself, as such; instead a sort of faint, misty nimbus suffused it, drawing it out of the gloom.

This thing belonged in her dreams of the grove; those were the only places it could or should exist. It didn't belong in anything like the real world, least of all here or now. She'd real enemies to fight, actual flesh and bone: James, Rose, Eric, Dr Reid.

No: this thing wasn't, couldn't be real. Jenna daren't believe otherwise, not in this situation. Even her sense of who she was had grown so threadbare. She had to hang on to the little she knew. She couldn't afford to lose her mind.

Yet here the thing was, revealed by the pitiless ghost-light. It was roughly human-shaped, but gigantic and completely skeletal: a skeleton that somehow lived and moved. Roots and creepers were twined around the bones, which looked overgrown and deformed: sharp curved spurs protruded from every joint, the fingers and toes ending in bladelike talons. It walked on all fours, spine arched and shoulders hunched, and flaps of tattered, rotting hide hung from it.

Mercifully, she couldn't see its face; the one thing resembling an item of clothing was a bolt of coarse material wrapped around the head into which the hazy glow enveloping the creature didn't extend; only the luminous eyes were visible. Finally, from its head, a set of huge, spreading antlers rose to brush the ceiling.

The shape moved forward with a terrible, ponderous grace, branchlike limbs stirring, rotten hides flapping like ruined flags. She heard other sounds too now, as it grew closer or more real: the gristly crackle of its joints, the hoarse labouring of breath drawn into non-existent lungs.

Once again, Jenna was unable to move. A spade-sized, clawlike hand reached out; in another second it would have touched her, but at the last moment her paralysis broke and Jenna threw herself backwards, tumbling over the mattress and scrambling back across the floor until she collided with the east wall.

The creature threw its head back, antlers grating against the ceiling, and made a sound like gas bubbling through tar, then hunched forward again and continued to advance. The nimbus around it intensified to form a pool of light that illuminated its immediate surroundings. Jenna saw the mattress crumple under the thing's weight, almost flattened completely. And then the beast was closing in on her; she wanted to run but felt so cold, so small and alone and afraid, and realised now that it only seemed unwieldy because of its size; it was moving with the slow, deliberate grace of a cat closing on its prey. Antlers or no, this thing was a predator, and a piercing cold radiated from its eyes. Cold that went deep into you, down to the bone: the cold light that saw everything, inside you and out.

She had to call it something for her own sanity, and so in that moment she gave the thing a name, supplied by some unknown instinct or buried race-memory:

Bonewalker.

It sounded like the name of a creature in one of the video games Holly liked to play, but even if it was, Jenna didn't care. It was the perfect name for this most personal monster of hers. She pushed herself backwards, scrabbling at the concrete with her heels till they bled, but there was nowhere to go. She tried to convince herself the brickwork behind her was softening, that with a little more effort she could force herself through it – so many other laws of physical reality had been breached today, after all – but it refused to budge.

It wasn't real. She was hallucinating. She told herself that, but was unable to convince herself. That cold was too familiar, and the thing was too real, too solid, too detailed. The yellow bones were striated, as if defleshed by knives, and pitted as though by time. She could see the tiny leaves on the creepers flutter in the cold draught of its breath. And its joints made a soft, gristly crackle as it raised its clawlike fingers to her face.

They brushed her cheek, light as cobweb; even so it stung, a warm trickle running down it. The thing – the *Bonewalker* – breathed out and she gagged, not only from the stench but from the arousal in its ragged panting breaths.

When its hand came away from her face, one claw-tip glistened red. It slipped the digit into the blackness within its cowl; the finger disappeared, its glow snuffed out, and there was a slurping, sucking sound.

Jenna thought she might actually faint. There was nowhere to run or hide, and how could you fight something like this? At least, unconscious, she wouldn't know or feel what it was doing to her, wouldn't know anything any longer. Even that might be a victory of a kind: she could cheat it, at least, of whatever gratification it got from her fear.

It was laughing again now, that appalling bubble of tar. If it leant forward it could kiss her, assuming it had lips; more likely, it would bite off her face. Instead, it leant back on its haunches, still chuckling, shook its antlered head, and receded.

She wasn't sure afterwards if it had moved backwards, if its glow had faded, or whether unconsciousness had finally delivered her from it, plunging her into a blackness deeper than the cellar's. Whatever the case, it was gone, except for a single bubbling word that followed Jenna into the darkness like a coin tossed down a wishing well, one she'd heard before in her dreams of the forest grove:

Soon.

14.

On her fourteenth night in the cellar Jenna woke suddenly, feeling lost and adrift as she hadn't in days, and very cold.

Her first impulse was to scuttle back towards the east wall, looking round in search of those luminous eyes. She'd tried again, afterwards, to convince herself the Bonewalker had only been a nightmare, like the grove, but it had been impossible, even after it had disappeared. It had been too vivid, too present, to be anything but real. And the scratch it had left on her cheek, the dried blood crusted there, was no product of her imagination.

That had been bad enough, but it wasn't the worst. The worst wasn't even accepting that she'd encountered it before. Oh no. The worst thing of all was accepting *where*.

That thing took Mum.

When it first sank in, she was afraid it would destroy her. It had come along and taken Mum, then casually returned after Jenna had slowly and painstakingly rebuilt her life to take her too. Why here? Why now? She'd no idea, but it made a joke of everything she'd done, all she'd achieved.

But all that had sustained her in this place was her anger at being robbed of her freedom and independence: on that score this thing was no different from James, and had taken her mother to boot. So once Jenna had accepted its existence, its greatest effect was to supply her with a fresh reservoir of rage. Beyond that, though, she'd no idea how to deal with the creature.

And so, in the end, she'd come full circle. The Bonewalker was a separate threat to James and Rose, Eric and Reid; it belonged to a different world. They were the ones who currently held her captive, so they were the ones she must focus on escaping. If the Bonewalker came after her after that, she'd deal with it as best she could: for now, she'd decided to dismiss all thought of the creature, as though it had been an illusion after all.

But now the cold was back, and with it the fear. The glow and the stench were absent this time, at least, and she had no sense of a presence in the cellar with her. However, a sound Jenna recognised came from directly overhead, through the wooden ceiling: a thick, dark noise like gas bubbling through tar. When she'd heard it before, it had sounded like laughter, but now the rhythm was different. It was irregular, almost like speech. And then a very ordinary, human voice – and a familiar one – answered it.

"Yes, of course I understand. But Dr Reid's keeping close tabs on her. If there were a real problem–"

Another tarry growl.

"No, I understand! I understand. I *know* she can't be replaced."

James, she realised. It was James, and he was talking, somehow, to the Bonewalker.

"But you see what she's like," James was saying. "Absolute nightmare to deal with. I could barely stand her for the month we were together, and you saw what she did, didn't you? I know you were watching. God knows what would've happened if Rose and Eric hadn't been on the ball."

The next rumble ended on a rising note: a question.

"No! No, of course not." James sounding genuinely afraid. "I'm perfectly capable of handling the situation, and I haven't forgotten our priorities." His voice took on a wheedling tone. "But you've seen how she can be. She has to be compliant, or bringing this pregnancy to term without incident will be almost impossible. Never mind future ones."

Future ones? Jenna clenched her fists and teeth. Not that she'd ever intended accepting James's bargain, but, as she'd suspected, he wouldn't have honoured it anyway.

More essential than ever, then, that she continue to resist.

Why do this, though, James? Why any of it, when by his own admission he loathed her? Although she'd resolved to push the issue of the Bonewalker to one side in order to focus on that of James and her captivity, for now at least she'd have to break the first resolution if only to keep the second, since something clearly connected the three of them. But what interest could it have in her? Finishing the job it had begun on Tallstone Hill? Maybe it had a taste for McKnight women, she thought; that was why James was determined to make her pop out a string of babies, to supply the monster with delicacies. Jenna bit her lips; she was on the verge of a full-blown hysterical laughing fit, and if that started she'd no idea when she'd be able to stop. Or even *if*.

The tar-voice spoke again. "Fuck Dr Whitecliffe!" James snapped. The tar-voice emitted a rising growl: a big cat might make such a sound, a panther or tiger. The image took Jenna back once more to that night on Tallstone Hill. It wasn't even directed at her, but she still shrank back against the east wall.

"I'm sorry!" James sounded terrified now. "I didn't mean to – but there's no need to involve Whitecliffe. I can handle this. No need for that cold, clinical stuff. It'll be done as nature intended. Eh?"

A thin, reedy laugh from James; a noncommittal rumble in response.

"All right," said James. "We'll bring her up from the cellar tomorrow. She'll have learned her lesson by now anyway."

Dream on, fuckstick. Jenna breathed out. The hysteria had passed. There was only anger again, and now it was as cold as the cellar air. That was good. Cold anger was so much better, so much easier to direct.

Overhead, the tar-voice purred.

"Soft restraints," said James. "Should be enough. She's already pacing up and down and talking to herself – probably half-bonkers already." Jenna could almost see him smirking. "Always the ones who talk a big fight who break first."

I have not broken. Jenna mentally replayed her fantasy of splitting him in half with an axe. Or better still, hanging him upside-down and using a saw instead, which she'd seen in a couple of gruesome medieval woodcuts. It was a two-person job, but she could probably get any woman who'd ever dated James to help out. *I will not break.*

The tar-voice growled again; this time Jenna thought she could actually make out the words, distorted though they were: *Very well.*

"All right, then. Tomorrow." James's voice became wheedling again. "And then–"

The answering growl was long and menacing.

"I'm sorry! I didn't mean any disrespect."

The growl became a chuckle, then cut out; warmth flooded back into the cellar again, so suddenly it now felt almost sweltering.

Overhead, James was panting in mingled exhaustion and relief. Then there were footsteps, a slammed door, and silence.

So, tomorrow this would end. Back to the light, the cottage, and the pretence that if she gave them what they wanted, she could take the money and go.

Jenna wondered whether James expected her to deliver a specific number of children or just to pop them out *ad infinitum* until it killed her or the menopause kicked in. Either way, a shallow grave awaited her as soon as she was no longer useful. To survive, in any and every sense, she must escape. That was the immediate priority: for now, at least, the Bonewalker was irrelevant.

Jenna's default response to a threat was to kick its teeth in and run away. That had been enough in the past, but wouldn't be here. Precautions would be tight; they'd expect her to try again. No margin for error, then: her next attempt had to succeed, and put her beyond James's reach.

Even when she escaped, James might try for her again. And from what she'd overheard, he wasn't the only person involved. Even though she'd still no idea why *her* producing a child should be so important to anyone. But all that would wait until she was free. She'd find Holly. Holly would help her; Holly would understand. Even if she'd left and found someone else – and she would've, because everyone did – she wouldn't abandon Jenna if she needed help, not when she knew the truth.

Act, not react, had to be the first rule. Watch, wait, gather information, and let them think they'd broken her.

That was a frightening thing, dangerous, because she mustn't let the act become reality; she had to keep who she was, what she wanted, safe at the core of her beneath the pretence, had to armour it in steel. But despite that fear, she felt calmer now, more centred, than at any point since finding herself here; in fact, she was coldly excited at the prospect of the game about to begin.

15.

Even so, after two weeks in the dark she screamed when they turned the light back on, and every sound was deafening; Rose murmured soothing words as they helped her up the steps, but might as well have been firing a gun in Jenna's ear.

Reid attended her the day she was brought up, and visited Cutty Wren Lodge each day for a week thereafter. When he did so, Jenna saw he was furious – not at her, but at those who'd reduced her to this state. But it was helpless fury: he was too cowed, too scared by whatever James was holding over him, to be of any help.

Rose was a constant presence, bringing soup, water and painkillers for the splitting headaches that initially plagued Jenna, bathing her with a sponge and easing a bedpan under her when she needed to relieve herself. Secured to the bed with soft restraints, Jenna couldn't even clean herself afterwards; Rose did that too. On the third or fourth occasion Jenna began crying with anger and humiliation: even Holly had never seen her so helpless.

"I know, lovey." Rose cleaned her hands on an antiseptic wipe. "I did warn you, though."

Jenna looked away. Rose squeezed her hand with what seemed genuine compassion. "Sweetie, I hate seeing you like this, honestly. I'll do everything I can, try and make things easier. But you've got to show you can be trusted. You have to be patient."

Jenna didn't feel capable of patience: she couldn't even exercise, meaning she grew more out of condition daily while the pregnancy continued developing, sapping her strength. Eventually she'd be too bloated to move. She had to get out of the restraints before then.

It was three weeks before they finally untied her, letting her move freely, first around the bedroom and bathroom, then other parts of the house. By now the pregnancy was showing. Her belly had expanded, making the jogging pants difficult to secure, and her ankles had started to swell. It made her hate the thing inside her even more. It was changing her; James was changing her by remote control. Pregnancy affected your mind as well as your body, one reason she'd hated the whole idea. It was James trying to break her down, force her to be someone she didn't want to be, given physical form.

Sometimes she thought James's child knew her hatred for it, and was working deliberately to make her incapable of escape, but that was true paranoia, real madness. Nonetheless, it underlined how little time she had.

And she'd have to escape through the woods. Oh, James had been a clever bastard there. Outside Cutty Wren Lodge and the grounds, she'd have miles of woodland to traverse, and probably barefoot, too. They still provided her with sweats and jogpants, but the trainers had been replaced with flip-flops, of all things, which she was regularly chided for failing to wear. You couldn't launch a decent Muay Thai kick in those, far less run.

But beyond all of that, there was the crippling fear that descended on her every time trees surrounded her. She might escape only to collapse in a gibbering heap a hundred yards from the cottage.

Rose and Eric were her constant companions; after the first week out of the cellar, Reid's attendance fell off to once or twice a week and James absented himself from the cottage for days at a time. She was pregnant and under guard, after all; what was left for him to do? When present, he kept his distance, watching her balefully, although his fingers were now no longer taped up and his voice had more or less returned to normal.

Even when Rose or Eric wasn't with Jenna, she was monitored constantly. They couldn't review every second of footage from the hidden cameras, but she could never be sure they weren't watching at any given moment. Her world was basically her bedroom and bathroom, the cottage's living room, which had a locked patio door looking out onto the garden, and the kitchen-cum-breakfast room. There was a back door there, likewise permanently locked. The rest of the building, especially the hallway to the front porch, was off-limits.

The shower was Jenna's sole sanctuary; when the steam grew too thick for the fans to dispel and the glass misted up, she held onto the armrests and performed squat after squat, trying to strengthen her thigh muscles. Even there she couldn't be sure she was unobserved, but it was the best she could do. Nowhere else was secure, even her bed at night. Her biggest fear was that she'd talk in her sleep and reveal that she hadn't accepted her lot and still planned to escape, if she could only find a way.

Eric and Rose treated Jenna with considerable kindness now that she was playing the broken, docile little girl. She had to remind herself they were the enemy, that if necessary she'd have to kill them to escape: she was afraid her anger would die if she kept smothering it, and the act become reality.

And then, one day, Rose asked if she'd like a walk in the garden.

"Bit of sun would do you good, lovey. And some fresh air as well. Mm?" The older woman raised her eyebrows. "Long as you promise to behave, of course."

"Of course," said Jenna, hiding her excitement as best she could. "I promise." She resisted the urge to cross her fingers behind her back.

It had been seven weeks since they'd let her out of the cellar, and she'd been out of restraints a full month. The leaves on the trees beyond the garden wall were starting to turn: it was almost autumn.

Which, whenever she'd dreamt of it, always seemed to be the season in the grove. Thankfully she hadn't dreamt of that place again, but it was hard not to think of it, or of the Bonewalker. *Soon*, it had told her. One more reason to escape.

Grass brushed her feet as she clomped along in the clumsy flip-flops. Rose stayed close behind her. The garden was surrounded by a nine-foot wall. Not impassable, especially as there was a rose trellis on the back wall above the rockery, but it was topped with cement embedded with broken glass. She'd need a blanket or similar to throw over the coping – it wouldn't be complete protection, but would guard her from the worst. In a pinch the hooded top might serve, if she peeled it off in time.

"Penny for your thoughts," the other woman said. Lightly, but she actually meant it.

"It's just nice to be out here."

Rose nodded, hopefully satisfied. Jenna continued pottering around the garden, smelling the remaining flowers and finally lowering herself into a lawn chair: thankfully she could still stand up again unassisted.

With a little help and preparation, she could get over the wall. For all she knew there was a ditch at the bottom that'd break her neck, but she couldn't afford to consider that, or what happened once she reached the trees. She'd just have to hope she could resist the panic attacks.

"What's she doing out there? Get her back inside."

James stood in the back doorway, glowering.

"Sorry, boss." Rose winked and stuck out her tongue, so quickly Jenna barely believed she'd seen it. "Sorry, lovey. Back we go, I'm afraid."

Again, her affection seemed genuine, however constrained by circumstance; Jenna knew she mustn't soften towards the other woman, but, just possibly, Rose no longer saw her as a threat. That was a weapon too. One by one, she was gathering them, and now she saw a way out. All she needed, from here on in, was a chance.

16.

Jenna woke around 7am – it was a habit by now – showered, changed into the jogpants and sweatshirt Rose had laid out, then stretched and limbered up as best she could.

Her belly was protruding further. Not much, but a few more weeks and she could abandon her already small hope of getting over the wall. She pictured her unwieldy bulk toppling back into the flowerbeds, limbs waving helplessly like an overturned tortoise's while the others watched, doubled over with laughter.

Enough. She shook her head. Then, remembering the cameras, she turned the movement into the start of a general body shake-out before forcing her feet into the hated flip-flops and opening the bedroom door. They didn't lock it anymore.

"Morning, lovey," Rose called, from the speakers in the bedroom ceiling. She was on watch this morning.

"Morning," Jenna called back; it had become a morning ritual.

She went down the hallway to the living room. Outside, a grey sky overhung the garden.

"Nice out," Eric called from the kitchen.

"You think?" said Jenna.

"Forecast says it'll tip down again later." It had rained heavily almost the entire week. "Enjoy it while you can."

He was at the counter, chopping meat and veg. Rose might

been the housekeeper, but Eric was the cook. he'd served in the catering corps, he'd told Jenna in a relaxed moment: he'd done other things in his army days, too, many of them far less pleasant, but always seemed happiest while labouring over a stove. Surprising how different he looked at times like that – cuddly, almost. She'd seen him dance around the kitchen when music came on the radio, surprisingly light on his feet for such a big man.

As Jenna went through into the kitchen, she realised something had changed. It took her a moment to realise what; when she did her heartbeat quickened and her stomach hollowed with excitement. A light, cool breeze was blowing from the back door.

It's open.

Wide open, in fact, and propped in place by a rubber wedge. Understandable enough – it was a mild morning, and the air very fresh – but also, at last, a lapse on her captors' part, a chance of escape.

"Bacon and eggs?" said Eric.

"Please," Jenna said absently. He had his back to the door; she had to act normal, not alert him to his mistake. She moved to the breakfast table, pulled a chair back and sat down. *What are you doing? The door's open. Move, you silly cow.* "What you making?"

"Beef bourguignon," he told her. "Eight hours in the slow cooker, it'll melt on your fork."

He put the meat and veg aside and rinsed his hands at the sink. Now he was side-on to the open door, and Jenna's breath caught. She couldn't let her anxiety show: if he saw it, he'd look for the problem, and it would be impossible to miss. It was unbelievable he hadn't realised yet.

Her one chance and she'd already blown it. No, she hadn't. The door was still open. And yet she remained seated at the table. What was wrong with her? Was she so acclimatised to this place she couldn't bring herself to escape?

No. She was still who she'd always been. Her determination to break out hadn't gone away, but she couldn't just run: she had to get over the wall, too. Over the glass.

She stroked the tablecloth. It was plastic, but doubled over, if the material was tough enough, it might work. Might. If she had the time. Slowly, one after the other, Jenna eased the flip-flops off.

"You all right?" Eric was looking straight at Jenna. The door was directly behind her. Any second now he'd realise. And then–

"Yeah." She gave the brightest fake smile she could. "Still half-asleep, that's all."

"No problem." Eric leant across the kitchen counter and switched the kettle on. "Now for those bacon and eggs. Best get a wiggle on. Got Reidy coming round any minute." He pulled an iron skillet onto the hob, poured oil into the pan and took a packet of bacon from the fridge.

"Eric?" Rose called. Jenna's stomach clenched. Were there cameras in the kitchen? Rose wouldn't miss the open door, even if Eric did. But there was no speaker in here. She was shouting down the hall.

"I'm just sorting Jenna's breakfast," he shouted.

"What?" Rose called back. Remembering how she'd once read that ninety percent of married life was shouting "What?" at one another from different rooms, Jenna almost laughed.

"Sorting Jenna's breakfast!"

"What?"

And then, the miracle happened; Eric turned and went out, into the living room. "What's that, love?"

Now. Or never ever.

No hesitation. Jenna caught the tablecloth in the middle, folded it in half, pushed back the chair and stood. Two quick steps took her to the kitchen door; then she was over the threshold and in the garden. Then, for the first time in months, she ran.

Grass brushed her swollen ankles. *Don't think about the woods.* The back wall rushed up to meet her. There was a muffled shout from the cottage; an alarm blared. A door crashed, and she felt as much as heard footsteps behind her.

Eric, coming to fetch her back. He was bigger, stronger, in better condition: he'd be on her in a second.

Then do something about it.

Could she, still?

One way to find out.

Jenna pivoted as Eric bore down on her, aiming a Muay Thai kick at the pit of his stomach. It wasn't her best – Ron would've shaken his head in despair – but it was good enough, largely because it caught him off-guard.

Eric practically ran onto her extended foot and jack-knifed, landing in a heap on the grass, but as Rose came out of the cottage shouting Jenna's name, he lurched upright again, red-faced and wheezing. All the affability was gone now: his eyes were piggy with rage.

Jenna ran for the trellis, clutching a corner of the tablecloth between her teeth as she cleared the rockery. Rose-thorns pricked her palms and feet, but she barely felt them; the trellis creaked but held, and then her face was level with the broken glass atop the wall. Clinging to the trellis one-handed, she slung the tablecloth across the coping.

As she hauled herself up, something grabbed her left ankle and pulled; she almost lost her grip but managed to grab the trellis with her other hand too.

Eric, clutching her leg, glared up at her as Rose dashed across the lawn. The other woman's face was hard, scrubbed of any warmth; Eric hauled on Jenna's leg again and the trellis cracked and shifted. It'd come away from the wall in a moment and that would be that.

Eric reached up with his other hand. Jenna didn't know what he was after; the waistband of her pants, maybe. Hard to run away with them round your ankles and your bits on display.

Game over. You tried, and you failed.

And then James stepped through the back door, arms folded, smirking, and leaned against the doorframe. He was going to watch Jenna being dragged back into the house, bare-arsed, exposed, kicking and screaming like a spoilt child who'd thrown a tantrum, and he'd laugh all the way through it. *What you want doesn't matter; only what I want does.*

It was like a spark igniting gas. *Whoomph*, and there was flame: heat, light, and most of all rage. Which wasn't worth much on its own, but when you paired it up with other skills, it counted for considerably more.

Jenna drew her right knee as far up as she could, then rammed her heel down into Eric's jaw. Pain shot up her leg, but Eric's grip broke and he tumbled into the flowers. His head hit the rockery with a loud, wet crunch. Eric went limp and rolled out of the flowerbeds; he came to a halt on his back, eyes and mouth fixed open.

Rose screamed. Jenna felt a minuscule twinge of remorse – Rose had been kind to her, in her way – but swept it aside. She and Eric had signed up for the kidnapping and all that went with it: whatever happened to them was their own fault.

Jenna scrambled the rest of the way up. The tablecloth hung over the coping, already stretched and tented by the sharp glass points. All of a sudden, it seemed no protection at all.

Too late to turn back.

Jenna knelt up on the coping and pivoted. Glass crunched, and she slid over the wall, holding onto the inside of the coping: more glass crackled beneath her forearms, but again failed to draw blood.

From her position she saw Rose huddled by Eric's body, a keening howl still coming from her. James was rushing across the garden, open-mouthed; behind him Dr Reid stood in the kitchen doorway, astonishment on his face – astonishment, and unless Jenna was imagining it, a hint of a smile.

Jenna scrabbled with her feet for a purchase on the outside wall, looking down. At the foot of the wall was a slope, then a shallow ditch; beyond that, the woods. If she landed badly and broke a leg, it would all be over.

Same story if you stay put.

So she let go, flinging up her arms so her hands wouldn't catch on the glass, bending her knees on impact and rolling. The wind flew out of her but she barrelled to a halt at the foot of the slope, shaking.

Out.

Behind the wall, James was shouting; the words were a blur of sound beneath Jenna's heartbeat thundering in her ears and the ragged sawing of her breath. Rose was still howling.

Jenna turned towards the trees. For a second she was back on the Panorama Road with Holly: *Not going. Don't want to.* Her stomach clenched; panic threatened to seize her.

Move.

Sometimes it really was that simple: one bare foot in front of the other. She couldn't let the fear stop her, any more than she could allow James or the others to. She jumped over the ditch, landed on crumbling leaf matter, scattered twigs and wet muddy loam. Then she was wincing and grunting as her feet caught on stones and roots, grabbing the rough-seamed trunks for support as she hauled herself forward with increasing speed: into a run, and into the woods.

17.

Rose had felt positively betrayed when she'd seen Jenna run. She'd honestly felt they'd come to an understanding and the girl had seen sense after her time in the cellar. But she clearly hadn't, and now there'd be so much inconvenience. Just when things had settled and they were all rubbing along fine, she'd gone and spoilt it all. It would be back to the cellar for her now, meaning more work all round and the end of the nice, civilised atmosphere they'd developed.

And then she'd been climbing over the wall. Eric had tried to pull her down, and then her foot had flicked out.

That had been bad enough – the girl hurting her Eric like that – but then he'd fallen and hit his head. The sound it had made; that horrible crunch. The way he'd rolled back onto the lawn, his eyes wide open, and lying so terribly still, in a position so awkward and jumbled it could only mean–

But she'd refused to complete the thought, refusing to believe.

So she'd moved across the lawn in silence at first, because it couldn't be real. Except then she'd seen the dent in the side of Eric's lolling head and his empty unblinking eyes and realised it was. Her Eric, her husband of twenty years–

That was when she'd screamed.

A howl. Agony. Disbelief. And the hope – forlorn, desperate, fading now to nothing – that if she played along long enough someone would tell her it had all been a trick. Eric would sit up laughing and say, *Got you, love, should've seen your face.* Jenna would climb, grinning, back over the wall. Everything would be all right. They'd go back inside, and Eric would get on with making his beef bourguignon, which was always lovely, a real treat. Rose had been delighted earlier when he'd announced it as the evening meal.

But he stared up at her, unblinking, and a fly crawled into his mouth and he didn't move, didn't even flinch. And now the sobs started, breaking the howl coming out of her into fragments, as the truth of it sank in: her husband was dead.

She heard Mr James shouting – Sir James now, of course, but he'd been Mr James to Rose all his life and she couldn't think of him otherwise. She was aware of Dr Reid beside her, too, but he would know even better than her that there was nothing to be done, not now.

Nothing to be done at all.

Except – the thought stirred cold and slow in her, like some reptilian predator in a swamp – for one thing.

And just like that, she stopped. No more screams; no more tears. She was calm now. She wiped her eyes. She knew what to do.

James grabbed her shoulder, tugging at her sweater. "Get *up*," he shouted. "Get on your fucking feet. We need to find the bitch."

"Yes," Rose heard herself say. "Yes, we do."

James pulled her round to face him. "We need her alive." Rose stared back at him; he managed to compose himself and put on a concerned expression. "Rose, I'm sorry about Eric. I truly am. I'll make things right when this is done."

How? But, of course, Rose knew the answer: money. It was all he understood. He had no time for people; he barely understood them. Grief, loss: he had no idea how to deal with someone in real pain. Not even himself. His father had been no different: no wonder, Rose thought distractedly, James had turned out as he had. Sir Alec had given him everything materially but provided nothing emotional, nothing of depth. No amount of money would replace the mother he'd lost, any more than it would replace Eric, but it was the only thing the Frobishers understood,", so they threw it at every problem.

She said nothing. Only nodded.

"She can't have got far," said James. "Not in her state. Get the tranquiliser guns. Chop chop."

Did he really just say "chop chop"? But of course he had.

In the kitchen, she stopped, staring at the counter where the beef bourguignon Eric would never cook still lay half-prepared. The skillet smoked and crackled; Rose went to the stove and switched off the hob, then went back through the cottage to the room beside the one Jenna had been kept in. She'd been in there minutes ago – had it really only been minutes, before she'd become the person she was now? Because she was different now. She knew that. Her former life was irrelevant. Only one thing still mattered.

Eric had been a soldier. She knew what he'd have done had Rose been lying dead on the lawn – and oh God, she wished she was. She might as well be. She wouldn't outlive Eric, not for long. But she had work to do first.

In the room beside the bedroom was a chair and desk; monitors; speakers; a control panel; a microphone; an alarm button. The monitors showed the inside of every room in the house, and also the garden. They didn't matter now either.

What mattered, now, was the steel cabinet bolted to the wall.

Rose took the keys from her pocket and unlocked it.

Inside were the guns.

There were deer rifles. There were shotguns. And there were three DanInject tranquiliser rifles, which Rose took out and propped against the wall. She removed a backpack, too, and put a box of tranquiliser darts inside. Animal tranquilisers were potentially fatal when used on humans, but each of these darts contained a dose of Propofol, which they'd used on the previous occasions they'd needed to subdue Jenna. It would knock her out within one minute of injection, and keep her under for ten unless a further dose was administered. Eric's idea: he'd believed in preparing for all eventualities.

But there was always one you missed.

Rose smiled tightly, as if in pain. Then she glanced towards the door, ensuring no one else was there, and reached inside the cabinet for the Paradox Gun.

She forgot why Sir Alec had ordered it, but it was a beautiful piece, custom-made to his exact specifications. Modelled on old poachers' shotguns, it was a single-barrelled weapon that folded in half. The last two inches of barrel were rifled, so it could be used as either a shotgun or rifle. Both at once: hence, a Paradox Gun. It was the gun Rose needed because, folded, it would fit neatly in the backpack. She put a box of rifled shells in too.

"Rose?" shouted James. "Where the fuck are you?"

"Coming," she called, zipping up the pack, but didn't leave yet. She took two more items from the cabinet: a hunting knife in a sheath, which she pushed down inside her boot, and one of several handguns on display. They'd been illegal to own under UK law for years, but Sir Alec had never allowed little things like *that* to get in his way. Which Rose was very glad of just now. She was taking no chances.

She chose the Beretta 84. It was an excellent gun. Compact, reliable, never jammed. And, despite its small size, the magazine held thirteen rounds. She'd prefer to use the Paradox Gun – stalk the girl like a deer, bring her to bay, then finish her – but if it came down to it, she'd no intention of letting Jenna McKnight get away for want of ammunition.

Rose loaded the magazine, inserted it into the pistol and racked the slide to chamber a round, then lowered the hammer and slid the Beretta into the back of her waistband.

"Rose!" James stormed down the hallway. "The fucking hell's keeping you?"

"I'm ready now," she called, then shrugged on the backpack, picked up the tranquilliser rifles and went to meet him. She didn't bother relocking the cabinet. It didn't matter anymore. Nothing did, except revenge. She could settle that, and then, for all Rose cared, she could die too.

18.

Jenna didn't know how long she'd been running; hopefully a while, as her feet were already throbbing, bruised and – she thought – bleeding, too. She'd lost count of how often she'd stubbed her toes on rocks and roots, and wondered if she'd broken any.

She'd focused so far on what lay right ahead of her, always looking for the next gap between the – *not trees, don't think of trees* – the next gap she could squeeze through in order to keep moving away from Cutty Wren Lodge.

She knew that wasn't enough: she needed to work out which way to go. But to do that, she had to put enough distance between her and James to buy the time to stop and think; James wouldn't let Eric's death delay his coming after her. She still didn't understand why she was so important to him, but Jenna wasn't sure any sane person could. He'd been talking to the Bonewalker, after all. Only a madman would do that.

The Bonewalker isn't real. Solitary confinement can make anyone hallucinate, never mind everything else you've been through. Only natural you'd associate it with what happened to Mum. You were kidnapped, like her, for no reason that made sense–

No. She'd have loved to believe that, had tried her hardest to, but she'd felt the thing's touch, heard its laughter. And she'd met it before.

A nightmare.

But it hadn't been only one, had it? How often had she dreamt of the grove over the years?

A recurring nightmare, then. Understandable, given what you've gone through.

She had to stay in the present. Keep moving. Holly. Think of Holly. That was something to cling to.

She'll be long gone, you know that.

Jenna realised she'd stopped moving; worse, she'd fallen to her knees. She hauled herself back up again, clutching at tree-trunks to pull herself forwards. She'd find Holly, after all this, and say, *Please come back, I love you.*

Could she really say *that*? Had she ever before in her adult life? But, after all, Holly loved her.

You believe that? When you were such a bitch to her?

The trees reared up around her: oak and pine, birch and aspen, branches interweaving, blotting out the dull sky. She was in the deep woods, like the one Mum's car had broken down in, where nightmares dwelled. Panic seized her, something she couldn't defend herself against or resist, and she was down on her knees, curling up on herself in a vain attempt to hide as she fought for breath, unable even to cry out as a red squirrel bolted from the undergrowth and skittered up the trunk of a nearby rowan tree.

She lay on the forest floor, feet throbbing; her right heel ached from where she'd kicked Eric. She'd killed him. Killed a man.

She knew that, but it meant nothing to her: it was a fact, nothing else, like the colour of her hair or eyes, or the little white scar on her left thumb. Or that she was nearly four months pregnant and pissed off about it.

Being up the duff does not agree with you.

Jenna started laughing, as she had when Holly had said it. She shouldn't. James and the others might hear. But despite her best efforts, the laughter kept coming. Till suddenly, it stopped.

Fucking hell, I was such a cow. Not exactly news, but still. And on the heels of that, another thought: Holly couldn't have been for real, couldn't possibly have cared for Jenna. She'd have had to be an emotional masochist for that to make sense. Look what a bitch Jenna had been when Holly had found the pregnancy tests.

An emotional masochist, or only with Jenna to get something out of her. The same thing James was after, maybe. Jenna could think of nothing else she had that people would want. She'd no idea why anyone would want *that*, but James did, and apparently not only him.

No. Jenna wouldn't believe that. She had to cling to something, and Holly was all she had.

Cold water trickled down the back of her neck. Rain hissed and rattled on the canopy overhead. But it was still biting cold, and the stench of decay and foul breath hung in the air.

She crawled to the nearest tree. The Bonewalker was here, or close. She had to move. She couldn't let it touch her again.

But the stench faded, and Jenna wasn't even sure any longer that it had been there to begin with. It had been cold – still was, her breath was pluming in the air – but summer was gone and it was raining hard, and the forest was far too like the grove of her nightmares. She couldn't stop thinking of the last but one, in which the Bonewalker had been gnawing that limp, naked body. It reminded her of something else she'd seen, but she didn't know where.

For Christ's sake, don't think, not now.

Jenna could hear voices, twigs snapping underfoot. *James.* She had to keep moving, if only to spite him.

She stood and took another shambling step, then one more. *You're already fucked. You're not going to get away. Give up now.*

"Fuck off," she screamed. She didn't know if some traitor part of herself had been talking, or the Bonewalker whispering in her ear; either way, she'd carry on.

Jenna stumbled through the trees, hands stretched out ahead of her, eyes squeezed shut.

19.

In happier times, Rose and Eric had catered to the late Sir Alec's privileged guests, plutocrats and oligarchs invited on exclusive deer-hunting retreats. They tended to be very male affairs in the least appealing ways, so Rose had usually stayed at the cottage or Sir Alec's hunting lodge like a dutiful little wife and been more than happy to do so, but larger groups were often divided into two parties, one led by Eric and the other by her.

Rose wasn't in Eric's league, but she was more than good enough to track Jenna McKnight. More than the equal, even in her grief, of a citified little bitch lost in the woods, quite literally barefoot and pregnant. The girl's trail had been so clear she might as well have left signposts. Even before she screamed.

"Fuck off!"

Small animals bolted, birds took flight, and Rose smiled. A scream meant Jenna was suffering, which was good: Rose wanted her to suffer everything humanly possible before she died. On the other hand, whatever the girl might be suffering, Rose wasn't there to see it. And that wasn't good enough.

Behind her, Reid's bleaty little voice rose. "Sir James, please – I can be no help to you here."

"Oh yes you can, doctor. We need every able body we can get, and that includes you."

"But Lizzie – please, Sir James, today she might–"

"You know what happens to your precious Lizzie, doctor. If. You. Do. Not. Do. As. You're. Told. Don't you? *Don't* you, Dr Reid?"

"Yes, Sir James."

"Then shut up and get on with this, and with a little luck you'll soon be home. Rose! Which way?"

She hadn't even realised she'd stopped until he called out to her. "Which way now?" James demanded again.

He was such a lazy little prick. If he'd just apply himself a little, he could find the girl's trail, but James Frobisher was, as he always had been, a pampered little shit who expected others to wipe his arse for him.

Still, his indolence was to Rose's advantage.

Maybe when this was over she'd kill him, too. After all, if not for him then none of this would have happened. Sir Alec, ruthless old bastard that he'd been, had had no shortage of skeletons in his cupboards – or, indeed, buried in these very woods – but there'd always been a sane reason for it.

It hadn't even been out of reverence for life. Rose and Eric's greatest, bitterest regret had always been her inability to have children. To spurn that gift, when Rose would have suffered Hell's own torments to receive it, was abominable. But James had been willing to risk the baby just so he could break Jenna, because he could always get her pregnant again. Because for whatever reason it had to be Jenna, and no other. If not for this stupid, pointless project, Eric would still be alive.

None of which let the girl off the hook. To kill her now would be to kill the unborn child too, Rose knew, but she no longer cared even about that. The girl had taken Eric from her, and so she had to pay. Pregnancy or no, Rose would kill her before sunset, if not within the hour – but James had set it all in motion. He wouldn't feel a moment's real sorrow or guilt over Eric, either; he'd just throw money at Rose as if she could order a replacement online. As if you could replace love at the click of a button. But then, he'd never really known love. You couldn't expect him to understand it.

"Well?" he demanded.

Rose took a deep breath and turned. "Ahead somewhere," she said. "You and Dr Reid go right, I'll go left. I'll drive her towards you if I can."

James peered back at her through the rain, frowning. "All right," he said at last, then moved away, Reid's dumpy figure stumbling in his wake.

Rose stopped when she was out of sight among the trees, listening to James grunt and curse as he followed the false trail. It would take them deep into a pathless tract of nettles and thorns that would make the going slow and painful, and ultimately lead nowhere. That took care of James for now. It should be long enough.

Rose propped the tranquiliser rifle against a tree, then opened the backpack, pocketed half a dozen rifle rounds, and unfolded the Paradox Gun.

She left the pack behind as well. She had the rifle, the Beretta and the knife: if she couldn't get Jenna McKnight with those, she didn't deserve to.

Rose slid a round into the Paradox Gun, snapped the barrel closed and set off along the trail, rain drumming on her scalp, a kind of cold, resolved peace in her heart.

20.

"*Still falls the rain*"; that was a poem Holly had read to her. The title was all Jenna could remember now.

What'd it been about? She'd asked Holly something like, *Nice poem, what's it mean?* But she'd only been half-serious; she hadn't found it that impenetrable. Jenna wished she could remember what Holly had told her. Not because of the poem; just because it was something Holly had said.

But still fell the rain, all right, leaving Jenna soaked and cold.

Not that she should care, anyway, about anything Holly had said. None of it was to be believed. Everyone had a knife behind their back. No one could be trusted.

Aw, poor Jenna. She heard the voice as if it spoke aloud. *Everybody feel sorry for her.*

"Piss off," Jenna mumbled.

Will I fuck. Listen to you, whining on. Stop feeling sorry for yourself.

She knew that voice. Where from?

So you're on your own. So fucking what? You gonna let the wankers win? Seriously? Pathetic.

"What the hell do you know?" Jenna's voice was thick and choked; she realised she'd been crying.

I know how it was when your dad died. You were all on your own then, weren't you? You'd already lost your mum, your nan, your house. You and your dad were stuck in that shitty little flat in Northern Moor. You had a shitty little day-job in a shitty little shop in Altrincham. Remember that?

117

"Course I fucking do." Unwillingly, Jenna opened her eyes a little: the nagging voice seemed determined to give her no peace. Squinting through the drizzle, she thought she saw someone on the other side of the clearing, but it could've just been the rain in her eyes.

And all he did was drink. That and gamble. Horses, scratch cards. Try to get it back. Till you got home that morning and–

She'd turned the key in the lock and all the familiar odours had washed out over her. Stale urine, spilt beer, rotten food, cigarette smoke, old sweat, unwashed skin. And – oh, joy of joys – it'd smelled like he'd thrown up again as well.

She'd gone through into the living room, because there was no choice: it was the only way to reach either her bedroom or the kitchen. The curtains were pulled so the only light in the room was a dull grey. Dad's drink-bloated mass had been a shapeless, silhouetted lump on the sofa – his weight had nearly doubled in the past year and a half. Glass and crumpled empty cans had glinted on the floor.

Then she'd realised how silent the flat was. The only sound had been a fly buzzing. When Dad slept, he snored like a pig; even awake, his hoarse, wheezing breaths could be heard throughout the flat. But there'd been no sound. And then she'd seen the morning light had glinted not only on the vodka bottle and beer cans, but on his open eyes.

You'd been kicked and kicked and kicked. No idea what to do. All on your own and barely eighteen. You could've curled up and died then. The voice took on a whining, hectoring tone: *Mummy, Mummy, come and get me.*

"Fuck you," Jenna snarled.

You didn't though, did you? Else you wouldn't be alive to whinge your arse off now. Remember what you did *do? Eh? Or are you too old?*

"Get stuffed, you cheeky little cow." Jenna got onto her hands and knees. Rain pattered on her back. The voice was ridiculously young and smug: a teenager who knew she knew everything. Jenna had been like that once. Time took that certainty away.

What did *you do, then? Come on, Jenna, what* did *you do?*

Her mobile had been dead, the battery flat. So she'd had to go down the street to the phone box outside Bargain Booze, with its graffiti-covered windows and its choking smell of piss, and ring 999 from there. And people had come and taken Dad away, but the vomit and beer cans and empty vodka bottles had been still strewn around the sofa, around an empty space that still lingeringly smelled of him. The police and ambulance people didn't clear those things up.

You had to do that yourself, and so much else.

She hadn't even known *what* she had to do, only that it needed doing.

But it got done, Jenna, didn't it?

She'd sat down at the kitchen table, after they'd taken Dad away, and made a list: everything that had to be done now, every question that needed an answer, and anywhere she could think of where those answers might be found. It had seemed huge at first, impossible, an infinite, flattening weight, but once it was written down it was finite after all, and began to look just a little more manageable. Above all, she had a place to start.

And bit by bit, scrap by scrap, she'd got it done; not only that, by the time Rose and Eric had jumped her at Castlefield, she'd had a life. Even a career. Not perfect, but hers. She'd got through it.

Jenna could almost see the other woman now, that blurred shape across the clearing.

"How'd you know all that, anyway?" she demanded.

Duh. Because it was me, *div-head.*

Pushing herself to her feet, Jenna blinked, and for a second she saw a lanky teenage girl with cropped spiky reddish hair and ripped jeans, army boots and a Korn t-shirt, last night's smudged mascara and a spiked collar round her throat. Hands on hips. For a second, the hard little face grinned, and then there was only a blur again, everything washed out by the rain.

"*Still falls the rain*": Jenna remembered the poem now. Edith Sitwell. Written during the London Blitz. When the world had seemed dark and hopeless, overwhelmed by irredeemable cruelty or about to be. It had been about finding a gleam of hope in all the blackness, and holding onto it. At least, that was what Holly had reckoned.

Still falls the rain, thought Jenna. *But I'm still going too.* That was her, not Edith Sitwell, and it wasn't a poem. But it would do for now.

You didn't give in. You got up and you fucking coped. So do that now.

But she was older – so much older, or so she felt – and so much more tired.

Stop feeling sorry for yourself. Get up. Walk. Keep moving.

"And then fucking what?" she snapped. "Don't even know which way to go."

Water, you silly cow. Running water.

"What about it?" Although admittedly she *was* thirsty.

Running water. Find it. Follow it. It'll lead you out of the woods.

Holly had told Jenna that. She'd told her a load of basic survival stuff, when they were driving to Wales. The kind of thing that seemed obvious when someone said it, but was easily forgotten in panic. If you got lost on a mountain, you looked for a path heading down. And if you were lost in the woods – Jenna had managed not to snap how that'd be a cold day in hell, because the mood had been good and for once she'd had sense enough not to spoil it – you looked for a stream, a river, any kind of watercourse, and followed it, because sooner or later it would lead you out. To people. To civilization.

Holly again.

Yeah, Holly. She knew her shit, didn't she?

Yes, she had. She'd talked Jenna into the holiday, and it might actually be a good thing she had gone.

Move it, then.

Jenna wiped her face on her sweatshirt sleeve and looked across the clearing. Her old self was gone, but there was someone else there now; only a blurred shadow, and it hadn't been there throughout because it was still moving towards her, through the trees. And then it stepped into the light and she saw it had a rifle.

"Hello, lovey," said Rose, through a terrible smile, a rictus of bared teeth. And then she fired.

21.

Never gloat, Eric had once told Rose; whether you were hunting an animal or human quarry, you didn't savour your triumph till after the kill. Apart from anything else, it tempted fate; more pragmatically, it gave the prey a chance to bolt, or pull some other trick that turned victory into defeat: a missed opportunity if you were lucky, your own death instead of the quarry's if you weren't.

Rose really should have remembered that. But she'd been unable to resist the desire to ensure the little bitch knew who was sending her to Hell, to inflict fear and suffering on Jenna McKnight before she died.

So even though she could've aimed and fired from among the trees long before the girl had snapped out of whatever spell of lunacy she'd been going through – she'd been talking to herself, which had helped Rose home in on her all the quicker – Rose had waited until the little bitch could see her and she was sure she had the girl's attention, that Jenna knew Death had come for her and had done so, most of all, in Rose's form. Then, and only then, had she raised the gun and pulled the trigger.

Half a minute earlier Jenna would have been too lost in madness to know anything about it; even a few seconds before, Rose could have taken her off-guard with a head or chest shot. She should've done so. A chest shot could have brought the girl down without killing her outright, and Rose could've had her moment's triumph without having to worry about the quarry bolting. But the girl had looked broken, incapable of another step, let alone any kind of swift movement.

But move she did, dropping sideways as Rose fired so the bullet smashed into an oak behind her, then scrambling up on all fours and bolting into the wood as Rose broke open the Paradox Gun to reload. The girl stood as Rose snapped the breech shut once more: for a second she was framed between two thin birch trees, a perfect silhouette; Rose shouldered the gun, but the girl dodged sideways and was gone again.

"Fuck." Rose almost never swore, and had said *that* word perhaps a handful of times in her entire life. But Eric was dead today, so none of the usual rules applied. Cradling the Paradox Gun, she followed the girl into the trees.

Still falls the rain, and now still fly the fucking bullets, apparently. Jenna ducked, stumbling between the trees through nettles and bracken, as a second shot missed her so narrowly she felt it part her hair. A tree-trunk ahead of her cracked; she flung her arm up in front of her face, but a bark splinter cut her cheek, just below the left eye.

All fun and games till someone loses an eye.

Behind her she saw Rose break open her rifle to reload again. The older woman's face was cold and set. Honest at last. And yet Jenna felt a funny kind of pity, too – or understanding, at least. *I'd do the same if I was her. If I'd had an Eric.*

If Holly had been for real.

She might have been.

Maybe she had, maybe she hadn't; either way, she was gone now. She wasn't here and Jenna would die in these woods unless she got away from Rose.

The wet air scorched her lungs, drenched clothes weighed her down, but ahead, to the right, there was a break in the trees and Jenna veered towards it.

* * *

Rose took aim, but the girl broke right and the wretched trees were in the way again. But she knew where the girl was heading: a clearer stretch where a gully passed through the woods. It wouldn't get her out, but it would leave her in the open, exposed.

Rose considered the pistol: she'd only have to get a little closer, and it had more firepower. Aim for the legs, bring the quarry down and then there'd only be the *coup de grace* to deliver. But the Beretta was a backup, to be used only if she must. No: Rose would use the rifle.

She knew the woods. The quarry didn't. Pointing the Paradox Gun down and away from her, Rose hared along the wet path after Jenna. The girl glanced back; Rose was gratified to see fear on her face.

Almost over now, lovey. I won't miss next time.

The girl was flagging. Her movements lost their rhythm, a desperate, losing struggle to keep going. Yes. Almost finished now.

Rose saw the girl burst out of the trees, then stumble to a halt as she saw the narrow clearing she'd emerged into, realising there was no escape. She turned back, then her eyes found Rose's and she was still.

But only for a moment: shaking her head, she backed away, slow and swaying as bracken and creepers caught at her ankles. She'd given up; was ready to die. The bullet would almost be a mercy.

For a moment, Rose thought to spare her: a return to the cellar to spend the rest of her life as James Frobisher's broodmare, till her body gave out and could pup no more, would be a far worse fate than a bullet to the brain. But Rose was done with any semblance of duty to him. He was as culpable in Eric's death as the girl. And Eric was what mattered here. This was vengeance. Blood for blood. Balancing the books.

Shouldering the Paradox Gun, Rose took aim.

* * *

Still falls the rain. Still falls the rain.

Still falls the rain, but I'm still going too. The phrase rattled in Jenna's head. A bolt in a can rolling down concrete steps. A hollow boast now.

A clearing, nothing more. She'd given up the slight protection the trees had offered and made herself an open target. But even back in among them, where would she go? Twenty square miles, James had said. Unless he'd lied. He had form in that regard.

Safety could be just across the clearing, through the next coppice. But she'd never know now. Maybe better not to: death would be all the bitterer if it came so close to safety.

The rain hissed down between Jenna and Rose, as if they were the last two people alive. A terrible intimacy. The killer and the killed; the revenger and the revenged-upon. It was all over, done, yet almost as a kind of reflex Jenna kept stumbling backwards over the uneven ground, through the clinging bracken.

Rose sighted down the rifle at her. Jenna supposed she'd see the muzzle flash. Would she hear the bang? They said you didn't hear the one that got you. *Who said that? How would they know?* Too late to find out now. Too late for so many things.

Rose's finger tightened on the trigger. Jenna kept going backwards. Then suddenly there was no ground, and she was falling. A glimpse of sky, then the bracken fell back into place, blotting it out. She didn't see the muzzle flash of Rose's gun, but she heard the shot after all.

Rose stepped out of the trees, breaking open the Paradox Gun and reloading one last time. It was the last bullet. After this, it would be the Beretta. Only a handgun, but at that range, with its rate of fire, it would be enough. Not that she could miss the little cow with the rifle this close to.

She slowed down as she advanced through the bracken, not wanting to fall into the same trap. The rain beat down unmercifully now, drumming on her head and shoulders and filling the clearing with a rattling hiss, but as Rose neared the spot where Jenna had vanished, she made out a sound of rushing water from directly ahead.

The gully wasn't wide, and its edges were overgrown with thick, lush ferns; a casual observer could easily miss it. Even more so if they were walking backwards. But if you were observant and knew the territory – and Rose met both criteria – it wasn't hard to see where the ground fell away.

Rose skirted to the edge of the crumbling earth bank and peered down, knocking the bracken aside with the gun-barrel. Below her was an almost sheer seven-foot drop, at the bottom of which a second lush growth of ferns almost completely hid the stream that sluiced along the gully floor. What she could see of the water was a muddy brown from disturbed sediment, except where it foamed white around the rocks. There'd been heavy rains the past few days: the streams and rivers were all in spate.

The girl lay groaning at the edge of the stream, still wheezing for breath where the fall had winded her. *She doesn't even see me*, Rose thought, and raised the rifle to her shoulder. She'd like to let the girl see her first, but look what had happened last time. *Aim and pull the trigger: one shot and get it done.* Go for the chest: even at this range, a headshot could still miss. Then finish the job with the pistol.

There was a loud *thwack* and something hit Rose in the back, just below the shoulder blade. There was a sharp white pain, then a spreading coldness. *Ignore it*, she decided. She wouldn't let the girl escape again. This ended now.

Then she swayed; she felt dizzy, and tired. Ridiculous she should feel like that now. But then she realised, and spun round.

James stood at the treeline, fumbling at the breech of his

tranquiliser gun. He threw it aside with a curse and grabbed for the one held by Dr Reid, who stood beside him. They struggled over it.

Ridiculous, Rose thought again, though for a different reason now. She turned away, her legs gave way, and she fell to one knee. Propofol worked fast: that was why they used it. But she only needed a few more seconds' consciousness. That would be enough.

Rose looked back down in time to see Jenna roll through the bracken on the gully floor and into the stream. The bracken swished back into place to hide her, the long legs moving frantically to push her along. Rose's vision was fogging, too hazy to see anything clearly, but she fired the Paradox Gun into the bracken one last time. There was a cry that might have been pain, or maybe only fright. But now even vengeance no longer mattered; Rose slumped head-down over the edge of the gully, watched the Paradox Gun drop from her hands, and closed her eyes.

22.

The stream was shallow, despite the rain, but freezing cold: already Jenna's teeth were chattering, her feet and fingers numb. Still, she was alive, even if a bullet had smashed into the bank above her head just after she'd fallen in. Before that, there'd been an odd *thwack*ing sound, like an air rifle. Either way, nothing had hit her.

And freezing or not, she'd found running water. Follow the stream and it would lead her out of the woods, to other people. Not that she couldn't usually take or leave those, in the normal run of things, but it would get her away from James.

She thought of Holly and how hot the other woman felt in bed at night. That kind of thing was usually a nightmare in the summer months, but perfect in colder weather. Just now she'd have gladly wrapped herself around Holly and hung on all night long.

There were voices above and behind her; she recognised one as James's, though the words were inaudible over the roar of the rain. *Tough shit, Jimbo. You're not getting me.* She crawled, awkwardly with her belly, keeping low to avoid disturbing the bracken above her, which meant she was half-submerged in the cold, murky torrent of the stream. Soon the voices were lost in the rain.

* * *

When the banks of the stream rose higher she stood up, hugging herself and shivering. Her clothes were wringing wet, adding to the weight she carried, and she couldn't feel her feet. She rubbed her hands together and tucked them under her arms in an effort to coax some warmth back into them.

She continued walking until the ground sloped downwards and the banks sank lower again. She looked behind her, but saw only the slope, and ranks of trees through veils of grey rain. No sign of movement; with luck, she'd shaken them off for now, so she could stay upright instead of having to crawl again.

They wouldn't stop, though. And they might be armed. Rose had been.

She'd a special reason to want you dead.

True. But Jenna remembered the *thwack*ing sound she'd heard while crawling away. Like an air rifle. The kind that fired tranquiliser darts, maybe. It would make sense.

The stream banks had now fallen level with her swollen ankles, so Jenna climbed out of the water onto solid ground. As long as she could see the stream, she could follow it. Her feet were caked in filth and blood, marbled blue with cold. But she could still walk, just about.

She followed the stream to the foot of the slope. Beyond that, the forest floor was relatively flat; the stream wound its way through the trees till she lost sight of it.

Jenna pushed her sodden hair back from her forehead, wincing as cold water trickled down her spine. She wanted to rest, lie down and shut her eyes, but if she did, she might never get up again. Putting one numb foot ahead of the other, she followed the stream.

23.

Rose resurfaced, drifting up through grey murk, vaguely aware of her arms being pulled behind her. Rain hammered on her scalp, pouring down the back of her neck. It helped wake her, at least.

She was sitting upright, her back against a tree – an oak, she guessed, from the acorns and acorn-cups strewn about. Her wrists had been bound together behind it. Something bit painfully into them.

Her shoulders and upper arms ached. She couldn't see much. At first she thought her vision was bleary from the Propofol, then she realised the air was misty with rain. She blinked a few times: in front of her was a long narrow stretch of wet earth, dotted with puddles and leaves, a thick band of bracken and bramble and then more trees beyond.

The gully. Jenna McKnight was still nearby – most likely following the stream, in which case Rose could still pick up her trail. She shook her head to clear it of the lingering brain-fog.

"Back with us, are you?"

Rose recognised the sneering, angry voice at once. She looked up and James Frobisher bared his teeth in a grin, then reached down and hit her back-handed across the face. She tried to duck, but tied as she was, she couldn't move out of its way.

"Sir James–" Reid bleated from somewhere out of view, sounding even more frightened of everything than usual.

"Shut up." James looked at Rose, shaking his head. "You've no idea what you almost did, have you?"

"Think I'm pretty clear. I'm not a complete moron." Rose pointedly looked him up and down. She didn't hide her contempt, because doing so no longer mattered. It was dizzying, liberating, to no longer care about that. "Unlike some."

That earned her another back-handed slap, then a forehanded one. Rose tucked her head down and James slapped at her shoulders and the back of her skull. Playground stuff, as ridiculous as it was ineffectual. Rose began to laugh; James stepped back and kicked her in the side.

"Sir James!" said Reid again.

"Stop fucking bleating," James said, "unless you want the same."

Rose looked up and followed his gaze to Reid shivering under a half-bare tree. He blinked wetly, but his pudgy hands tightened on his tranquiliser rifle. Rose wondered detachedly if the worm might be about to turn, and if so whether he'd shoot James before James shot him. But he bowed his head; a whipped dog, it seemed, to the very end.

James, meanwhile, had recovered some of his composure. "As for you," he told Rose, "the only reason you aren't dead yet is that you lost that fucking gun. Otherwise I'd blow your head off."

He'd struggle to do that, with no more bullets. As James would have known if he'd searched her. He'd also have found the pistol and knife. So if he didn't know about the bullets...

Rose shifted position, pressing the small of her back against the tree, and felt the Beretta dig into her spine. Still no use to her, though, with her hands tied. She tugged at the bindings on her wrists, felt a thin sharp plastic band cutting into the skin. *Cable ties.* Hard to get out of normally, but the hunting knife's serrated upper edge would snap them easily.

Assuming she still had it. A big if, that. James might have found that, though he'd probably blench at using it: it was a different, more intimate kind of violence than a gun's. Rose would have to wait and see if it was still in her boot.

When she glanced up again he was pacing up and down the gully's edge, wittering on about her ingratitude after all his family had done for her. And with every second he so wasted, Jenna got further away. *Idiot.* Rose sneaked a glance at Reid, whose expression clearly stated he wished he was anywhere but here, including quite possibly the Antarctic.

James broke off mid-sentence, looked up and nodded to himself. "Come on, doctor."

"What are we–"

"What do you think, man? Same as before. Find the little bitch and bring her back. God's sake, Reid, you've the attention span of a gnat. Now come on."

"Sir James, I'm no use for something like this–"

"You're not particularly impressive at the best of times, I assure you, doctor, but for the last time, you're not going home to your precious *Lizzie* until this matter's resolved. I'm more than capable of tracking the little bitch down." James gave Rose a sulphurous glare. "And you, you treacherous cow, I'll deal with once she's back in the fucking cellar. Now come *on*, Reid."

He turned and stalked off along the top of the gully, following the stream. With a last miserable glance at Rose, Reid scampered after him.

Water dripped from the trees; a light drizzle still floated down to earth, but once the two men were out of sight, birds began twittering again and small creatures resumed their scuffling in the undergrowth. After a few moments, a young fox broke from cover, padded a short distance, then stopped to study Rose with gleaming topaz eyes.

"You're up early," she murmured.

She was, for the moment, completely helpless, weapons or no, and foxes could be vicious – though usually, only when cornered. Nonetheless, Rose was acutely aware of her own vulnerability, and relieved when the fox padded on into the trees and disappeared from view. She couldn't die yet. She had work to do.

James, unfortunately, was right about being able to track the girl. Much as Rose would have liked to picture him getting lost in the woods, going slowly mad with thirst and hunger before falling fatally into another, much deeper gully, he knew these woods; he just couldn't be bothered to do the hard work unless he had to. But that shouldn't be a problem: she'd no doubt at all she could find Jenna first, and deal with young Master Frobisher if he got in the way.

All depending, of course, on whether she could actually get free. But that was an easy enough question to answer. Rose arched her back, trying to hook her leg behind the oak tree, to bring the knife at her ankle within her fingers' reach.

24.

The stream widened and Jenna walked along the left bank, occasionally glancing behind her for any sign of James.

The treeline was several yards from the river's edge on either side of the water, only bare earth and a little grass in between. She felt vulnerable and exposed, so after one last backward glance she moved into the woods again, weaving over the uneven ground between the trees. It was slower going, but felt safer.

Her stomach growled. She hadn't had time for breakfast before escaping. Eric had made good bacon and eggs. Pity she'd had to kill him.

Jenna laughed shakily. Feeling had begun to return to her feet; the right one was throbbing badly, making her limp. She found a fallen branch to lean on for support, but the pain brought back the memory of her heel hitting Eric's jaw, the sound of crunching bone as his head hit the rockery. None of her pent-up rage and aggression, none of her martial arts training, had prepared her for the actual act of killing another human being.

And Eric hadn't been a faceless enemy, either. Not by then. When he and Rose had abducted her in Castlefield, he'd just been a nameless thug in a balaclava; maybe if she'd killed him then it wouldn't have troubled Jenna at all, although she doubted it. Yes, Eric had drugged and kidnapped her and all the rest, but he'd ultimately treated her with kindness and respect within the limits of his role. He'd told her about his childhood on a Dorset farm, the red setter he'd owned when he was sixteen, funny stories from his army days.

She wasn't as cold as she'd wanted to be in the past. Didn't want to be anymore, either, not if Holly was there. But she mustn't think of Holly. Holly might be the enemy too. There was no knowing if Jenna could trust anyone.

Hey. Eric took the money and made his choice. No one put a gun to his head and made him kidnap you.

Not necessarily. He and Rose could have been coerced or threatened.

Bollocks. They both trotted out all that "pro-life" crap at you. They were on board for this.

"Point," she muttered, leaning against a pine tree. Little pellets were littered round it, and small grinning bones: mouse skulls. An owl must have made its nest there.

More than anything else, she wanted to lie down and sleep. But if she did, she'd wake up back in the cellar. Assuming James and Reid found her. If Rose did, she wouldn't wake at all.

Jenna pushed on. She was still battling the weariness, but when she next closed her eyes, she saw Eric's head snapping back from the impact of her heel against his jaw, heard his skull crunch, and that helped her keep them open.

He held you prisoner. Stopped you escaping. Locked you in the cellar. Would've made you give birth, then helped James get you pregnant again. And again. And again.

All true. She walked faster, leaning on the branch. Fuck Eric, she told herself, and fuck Rose too. They'd both helped James, both tried to force Jenna under his control. Fuck the pair of them.

The stream was narrowing again, sinking between steeper banks. Up ahead there was a bend, and it disappeared into the trees. With another brief glance behind her – no sign of anyone following – Jenna came out of cover onto the bank, limped to the bend and around it.

She almost cried out as there was a sudden movement in front of her, but its source was probably more frightened of her – a young deer had been drinking from the stream, but bolted away from her, into the trees. She breathed out, laughing weakly; then she took in the sight ahead of her, and the laughter stopped.

The stream, still narrowing and sinking into an ever-deeper channel, ran on for another dozen yards or so before vanishing into rocky ground. Jenna staggered forward, feet squelching in muddy earth, and saw a hole gaping among the rocks. The stream rushed into it, fast and foaming, and disappeared underground.

Jenna's first emotion wasn't fear or despair, or even confusion: what she felt was pure, cheated rage. She'd played by the rules – had *remembered* the rules, which by rights she should have long forgotten – followed the water, and the water had pulled a mean, cheap trick to leave her stranded as James and his people closed in.

Bastards, all of them. James, Eric, Rose, the woods, Dad, the whole fucking world.

Jenna screamed: it rang and echoed, birds scattering from the trees, clattering away into the dull grey sky.

Shouldn't have done that, babe. Really torn it now.

If Jenna hadn't been clinging to the branch, she'd have fallen. She listened; she couldn't hear any voices, but it was only a matter of time. No way James couldn't have heard that scream. Nor Rose, if she was still on the loose too. Maybe Jenna should hope Rose found her first: at least then James wouldn't get what he wanted, either.

Or finish it yourself. Then they all lose.

Jenna resisted that idea, but not as hard as she should. No baby for Jimbo that way, no vengeance for Rose: a last extended middle finger to them all.

But then Jenna wouldn't get what *she* wanted. She wouldn't get away.

Yeah, but that's not on the table, is it?

"Bollocks it isn't." She'd keep going through the woods and hope for the best; hope to find a way out.

You've no chance and you know it.

Jenna closed her eyes for a second, holding tight to the branch so she didn't fall. *Don't sleep. Mustn't sleep.*

And then she heard it.

A sound of rushing water.

Jenna opened her eyes, blinking. A hallucination; an aural mirage. That was all it could be. It couldn't be anything else–

No. She still heard it. She wasn't sure how distant it was, but somewhere within earshot, the water must come out from underground again – and, by the sound, with some force.

Jenna swayed, but steadied herself. She'd very little strength left, she knew. But she could always keep going, just a little further, given the slightest hope of escape.

She closed her eyes again, but not out of tiredness this time. She listened until she could tell which direction the sound was coming from, then set off towards it, leaning on the branch.

25.

When James heard the scream, he went still, suddenly afraid. Not for his personal safety: nothing in these woods could hurt him, or at least nothing a well-aimed rifle dart couldn't deal with. It was the fear that something had happened to Jenna. If he failed to deliver on the promise he'd made, he wouldn't get what he wanted.

And he wanted what he wanted very badly, or he wouldn't have done all this. After all, he was going to live forever. You'd go to any lengths to achieve that.

But if Jenna died, he'd be cheated of that.

Not to mention the fact that a certain person would be very, very angry, in which case James might lose out not only on immortality, but even a normal human lifespan.

As the scream went on, though, he realised it wasn't pain or fear, but anguish. Despair.

She's giving up.

He grinned first to himself, then at Reid. "Come on, doctor. We're almost done."

He broke into a run along the bank. Following her was easy now. He might not know these woods as well as Rose and Eric, but he knew them well enough. Certainly better than Jenna. And he was a decent enough tracker in his own right. Daddy would have been proud to see James today. For once.

Her trail left the bank and disappeared into the trees, but that didn't matter: she'd be following the course of the river, so he did the same, grinning as Reid panted and whimpered behind him, struggling to keep up. Her footprints soon reappeared, by the Devil's Hole.

That was what Daddy had called it, when James was little: he'd no idea whether or not that was really its name or just his father's invention to scare his milksop son. *The Devil was hot, you see, down in Hell,* Daddy had told him, *so he clawed a hole up through the earth to the riverbed, so the water would pour down and cool him off.*

But there's no steam, little James had said – bright enough to spot that, even at that age.

It's a long, long way down to where it's going, Daddy had said, then grabbed him. *Want to see?*

James knew now he'd only been playing, but hadn't at the time. Trying to impress Daddy in any way had always been a constant losing struggle, never mind actually making him proud. He'd so often felt he was being constantly tested and found wanting, that his status as Sir Alec Frobisher's son was only ever a probationary one which might be revoked at any second, so at that young age it hadn't seemed impossible Daddy'd finally had enough and decided to get rid. As a result, James had not only screamed in real terror – bad enough – but had actually wet himself.

The fucking shame of that now. He still remembered, with appalling clarity, the revulsion on Daddy's face. His father had thrust James away, wiping his hands on his coat. *For God's sake. Disgusting boy. Stop snivelling, for– All right, all right, come on. Back to the lodge. Get some clean clothes.*

James's eyes stung; his face was hot. He was walking very fast, with an angry, determined stride – away from the Hole, from Daddy, from that shameful memory. But not only for that reason; not just to get away from something. There was something to go towards as well.

Fuck you, Daddy. I'll show you, Daddy. I'll make you proud of me, Daddy, even though I don't care what you think anymore – no,

I don't. I don't! I don't care, but I'll make you proud, you'll see how great I am. If you were alive you'd grovel to me, when you saw what I'll achieve. If I could I'd bring you back to life so that you could and then I'd kill you again.

Jenna's trail carried on around the Hole, up through the sparse silver birches that grew above the rocks the Hole was set in. Through those trees and out again, towards the roaring water.

Once on the high ground, she wasn't hard to find, especially as James already knew where she'd go. He glimpsed movement among the trees – her dull grey clothing, pale face, reddish hair – and shouldered the rifle as he watched her stumble-jog down the slope. The soles of her bare feet, he noted with detached disgust, were black with dirt. But she could be cleaned up later, back at Cutty Wren Lodge, when under restraint. When she was back under control.

James had her in his sights. He began squeezing the trigger, aiming for her back rather than for the head as he would when going after a stag with a real gun. But then the blasted trees were in the way again. No way to get a clear shot.

James swore between his teeth, then shrugged. It didn't matter. He had her now. He just had to close in, till he had her at bay. She'd collapse from sheer exhaustion eventually, even if he didn't put a dart in her.

He was almost tempted to just stroll after her and wait until her strength gave out, but decided against it. No knowing what the mad cow would do when cornered. Besides, he *wanted* to pull the trigger and bring her down. He still remembered her arm around his neck, that punch to the throat. He rubbed it automatically; it no longer hurt and he spoke normally again, but he owed her for it nonetheless. Before, he'd relied on Rose and Eric. That was the intelligent move: give the order, send people you knew you could rely on to carry it out. Daddy would've approved. But at the same time, he saw Daddy shaking his head again, as when James had wet himself at the Devil's Hole: *Disgusting boy*. Daddy's eyes, Jenna's eyes: the same contempt. He'd show them both. Do this himself. Finish the job. Pull the trigger on her and Daddy's eyes.

"Come on, doctor," he called over his shoulder to Reid. "Need your help in a moment."

He went carefully down the slope, weaving through the dripping trees.

26.

A misty haze hung beyond the treeline, and Jenna smelled the yeasty odour of fresh water. She broke into a stumbling run, biting her lip against a cry of pain as her foot hit a half-buried rock. Her toes throbbed, but she used the branch to hobble along at speed. She almost missed being unable to feel her feet.

She saw water up ahead, she was sure of it. And then she was out of the trees and stumbling forwards. Dampness sprinkled her face, and the ground before her dropped away into white haze and empty space.

Jenna lurched to a halt and swayed, fighting to keep her balance; her stomach seemed to drop away into nowhere. Below her was a rocky cliff with a horseshoe-shaped bite taken out of it, out of a hole in which a huge cataract surged in a white foaming spray, with far greater force than the stream Jenna had followed.

The sides of the cliff were about thirty feet high, streaked with glistening moss, tangles of thin creepers and tufts of grass clinging to small, dryer shelves; the water overflowed from a deep, rocky pool at the bottom and down a channel to join a much larger, wider flow up ahead. High banks and fast-flowing water the colour of badly stewed tea, loose twigs, leaves and branches swept along on its surface.

Jenna broke into another run as she reached the trail leading down to her left. That was due less to excitement than gravity; nonetheless, she began to laugh. It wasn't a stream up ahead but an honest-to-God *river*, which sooner or later had to lead her to other people. But it could still be miles to the nearest settlement; still a substantial distance in her state, with or without James and Rose behind her.

She steadied herself against one of the Scots pines that clustered along the side of the path. The distance didn't matter: one foot in front of another, that was all it took. She'd have to stay off the path along the banks, however appealing it was, however much easier. Slip into the woods alongside, keep the river in sight, use the trees for cover.

Fuck me, babe, you actually sounded like you knew what you were doing there.

Jenna laughed to herself, gripped the branch tighter, focused on the river and stepped forward.

There was a loud *thwack* and a faint breeze upon the back of her neck, as if something had disturbed the air, then a shuddering impact as something thudded into the tree behind her. As she spun, ducking low, she heard James cursing.

He was at the top of the path, dropping what looked like an air rifle and turning to snatch another one from Reid. Before Jenna could turn, the second rifle swung towards her, braced against James's hip. She realised she'd heard the *thwack* before, when Rose had been about to shoot her. She looked at the tree behind her; there was a dart embedded in it.

James was still holding the gun on her; he nodded down at the one he'd dropped. "Reload that," he shouted to Reid over the water's roar. He wasn't taking chances.

Jump. Into the trees, into the river. Do it now.

But she couldn't look away from James's eyes, and suddenly she was exhausted. James smiled. *Fuck you, Jimbo*, she wanted to shout, but hadn't the strength even for that.

The bastard was going to win.

James raised the rifle to his shoulder, and began to squeeze the trigger.

The shot, when it came, was far louder than the previous *thwack*, and nothing hit her. Instead, James staggered forward, surprise on his face. He straightened up, frowning, and blood trickled from a hole in his chest. A second shot rang out, and James pitched forward; the rifle clattered over the edge of the cliff into the white haze below.

Reid stood, gawping, the other rifle broken open in his hands, as a figure emerged from the trees, one hand covered in blood, a pistol in the other.

Rose's face was blank until she saw Jenna; she smiled for the briefest instant, then became expressionless again. Reid was staring at her, mouth agape; Rose turned towards him and pointed the pistol at his head, and then her face softened for an instant.

"Run," she told him. "Run home to your Lizzie."

Reid threw down the tranquiliser rifle and fled into the trees, crashing through the undergrowth. The sounds faded till there was only the thunder of the waterfall, and Rose returned her gaze to Jenna. She smiled again. It was warm, genuine, even as she took aim.

27.

No two ways about it, Jenna McKnight was a most resourceful quarry. Quite literally, in fact. Whenever Rose thought the girl's last reserves had given out and she'd nothing else with which to fight or run, Jenna always somehow found more.

She'd been staring up at James and his tranquiliser gun with dumb, dull, cowlike eyes: exhausted, finished, waiting for the axe to fall. Even when Rose shot the spoilt little bastard, Jenna had just stood there, blankly staring. Rose had been disappointed at her absence of fear, cheated that there'd be no pleas for mercy before the end.

Even as Rose aimed the Beretta, the girl's expression didn't change. Yet as the trigger pulled and the hammer fell, something flared in the extinguished eyes and Jenna flung herself sideways into the trees, the bullet tearing a divot from the path behind her. The shot re-echoed from the cliff walls, the faint haze of gunsmoke dispersed, and Jenna was gone.

Rose sighed in annoyance, but smiled nonetheless. There was no pleasure in killing an empty husk. The victory would mean more if the girl still had some fight left. She moved towards the path, then stumbled as something caught her ankle.

She kicked out reflexively, almost overbalancing, but her leg was freed. She looked down to see James Frobisher lying on his back, pink lung blood frothing from his mouth and nose and with one arm outstretched, fingers clasping and unclasping.

Unlike Jenna, though, he'd clearly spent the last of his strength. It would've been easy to leave him to drown in blood, but Rose decided against it. With Eric dead, this was the end for her in every sense that mattered; now was the time to settle all accounts.

When she took aim, James's eyes widened and he emitted a bleating moan that might have been terror or a plea. Rose took a second to relish the disbelief in his eyes, that this could actually be happening to *him*, then pulled the trigger.

The bullet punched a hole just under James Frobisher's left eye, forcing it from its socket. His head snapped back and to the side; his limbs jerked once and were limp. The remaining air in his ruined lungs escaped in a bubbling rattle.

He was still.

Rose hooked the toe of her boot under his ribs and tipped him over the edge of the cliff. He caromed off a couple of outcroppings; both legs and an arm were askew at knees and elbow, like those of a broken doll, before he vanished into the frothing white pool.

Putting an end to that dreadful brat, throwing off the last shackles of duty and obedience after all these years, felt strangely liberating. Rose couldn't remember when she'd last felt so light and free. Everything felt a little unreal; perhaps it was the lingering effects of the tranquiliser drugs.

The girl, Rose remembered; she'd almost forgotten Jenna. The track ahead was empty, but Rose could hear her floundering through the woods. Then the sound stopped. So, the girl was waiting for her. All right, then. Rose went down the path, smiling.

28.

Jenna leant back against a pine, gripping the branch till her hands ached.

She'd felt Rose's bullet whip past her head with an angry wasplike buzz as she'd moved, feeling vaguely surprised she'd managed to do so. *Life in the old dog yet.* But whatever final reserve she'd somehow accessed was limited, and wouldn't carry her far. It would run out, and when it did, Rose would be there, patient and relentless, to finish things.

So running was useless: nothing more than a brief delay. But given the choice between fight or flight, Jenna had always preferred the first option anyway. She had a branch against Rose's gun, but when Rose had first tried to take Jenna she'd had the advantages of surprise, Eric to back her up, plus syringes loaded with sedatives. Jenna had only had her hands and feet.

They still won, babe.

But not without a fight; against Rose on her own, Jenna would've stood a chance.

Yeah, but she's got a gun now.

"Just fuck off," Jenna muttered, then bit her lips, grasping the branch tighter. She doubted it would have been audible at a distance, but you never knew. Her only chance was to catch Rose off-guard, and the other woman knew all too well what Jenna was capable of by now.

Footsteps crashed through bracken. Jenna drew a breath

and was still, pulling her shoulders in tight to make herself as narrow as possible so the tree's bulk would hopefully conceal her.

She couldn't hear the footsteps now, just the distant roaring of the falls. There was silence; even the woods were still. Waiting. Jenna flexed her fingers on the branch. Maybe she should peer round the trunk, try and spot Rose. Maybe Rose was waiting for Jenna to try exactly that.

As she deliberated, a voice behind her said, very calmly and softly, "Jenna."

She didn't turn, just dropped, and once again a bullet meant for Jenna punched into a tree. But a bramble caught her right foot as she fell, her ankle twisted and an explosion of white pain made her scream.

Jenna rolled onto her back. Rose stood over her, smiling, smoke still wisping from her pistol's breech; Jenna lashed out at her with the branch, but the blow didn't come close. Rose just smiled.

She thinks it's all over.

Jenna wriggled backwards, drove the branch into the ground and tried to stand, but fresh pain exploded in her ankle and she went down again. Rose's smile widened to show those yellow, horsey teeth.

It is now.

The branch had rolled away. Jenna's ankle was throbbing in agony; she didn't even try to stand, but pushed herself backwards. Rose smiled and watched.

Jenna rolled onto her stomach, clawing at the ground and dragging herself towards the path. Behind her Rose sighed and said, "Lovey", in an almost pitying tone. *It's over*, that tone said, *and we both know it. Just accept it, and have some dignity.*

But Jenna hadn't been able to afford dignity in years, certainly never in her adult life. She'd done many an undignified thing, but was still here; that mattered more. If she'd stopped to worry about her dignity, she wouldn't have lasted this long.

Hopeless, yes, but if nothing else, she'd make it out into the light. That would be something: not to die in the woods like an animal, or Mum. The woods were the Bonewalker's, and she wanted to feel light and open air on her face one last time.

If she was denied everything else she wanted, she'd have that one last thing.

Behind her, Rose tramped slowly and deliberately through bracken and loam, closing in for the kill.

29.

Jenna dragged herself out onto the path. The falls roared; as she rolled onto her back, looking up at the sky, water-mist settled on her face. She wriggled further back, pushing herself into a sitting position with her elbows.

Beyond the falls she saw the woods. Her least favourite place on earth, but at least she'd made it out of them, whatever that was worth. Irrelevant now, anyway. All that mattered was Rose, coming towards her, pistol at her side. Smiling and crying as she raised it, all at once; steadying it in both hands.

Jenna idly wondered what kind of gun it was. The things you thought of at the end; the things you wanted to know. Not what had happened to Mum, not what the Bonewalker was, not even why James had done all this. Just the gun that was about to kill her.

She thought of asking Rose, by way of a last request, and then the air grew colder. She'd been cold already in her sodden clothes on this grey day, but this was depths-of-winter cold, the kind that turned water into ice. And with it came an appalling, foetid stink, so overpowering she almost retched.

Rose smelled it too; she grimaced, then frowned and almost looked around to find the source of it before remembering Jenna and focusing on her once more. She felt the cold as well, because her teeth were chattering, just like Jenna's.

Jenna touched her hair; it felt stiff and brittle and seemed to snap at her touch. When she stared at her hand, hollow quills of ice were melting there. She looked from that to Rose, who'd lowered the gun, now looking less perplexed than annoyed – that something had distracted Jenna from her, perhaps – before raising the weapon again. Her finger tightened on the trigger, and she opened her mouth to speak. Some last *bon mot*, presumably. Or just the obvious *This is for Eric, bitch.*

But Jenna had recognised the stench from the cellar, from her dreams of the grove, and most of all, from that night on Tallstone Hill. A crash and crack of splintering wood came from up the path; Rose turned, the gun sweeping round, and Jenna looked too, both wanting and not wanting to see, as the Bonewalker emerged from the woods.

Rose moaned faintly, in incredulity and terror. Jenna couldn't blame her: previously, she'd only glimpsed the Bonewalker dimly in her dreams, or glowing hazily in the cellar, and had felt much the same way. Now it was in the open, in daylight, walking in the real world, and she was squirming backwards down the path, no longer so apathetic about her fate after all.

It was bigger than it'd been in the cellar. Its back was bowed, as if by the weight of the crown of antlers emerging from its hooded skull, and it walked on all fours, like a gorilla.

It crouched there on the path, letting Jenna see it, then stood upright: it was easily twenty feet tall, not counting the antlers. It raised its arms in a somehow preening gesture, as if saying, *Look? See? Aren't I magnificent?* Jenna started laughing: looked like the thing was no different from so many other men she'd known. Maybe it was related to James.

She couldn't stop laughing. It wasn't a pleasant sound, wheezing, gasping and borderline hysterical. Rose looked back at her, blinking in confusion.

The Bonewalker strode towards her. Jenna felt the ground shudder beneath its steps. *Heavy fucker*, she thought, *considering it's literally just skin and bone.* Again the laughter. It wouldn't stop. She pushed herself backwards and tried to get up, but her twisted ankle sent another flash of white pain through her.

Jenna stayed on the ground, wriggling away as best she could. She wanted to turn away, afraid to see what was happening, but was even more afraid not to.

The Bonewalker advanced on Rose. She screamed at it, although her words were unclear, then opened fire.

It's a walking fucking skeleton, you silly cunt. What do you think you'll do, hit a vital organ? All you'll do is piss it off. Still, have fun. This way maybe you won't have any bullets left for me.

The gunfire stopped; the pistol's slide had locked open. Rose screamed something and threw it at the Bonewalker, but didn't try to run. Even Jenna was forgotten now, it seemed; Rose stood, legs shaking as if she was fighting the urge to kneel and grovel to the beast.

The Bonewalker's hooded head lifted and Jenna stared into the black void of its face; a moment later the pale blobs of its eyes took shape in that darkness, staring into her. Rose was irrelevant now; for a moment Jenna thought the Bonewalker would simply brush past her, at worst swat her casually aside. But the luminous eyes left Jenna and came to bear on Rose, and Jenna felt the air darken with the Bonewalker's fury. Rose moaned; it became a wail and at last, Jenna thought, some kind of plea, but one that went unheeded.

The creature extended its right hand; Rose tried to avoid it, but it closed around her upper body and lifted her screaming into the air. Its left hand fastened around her hips, and then the hands twisted in opposing directions, as if wringing out a wet towel. The sound of flesh and skin tore, cartilage crackled, bones broke with muffled snaps and Rose's scream reached a pitch Jenna wouldn't have believed possible from a human throat. Blood fell and splattered on the path, along with other, more solid things.

The Bonewalker tossed the pieces of Rose away in opposite directions, the lower half into the trees and the upper off the riverbank. The worst thing was that Rose's top half was still screaming, even then. It stopped when she hit the water;

the torrential current swept it away, but Jenna thought the arms might still have been moving weakly. Beyond it, she saw another body floating. James, presumably, but it was already too far downstream to identify.

The sheer casual violence of it was such it took Jenna a few seconds to once more become aware of the gnawing cold and ripe stench emanating from up the path. The Bonewalker squatted on its skeletal haunches, hands outspread, presenting its fleshless palms, smoking and scarlet, to Jenna. *Look. See?*

They faced one another, neither moving. The only sounds were the river, the falls, and Jenna's laboured breathing, steaming in the freezing air.

"So," she said at last. "What now?"

For a moment, the Bonewalker remained impassive, then it tilted its head slightly back and to one side; Jenna could have sworn it was signalling some form of amusement, perhaps even respect. But then it rose to its full height, standing as straight as its hunched spine allowed, flicked its hands twice, sending spatters of blood flying into the trees, flexed its bony fingers and began to advance.

She thought of her mother: the Bonewalker had taken her, of course it had, and Mum's last scream had been worse, far worse, than even Rose's had been. Jenna didn't know what it had done to her mother and was determined in that moment that she never would, because she knew already it was far worse than what it had done to Rose; knew it was the worst end of all.

She wriggled backwards. Her feet were filthy with soil and blood. The pains that filled her body had faded to murmurs and rumours; what mattered was the Bonewalker, which mustn't, at any cost, get hold of her. Whatever it took, she had to deny it that.

Somehow she was standing; somehow she'd managed to do that. She knew her ankle was screaming its agony, but in a distant, almost theoretical way.

The Bonewalker was closing in. It walked slowly, unhurriedly, knowing the game was at an end. Jenna smiled, and it hesitated for a moment. Not afraid, but wary, because she shouldn't be smiling, not here, not now.

And then it was moving forward again, faster now, having realised what she had in mind.

But it still had a gap to close, however small, and for Jenna freedom was only a step away. Or rather two.

The Bonewalker reached for her, and she pivoted left. One step took her to the path's edge; the second propelled her out into space, and the huge bone hand closed on empty air.

The bank was sheer, and the water rushed up to meet her. The impact was like a slap, and icy coldness washed through her. She didn't need to do anything after that. She was swept out into the middle of the river; the current caught and carried her away.

None of them had had what they'd wanted from her. Cold comfort, maybe, but better than none. She'd won.

Jenna rolled onto her back, looking up. The Bonewalker ran along the bank, with a speed she wouldn't have believed anything so corpselike capable of, its rotting hide flapping like banners as it went. Perhaps it meant to dive into the water and fish her out.

Can't have that, Jenna thought detachedly. So she rolled over in the water again, facedown, dived as far beneath the surface as she could, and then inhaled.

THE BEAST OF CHORAZIN

In the twelfth century, shortly after the Order of the Knights Templar was founded, a creature terrorised the area around a certain hill near the ruined city of Chorazin, on the northern shore of the Sea of Galilee. Human in appearance but demonic in nature, it preyed on Christian and infidel alike, and was seemingly invulnerable.

When word of the Beast's depredations reached Jerusalem, the Knights Templar despatched an expedition to investigate the matter and to put an end to the creature's ravages. On reaching Chorazin, they encountered a Saracen force, comprised of both warriors and scholars, sent to achieve the same goal. After unsuccessfully trying to slay the Beast separately, the two sides declared a truce, and joined arms against their common foe.

After a long and bloody battle, they overcame the Beast and hacked it into pieces. But even dismembered, it still lived, and its fragments tried to join back together.

Unable to destroy it despite their combined faith and knowledge, the Templars and the Saracens sought instead to contain it, to ensure it did no further harm. Its portions were enclosed in reliquaries, sealed with every ward or sigil that Christian and Muslim could devise, to contain its malevolence.

After much discussion, the safekeeping of the reliquaries was finally entrusted to the care of the Templars. After that, what happened to the Beast is a matter of speculation. Some say its remains became the "holy of holies" the Knights guarded at the Dome of the Rock in Jerusalem; others that they were "Baphomet", the idol they worshipped. Some say they were both.

According to one account, the reliquaries were transported to Acre after Jerusalem fell, but were lost when Acre was taken. Another source claims they fell into the Templars' possession one last time, following a daring raid on the Syrian port of Tartus, and transported to the island of Ruad. The Order sent Jean de Messins, one of their foremost scholars on demonology, to ensure the various protections on the reliquaries remained intact before the return to Cyprus. Before de Messins could depart with the relics, however, the Mamluks blockaded the island.

De Messins was a very old man, and in frail health; astonishingly, he survived almost the entire siege, but died the day before the surrender. Whether Marshal De Quincy had time to appoint another keeper in his place, or who it might have been, remains a mystery. And so does the fate of the Beast of Chorazin.

PART TWO:
Walking the Greylands

30.

There was a white ceiling above her, and she wasn't dead.

That was about all there was to be said for it: Jenna's entire body ached, muscle-deep, and her throat felt scorched. No wonder, really: the last thing she'd done was inhale a river. God alone knew how she'd survived, but she seemingly had.

She looked blearily around the room she was in. To her left, a window with a partly lowered blind, above a low chest of drawers. Trees outside. *Trees. A wood*. But they were in the distance; she could see a lawn below the window, which she guessed to be two or three floors up.

Jenna took stock of the room itself. It was small, neat and clean. A gleaming floor; plain walls. A desk and chair in a corner. An IV in a stand; a needle in her arm. The air smelt antiseptic.

Hospital, she thought. *I'm in hospital.*

She smiled, and laughed – or tried, at least. It became a gasp and groan, then an indrawn breath. Laughing hurt too much, and the gasping and groaning weren't much better.

Funny, even so. She'd always hated hospitals, especially since Mum. But today was different. Hospital meant she'd been found and rescued. Hospital meant she was safe. They'd got her out of the river, and she was safe. She could go and find Holly, explain what'd happened. Probably too late to do any good, but Jenna at least wanted her to know her absence hadn't been a matter of choice. To tell her – what? *I love you*?

159

She would have if Holly had been there in the woods with her, but she wasn't in the woods any longer. *Thank you*, maybe. That if nothing else.

She remembered why she'd gone into the river in the first place, but her mind recoiled from it, back into the dark. She closed her eyes. It didn't matter. Wherever she was now, she was safe.

She was sitting up in the bed, and it no longer hurt when she breathed. Her throat was a little dry, but nothing worse.

The door opened, and a round-faced woman with short, dyed-blonde hair came in, wearing a white uniform. She looked at Jenna; smiled. "Well, look who's back with us."

"Hi." Jenna wasn't sure what else to say. Her voice was a croak. "Got any water?"

"Course." The nurse pulled up an overbed table with a carafe and glass on it. Jenna thought of Rose and the bedroom in Cutty Wren Lodge and sucked in a breath through her teeth.

The nurse frowned. "Are you all right?"

"Fine."

"You sure? If you're in pain–"

"I'm fine."

A short pause, then the nurse nodded. "Okay. Just let us know if you're in any pain or discomfort."

"Will do."

"I'm Angela, by the way."

"Hi." Jenna reached for the carafe; Angela tensed slightly, watching closely, but let her pour herself a glass of water, relaxing when Jenna set the carafe back down without incident. "Just making sure," she said. "You've been through a lot."

"No shit." Jenna felt a brief impulse to apologise. Apart from anything else, she was weak and struggling to move; she'd need help and it was better not to antagonise people you'd have to rely on for it. But words like *sorry* didn't come naturally to her. It didn't seem to bother Angela, though; she just smiled, and it looked more genuine than the first one.

Jenna drank off the water, then refilled the glass. "Go easy with that," Angela said. Jenna looked up, annoyed – she was a fucking grown-up, for Christ's sake. The nurse shrugged. "You gulp it, you could make yourself sick."

"Right," said Jenna. Then, after a moment, she added "Sorry", in an awkward mumble. She hated being helpless, reliant on others. One of the many reasons she hated hospitals, along with all the memories the smell of the place brought back: Dad sobbing helplessly beside her bed, as if she wasn't even there; the police talking to her about Mum with sad, awkward faces.

Jenna looked down at herself. Everything seemed in place. No bandages or casts. She remembered the twisted ankle and flexed it; there was the faintest twinge of discomfort, but nothing more. She waggled her toes; they all moved freely, without any pain. Looked as though she hadn't broken any after all. With any luck, she'd be out of here soon.

Out of here, and into the NUPAS clinic. Or perhaps the hospital could help her with that issue. She moved her hand to her belly. "How long have I been here?"

"Couple of weeks."

"Jesus, was I in a coma?"

Angela shook her head. "Nothing like that. You were pretty sick – exhaustion, blood loss..." Her gaze shifted to Jenna's abdomen; she smiled again, this time nervously. *Puts a lot of range into her smiles*, Jenna thought, forcing one of her own in return. "Mild respiratory infection, too, on top of all that. Luckily they dosed you up with antibiotics and knocked that on the head before it could turn into something worse, but you were delirious for a bit. Or just out of it completely. You were exhausted, like I said – physically and mentally. You'd proper been through the mill."

She was still looking at Jenna's stomach. Jenna took her hand away, and Angela's gaze returned to her face. "What about the pregnancy?"

Angela looked surprised; she'd no doubt expected to Jenna to say *my baby* or *my child*. "The doctor'll talk to you about that."

Did the fucking thing have horns and a tail, or something? Anything was possible, she supposed, in this case: Jenna remembered the Bonewalker showing her its scarlet hands, and shuddered. "Why? What happened? You said something about blood loss."

"The doctor," Angela said again, then shifted backwards towards the door. "I'll get her now."

"Wait–" But she'd already gone. The door swung shut and locked with a clunk.

Jenna filled the glass again. This time she sipped the water slowly, moistening her lips with it and swilling it round her mouth before swallowing.

A minute or so later, there were footsteps outside. The door opened, and a woman entered. She was very tall, well over six feet, and also very thin, making her look taller still. She had pale-coloured hair scraped back from a sharp, ascetic face and wore a white coat over scrubs, together with thin, wire-framed glasses that glinted as she studied her clipboard. She wore no make-up and when she looked at Jenna, her eyes were a dark, stony grey. "Ms McKnight?"

"I should hope so."

The woman's face twitched in the vaguest approximation of a smile.

"You the doctor?"

"If I'm not, my husband's in for a hell of a shock when I get home." The doctor's mouth twitched again. "I understand you were asking about your baby."

"The pregnancy," Jenna said. "The nurse said I'd lost blood?"

"Yes." The doctor removed her spectacles and massaged the bridge of her nose; there were small red marks where the nose pads had rested. She replaced the glasses and clasped the clipboard to her stomach.

"Just tell me," Jenna said quietly.

The doctor's mouth twitched again. "Direct, aren't you? I like that. Makes a nice change. All right, Ms McKnight. I have some bad news."

"Hit me with your rhythm stick."

This time the twitch was a little more uncertain. "I'm afraid we couldn't save the child."

"It's gone? I miscarried?"

"Technically, after twenty weeks it's a stillbirth."

Twenty weeks. She'd been carrying James's child that long. No, not child. She wouldn't think of it that way. Jenna lay back, closing her eyes. "Thank fuck for that."

A long silence. "The good news is, no permanent damage."

"Oh, good. I'll be able to play the violin, then?"

"Not if you couldn't before." Jenna opened one eye, and the doctor gave another twitchy little smile. "Sorry, Ms McKnight. Heard that joke far too many times." The smile faded. "I meant your reproductive organs. You'll be perfectly capable of having children in the future."

"Pity," said Jenna. "You could've whipped them out while I was under."

"I'm afraid I couldn't. We normally discuss that sort of thing with patients first, wherever possible, and we certainly don't perform major surgery without good reason. If you've made up your mind not to have children, the appropriate procedure would be a tubal ligation, which I take it you've been considering?"

"Yes."

"Mm." A sympathetic smile. "All but impossible to arrange, though, isn't it? Women's healthcare in this country is still a minefield in many respects, though still not as bad as others. But I digress. Can I ask why?"

"Why do you think?" Jenna was annoyed. "Because I don't want kids. Now or ever."

"Yes." Again the twitchy smile. "Thought so." The doctor went to the window and laid her clipboard down on top of the chest of drawers. "I'm hoping I can change your mind about that."

31.

The doctor stood, her back to Jenna, hands clasped behind her, looking down at the lawn.

Jenna, sitting up in bed, was very still. Her stomach felt hollow, and not from hunger. It was hard to breathe: no pain, just constriction. For almost a full minute, she didn't trust herself to speak. The doctor said nothing either. Only her long thin fingers moved, clenching and unclenching. They were waxy, white and slightly wrinkled, as if from cold.

"What did you say?" Jenna said at last. She kept her voice level and steady, although her heart rate had accelerated.

"I said," the doctor replied, "I hope to persuade you to change your mind."

"About the operation?"

"About not having children."

A horrible suspicion formed. Jenna wondered if she'd be able to fight, if it came to it. Doubtful, somehow. She wasn't sure she could get out of bed unassisted. "What's your name, doc?"

The doctor turned, looking faintly surprised. "My name?"

"Wouldn't be Whitecliffe, would it?"

"Ah." Another twitchy little smile. She nodded. "My fame goes before me."

"Yeah. James Frobisher wasn't a fan, I remember that."

"I'm sorry, who? Is that a relative of one of my patients?"

Jenna folded her arms. "Let's not bullshit each other, eh?"

Whitecliffe studied Jenna for a few seconds, drumming her pale fingers on her thighs. "All right, then, Ms McKnight. Cards on the table, hm?"

"Why not?"

Two plastic chairs were backed against the far wall; Whitecliffe pulled one over and sat down. Close to the bed, but out of punching or kicking range. Obviously Jenna's fame had preceded her, too. "So, Sir James Frobisher mentioned my name."

"Yeah. Like I said, he didn't like you much."

"Huh." Jenna realised the snort had been a brief, humourless laugh. "I assure you the feeling was mutual."

"Two points in your favour, I suppose."

"Glad to hear it. We're off to a good start, then." Another snorting laugh.

"So whereabouts are we?"

"Oh, yes. Welcome to Stonebrook. It's a privately owned clinic. Owned by me, I should add."

"And where's Stonebrook, when it's at home?"

"Cumbria. Just this side of the Scottish border. Lovely part of the world."

"Quite a distance," Jenna said. *Be calm, be steady, be ready to fight.* "So what am I doing here? I mean, I'm grateful and everything, but I'm not an expert, and I'm pretty sure they have hospitals in Scotland."

"They do, and good ones on the whole."

"So? What happened? What's going on?"

"What's the last you remember?"

"Last thing I remember's going into the river." She didn't add that she'd thrown herself in, or what she'd been trying escape. Far less how she'd dived down deep and breathed the water in.

Whitecliffe smiled. "All right, I'll fill in some blanks. You were very lucky the river you fell into was in spate. You were washed downstream very quickly and found far sooner than you might've been otherwise. You were clinically dead, you know. I take it you've no memories of going towards a bright light or any of that sort of thing?"

"Nope."

"Shame. We're told near-death experiences are simply caused by the brain shutting down through oxygen deprivation, but I'm always hoping to find one that can't be so easily explained away. Irrefutable proof of an afterlife would be nice, you must admit."

"No luck so far, I'm guessing?"

"No, but as I say, one lives in hope. You were lucky the river was so cold. Slows tissue deterioration, which sets in very quickly in the old noggin–" Whitecliffe tapped her forehead "–*sans* an oxygen supply. Probably stopped you getting irreparable brain damage."

Jenna sagged back against her pillows. "Jesus."

"Didn't prevent the stillbirth, though. Given your condition when they brought you in, it's a minor miracle it hadn't happened before."

"And they brought me all the way to Cumbria?"

"No, you were initially treated at Craigland Hospital in Inverness. I became aware of your case and took an interest. Obstetrics, you see. My area of expertise."

"There wasn't anyone that side of the border?"

"Not in my league."

"Modest."

"Accurate."

"I was in that bad a way?"

"Oh, you were long out of danger by the time I got involved – you've only actually been here at Stonebrook for the last four days. It's the latest in a series of clinics I operate throughout the country. So new, in fact, it's not officially open yet. You have the honour of being the first patient. Skeleton staff, I'm afraid – just myself and four nurses. But my staff, like my facilities, are top-notch. Don't get me wrong – the obstetrician at Craigland was perfectly competent, and there was no reason to fear any complication that might prevent your bearing a child in the future. But I like to make sure of these things."

"I said already, I don't want kids. Ever."

"People can change their minds."

"Not me."

"Well, as I said, I'm rather hoping to change yours."

"Not going to happen."

"Well. We'll see."

"No, we fucking won't."

"There's no need to be rude."

"Isn't there? I don't like being told what to do with my body."

"No one's *telling* you."

"You just don't like the decision I've made and want me to change it." Jenna gave Whitecliffe a cold grin. "When I say no bullshit, doctor, I mean it."

"So I see."

"So, what's your pitch? You another anti-choice arsehole?"

Whitecliffe snort-laughed several times. "Nothing of the sort, Ms McKnight, I can promise you that. I've no religious faith at all. Sometimes wish I did. Be a lot easier to get through this life if I could believe there was another one awaiting me."

"Oh yeah, course. You and your near-death experiences."

"I've normally no moral objection to abortion or sterilization, if that's what a woman wants, or needs. But this isn't an abstract question. This is about you in particular, Ms McKnight – Jenna, if I may."

"You may not." Jenna was quite proud of that comeback. "So, what's so special about my eggs?"

"Your... eggs?" This time Whitecliffe's smile pulled up one corner of her mouth and hung stiffly on her face.

"Got to be that, isn't it? No one's going to put me down as a future mother of the year."

"You'd be surprised. You've many qualities that would be worth passing on."

"I'm not going to tell you again about the bullshit, doctor."

Whitecliffe's lips thinned as she pressed them together and the stony eyes glinted, but she didn't speak.

"Come on," said Jenna. She was thinking as she spoke, now. "You, James – you both wanted something from me. The *same* thing. He got me pregnant by stealthing me somehow. You want to do it the fancy way, but it's the same thing, isn't it? So what's the link? What is it you're after? What could a wanker like James be after that you'd be interested in?"

"All right, then. You have certain rare... factors, Jenna. Properties. Qualities, even. Very rare qualities, Jenna. Perhaps even unique."

"What qualities? What's so special."

"Ah." Whitecliffe sighed. "It's rather complicated. But they could be extremely valuable in the treatment of certain health conditions – conditions which we currently can do nothing to cure."

"Such as?"

"Huntington's Disease, Parkinson's Disease, that kind of thing. Degenerative neurological conditions." Whitecliffe smiled, but there'd been the slightest pause before she'd spoken. A hesitation. She'd had to think of an answer, which meant she was lying. But she went on: "Sir James wanted to exploit them. I'm afraid that's why he initiated his relationship with you in the first place. You used protection, of course, because you always do, especially with men–"

"Whoah, hang on, how do you know all this?" The intrusiveness of it all was enraging and frightening in equal measure, the way they'd made it their business to know her life seemingly inside-out. *Trying to get inside your head.*

"–but young Frobisher got to the condoms. Used an ordinary pin, to put a few holes in the rubber. Simple but very effective, unfortunately. It just took one little prick, in more ways than one. I think he planned to get you to surrender all custody, on the assumption you'd want nothing to do with the child – and then, well, use it as he saw fit."

"Only I kicked him to the kerb."

"Yes. So he kidnapped you."

"He said he'd let me go once I'd had his kid." It felt good to unburden herself, even to Whitecliffe. "He didn't mind me losing the one I was carrying, as long as he got one out of me in the end. But he wouldn't have stopped with one. Not when he could keep me and my magic baby-maker on tap."

Her voice was shaking. She mustn't crack, not in front of Whitecliffe. She already regretted telling her. It'd been a mistake. Holly was still out there somewhere, even if she'd left. Better to save her story for her.

Whitecliffe shook her head sympathetically. "Appalling. And I'm afraid you're probably right. The more children he could get out of you, the better, from his point of view. As far as he was concerned, you were – forgive the expression – a cash cow. As I told you, Jenna, what you have is very rare – and, therefore, very valuable."

"And I told you to call me Ms McKnight."

"As you please."

"And now you want me to pop a sprog out for *you*."

"Not to beat around the bush, yes." Dr Whitecliffe leant forward. "I completely understand your not wanting to be a parent. I completely understand your wanting a tubal ligation to ensure that possibility never arose. I wish many other women, and men, had the courage to admit it. And if there was another way to get what I need, I'd honestly respect that wish. I'd help you achieve it, in fact. Indeed, I *will*: I can carry that procedure out for you, Jenna, here at the clinic. You won't find finer facilities anywhere in this country. Our equipment's state-of-the-art. Not only will I perform that operation gratis when the time comes, I'll compensate you quite handsomely – but first, I require at least three children from you."

Jenna opened her mouth to speak; Whitecliffe held up her hand. "I have various drugs that will increase the odds of multiple births. It may only take one pregnancy. The procedure will be off the books, so your details won't appear on our records. We'll falsify details or those of existing clients. None of the resulting offspring will be able to trace you."

"You finished?" said Jenna.

Whitecliffe sighed. "I know it's not ideal. You've never wanted to carry a child or give birth. In an ideal world, we'd simply go the surrogacy route; harvest a few of your ova, carry out IVF and implant them in a willing host. It's a minimally invasive procedure – would've taken us a quarter of an hour, twenty minutes at most. Unfortunately, that isn't an option here."

Jenna hadn't liked the way any of this had been going; she liked this latest turn of the conversation even less. "Oh? How come?"

Whitecliffe sighed. "We found one other person like yourself. Sadly she's no longer with us, but before her untimely passing we were able to harvest some of her eggs and implant them in surrogate mothers. However, not one embryo developed to full term. They all developed malformations and abnormalities – the most appalling I've seen in my career – and miscarried. It isn't just a matter of genes and chromosomes, that's the trouble. A child with the qualities we're trying to replicate can only gestate in the womb of someone who possesses those same attributes."

"And now I'm the only one in town? Right?"

"Sorry." Whitecliffe shrugged. "But I'm afraid so. Which is why Frobisher attempted to steal a march on me, with methods that were crude to the point of barbarism. Unfortunately, we – I – still need those children, hence the very generous terms I'm prepared to offer in exchange for your cooperation. Fair exchange, no robbery, and all that. Enough money to live on for years, maybe even the rest of your life if you're prudent." Whitecliffe rose. "I'll let you think about it."

She made it sound so reasonable. So tempting. Who could refuse?

Only me.

"Don't bother," Jenna said.

"Excellent." Whitecliffe smiled. "I'll prepare the necessary paperwork, and we can discuss your compensation in due course–"

"No," said Jenna, "you won't, and we fucking can't."

Whitecliffe sighed. "Jenna–"

"The answer's no."

With a longer, deeper sigh, Whitecliffe sat back down. "I really had hoped you'd be reasonable."

"Is that what you call it? You fucking hypocrite."

Jenna had known enough controlling or abusive partners to know that. You were oh-so-reasonably talked out of this, or oh-so-gently pressured into that. Logical arguments or emotional blackmail, facts and figures or withholding of approval. They were all tools from the same kit, with the same overall purpose: to chip away at your will, to separate you from anyone or anything you drew strength or certainty from – and Jenna had little enough of either – till you weren't sure of anything, second-guessing yourself to the point of madness, till you barely knew who you were anymore.

Oh, Jenna had been there before. Had spun adrift, unanchored, in the years since losing Mum, losing Dad, losing everything else. Only one compass to guide her: her own instinct, her own will. And there'd been so many people, over the years, out to subvert that, to rob her of it, sometimes for what they saw as the best possible reasons and sometimes for their own selfish gain.

At the end of the day, this wasn't a choice. Whitecliffe was just dressing it up as one. She wanted what Jenna had and meant to have it by any means.

And for that very reason, Jenna would deny her.

Whitecliffe's lips tightened again. "Ms McKnight, I have asked you before to refrain from abuse."

"You call *that* abuse? I haven't even fucking started, you stupid c–" Whitecliffe's face darkened, and Jenna broke off. "Look," she said, "let me make it so crystal clear to you, doctor, that even a five year-old can understand. I do not want children. I do not want to give birth, adopt, foster, *or*, for that matter, donate my eggs. I. Said. No. Is that clear? Do you need any complicated bits explaining?"

Dr Whitecliffe breathed out, eyes closing. "I see."

"Do you? Oh good."

"Can I ask why?"

"No, you can't. It's none of your fucking business."

"Perhaps if you talked to one of our psychotherapists–"

"Jesus Christ, do you not understand *no*, or do you just not want to?" A part of Jenna was almost enjoying this. The steps of the game. She knew what was coming. The goal was to make Whitecliffe admit it, to show herself for what she was. "What happened to the woman's right to choose? Aren't you supposed to be all about that?"

"In normal circumstances, yes," said Whitecliffe. "But there are, sometimes, exceptional ones."

"Well, you know where you can shove your exceptional circumstances," said Jenna. "Sideways."

Whitecliffe closed her eyes and shook her head. Mum used to do the same when she'd thought Jenna was being a "little madam", so the gesture only made Jenna angrier.

"I'd like some clothes, please," Jenna said.

Dr Whitecliffe opened her eyes. "I'm sorry? Clothes?"

"I'm discharging myself," said Jenna. "So, I'll need clothes. If necessary I'll pay for them – should have some savings left, so yeah, first of all I'll need access to the internet or a phone to contact my bank. Okay?" She clapped her hands together. "Chop-chop, sweetheart. Set it all in motion."

She knew she was being obnoxious, but couldn't stop herself.

Knew, as well, what Whitecliffe's answer would be.

Dr Whitecliffe removed her spectacles again and once more massaged the little red marks on the bridge of her nose, then slowly, carefully replaced the spectacles and looked up at Jenna, her grey eyes more like stones than ever. "No."

"What?" said Jenna, with all the menacing softness she could muster.

"I said no," said Whitecliffe. "I'm sorry, Jenna, but that won't be possible."

"And why's that?"

"Because legally, I can't." A distinctly unsettling smile hovered round Whitecliffe's lips, neither a nervous twitch nor fixed fake grin. "You see, Jenna, you've been detained under the Mental Health Act." She contemplated Jenna for a moment, seemingly half-relishing and half-studying her shock. "Sectioned. You're a danger to yourself or others. The trauma you've been through, the stillbirth. There may even be a form of puerperal psychosis involved."

"This is bollocks," said Jenna. She hadn't bargained for that, but knew she should have. It all boiled down to the same thing in the end. Whitecliffe had shown herself for what she was. Jenna had won the game.

For all the good it did her.

"Well, I suppose male genitals *were* a contributory factor. But otherwise, Jenna, it most certainly isn't." Whitecliffe twitch-smiled. "At Stonebrook, we provide psychiatric as well as obstetric care for our patients. I like to cover all the bases here – people do forget how gestation, birth and/or abortion can all take a psychological toll on the women involved, and, of course, that's before we take account of your pre-existing mental state. Even axe-murderers sometimes need to give birth."

"I'm not crazy."

"Well, you know that and so do I, but good luck convincing anyone else. Your medical records very clearly state you have a history of violent and suicidal behaviour, not to mention extreme delusions – such as insisting your name is Jenna McKnight, rather than the one we have you registered here under. I'm afraid it's a little precaution I arranged, in case you did prove unreasonable about all this. Apparently you have a reputation for that."

"You hypocritical bitch." Jenna tried to sneer, but it came out as a compound of fear and anger.

"For a supposedly intelligent young woman, you're being very silly. You really should be trying to get on my good side."

"You have one?"

"As you'd see if you only gave me a chance."

"Go and fuck yourself."

"Maybe later, when I'm off duty. In the meantime, I've work to do, including providing you with the care you so desperately need. As I said, we have all necessary facilities here."

Jenna's hand moved towards the carafe. If she slammed it into Whitecliffe's head, she could stun her; if it broke, she'd have an edged weapon.

"Said facilities include restraints, of course," Whitecliffe added. "And qualified staff on standby, keeping an eye on things." She pointed up to a corner of the ceiling, near the window: Jenna saw a small camera, a little red light glowing above it. "They'll be in here at the first threatening move from you."

"I see."

"Our facilities for disturbed patients are absolutely excellent quality, I can assure you. Among the best in the world. But I do feel duty-bound to point out you won't find them as pleasant as these." She motioned to the room around them.

Jenna grasped the handle of the carafe. Whitecliffe stared at Jenna's hand and, despite everything, some of her smug assurance left her. When the doctor licked her dry lips, Jenna grinned, refilled her glass and settled back against the cushions. "Think you've got it all figured out, don't you?"

Whitecliffe recomposed herself. "I know I have," she said.

"Keep telling yourself that."

"I don't think there's much point continuing this discussion at this time." Whitecliffe stood, reaching for her clipboard. "You should bear two things in mind, though."

"What's that?"

"We offer pre- and post-partum care here, so once you've given birth, we'd be able to continuing caring for you as long as necessary. Uninterruptedly. Through several other pregnancies, if it came to that. That's the first thing."

"And the other?"

"Persecutory delusions are not uncommon in cases of psychosis. So, of course, if you *were* a patient here for an extended period under the MHA and later released, no one's likely to believe you if you accuse us of forcibly impregnating you. Whether we did or not."

Of course. And Jenna was hardly a poster child for mental health in the first place. "Aren't you a treasure?"

"I like to think so."

"What's so special about me?" But Whitecliffe headed for the door, without replying, or even any sign she'd heard. "Hey!" Whitecliffe reached for the door handle, still ignoring her. "What's the Bonewalker giving you for my children?"

Whitecliffe slowly released the door handle; for a full three seconds – Jenna counted – she was still, then turned, face blank and composed. "I'm sorry?"

"You heard."

"I did, not that what I heard made any sense."

"Maybe you've got another name for it." Jenna maintained eye contact, refusing to look away, but was already beginning to doubt herself. She mustn't; she was the only resource she had. She reminded herself how Whitecliffe had reacted; she must have struck a nerve somewhere. "I don't know what that thing calls itself, but I know James was trying to make some kind of deal with it. It turned up and saved my arse at the end, when Rose was going to kill me." Despite herself she flinched when she remembered the sounds Rose had made when the Bonewalker tore her in half. "Big fucker, looks like a walking skeleton with antlers and a hood on. Stinks like shit. You can't miss it."

Whitecliffe frowned as if puzzled, then sighed and put on a pitying expression. That only made Jenna angrier, which was at least better than the growing uncertainty she felt. "James was slagging you off to it. Where do you think I got your name?"

Whitecliffe shook her head. "I'm so sorry," she said. "Obviously all you've been through affected you worse than we thought. But don't worry. We'll take good care of you, Jenna, until you're well. We can revisit the topic of motherhood then. In the meantime, try to get some rest." She turned and reached for the door handle again.

Jenna was insane; of course she was. What else could she be, babbling of monsters with horns? But Rose hadn't killed herself, and Jenna had heard James saying Whitecliffe's name, heard the rumbling tarry voice he'd conversed with. Whitecliffe was just trying to convince her it was all in her head. The final insult. Even so, she sounded far more defiant than she really felt when she called: "What happened to not bullshitting me, doc?"

For a moment, Jenna thought Whitecliffe would turn round and come clean, but instead she opened the door and stepped through it without looking back. It clicked shut behind her, then locked again. And Jenna was alone, a prisoner once more.

32.

So it wasn't over; in fact, it had begun all over again. Jenna lay in the bed and tried to take stock. She was rested and her injuries had healed – there wasn't even a twinge from her twisted ankle – but her hand shook when she reached for the water again.

James had abducted Jenna and locked her in a cellar to make her give birth, with additional inseminations by turkey baster to follow. Whitecliffe, in contrast, was keeping everything outwardly legal and above board. If Jenna accepted Whitecliffe's offer, she'd immediately be pronounced *compos mentis*; if she said no, Whitecliffe would use her anyway. And either way, if Jenna tried to report it afterwards, everyone would feel sorry for her, but no one would believe her. *Never got over what happened to her parents and what the Frobisher boy put her through. Sad business. Poor thing.*

No choice, either way.

The worst part was, Jenna was even beginning to doubt herself. After all, what was easier to believe: giant horned monsters made of bones that appeared out of thin air and tore people in half, or that she was delusional?

Well, something *killed Rose*, a small, still and oddly familiar voice piped up, *and it wasn't you*.

But for all she knew, it had been. With her memory full of impossible monsters, she couldn't be sure of anything that had happened in the cellar or the woods; about anything connected with the Bonewalker.

You didn't pull Whitecliffe's name out of your arse. You heard James say it.

Maybe: but perhaps he'd been talking to Reid, Rose, or Eric, and her fucked-up mind had twisted it into something nightmarish. Or even more nightmarish: solitary confinement and sensory deprivation could be massively damaging to mental health at the best of times, after all. Maybe she hadn't coped with them as well as she'd thought.

I'm mad, or the Bonewalker's real: which one sounds more likely?

She almost wished herself back in the cellar: at least there the enemy had been outside her, to be outwitted, escaped and, if necessary, destroyed. Now it might be between her ears, behind her eyes, warping all the information that went in so she couldn't trust her own perceptions.

Babe, you've got to trust yourself, the little voice piped up again, and Jenna realised it sounded very much like Holly. *You're all you've got.*

She lay down after an hour and tried to sleep, which wasn't hard: the state of desperate anxiety she'd been in since Whitecliffe left had exhausted her. Sleep was an escape from all that, at least.

Unless it wasn't, she realised as she was about to go under: what if she dreamed of the grove? Better the anxiety and the fear of going mad than facing the Bonewalker again, even in dreams. But sleep had her in its tentacles and pulled her under, down, down, down into a wine-dark sea.

33.

She didn't dream; there was that small mercy, at least. When she woke she was lying on her side, facing the window; the curtains were open, but it was dark out, and the light in her room was on. She'd no idea if it'd been morning or afternoon when she'd first woken, so it was impossible to be sure how long she'd slept. It could've been an hour; could've been ten.

Why's the light on?

"Jenna?"

"Fuck," she mumbled, and twisted round to see Dr Whitecliffe sitting in the plastic chair, now backed up against the far wall, a paperback in her hands. Jenna rubbed her eyes and Whitecliffe folded down a page corner, slipping the book into her coat pocket. As she did, Jenna glimpsed the cover. "Mills and Boon?"

Whitecliffe twitch-smiled. "My guilty secret. I'm a sucker for romance. Especially hospital ones." She attempted a Cockney accent: "It's a fair cop, guv'nor." She snorted with laughter then sat, fidgeting. An awkward silence, then Whitecliffe sighed.

"All right," she said. "We agreed not to bullshit one another, as you said. I've just become very used to... not discussing a certain subject. Or even acknowledging its existence."

"The Bonewalker," Jenna said. "Right?"

"Not his actual name, but yes. Quite an extraordinary being, you know."

"One way of putting it." Jenna folded her arms. "It killed my mother, didn't it?"

"Not the word I'd use."

"I wonder what word *she'd* have used?"

Whitecliffe sighed. "You're not making this any easier."

"Why should I?"

Bite your tongue and listen, babe; might actually find out something useful.

Extraordinary how like Holly that inner voice sounded. Jenna controlled herself with an effort: she needed the determination she'd found in the woods, to get out and see Holly again. "I'm sorry. Please. Go on."

"All right, then." Whitecliffe removed her glasses, massaged the bridge of her nose, then replaced them. She paused, gathering her thoughts, then nodded and began. "Quite simply, Jenna, there's a way to live forever."

Jenna leant back against the pillows. What Whitecliffe had just said might be sheer madness, but if it was, she was in good company: if Jenna hadn't already been sectioned, repeating what she'd seen and experienced thus far would rectify that.

She kept her mouth shut and continued listening.

"You could say it's been my life's work," said Whitecliffe. "My life's obsession might be more accurate. Longevity, that is. There aren't enough hours in the day, or years in a lifetime, to do everything you want to do or achieve everything you want to achieve."

"And no afterlife, right?"

Whitecliffe sighed. "I've wanted to believe otherwise for as long as I can remember. When I was a very tiny girl, of course, I did. My father was an Anglican priest. I was very happy when I was little. When I still believed. But…" She sighed and shook her head. "Didn't last."

There was real sorrow in her voice, and for a moment the stony eyes were focused on some point in the distant past. Then she shook her head. "So I turned to science instead. I thought that would give me answers, or at least work of real social benefit. I married, had children, and all the rest. Immortality of a kind, or so people tell us. Some part of ourselves continues if our genes live on."

"So I've heard," said Jenna. "Never my thing, though."

"Yes. You are a strange one, aren't you?"

"Not *that* strange."

"True. Not as if every woman feels that need. Pretty common, though. I certainly hoped it would be enough. But it wasn't, Jenna, not at all. You see, what I wanted – what I *want* – isn't some airy-fairy, metaphorical immortality. And I don't want it in some metaphysical never-never land. I want the real thing. Personal immortality. Here. Now. On earth."

"Good luck with that."

"I'd exhausted all scientific options. Couldn't find anything. Oh, there were possibilities, but nothing I was likely to see in my lifetime. And even then, nothing that was guaranteed."

"Nothing's guaranteed, sweetheart," Jenna told her. "Could have told you that a long time ago."

"I thought you wanted me to get to the point?"

"Sorry. Go on."

"Science couldn't help me, and I'd abandoned religion. So I looked to the occult for answers. Which isn't as an uneasy a bedfellow with science as you might think. Isaac Newton wrote books on alchemy and magic when he wasn't discovering gravity or inventing calculus. And when you go back to Greece, or Ancient Rome… anyway. I began wondering if some of those ancients might have known something we rational, scientific types have forgotten or discarded."

"And they did, huh?"

"Oh, yes. Quite definitely. It took years of research, tracking down unbelievably obscure manuscripts, but at last I found it. Or rather, I learned of its existence. The Rite of Cronos, Jenna. How well do you know your Greek mythology?"

Jenna shrugged. "Bits."

"Know who Cronos was?"

"One of their gods?"

"The first of the Titans. The Romans called him Saturn. He overthrew his father Uranus and ruled creation in his stead. To ensure *he* couldn't be overthrown in turn, he devoured each of his children when they were born. But his sister-wife Rhea hid one of his sons, Zeus, who defeated Cronos and became king of the gods in his place."

"Saturn," said Jenna.

"As I said, that's what the Romans called him." Whitecliffe gave another of her twitchy little smiles. "I thought you'd make one of those infantile jokes about Uranus. I've heard them all."

That dream she'd had, a couple of years before: the figure crouching in the shadows with a body in its claws, the head and one arm gnawed away. There'd been a dreadful familiarity about the image, and it was absurd it had taken her so long to place it: Francisco Goya's painting *Saturn Devouring His Son*. She'd seen it in an art class when she was fourteen. The old, mad god, all wild eyes, matted hair and ravening mouth, ogrish and grotesque; the naked body half-eaten in his grasp.

"That's how the Rite got its name, anyway," said Whitecliffe. "That's the basic principle."

Jenna snorted. "What? Eat your kids and live forever?"

"No. Well, not just, or not only, your children. It's not a one-and-done sort of thing. Each... absorption brings a new lease of life, as it were, lasting–"

"Absorption? That's what you call it?"

"It's a word, Jenna. It describes a process."

"What's wrong with good old-fashioned cannibalism, then? Or is that too near the knuckle for you? Do you not like thinking about it too much?"

"Cannibalism is *not* the correct term."

"Looked like it to me."

"Really?" Whitecliffe looked genuinely fascinated. "When did you witness it?" When Jenna didn't answer, the older woman nodded. "A dream? Is that it? I read in the documents I studied that could happen, but I didn't know for sure. The Progenitor's rather close-mouthed on certain details."

"That's what it calls itself?"

"He likes to cover his tracks. The less I know of his origins, the less chance I'll find out what I want without his help." Whitecliffe sighed. "Sadly, he's done far too good a job. To get the information I want, I've no alternative but to help him. But that's no great hardship. The work I'm doing on his behalf will be just as beneficial to me."

"You've completely lost me now."

"I forget I'm so familiar with all this. The process of absorption – I'll keep calling it that, if you don't mind – is what makes the Progenitor immortal. By completely absorbing his offspring, or rather descendant, he renews himself. And by repeating the process every thirteen years or thereabouts, he can extend his lifespan indefinitely. Even infinitely."

"So what's the catch?"

"The 'catch', as you put it, is being *able* to repeat the process. As long as he still has descendants, it doesn't matter how many generations removed they are: all that matters is that they carry his bloodline. Unfortunately, while the Progenitor himself is invulnerable, his descendants are just ordinary, mortal humans, with all the weaknesses that go with that."

Jenna laughed. "Are you saying he's running out of kids to eat?"

"At the last absorption, which was a couple of years ago now, the numbers were beginning to run low, but he wasn't overly concerned."

A couple of years ago: around the time she'd last dreamt of the grove before it had all started up again. The half-eaten body dangling in the monster's grip; she must have caught the briefest glimpse, on some level, of the last "absorption" taking place.

"There was, you see," Whitecliffe went on, "a fairly substantial branch of the bloodline at that time in Ukraine, of all places. Unfortunately they were in Mariupol, and during the bombardment that followed the Russian invasion earlier this year they were wiped out *in toto*. Every last man, woman and child. And that left you alone, Jenna. The Progenitor's very last living descendant. He can absorb you, which will keep him going for just under another decade and a half, but after that–"

"He's fucked."

"If you must put it like that, then yes."

"Can't he just get some other poor cow up the duff?" Not that Jenna would wish that on anybody else.

Whitecliffe smiled sadly. "An unfortunate side-effect of the Rite of Cronos is sterility. It's a trade-off, I suppose – immortality through your children in exchange for the real, literal thing. So before carrying out the Rite, you need to make sure you've sown your wild oats far and wide. The small number of people who've successfully performed the Rite have almost all been men. They've always had an unfair advantage in that regard. Until now, of course."

"You've already taken care of that, then?" said Jenna.

"My particular discipline's stood me in perfect stead for it. I've three daughters, and grandchildren through all of them. Very fond of them all, of course..."

"But you'd eat the lot of them without a second thought?"

Whitecliffe chuckled. It sounded like a hacking cough. "You'd be well-advised to consider it, if only in terms of simple self-preservation. If there are more descendants out there, the Progenitor doesn't need you. Being his descendant doesn't automatically mean you'll be..."

"Absorbed."

"Yes."

"Because he can do it to a baby instead?"

"No. He won't need to repeat the process for another ten or eleven years at the present time."

"Ah, great. He can kill a schoolie instead."

"As I said, killing isn't the right word."

"Oh? You mean they're still alive?"

"Well, not as such, but–"

"So he kills them."

Whitecliffe sighed. "If you must be sentimental..."

"I was there when he took my mother, doc. I heard her scream. And there wasn't even anything left of her to bury."

"We can't do anything about that now, can we?" Whitecliffe sounded so maddeningly reasonable Jenna wanted to leap out of bed and hit her. "We're talking about eternal life here. If I ensure the Progenitor's bloodline continues, he'll show me how to perform the Rite of Cronos. However, I've always been pro-choice. It goes against the grain to violate that principle."

Choice; that word again. If it had been an actual, proper choice, would Jenna have agreed to it? She'd done her share of questionable things in her time. But she was fairly sure that producing children to be sacrificed would've been a bridge too far for her, even on her worst days. "But you will," she said to Whitecliffe. "Right?"

"Quite simply, yes. That shouldn't be a shock, Jenna. Most people will abandon their principles, given sufficient temptation. Don't tell me you're so holier-than-thou you're incapable of it."

"Never claimed to be. But then I'm not a hypocrite. Unlike some."

Whitecliffe's mouth twitched, and this time it wasn't a smile: that particular barb had hit home. "Be that as it may. If you agree to the procedure, you'll have a far easier time of things, and I'll pay you very well."

"All you're coming out with, doc? Just a fancier version of what James said. All boils down to *do what I want or else*." Jenna needed to remember that. It would keep her angry and focused, however hard Whitecliffe tried to muddy the waters.

"Again, be that as it may. Debating morality won't get us anywhere. You seem a pragmatic young woman, Jenna. I can offer you another inducement."

"Oh?" Jenna's stomach tightened.

"Only a handful of people, over the millennia, have successfully carried out the Rite of Cronos," said Whitecliffe. "I don't know exactly how many, but as I said earlier, they've almost exclusively been men. I'd say it's past time to redress that balance."

"Starting with you, right?" Jenna hoped she was hiding her relief: her real fear had been that Whitecliffe would threaten Jenna with Holly. *You can have her back, or she can die. Which would you prefer?* Despite everything, Jenna realised, that might actually have worked. Christ; it must be love, after all. That was what was so terrifying about it, why she always tried to keep a distance with any partner. They could get inside you and warp you out of true. But that approach, it seemed, had no more occurred to Whitecliffe than it had to James.

"Or *us*."

"Are you serious?"

"This isn't a zero-sum game, Jenna. There's no reason I couldn't share the secret with you. And it's cheap at the price. It's taken me decades of searching and planning to get here. You can have it on a plate."

"That's what you're offering?" Jenna began to laugh. "Fucking hell, love, you don't know me at all, do you?"

"Apparently not. But you wanted to know what this was all about. Now I've told you." Whitecliffe stood. "You're fully recovered, so we can begin the necessary treatments in the next two or three days. Think about my offer, anyway. I'd much rather resolve this in a way we're both happy with."

Jenna could normally manage a suitable parting shot even in the most trying circumstances, but this time around she was genuinely stuck for a reply. Whitecliffe flung the door wide as she left, either in a grand gesture or straightforward irritation, but it was on a hydraulic hinge, and swung smoothly and quietly closed again. The lock clicked, and the light went out...

Jenna glared at the door for a few moments, then threw back the sheets and climbed out of bed. She wanted to get out of here – outside, away, free. But the best she could manage was to stalk to the window and gaze longingly out onto the lawn.

Most of it was in darkness, with the trees a high, ragged black line against the deep, star-speckled blue of the night sky, but the light from the building illuminated most of the lawn, and drew even its edges into a dim twilight. And in that grey, twilit area, Jenna saw, a woman was standing, just at the edge of the trees. She was plump, stocky, wore black clothes, and was staring up at Jenna's window. She tensed, mouth opening, and Jenna realised the woman had seen her gazing down at her.

The woman in black moved back towards the trees, and moonlight glanced off her features. A round, dimple-chinned face, and a wing of dark hair falling over one eye. She looked just like Holly, Jenna thought. Then realised, in the instant before the woman disappeared into the shadows, that it was.

34.

Jenna lay back on the bed and shut her eyes, but sleep was as impossible as Whitecliffe's story. And as true. Strangely it made such sense, once she accepted it.

The Bonewalker was real, and she mattered because she was the last of its blood. The only real surprise was that it had taken Whitecliffe this long to get hold of Jenna.

And then there was Holly.

Jenna put both hands over her mouth to muffle her sobs as her worst suspicions and paranoid imaginings from the cellar returned. Holly had been working for Whitecliffe all along. Or, like James and Whitecliffe, she wanted the Bonewalker's prize, and was playing her own long game to get it.

Jenna didn't want to believe that; the thought hurt, and threatened to taint every memory of the relationship. That wasn't usually a problem: while every liaison she'd ever been in ended in an emotional car-crash of one kind or another, that part usually faded with time. But Jenna was only now realising how different it had been with Holly. Or how badly she'd wanted it to be. And now it seemed every memory that had sustained her in the cellar, from walking on Dinas Oleu to watching movies on the sofa, had been a lie.

She shook her head, but the pain wouldn't go away and she doubted there was a drug in the clinic that would make it, except the kind of stuff that turned people into junkies, that made reality disappear when you couldn't bear it anymore.

This is why Dad drank.

"Fuck." Jenna opened her eyes and took deep breaths, in and out. No. She wouldn't go that way. Wouldn't end up like him. She dragged her sleeve across her eyes and glared at the little red light glowing in the upper left corner of her room, where the CCTV camera kept watch on her. They loved their little electronic I-spies, all the wankers who clustered round the Bonewalker, clamouring for its secret at any price.

If – when – she broke out of here, the police would be hunting her too. *Jenna McKnight, escaped nutter. Don't believe a word she says, just break out the butterfly nets and cart her back to the clinic. That nice Dr Whitecliffe'll take care of her.*

Well, she'd deal with that later. And with Holly, one way or the other. The first step was getting out.

A few more deep breaths steadied her for now. She'd escaped Cutty Wren Lodge; sectioned or not, she'd break out of here too, even if she'd no idea how, as yet. Jenna threw the sheets back and slid clumsily out of bed. Her legs tremored. *Jesus.* But she steadied quickly enough. She'd retained her fitness as best she could while confined at the cottage, as her escape had proved; two weeks flat on her back had taken something out of her but not too much, and at least she wasn't burdened with the pregnancy any longer. She squatted a couple of times, testing her strength.

She'd be able to run, Jenna decided; she could fight too, if it came down to it. She made her way over to the window, peering out over the dim-lit lawn. She was about three floors up, or so she calculated, and the side of the building was flat and painted smooth, with no gaps sufficient for hand or toeholds. Not that she'd likely be able to climb, in her state, even if she'd been willing to risk it, which she wasn't. The window was shut anyway, and the handle locked; it wouldn't turn. So she couldn't even get out to try.

You've got to think of something, though, else you're fucked.

Across the room, the lock clicked. The door swung open. Jenna stumbled back towards the bed, groping for the carafe.

Someone appeared in the doorway, silhouetted by the corridor light, then stepped into the room, swallowed by the dark again as the door swung shut. Jenna grabbed the covers and heaved them in the intruder's direction.

The intruder was cursing and throwing the covers aside as Jenna moved towards her. If she was quick, and lucky, she could get in a kick, or a strike to the throat.

But she knew the voice, had recognised the silhouette. She knew who it was.

The intruder reached back through the open doorway. There was a click, and the lights came on.

"Hey, babe," said Holly.

35.

She wore a backpack over a hooded top and a pair of cargo pants. When she brushed the wing of hair back, Jenna saw both her eyes were glistening. *Tears*. What the fuck?

Holly tried to smile, mouth trembling. "Oh, sweetheart," she whispered. She moved forwards, arms outstretched, but Jenna moved back, hands raised ready for combat – weak or not, she'd fight.

"Get back, you fucking–"

Holly looked as though she'd been slapped. "Jenn? Jenn, it's *me*. It's Holl."

"I know who you are."

"Show some fucking gratitude, then." That was the Holly Jenna knew – the tears were gone as though they'd never been, replaced by sudden anger, and her hands were on her hips. She threw the backpack at Jenna. Jenna ducked to avoid it and moved to launch a kick in response, but her legs betrayed her and she grabbed at the bed for support.

"You okay?" said Holly. Jenna didn't answer, just glared. Holly shook her head. "Hurry up and get dressed for fuck's sake."

"What?"

"Jesus, Jenna, how doped-up are you? I'm trying to get you out of here."

A shrill electronic tone sounded, a klaxon of some kind, deafeningly loud. Holly looked ceilingward and mouthed

"Finally", then returned her gaze to Jenna. "Come *on*, for Christ's sake!" she was shouting now, over the alarm. "Get dressed."

No time to dither; only a moment to decide. Jenna bent and fumbled at the backpack. Couldn't be real. Had to be a trick. But the bag contained a sweatshirt, jogpants, trainers, underwear, a bra.

Fine. She'd go along for now.

She flung off the hospital gown, pulled on the pants and top and donned the trainers, grimacing at the alarms' clamour as she laced them up. It would get her away from Whitecliffe, anyway. And she could find out the truth about Holly. If she was on the level after all, well and good–

Oh come on, you don't really believe that.

And if not, Jenna would have a chance of escape. And if necessary, for revenge.

Holly was by the door, which she'd opened an inch or so, right hand in one of the cargo pants' pockets. Her left was fumbling at another, longer pouch on the other leg, unfastening the flap that secured it. "Come on, babe. No time."

She pulled the door open. Jenna followed her out into the corridor outside. "Just walk, Jenn," Holly said. "That's all you've got to do."

Jenna tried, but was shocked to realise how unsteady she still was. Holly circled around behind her back and linked her left arm through Jenna's to support her, right hand still shoved in her pocket. Jenna squirmed, but Holly's grip tightened. "Don't be stupid, babe."

Jenna gritted her teeth. But Holly was right. "Fine," she said. If nothing else, she could play along for now. "What's the plan?"

The corridor outside her room was short. There was another door in the wall in front of her. At each end of the corridor was another still, with a panel of glass reinforced with wire mesh. The one to Jenna's left looked into another corridor; beyond the one to her right, she could make out the night sky. It was marked FIRE EXIT – EMERGENCY ONLY.

"This-a-way," said Holly. "Think you'll agree this counts as an emergency."

Jenna grunted out a weak laugh.

"We use that, cut across the lawn. Then we'll have to go through some trees. Think you can handle that?"

"I'll manage." This couldn't be real. Couldn't be. She was dreaming. Hallucinating from the drugs they'd given her. Or she'd gone mad in the cellar after all and none of this was happening; maybe the story Whitecliffe had told her earlier had all been a lunatic's fever dream as well.

She's tricking you. Don't trust her.

Jenna knew she shouldn't. Yet how she wanted to.

"My car's parked up outside the fence," said Holly. "Just get through that and we're away–"

The door at the other end of the corridor crashed open. Jenna lurched round to face it, almost tumbling over. A louder clamour of alarms blared through the open doorway, and with them came Angela.

Her earlier friendly manner was gone; she came barrelling towards them at speed, head down. Something seemed to be wrong with her face, but Jenna couldn't quite tell what. "You, you bitch," Jenna heard her shout. She pointed as she ran. Not at Jenna, but at Holly.

Holly pushed Jenna aside and went to meet her. Her left hand dipped into the pouch and came out holding a long, narrow tube. She flicked her wrist with a loud *snap* that Jenna could hear even over the fire alarms, and it suddenly tripled in length.

Extendable baton.

Holly swung the baton at Angela's head. Jenna winced; it was a wild, clumsy blow that had no hope of landing, and it didn't. Angela dodged it easily. But Holly's right hand came out of her other pocket clutching what looked like a small aerosol spray, and when she thrust it into Angela's face and pushed the nozzle down, the other woman had no chance to avoid it.

That was what had been wrong with her face, Jenna realised. It had been red, the eyes streaming and bloodshot. As if sore, and stinging.

A hiss and a reddish mist, and then Angela reared back, clutching her face and screaming. Holly went after her, still spraying her, then scrambled backwards, stuffed the aerosol back into her pocket, and grabbed Jenna. "Come on!" she shouted.

Jenna let herself be steered towards the fire escape. "Was that fucking pepper spray?"

"No, it was Chanel No.5." Holly kicked at the fire door. "Course it was bastard pepper spray."

Jenna looked back. Angela was writhing on the floor, clutching her face and bellowing obscenities between her fingers. There was a crash and cold wind blew into the corridor; Jenna spun round in time to see the fire door swing open.

Holly turned back to Jenna with a shaky grin and nodded to the fire door. "Come on, princess, let's fucking motorvate, eh? Or d'you want me to carry you down?"

"In your fucking dreams, darling," said Jenna, and stepped through the door into the cool night air.

36.

A small concrete platform surrounded by railings overlooked the yard beside the main building; steel steps zigzagged down the whitewashed brickwork to the ground. Ahead of them was a gravel forecourt, then the lawn.

Jenna stumbled down the steel steps, clinging to the railing. Holly followed, still clutching the baton. Jenna ducked; the way the other woman was brandishing the weapon, she seemed far more likely to do herself or Jenna an injury with the thing than anyone else. Nonetheless, as they reached the bottom of the steps and crossed the forecourt onto the lawn, Holly's face was pale and set and determined. "With me, now," she said, then took off in a straight line towards the trees.

More fucking trees.

Jenna didn't move. She'd no idea who this Holly was, what relation she bore to the woman Jenna had first met at Ron's gym. Maybe that woman had never existed. Not a new thought, but it seemed far more credible now. She'd never suspected the existence of this ruthless, determined version of the woman she'd thought she'd known. That woman had to have been a trick. A long con. The only question was whether she was in business for herself or a professional, hired by another Whitecliffe, another James.

Either way, she could only be leading Jenna out of this particular frying pan and into a fresh fire.

Holly, realising Jenna hadn't followed, turned back and stared. "Jenna, for fuck's sake!"

Any minute now she'd drop the mask and get out the pepper-spray again, or come at her with the baton. *Move, bitch, now.* But while she looked annoyed, exasperated, desperate, there was something else there, very like the Holly Jenna remembered. Something like the hurt that had been in her eyes during the row about the pregnancy tests; something like the tenderness that'd been in them afterwards, as she'd cradled Jenna in her arms.

Maybe, just maybe–

No. It wasn't real. Couldn't be. Whitecliffe behind her, Holly in front of her: Jenna needed to strike out on her own, but which way was that? Holly was her only way out, but that was just leading her to another trap. Unless–

Holly looked up, past her. "Jenn!"

Jenna half-turned, but too late; someone piled into her from the side and drove her to the ground, pinning her arms behind her back. "Got her," a voice shouted. A woman. Her breath smelt of Juicy Fruit gum.

"Nice one, Zoe." Another voice. A man.

"Yeah," Zoe grunted, wrestling Jenna to her feet. "Sort the other bitch out."

Two more white-overalled figures moved past Jenna towards Holly – men, this time. She couldn't see their faces.

"Get the fuck off her!" Holly bellowed, and Jenna saw her advancing, the baton raised. Moving apart, they bobbed and weaved, so Holly had to swing clumsy, flailing blows at first one and then the other of them. One man laughed.

"Get the fuck back," shouted Holly.

The one who'd laughed moved closer. "Why? What'll you do if I don't?"

Holly swung the baton towards him, but he didn't flinch. He was redheaded, with a scarred, thickly bearded face. Probably ex-army, in which case he'd faced people with weapons before – far more lethal weapons, and people far likelier to use them than Holly.

"Go on!" yelled Redbeard. Holly jumped, stumbling back. "Go on, then." But still she didn't; the baton shook in her hands, almost slipping from them.

Redbeard stepped forward and she swung at him, but it was, once again, a clumsy sweep and Redbeard dodged it easily, then slapped the baton, almost casually, out of her grip; his companion, a pig-faced man with greasy yellow hair, jumped aside and muttered "Fuck" as it flew past him. Redbeard's hand swung back, cracking Holly across the side of her face. She went sprawling with a shocked, childlike cry.

Don't you fucking do that to her, Jenna thought.

"That's what you get," said Redbeard. "Big boys' games, big boys' rules."

Holly looked past him at Jenna, eyes streaming tears, and opened her mouth to speak; Jenna wasn't sure what she'd have said and she never said it anyway, because Redbeard said, "Stupid cow," and kicked Holly in the stomach.

Jenna was sufficiently dazed, so much having happened so fast, that she might otherwise have been dragged unresisting back to her room, but the sight of Holly kicked when she was down and helpless broke through the fog. Even more than the kick itself, there was the noise Holly made – a winded cry of pain and a hurt, sobbing wail. It wasn't a sound a trained, cold-blooded professional would make; it was the cry of a woman who'd taken a step off the path into a world that was strange and dark and frightening.

Jenna recognised it, because that had once been her too.

It felt like waking up.

I know who I am.

And I know what to do.

Jenna lifted her right foot and raked the heel down Zoe's shin before slamming it into the other woman's instep. Zoe cried out in pain, her balance going, grip weakening. Jenna hit her in the ribs and stomach with her elbows – half a dozen blows, as fast as she could.

Redbeard and Greasy Hair, as if in slow motion, turned.

Zoe's grip went slack. Jenna stepped forward, breaking free easily, but the other woman was still on her feet. Jenna pivoted and saw her opponent for the first time: a mixed-race woman with cropped, frizzy hair and a square, determined face. Zoe moved towards Jenna, but Jenna was already aiming a roundhouse kick at her jaw. Zoe's head snapped sideways and she fell.

Ron would have found a hundred things wrong with Jenna's technique, but, she thought – letting the kick's momentum spin her back round before falling into a halfway decent fighting crouch – she was a little off-form. Besides, she didn't need Zoe dead. Just down and out. Which she now was.

All of that felt as though it had taken several minutes, but Redbeard and Greasy Hair had only advanced a couple of steps, their hands outstretched. Bullet time, soldiers called it: everything happening both grasshopper-quick and treacle-slow as the adrenaline kicked in. Reflexes, responses and perception all sped up, slowing the world around you to a crawl.

Redbeard and Greasy Hair spread out as they ran in. Tackling one would mean turning her back on the other.

Two-to-one odds. Not good in your state, babe.

But an equaliser lay a few feet away in the grass: the baton. Jenna took a step towards the two men, then dived and rolled. Her hand clawed through the grass and found cold metal.

Greasy Hair barrelled towards her, swinging his foot back for a kick. Jenna tucked and rolled forward, cannoning into his other leg, and he flew over her with a cry of pain, thudding into the grass.

Jenna collided with something warm and soft and yielding, that gave a little squeak of pain and fright. When she opened her eyes, Holly stared back at her, red-eyed and crying. For that moment, at least, there was no doubt: this was the Holly she'd met at the gym, the one she'd gone camping in Wales with, who'd held her all night after the pregnancy test, whose memory had got Jenna through the nights in the cellar.

And Redbeard had kicked her when she was down.

Bastard.

Jenna scrambled to her feet, suddenly clumsy again now, as Redbeard studied her. For a moment he was quiet, still, then he held out a hand. "Give me that."

She was holding the baton left-handed, by the wrong end. She grabbed the handle with her right, then wrapped both hands around it.

"Put it down," said Redbeard. "Before you get hurt."

"Won't be me getting hurt," said Jenna, hefting the baton.

"Yeah, right, love." Redbeard laughed and extended a hand, fingers grasping. "Come on, before I get pissed off."

Just myself and four nurses, Whitecliffe had said. Three of the nurses were here. Zoe was down on the ground; Greasy Hair was now getting up again. Angela made four; she was hopefully still rolling around in the corridor with her eyes on fire, but then again, she'd recovered once already. And then there was Whitecliffe herself. That made two more opponents who could show up at any moment; she and Holly had to be on the move before they did. "Last chance," she said, and stepped forward. "Move."

Redbeard stepped forward. "We both know you're not gonna–"

They obviously didn't tell him anything about me, Jenna thought, then swung the baton with all her strength. The blow connected with Redbeard's upper arm; he yelled in pain and staggered, clutching his shoulder. "You fucking bitch," he said, and charged.

Jenna dropped to one knee and swung again, aiming lower. The baton caught Redbeard across the shins, and he screamed and crashed to the ground.

Greasy Hair came at her from the side, maybe hoping she was too shocked by what she'd just done to react. If so, he was wrong. Jenna surged up onto her feet, driving the baton up ahead of her like a spear. Greasy Hair doubled up screaming, clutching his belly.

Jenna stood, and got her first proper look at Stonebrook. It didn't look like a clinic; it was a big, whitewashed farmhouse, with a stone outbuilding over to one side of it at an angle. But that was a detail; there were more important things to deal with. If Whitecliffe hadn't already guessed where she was, these two were screaming their heads off. Zoe lay motionless in the grass – still out for the count, with any luck, unless Jenna had broken her neck. Be hilarious if the men she'd belted with a club survived and the one she'd kicked didn't.

Holly grasped her hand, scrambling to her feet and pointing towards the trees. "This way."

They dashed across the lawn, Holly clinging to Jenna's arm and setting a decent pace despite the kicking she'd taken. Jenna slowed as they reached the treeline and the scent of pines enfolded her, but aided by Holly's momentum, managed to keep going. *You can do this, babe. You got over the wall and through the forest before, even with James and his dickheads after you.*

"Jenn!" Holly shouted. Jenna turned and blundered through the trees. Holly crouched by the fence, pulling at the wire; as Jenna reached her a huge flap of the chain-link peeled back. "Go. Quick."

Jenna squirmed through the gap on hands and knees, nearly pitching headlong down the grassy embankment beyond before landing in a heap on a tarmac roadway. Holly tumbled after her, then grabbed her arm to help her up. "Soz," she wheezed. "Should've warned you 'bout that." She pulled Jenna after her, across the narrow lane.

Branching off the lane was the entrance to another one, and the two of them stumbled down it. The night was clear and cloudless; in the moonlight Jenna saw a couple of houses that were either half-built or half-demolished, and a row of vacant lots each side of the street, thickly overgrown with grass, behind yet more wire fencing.

Holly pulled her down one house's driveway, and Jenna saw a Kia Sportage parked there. There was a bleeping sound, indicator lights flashing, and a *thunk* as the locks unfastened. "Get in," Holly puffed.

Jenna obeyed, running on a kind of autopilot now, dazed and numb, slamming the door behind her. She fumbled for her seatbelt as the engine roared into life, then realised she was still clutching the baton. She put it on the dashboard, but as Holly drove the Kia into the lane it clattered into the footwell between her feet. "Fuck."

Holly glanced at her, eyes wide, then turned right and accelerated up the lane, away from the direction they'd come. "You okay?"

"Yeah. Just dropped the baton."

"No problem. We'll get it back later." Holly glanced at her for a second. "Hang onto it if you want, if it'll make you fucking trust me."

The lane ended in front of them in a kerb and a low embankment, beyond which lay an empty field. The Kia bounced and jolted over the kerb, mounted the embankment, then slewed down onto the scrubby vegetation and rutted ground, slaloming across the uneven terrain.

Holly, glaring straight ahead, kept the accelerator floored, the speedo needle climbing past 70mph. Jenna hung onto the handle above the passenger door as she was flung about in her seatbelt. Then the field ended in a slope leading down to another road – a country lane, winding and empty and sparsely lit – and the Kia shot down it at full speed. It jolted and shuddered as they hit the tarmac, fishtailing wildly, but Holly spun the wheel and the car's rear end swung back into line as she accelerated on into the night.

37.

With the immediate danger past, exhaustion swept over Jenna and she slumped in her seat, closing her eyes. She didn't fall asleep, but instead entered a sort of grey twilight between wakefulness and slumber; she didn't know how long she spent like that, but when she opened her eyes motorway lights were shining down through the windscreen.

She rubbed her eyes. Road signs flashed by, but she was too bleary to register any details. "Where are we?"

"Hey." Holly glanced at her, smiled weakly. "You're back."

"Just about." Jenna rubbed her eyes again. *Wake up. Stay alert. Still don't know you can trust her*. No matter how much she wanted to. "Where are we?" she said again.

"Motorway."

"I can see *that*."

"Heading for Wales," Holly said.

"Wales?"

"Why not?" Holly gripped the wheel, shaking, knuckles white. She didn't look like someone capable of playing a long con, of cheating or betrayal: she looked terrified, like an innocent way out of her depth. That was the Holly Jenna knew.

An act. It's all an act.

Jenna shook her head to dispel the voice. "You okay?" she asked.

Holly nodded. "Think so."

"How'd you get in there?" And now all the questions tumbled out of Jenna. "How'd you find me? Why'd you get me out?"

"Why do you think, you stupid cow?" Holly glared at the road ahead. "Christ's sake, a little fucking gratitude, but no, way too much to expect…"

Either the hurt and outrage were genuine or Holly was a world-class actress, and as Jenna had seen her audition – unsuccessfully and very painfully – for an amateur play, she knew that was unlikely.

All part of the act.

Jenna didn't believe that.

Because you don't want to.

"I'm sorry," she said at last.

"Forget it." Holly wiped her eyes again. "You've been through a shitload lately." She reached into the sidewell for something. "Look, I'll tell you whatever you want to know, but not right now, okay? I need to make sure we're in the clear."

She fiddled with the item she'd picked up, which at first sight resembled an old-fashioned mobile phone. Then there was a crackle and voices emerged from it.

Jenna stared. "Is that a police radio?"

"AirWave. What they use instead of walkie-talkies now."

"Where'd you get that?"

"Hang on." Holly held the AirWave to her ear for nearly a minute, listening, then returned it to the sidewell. "Still nothing."

"You mean about us?"

Holly nodded. "I've kept checking as we've gone. Put the news on a few times, too – nothing there either. Think Whitecliffe might be keeping a lid on things. She's got friends in high places, her. Even if she is a nutter."

"Nutter?"

"Kidnapped you, didn't she? I couldn't make much sense of what I was told. What I could make out, she wanted to steal your eggs or something, because she thought they were special somehow? Like you've got some sort of rare blood factor or something?"

It was, of course, far more complicated and insane than that, but Jenna had no idea where to begin explaining it, not without Holly thinking she really *had* suffered a breakdown. For now, that explanation was close enough. "Basically, yeah."

"Is that why that little prick James kidnapped you as well? I mean, that's what I heard, but since when's he into anything medical?"

"He thought he could make money out of it," said Jenna. A lie, and she hated having to do it, but once again there was no sane-sounding way to tell the truth. "He didn't know one end of a test-tube from another, but people like him don't have to. They just hire someone to do it."

"Sounds about right," said Holly.

None of this made sense. "How do you know all this?"

"Bit of a long story, babe. I'll explain everything once we're safe."

"Good luck there."

"Trust me, all right? I've got it worked out." Holly shrugged. "Hope so, anyway. I'm not exactly a professional at this."

Don't believe her.

"Could've fooled me," Jenna said.

"Beginner's luck. Plus, I couldn't even use that sodding baton."

That was a point; that would've been taking the act too far.

Holly grinned tightly. "Should've known you'd manage."

Jenna chuckled, almost against her will, and then was cackling near-hysterically, unable to stop for almost a minute. "You all right?" Holly said at last.

"Define 'all right' for me first." Jenna managed a smile, though God knew what it looked like. "But yeah, not too bad. I think."

"You didn't even hesitate."

"Yeah. Well." Another shrug. Different backgrounds, different lives.

If you believe her.

Jenna ignored the voice for now. Watch. Listen. Then decide. Although that was easier said than done right now; the weariness was sweeping over her again. "So where we heading?"

"Told you. Wales."

"*Where* in Wales? Tell me we're not camping out in Criccieth again."

"No. I'm not thick."

"Thank fuck for that."

"Got us a static caravan near Harlech."

Jenna had no idea if Holly was joking or not, and by this point she no longer cared. She settled back in her seat.

Holly's hand found hers and squeezed. "I'm glad you're all right."

Define all right, Jenna thought again, but just said, "Me too," squeezed Holly's hand in return and shut her eyes. The car coasted along the motorway at a fast but steady pace, and the purr of the engine lulled her, finally, into sleep.

38.

Loam, brittle leaf matter and old twigs crunched under her trainers; close-packed trees, russet and gold with autumn, surrounded her. Jenna's first, horrible thought was that Stonebrook, Whitecliffe and Holly's rescue had all been a dream and she was still in the woods around Cutty Wren Lodge with James and Rose stalking her.

But the air was biting cold, and she gagged on a rank stench that had nothing to do with mulching leaves. The trees formed tight ranks on either side of her, tapering to a point behind her and vanishing into a thick mass of shadows up ahead. And in that darkness, something stirred.

There was a thick growl, gas bubbling through tar, and two vague grey blobs emerged from the darkness, slowly gaining form, resolution and brightness.

No: this *is a dream, but the Bonewalker's real.*

As well as the growling, faint soft whispers were coming from the trees. It might have been the wind in the leaves. But she didn't think so.

The glow was brightening; the pale eyes shone in the dark. A looming, familiar shape coalesced around them, then stirred and leant forward, antlers scraping bark from adjacent trees. The eyes burned brighter, the thick, tarry rumble continued, and she realised she could make out words.

Tell me where Tell me where Tell me where. Those three words, over and over. *Tell me where Tell me where Tell me where.*

She had to turn round, had to get away, but the paralysis she'd experienced the other times she'd dreamt of this place was on her, and she could do neither. Indeed, she took a step *towards* the darkness where the Bonewalker waited.

This isn't a dream. It never was.

The pale eyes blazed, chilling and numbing her. *Tell me where Tell me where Tell me where Tell me where Tell me where.*

The cold crept through her, and Jenna realised it wasn't a case of whether she spoke or not: she'd have no choice. The Bonewalker's stare was like an X-ray in slow motion, penetrating not only her body but her mind. Her soul, even, if she had one: she'd never believed in those before, but knew no better way to describe the most secret, fundamental corner of herself, the part that made her Jenna McKnight. When the Bonewalker's gaze reached *that*, it would know every detail of her, inside and out, including her present, physical location, even if Whitecliffe or the police couldn't find her.

She'd felt the same marrow-deep cold the night of Mum's disappearance, and more than once in other dreams of this place: no doubt she'd been subjected to the same all-invading scrutiny then, but she couldn't allow it now. She didn't even let her lovers that far inside, except maybe Holly. Even that might have been a mistake. But allowing this thing such access would be an obscenity.

Jenna strained to move herself out of that glare's focus. At first she thought the paralysis would be unbreakable, but then something shifted. Perhaps it was because she'd realised she wasn't dreaming, that the grove was in some sense a real place and separate from her; that however futile it might be, she had control at least of her own body here.

One moment she was taking another unwilling step towards the end of the grove; the next, she realised her upraised foot hadn't descended to the ground, and her leg began to shake. Tension; conflict; strain. Two opposing forces at play: the Bonewalker was still trying to make her move, but she was, at last, able to resist.

There was a moment of screaming tension – again like sleep paralysis, where the will to move fought against her body's stubborn immobility – and then something gave. Her foot came down behind her; Jenna stumbled, off-balance.

The Bonewalker's eyes flared like headlamps through fog; its voice grew in volume to a rhythmic boom – *TELL ME WHERE TELL ME WHERE TELL ME WHERE* – and the cold, which had lessened for a moment, intensified again.

Move, now, or you never will.

Still swaying, Jenna swung her arms wildly and pivoted on her heel, turning her back on the Bonewalker. She put a foot in front of the other, then did it again, stumbling towards the narrow end of the grove. The refrain of *TELL ME WHERE TELL ME WHERE* became a wordless scream of rage.

There were gaps between the trees at the edge of the grove. Not big ones, but wide enough for Jenna, lean as she was, to squeeze through. Behind her, heavy footsteps crashed through loam and leaf-litter. Jenna forced herself on through the trees; as she did, the soft rustling she'd heard before became louder. But it wasn't rustling: they were voices, and whispering to her.

This way, girl. Through here, girl. Your left, girl. Now your right.

Each gap they guided her to was easier to slip through than the last. The Bonewalker bellowed in triumph: Jenna turned to see a huge, skeletal hand lunge through the trees towards her. She threw herself backwards; its curved white talons halted inches from her face, at the limit of their reach. Between the tree-trunks she saw the cowled and antlered head. The Bonewalker roared again.

This way, girl, the voices whispered. ***Move.***

The trees became more widely spaced, at least compared to before. Jenna could move freely now, pressing on deeper into the woods.

39.

The whispers urged her on. She'd still no clue where she was going, but for now all that counted was putting as much distance between herself and the Bonewalker as possible.

It shrieked again in cheated fury, more deafeningly than before. The whispers faded, fearful; frost crept over the fallen leaves, which splintered like glass underfoot.

A shadow fell; the Bonewalker loomed above her, now grown vast and towering above the forest canopy. Its eyes were white suns; it bowed its head and a hissing, crackling sound rose where their light fell. Trees broke apart; vegetation crumbled away. The soil turned black, then grey and hard, cracking like droughted earth. As the Bonewalker's head turned, the light swept across the forest, leaving destruction behind it.

When Jenna ran now no voices guided her; the woods were open enough that she could keep going, but she'd less idea *where* to go than ever before. Maybe there *wasn't* anywhere; maybe this entire dreamworld belonged to the Bonewalker.

And yet it's fucking up the landscape to find you, babe. Maybe you've got it worried somehow.

The Bonewalker bellowed again: its eyes' killing light hissed and crackled behind Jenna, louder than ever. When she looked back a vast stretch of ground lay bare and grey behind her; above her, the Bonewalker turned its head back the way it had come. It was sweeping the forest in methodical arcs, clearing it swathe by swathe.

A root caught Jenna's ankle and sent her sprawling. She had to get up, had to keep ahead of its eyes for as long as she could try: however hopeless, there seemed no other option.

But the whispers were back – very close now, like tiny mouths breathing in her ears. She felt hot breath on her face, all the warmer in the cold.

Hide girl, crawl girl, take cover from the light.

All very well in theory, but where?

Here girl, your right girl, quick girl, under here.

To her right, half-hidden under bracken, was a stream; only a thin rivulet, but in a deep channel. Roots straggled out over the far bank, where a huge oak straddled a horizontal slab of rock.

Down here girl, through here girl, hide beneath the stone.

The sound of vegetation disintegrating under the Bonewalker's glare was deafening now. If the light fell on Jenna, would she be scorched to dust like the bracken and trees, or just pinned, helpless, as it reached down to claim her?

She'd no idea, and less desire to find out. She rolled into the stream, soaking her right arm and shoulder, then crawled under the rock.

White frost sped across the ground; the stream turned hard as glass. The hissing and crackling was now so loud it hurt, the light so bright it burned the eyes.

My eyes might freeze. Break like glass. There was something uniquely horrible about that thought, so she squeezed them shut. She remembered a film she'd seen about nuclear war, how everything had turned a brilliant, soundless white when the bomb fell. A second of silence before the explosions, the fires, the screams of the dying and the maimed.

Her teeth chattered, her fingers numb, as the light blazed down around her. Around, but not on: she had to hope that would be enough. Even with her eyes shut she saw the light; even under the rock she felt the cold, which grew searingly intense on her soaked arm and shoulder, till she screamed aloud. The rock shuddered as the oak above it came apart.

She couldn't bear another second of this. But there *was* another second to bear; then another, and another, and another. Until, at last, the light faded and the crackling diminished; till at last she dared open her eyes.

The cold took longer to go, especially in her right arm. When she looked, she saw a shell of ice covering it from shoulder to wrist, where the water had soaked her sleeve. But it was already starting to melt, and when she pulled at it, it fell away in pieces.

Ice popped and cracked in the stream as it began running again. In the distance, the Bonewalker thundered and its footsteps crashed, but it seemed to be moving away. Venturing out from under the rock, Jenna peered upwards.

The grey earth darkened and softened before her eyes, becoming moist black loam again. Green shoots grew, uncoiling into fresh bracken; saplings thickened into trees. She jumped as a set of roots dropped over the slab, and looked up to see the big oak had been restored, as quickly as it had been destroyed.

This is **His** *place, girl,* the voices whispered. *All things to His will here, girl; get out, girl; walk the Greylands.*

"The what?" she said aloud, then covered her mouth lest the Bonewalker hear.

The Greylands, girl; follow the stream, girl; get out of His woods.

"Less of the 'girl'," Jenna muttered, but it seemed good advice nonetheless. She crawled along the streambed, moving as quickly and quietly as she could. It was like being back in that other stream, in those other woods, trying to evade James and Rose. Again, the fear she'd never escaped those woods at all; again, the uncertainty about what was real and what was only dream.

Doesn't matter, babe. In a dream or out of it, you don't want that thing catching you. Now follow the river; follow the stream.

The Bonewalker roared again, Jenna couldn't tell if it was closer or further away. Didn't matter. She kept going. The silty streambed mud slid between her fingers as if it were liquid itself. *Soil puree.* She laughed weakly.

No time for laughing, girl, said the whispers from the banks above. *And no dream either; It's real, girl; All real, girl; As we learned to our cost, girl;* **He** *took us, girl; To sustain Himself, girl; Like your mother, girl; Like your daughters, girl; Like you if you don't get away.*

"Not having any daughters," she said through her teeth. "Or sons. No kids, ever. And stop fucking calling me girl."

The stream wound on and on. At each turn she hoped she'd see something different but each time there was only more shallow running water overhung with trees and ferns and the forest still swaying overhead. No sign of the Greylands, whatever they were. If they even existed. For all she knew, the voices were leading her into a trap of some kind: even if they were the Bonewalker's enemies, they weren't automatically her friends. If Whitecliffe had been telling the truth, the whisperers might want Jenna dead, to snuff out the Bonewalker's line once and for all and ensure the beast's destruction.

No, girl, the whispers said. *Trust in us.*

Had she spoken aloud?

No, girl; But we know you, girl; We share your blood, girl; His blood, girl; He took us, girl; As He took your mother, girl; This grove is His place, girl; He raised it, by time and will, from the Greylands' dust and ash.

None of which made much sense. She followed the apparently unending stream.

Now we walk, girl; Souls imprisoned, girl; Trapped eternally, girl; Until, perhaps, He dies.

Again the fear: they'd every reason to want her dead, if it was their one chance of escape.

Not us, girl. There was a sincerity in the voices Jenna didn't believe could have been faked. *Just don't be like us, girl; Find the Greylands, girl; Command the dust.*

"Command the dust?" she muttered to herself. "What the fuck?" She felt a little reassured, but surely the whisperers couldn't speak for every soul trapped in the forest. Jenna had no idea as to the Bonewalker's age. No guessing how many lives it must have devoured in all that time.

And then, thinking of that legion of whispering ghosts as she crawled along the endless windings of the streams, another thought occurred to her. "Is my mother there?"

The whispers grew indistinct, as if talking among themselves. "Mum?" Jenna said, hearing her voice crack. Stupid to hope, even for a moment, that the loss she'd resigned herself to fifteen years earlier could be restored, but she couldn't prevent it filling her, however briefly.

Stupid. Stupid, stupid cow. Just keep fucking crawling. Might get you somewhere in the end. Even if it doesn't, what else can you do?

The whispers faded and didn't come back. Maybe better that way. No need to wonder whether they could be trusted. Or maybe they were looking for Mum, one ghost among the horde. Maybe they'd given up on Jenna. Or–

Or something else had changed. Like the bed of the stream.

The watercourse had slowed to a trickle, the streambed turning first to mud, then dry loose soil. Now it was baked hard as brick, and cracked. And when she looked down, it wasn't yellow like sand nor black like loam, but grey like ash.

The last of the stream petered out a few yards from her, a channel of dry cracked earth stretching on ahead. The banks on either side were as grey, hard and cracked as the streambed. The few trees overhanging them were stunted, dead, or both, and the same ashy grey in colour.

The whispers were gone; the only sound now was a low, moaning wind, and the Bonewalker's far-off bellows as it hunted her.

Jenna stood. The dry ground cracked and crumbled underfoot; the embankments became just as fragile to the touch. The dust they collapsed into was like finely milled flour, or cigarette ash; it blew through her fingers and dispersed on the wind.

The remaining trees thinned out and disappeared. The channel sloped down, and the embankments lowered, finally sinking level with the streambed. And then Jenna was stumbling down a low incline to a flat, almost featureless plain, streaked with mist and stretching as far as she could see.

She'd found the Greylands.

40.

Jenna quickly realised her first impression had been wrong: it wasn't a plain, but a desert.

The ground quickly lost all remaining firmness, becoming like loose sand on a beach. Nor was the landscape as flat or featureless as she'd first thought. The terrain rose and fell, like waves or dunes, and in places more regular outlines were visible, although mostly fragmentary and standing alone: she saw sections of walls, and what looked like a statue. Ruins: lost, half-buried remnants of what had once been.

Anything but an inviting landscape; crossing it looked to be a nightmare on every level, but if the voices had directed her, presumably it was survivable.

Then again, how could they be certain, trapped in the grove as they were? They could see the Greylands in the distance, but nothing more. Even desolation could resemble a promised land, under such circumstances.

Nonetheless, Jenna had nowhere else to go. She took a deep breath and set out across the desert.

Whenever she'd dreamt of the grove, she'd been clad in whatever she'd been wearing when she'd fallen asleep, so she was glad she'd done so this time in sweatshirt, jogpants and trainers. Although the soft, thin-soled shoes sank unsteadily into the dust – not to mention letting plenty of it leak in – she could at least pull the sweatshirt's crewneck up over her mouth and nose.

The mist hanging over the Greylands was in fact a haze of fine, ashy dust: the desert's surface was easily disturbed, even a light breeze sending clouds of particles airborne. Jenna's trudging across the landscape sent more dust still billowing in her wake, no doubt leaving the clearest of possible trails. Hopefully the Bonewalker was still laying its own forest to waste in search of her.

Despite the covering, her mouth and throat were parched; she had to pull down the crewneck to cough and spit, trying not to inhale as she did. With every step her feet sank almost ankle deep, making progress slow and exhausting.

Nonetheless, she covered ground, and as if to reward her the landscape shifted in the winds, a dune thinning and blowing away to reveal, to Jenna's disbelief, the fuselage, wing and tail of a wrecked aeroplane. The dust continued to disperse; a deep depression appeared in the ground, exposing the bulk of the wreckage formerly buried under the surface.

It was the biggest aircraft Jenna had ever seen, or heard of, with four propellors on the surviving wing. The fuselage was at least two hundred feet long; it had been torn open along one side, revealing three or four levels within – decks, like an ocean liner's. Jenna could see cabins with double beds, dressing-tables and baths, a huge Art Deco dining room. No such plane had ever taken to the skies, except in the dreams of geniuses or lunatics.

In dreams, thought Jenna, and in that moment felt close to understanding the Greylands and their nature, and perhaps the forest she'd just escaped as well. With such knowledge she might understand what she was dealing with, and perhaps how to protect herself. And in another moment it would have come to her, but then a familiar roar sounded, loud and terrifyingly close, and the ground around her exploded in a shrieking haze of dust.

She cried out, choking, staggering blind in the smothering cloud, but there seemed to be no escape from it. Then the ground slid from under her and she pitched headlong down a slope towards the wreck.

She slewed to a halt in the dust, thankfully before she could brain herself against the fuselage. Above her the dust was settling, but was illuminated by a great ray of searing light that swept towards her, radiating the bitterest cold imaginable. The Bonewalker howled again; then the dust shuddered and slid as something vast and heavy walked the plain of ash.

Jenna supported herself against the fuselage. Dust blew everywhere and she pulled the sweatshirt up over her mouth and nose again, dragging her sleeve across her eyes in an effort to see. Almost everything was a grey haze now, but just before the outside world was completely lost to sight, she glimpsed a huge silhouette looming through the dust – fifty feet tall, antlers spreading from its head, tramping across the desert, vast pale eyes burning.

No voices to guide her now; she could only seek shelter and hope that would be enough. It had worked before, after all. Even in the Bonewalker's forest, she'd been able to hide. She'd just have to hope the wrecked aircraft offered the same protection.

Jenna groped along the fuselage to where the side had been ripped open. The edges, once jagged, had been worn smooth, else she might have lost fingers to them. She wondered if she'd carry such a wound back into the real world – or whatever she should call the world she'd come from, as this one felt no less real.

She slithered down a heap of dust into the plane's dining room, floundering through thigh-deep ash as the icy searchlight of the Bonewalker's eyes tracked across the wreck and shone into its interior. There was a brief, excruciating chill as it brushed her. She staggered and pitched forward then lay there, fingers hooked into the ash. She couldn't move; she was paralysed with the dread that momentary touch had been enough to tell the Bonewalker where she was.

It bellowed again, in frustration; the desert sands shook. It was advancing, but she wasn't sure if it was coming towards the plane or not. The light hadn't returned, so she crawled towards one of the exits, still visible at the far side of the half-buried dining room. She might be able to hide successfully if she could get deeper into the plane's interior.

But it was getting harder to move. Between the cold and crossing the ash-desert, Jenna's strength was all but gone. A dream that exhausted you; that was a laugh. But then, once more, whatever she called this, it wasn't a dream.

The white glare lit the ruined dining hall again in all its faded grandeur: leather chairs and wooden tables, inlaid with mother of pearl, lacquered wood panelling with stylised bronze bas-reliefs and fluted glass columns. This time, though, the light came nowhere near her; at least for now, she was out of its reach. Nonetheless, Jenna kept crawling, using her last remaining energy to reach the exit.

She slid down another pile of ash, coming to a halt by a cabin door which opened into a double bedroom. Time and dimness had faded the once-bright furnishings and everything was filmed with ash, but none of that mattered.

She dragged herself inside the room and closed the door as fully as she could. The inside of the room grew almost black. A thin trickle of light came in through the door; the porthole window was blocked by a wall of dust.

Jenna would have liked to haul herself onto the bed, but hadn't the strength. The floor would be enough. She was tired beyond words; even when the Bonewalker seemed to howl directly overhead, it couldn't arrest her descent into sleep. She'd done all she could; she could go no further. Jenna curled into a foetal position, pillowed her head on folded arms, and closed her eyes.

41.

"Jenna. Jenn!"

Someone was shaking her; she woke, gasping for breath.

"Babe?"

This wasn't the forest, or the Greylands. She was back in the car. Nothing was bellowing; the only light came from overhead, from an electric bulb in the ceiling of a building they were parked inside. Concrete walls and floor. A Land Rover was parked next to them; in front of the car was a metal shutter, which stood half-open onto a narrow street lit by sodium light. Across the road were more shuttered buildings. Low, single-storey structures: units on an industrial estate.

"Babe?" Holly was looking at her, the round face and dark eyes full of concern. "You okay?"

"I'll live." Jenna felt fairly certain of that – for now – if nothing else. "Where are we?"

"Industrial estate near Wrexham. Get a wiggle on."

Holly climbed out of the car, aiming a key-fob at the Land Rover to unlock it. Jenna did the same, swaying, not remotely rested after her sleep – no surprise, given where she'd been – then stumbled after her.

They pulled onto the road outside, which could have been on any of a hundred identical places in Britain: brick and concrete, high lampposts, a railway viaduct. Holly climbed out of the car and ran back to the lock-up. She pulled the steel shutter back down again and locked it, then jogged back to the Land Rover.

"Buys us some time. Don't worry, there's no CCTV…" Holly bared her teeth in a taut grin. "Why I picked this spot."

She drove till they reached a bigger thoroughfare, an A-road of some kind. Holly continued along it for a while, then turned off onto one of the small, winding B-roads so common in North Wales. "Best staying off the main routes," she said. "Just to be on the safe side."

She was jittery with excitement again; in a way that was a relief. This shy, nervous Holly was more familiar than the determined, capable version of her, although some lingering uncertainty on Jenna's part still remained. "We really going to Harlech?"

Holly nodded. "Had to go somewhere, and I figured we both liked that bit of the world."

Jenna shook her head. "And did you say a caravan?"

"Static one, yeah. Rented it for a couple of weeks."

"A caravan, pepper spray, a police baton, a police *radio*–"

"AirWave."

"Whatever. And two new fucking cars? How the fuck did you get all that, Holly?"

"How do you think? Money."

"And where did you get *that* from?" Neither of them had any real savings to speak of, and nor had Holly's family. Jenna wanted to believe in her, but–

"Reid," Holly said.

"*What?*"

It emerged as a shout; Holly flinched, then glared back at Jenna angrily. "Reid, I said! Yeah, the doctor that prick James had looking after you. He helped me find you and gave me money so I could try and get you out."

"The fuck?" Jenna felt sick, and frightened. "Are you both trying to use me as a fucking broodmare too?"

"No! Jesus. Reid's *dead*."

This world was becoming no less unreal than the Greylands. "What? Holly, what the fuck?"

Holly reached across and gripped her hand. Jenna tried not to flinch from the contact. "Babe, I know what a nasty suspicious mind you've got, but I'm on your side. No one else's. I'm just trying to get you safe. Fuck knows if I can, but I'm trying."

Don't trust her. Don't trust anyone. You can't. Don't let anyone in.

"But how do you know Reid?"

"Well, if you can wind your neck in for five minutes and try listening for a change, I'll tell you."

Which seemed a reasonable enough request, so Jenna did.

42.

"When you didn't come home that day, I went to the NUPAS clinic, but you'd never shown up there either," Holly said. "Couldn't get you on your phone, and no one else we knew had seen you, so I called the police. Reported you missing as soon as I could. Anyway, about a fortnight ago I get a phone call from someone in Manchester CID. You'd no surviving family, so I was their only contact. They wanted to know if I could identify you."

She shook her head, glaring down the road. "Thought she meant you were dead at first. But she said there'd been a woman admitted to Craigland Hospital, up in Inverness – matched your description, but she was unconscious, didn't have any ID, and could I take a look at some photos. So I said yes, and..."

Holly took a deep breath. "Sorry. Not a nice memory, that, state you were in. Anyway. I said yeah, that's Jenna, what the fuck happened? The copper I was talking to told me a bit – she could see the state *I* was in. Suppose she felt sorry for me. She told me where they'd found you and about James – that it'd been him who'd kidnapped you, but he was dead. They didn't know exactly what'd happened, since all they'd found were bodies."

"What happened then?"

"I asked when I could visit you, she told me she'd check and get back to me. But days went by, I never heard jack-shit, so I gave 'em a call back and all of a sudden they were trying to tell me I'd made a mistake and it wasn't you. Said they'd run the woman's fingerprints and it was someone else, crap like that." Holly bared her teeth in an angry grin.

And under most circumstances, no help would have come; no one would have been sufficiently bothered about Jenna's fate. But Holly had.

If you believe her.

"How'd you find me?"

"Took some time off work, raided the savings account–"

"Since when've you got a savings account?"

"Had. Past tense." Another shrug. "Wasn't much in it anyway. Enough for a bit. I headed up to Inverness, tried to get to see you at Craigland. Only that patient wasn't there anymore. I made as big a pain in the arse of myself as I possibly could, and worked my way up the totem pole to the hospital registrar. They'd have needed him to pull it off, alter your records and the like."

"Pretty deep pockets, our Dr Whitecliffe," muttered Jenna.

"Yeah." Holly snorted and shook her head. "Funny, really. I thought Reid would be the toughest one to get anything out of, but after all the drama, when I confronted him he just spilled the lot."

"Reid?"

"Did I not mention? He was the registrar at Craigland."

"Fucking hell. So what happened? You're not telling me Reid just told you everything?" It made no sense, thought Jenna.

"Oh, he was fucking glad to. See, the day you escaped, he'd just gone to the cottage to do your weekly checkup but he got shanghaied into going after you with James Dickhead Frobisher. Thing is, while all that was going on, his partner died. And he wasn't there."

Jenna now felt completely lost. "Wait, what? What'd Reid's partner have to do with anything?"

"She had pretty much everything to do with it, babe. She'd been ill, see. Cancer, terminal. Hadn't had long left. James Frobisher offered him thousands to pay for better treatments–"

"If he helped with me."

"Yeah. Again, I couldn't follow the details. I'm not sure Reid'd been able to, to be honest. But like I said, the bottom line seems to be that you've got some sort of rare blood group or gene or something that's worth a lot of money to the right people. Whoever they are. I mean, fuck knows what the little dickhead needed it for. Had money coming out of his arse as it was."

"Some people never have enough," said Jenna, rather than outright lie again; this version of events would do for now. "Or maybe he just wanted to make his own mark or something."

"What, cos Daddy never loved him?"

Jenna thought of James, for once, with something like a twinge of pity. "Basically, yeah."

Holly grunted. "Thing is, Reid said no."

"Huh?"

"True story. He was a doctor himself, babe. He knew there was nothing anyone could do. He was caring for his partner at home – that was where she'd wanted to be. All the poor sod wanted was to look after her till the end. So James changed tack. If Reid *didn't* help, James would take her away from him and hold her somewhere else, so that she'd die alone. And he told Reid he'd ensure she didn't receive any drugs. No morphine, not even a fucking aspirin for the pain."

"Jesus Christ." But that sounded entirely like James; charm and bribery quickly giving way to threats and coercion. "So Reid never had any choice."

"None." Holly's eyes glistened; she'd always been soft, which made all she'd done tonight – and over the preceding weeks – the more unbelievable. If this was an act, it was an impossibly good one. And wasn't it easier, wasn't it simpler to believe that this was the Holly Jenna had known, that she was telling the truth now? "They weren't married, but they'd been together over thirty years. Literally all either of them'd wanted was to spend her last few days together at home. Nothing else. Nothing fancy. And James took that from him. He really was a fucking shitbag, wasn't he?"

"He really was."

"And so Reid told you I was at Stonebrook?"

"Yeah. Apparently what'd happened was one of Whitecliffe's pet gerbils turned up–"

"Gerbils?"

Holly shrugged. "Politest word I've got for the fuckers. Anyway, one of them turned up and demanded all Reid's patient notes on you, and that he make arrangements to transfer you. Change your details, too, so they could say the patient was someone else. He recognised the name Whitecliffe, and remembered hearing James bitching on about her as well. Again, he wasn't given much choice in the matter. Naturally, he got told to keep his trap shut or else by Whitecliffe's lot, too. Police had been taken care of, blah blah blah. They paid Reid off too, of course. Thought that'd be it, they could forget about him after that. Just because he was quiet and scared easily. But he loved his missus. None of them seemed to get that."

Jenna wasn't sure she did either. However close to Holly she felt, she couldn't fathom a commitment that kept two people together for so long. Was it love, or did you just get tired of shopping around? "You did, though. Right?"

"Yeah. Poor old sod hadn't wanted anything special, just to be with his Lizzie when she went. We understood each other."

"And he just decided to help you?" said Jenna. Could it really be as straightforward as that?

"Pretty much. It was a way of getting back at them all, I suppose. Dunno how he found out about Stonebrook, but he told me that was where they'd taken you."

"And he gave you money?"

"Between James and Whitecliffe, he'd more than he knew what to do with. Whatever it is you've got, babe, they clearly expect to make a bloody mint from it. Anyway, all I needed after that was to work out how to get you out of Stonebrook, and what to do when I did."

"And you came up with a caravan in Wales?"

"It'll do for now."

Jenna had no answer to that; it was, after all, further ahead than she'd managed to plan. To put herself in someone else's hands was anathema, but she didn't see much choice. Just as she saw little choice but to trust Holly; to do otherwise would be too exhausting. She needed help, and she wanted to believe.

If you're wrong–

Jenna ignored the carping voice, then settled back in her seat and looked out of the window. Trees flickered by, little more than spiky menacing shadows; unable to tell how far beyond them the woodlands reached, she shuddered and closed her eyes.

43.

A few more miles passed in silence before Jenna sat bolt upright. "Holl?"

"Yo."

"You said Reid was dead?"

"Yeah."

"Shit. Who got him? What if they made him talk?"

"No one got him."

"How'd you know?"

"I was there." Holly's voice was flat. "He killed himself. Said nothing really mattered now. Just wanted to be with his Lizzie again. He'd planned it all out – pills, whisky, bag over his head, the lot. Just wanted someone with him at the end. Make sure it all went off quietly. And maybe he just didn't want to be alone."

"Jesus."

"Yeah. Anyway, that was the price." Holly focused on the road ahead, tears trickling down her face; she wiped her eyes on her sleeve, almost angrily. "Poor bastard. Anyway." She began to speak faster. "What I'm gonna try and do is get us over to Ireland. My nan's from there, remember? Did I tell you that?"

"I thought she was Welsh."

"That's my granddad, on my dad's side. Nan was County Kerry born and bred. Means I can claim Irish citizenship – which I did, back in 2017 after the Brexit vote. *Ich bin ein European*

228

and all that. Get across the water and we can figure out where to stay and what to do. I was pushed for time by the end, see – wanted to get you out soon as I could. Reid said Whitecliffe'd want to get started on you ASAP. And I'd enough to take care of planning everything else. The caravan, the cars, the gun, the lock-up – needed to make sure this–" she rapped the Land Rover's dashboard "–didn't get caught on camera. No point switching cars if the dibbles know we're in this one now–"

Holly broke off, out of breath. When she started talking again, she was calmer. "This all ought to get us a few days' grace if nothing else. Long enough to sort Ireland out. Get us out of the country. Once I knew whereabouts at the clinic you were, I just had to sneak in and set a fire in a cleaning cupboard. All the alarms go off, panic and shit, and I get you out in the confusion. I'd already cut a hole in the fence. Their security wasn't all that. Even so, it was all a bit mental, getting out of there." Holly sagged back in her seat, exhausted by her monologue. "Good job you didn't mind twatting people."

Jenna laughed weakly. "It's one of my better qualities."

Holly laughed too. Jenna found herself joining in, more loudly this time, and they cackled half-hysterically together as they drove on into the night.

Jenna wasn't normally chatty, but she broke that rule repeatedly over the next two hours, as they drove through the North Wales countryside. The silence that filled the car when they weren't talking was never comfortable, because she was still bone-tired and the lack of activity made her eyelids droop. If she let them close for more than a few seconds, sleep would claim her again, and Jenna was afraid to sleep. Or, more accurately, to dream.

Except that dreams weren't real and the Greylands were, and Holly couldn't help her there. And if the Bonewalker found her in the Greylands…

What *would* happen then, exactly? Could it "claim" Jenna, as it had her mother? She'd no idea. It could manifest itself in the "real" world, as it presumably had when it took Mum. But doing that to Jenna would leave it alone and without descendants and, if Whitecliffe was to be believed, doomed to extinction. No; the Bonewalker wouldn't want that.

It could obviously appear in other circumstances, as when it had saved her from Rose. The Bonewalker wasn't solely reliant on its human allies or servitors or whatever she should call them. So where was it?

She remembered the eyes on her in the grove, the murmuring in her head that had grown to a thundering demand – *TELL ME WHERE TELL ME WHERE TELL ME WHERE* – and realised:

It doesn't know where I am.

Not yet, at least. But it would find out if it could. If she hadn't managed to break away from it in the grove it would have had its answer.

Jenna's eyes closed; she forced them open again almost at once, but not quickly enough to evade a vivid slow-motion replay of the Bonewalker tearing Rose in half, only this time the victim was Holly. And the worst of it was she couldn't be sure whether the image had come from her imagination, or whether the Bonewalker, lurking on the edge of sleep, had slipped it across the threshold of her consciousness as a threat.

One thing she was certain of, at least: if the Bonewalker found her in the Greylands and turned those eyes on her for any length of time, it would find her in this world too. Even at its "normal" size, the Bonewalker's glare had penetrated to the marrow of Jenna's bones. Now it was a behemoth with eyes like lighthouse lamps; if those eyes pinned Jenna she'd no idea what would survive of her. Maybe she'd be reduced to a vegetable, a body without a mind. That would suit them, wouldn't it? All of them: the Bonewalker, Whitecliffe – God, she'd have probably been the ideal girlfriend for James in that state. Position it however you wanted. Do whatever you wished with it. Insert this, remove that. She shuddered again.

"Cold?"said Holly. "Can put the heater on if you want."

Jenna shook her head. "I'm okay. Thanks," she added, worried she'd sounded too sharp.

Bloody hell, get you. Actually worrying you sound like an arsehole? You really aren't *feeling well.*

"How much further?" she asked.

Holly grinned. "*Are we there yet?*" she said, mimicking a whining child. Jenna experienced a flash of annoyance – not least because it took her uncomfortably back to that night at Tallstone Hill – but before she could express it Holly was nodding through the windscreen. "Matter of fact, babe, we are."

Jenna looked ahead and glimpsed a sign that read *HARLECH* in the Land Rover's headlights before they swept past. Rain spotted the windscreen; Holly turned the wipers on.

They drove past the low stone cottages on the outskirts of the tiny coastal town, the huge hollow bulk of the castle, the derelict Theatr Ardudwy and Coleg Harlech campus and the tower-block that had served as its halls of residence, and then they were leaving the town behind them. Rows of bungalows stood along an embankment above on their left; below and on their right were the dunes and sea.

The last of the bungalows fell away and Holly turned left, up a narrow lane heading inland. They rounded a bend, then reached a heavily overgrown turn-off leading down into a field several feet below the level of the road. Jenna gave a short, muffled cry. It'd seemed Holly was swerving off the road into a ditch. "Soz," Holly muttered, touching her shoulder. "But here we are."

Jenna saw a flaky wooden sign reading *CARAVAN PARK*, a

dirt track and about a dozen numbered static caravans. "Five... Six... Here we are," said Holly, and braked. "Lucky number seven."

What Jenna saw in the headlights' glow before Holly switched them off didn't look particularly lucky: old, battered and worn, with greenish moss smeared around the base of the structure. But it had four walls and a roof; that would do for now.

"End of the rainbow," Holly said. "Well, to be going on with."

"Jesus," Jenna said. "This place condemned or something?"

"Not quite," said Holly. "Pretty much on its last legs, though. Owner lives up near the castle somewhere, and we're the only ones booked in here, so we've got the place to ourselves."

"Whoop-de-do," said Jenna.

Holly laughed. "Come on, babe. I'll get the kettle on."

The caravan was cold and draughty, the furnishings worn. The big space they entered was a kitchen on the left, with a stained linoleum floor, and a fairly new-looking washing machine under the sink. A pleasant surprise, given the state of the place – Jenna wouldn't have bet money on it even being connected to a mains water supply. To the right was a sitting room, with worn grey carpet tiles, a threadbare three-piece suite and a coffee table that must have been 1980s vintage. The doors to two other, smaller rooms stood ajar: through one of them she glimpsed a toilet and – another welcome surprise – a shower cubicle. The other, she guessed, led to the bedroom.

Well, Jenna had stayed in far worse; besides, she was too exhausted to care. She collapsed gratefully onto the sofa, relaxing as she'd been unable to in weeks. They were hunted, but for now they were free: no CCTV cameras, no Rose, Eric or James, no Dr bloody Whitecliffe. No Bonewalker, either.

Not until you sleep.

She grimaced.

"You okay?" said Holly.

"Yeah." Jenna sipped her tea. That was nothing particularly distinguished about it – bargain-bin teabags, UHT milk – but it tasted far better than it had any right to. Maybe it was the company.

"Hungry?"

"Bit."

"Hang on." Holly went to the fridge and came back with a couple of mini pork pies and a chunk of cheese; she dug out her Swiss Army knife, unfolded the blade and sliced the cheese. "Here."

"Thanks."

Holly stood in silence, watching Jenna eat, then finally said: "Mind if I sit with you?"

"Course not," said Jenna, meaning *you better bloody had*. For her, *Course not* was pretty warm. *Can if you want to* was her usual, noncommittal response. Or would have been, before.

Holly sat awkwardly beside her, not touching; her hand hovered over Jenna's knee, then withdrew. "How you doing?"

"Better." Suddenly Jenna's voice was choked; the mug of tea shook in her cupped hands. Holly gently transferred it to the nearby table. They faced one another in silence for a moment or two, then Jenna leant towards her, hoping that was a clear enough signal. It was: Holly's arms slipped around her, and Jenna hugged her back.

She let her head rest on Holly's chest, as she'd fantasised about so often during her captivity, and felt her eyes close. She sat up again. She couldn't sleep. Mustn't. The Bonewalker was waiting.

"Jenn? You okay?"

"Yeah. No. It's not you. I've been getting these really bad fucking dreams. Nightmares. Worse than ever." More than dreams, of course: far worse. But how did she tell Holly that?

"I bet, after all this." Holly squeezed her hand. "It's gonna be okay, hun."

"Is it?" Jenna hated the plea for reassurance in her voice. *Tell me everything'll be all right, Mummy.* She hadn't been so dependent in years, it hadn't been an option, but she needed it now. She'd always prided herself she could hack it alone, but you couldn't, in the long run. No one could. You needed other people, if only for when it was all too much to bear. But she'd always held back: no wonder every relationship had crashed and burned. Except this one; except, maybe, this one. *I want this to last. I don't want her to go.*

"Yes. Look, this'll keep us ahead of them long enough to get out of the country. After that we've got time to, I don't know, expose them. Whitecliffe, I mean."

"What?" Now she felt more exhausted still, and a little scared. Holly was talking about some sort of crusade, sending Jenna's life spinning out of her own control once more. "I just want my fucking life back, Holly. I don't wanna take on the big bad establishment or whatever."

"I don't fancy it either, babe. But you were *detained*. You know, officially. Long as you're in the UK, they're gonna be trying to find you, same as if you're a criminal. And if they catch you, they'll send you straight back to Stonebrook."

She was right, and in that moment Jenna hated her for it. "Fine."

"I dunno how long we'd be able to stay in Ireland. I'm okay, I'm a citizen, although they might try extraditing me – arson, assault, probably GBH as well."

"Most of that last one was me."

"Yeah, but that just puts you even more in the shit, dunnit?"

Jenna felt a dull, miserable anger. She didn't want to plan more battles or think about the need to do so. She just wanted to rest, to hide. To be left alone. Was that so much to ask?

Alone? Careful what you wish for.

That was a point. She turned back to Holly, forcing a smile. Holly took her hands. "We've got to prove what Whitecliffe was up to. Otherwise she can just keep coming after you, and she can do it legally."

"Okay. Okay." Jenna nodded; she wanted to hold her hands up, a warding-off gesture against the world – *Okay, stop, please, enough* – but didn't want Holly to think she was pulling away from *her*. More selfishly, she didn't want to let go of the other woman. "Can we leave it, though, just for now? I can't handle it right this second."

Holly held her arms out. "No problem, babe. We can take it easy for tonight."

Jenna rested against her again; Holly's arms folded around her, those small soft hands stroking her hair.

"Need to find out what they're after from you, though."

"Huh?"

"Whitecliffe, James. Just – what is it about you that's so special to them?"

Again, Jenna contemplated the sheer impossibility of telling Holly the truth – no, not of *telling* her, because if anyone had a right to know what this was all about it was her, but of convincing her it was true. "Let's not talk about it tonight, okay, love? Please?"

"Sure. I'm sorry. C'mere."

The hands drew her down again. Warm. Safe. Jenna closed her eyes. No. She mustn't. She wasn't safe. Mustn't sleep. The Bonewalker waited in the Greylands, in the dark of her dreams. Except they weren't dreams. That was the problem. She had to stay awake. *Open your eyes.* But they wouldn't open. She was so tired; Holly was so welcoming and warm, and Jenna was safe as she hadn't been in months. *Only physically,* she screamed at herself. *Not if you sleep.* But that voice sounded very small and faint and distant and not remotely persuasive, and a moment later she was gone.

44.

Jenna woke alone in the dust, and felt so desolate she began to cry.

A dim grey light, almost darkness; a keening moan of wind.

"Holly?" she muttered.

She was cold, and lying in the ash on the cabin floor, beside the double bed.

Holly's not here. Be glad. Wouldn't wish her into the Greylands.

Outside, the wind moaned on. She couldn't hear the Bonewalker. Maybe it had given up, at least for now; that, or lost her trail and was wandering the dreamscape in search of her.

Jenna breathed out and sat up.

The plane juddered and lurched from the impact of first one, then another giant footstep. Loose dust slithered and billowed around the cabin, and a familiar roar shook the fuselage, this time exultant and full of triumph.

The battered airframe creaked and shook. Accumulated ash slid away from the porthole, admitting the pale, dust-dimmed light for the first time in an age. The wreck shifted: Jenna cried out, but it was lost under the groan of rending steel and the machine-gun clatter of rivets popped from their housings.

The cabin ceiling tore open. Dusty light spilled in. Jenna's paralysis broke; she scrambled on hands and knees for the doorway, across the tilting floor. She looked up as another bellow sounded overhead, to see the Bonewalker squatting over the aircraft's tailplane, its claws digging into the roof and cracking open the fuselage along the top.

Its decaying pelt boomed and crackled like sails in the wind; lightning played around its antlers. Its face remained concealed inside the ragged hood, except for the white moons of its eyes, which were slowly moving up along the length of fuselage towards her as it methodically scanned her hiding place inch by inch.

Jenna hauled the door open and slithered out into the corridor, clutching at the walls to pull herself upright. Logically the best course seemed to escape the wreck the same way she'd entered, rather than crawling deeper into it, but sheer instinct already sent her stumbling forward, up the corridor.

A brilliant glare erupted behind Jenna, flinging her distorted shadow ahead of her through the dust; she turned to see the rays from the Bonewalker's eyes moving from the cabin she'd just vacated and across to the dining hall. If she'd gone that way, it would have had her.

Still might, if you just stand there. Crack on, babe.

The corridor grew dimmer. There was a squeal of metal being wrenched asunder from overhead. Dust trickled down. A door to her right opened into a saloon: it had the same lacquered wood panelling and glass columns as the dining room, a chromed steel bar with a red-and-black marble counter and a floor-to-ceiling window from which passengers could have gazed out at the world below, a drink in hand, as if standing on a cloud. Sadly, all she could see now was ash.

The plane's nose and cockpit hadn't been visible: they must be buried in the dust. Perhaps she could hide there till the Bonewalker gave up. She'd no idea. She could barely see ahead of herself now: even the dim light available before was gone. She extended her arms, finding her way by touch.

A thin beam of light appeared ahead of her; Jenna went towards it. The corridor tilted further as the Bonewalker grappled with the wreck, and she fought to keep her balance.

The corridor was choked with dust from floor to ceiling; at some point it had poured through the fuselage to flood the passageway. A half-buried flight of steel steps protruded from it, leading upwards to a hatchway, beyond which a long tubular shaft led up through the plane's various decks.

Jenna climbed the steps, clinging to the guardrails as the plane shuddered and rocked. There was another hatchway at the top of the shaft; as Jenna neared it she saw a chair lying on its side, and a table of some kind. Above them was a curved, bare metal ceiling. Jenna still couldn't see the source of the light.

She climbed through the hatchway, into a room with riveted steel bulkheads. Large, but functional and unadorned, with none of the dining hall or saloon's elegance or grandeur. A protractor and pair of compasses lay on the table, beside a huge paper chart that depicted no continent Jenna recognised. Across the room was an intricate radio apparatus with a microphone and headset.

It was more like a ship's bridge than an aeroplane, but that seemed the point of the design. An airborne ocean liner.

The beam of light was almost directly above her. Beyond it, the forrard half of the room was in near-total darkness.

Steel racks bolted to the bulkheads held a couple of rifles, though too rusted to be of use, and a row of old-fashioned handheld lamps with heavy, round glass lenses. What they used to call bull's-eye lanterns. After some fumbling, Jenna found and pushed a switch at the back of the nearest one's casing: a dull, embery glow developed in the lens.

Though weak, the reddish beam illuminated the forrard section, shining through an open door ahead of Jenna to reveal instrument panels, two fixed seats, a pair of old-fashioned wooden steering wheels and a huge windscreen, choked with ash like the saloon windows. No way out there. But just ahead of her was a ladder, leading to yet another hatchway marked with a sign saying OBSERVATION DOME.

The ladder led up through a small chamber above the chartroom, to a final hatchway in the ceiling, crowned by a plexiglass dome wide enough to accommodate Jenna's head and shoulders, through which the light shone down.

The groans and cracks grew louder, and dust sifted down from the edges of the observation dome. Coughing, Jenna raised the lantern and saw a handle, with a sign reading *EMERGENCY RELEASE.*

She wrenched it down, and there was a splintering crack: a gap opened between the observation dome and the hull and dust poured in. Jenna coughed and spluttered, but the cascade trailed off.

The plexiglass cover was on a hinge. She pushed it and it rose stiffly till she could squirm through, rolling down the ashy slope beyond.

45.

She could still hear sounds of destruction behind her and the Bonewalker bellowing its anger yet again as it failed to find her; the howling wind almost drowned it out, but Jenna could hear the thwarted rage in it.

It had either lost patience with the search or suspected she'd escaped the plane. In either case it would begin looking further afield for Jenna before long. Hopefully the ash-clouds would restrict its vision as much as hers, but if it even suspected her whereabouts, she'd no chance of outpacing it, and the desert, bare and empty as it was, offered no cover.

Jenna needed a fresh hiding-place, and quickly.

Good luck with that.

There has to be somewhere. Must be somewhere. There will be somewhere.

They don't just grow on trees. Or out of the desert.

But as if to prove that inner voice wrong, the ground underfoot was changing. There was something solid beneath the dust. And then there was no dust at all, only a hard, flat surface. *Stone?*

The wind continued to howl, but visibility had begun to improve. Jenna wiped her eyes, partly to clear them of tears and grit but mostly out of disbelief.

She was standing on tarmac in the middle of a road, with a kerb, pavement and buildings on either side of her. Dust covered everything, but it was a very thin patina; when

Jenna wiped her hand across a parked car's bonnet it was swept away at once to reveal bright red paint underneath.

A little suburban village. A main road. Cars parked at the kerb; others seemingly abandoned in the middle of the street, doors open. Bus stops. Shops and eateries of all kinds: a butcher, a cheese shop, bistros. A well-to-do little place.

It was familiar, and as Jenna progressed along the deserted high street, she realised why. This was the centre of Didsbury Village, where Wilmslow Road crossed Barlow Moor Road on one side, School Lane on the other. Jenna had passed through it countless times on buses between Manchester and Altrincham, when she'd lived in Timperley; the same buses had operated between the city and Northern Moor when she'd lived there.

Before Mum was taken, before it all fell apart, Didsbury had been a refuge of a kind to Jenna. It had all Timperley's comfort and security, but was busier and more exciting. There was more to do, and it was far easier here to avoid all the prying eyes who'd tell your parents the moment you did anything remotely fun. When she couldn't get into Manchester for whatever reason, she'd come here. Later, when she and Dad were in Northern Moor, it had combined the qualities she'd always loved it for with just enough echoes of the life she'd lost to be bearable.

After Dad died, she'd attended the FE college at Fielden Park, less than a mile from where she stood now. And in later years she came here to soften bad times or prolong good ones. She'd even meant to come here the day she was kidnapped, after waiting out the lunchtime rush in Castlefield.

She'd no idea what it was doing here in the Greylands, but it was best not to look a gift horse in the mouth, especially as it somehow seemed to be holding back the storm. About a mile from her a grey wall of churning ash hung in the air. It was the same to her right and left, and behind her too. She was in the still centre of a dust cloud swirling around her.

There were no people in sight, no life of any kind other than a few dead-looking trees dotted along the roadside. The state of the buildings varied widely: many were in perfect condition other than their coating of ash; others were missing windows or even roofs. In some cases, examples of each stood side by side.

Bizarre, but here it was. A place to hide, as she'd wanted. As she'd wished for.

As you willed *it.*

No, that was ridiculous. It couldn't be true.

As if in answer, ash blew thickly down the street, as if whatever held back the storm had begun to fail. The wind rose.

Now look what you've done.

But this couldn't be connected with her. It made no sense.

And exactly what makes sense about any other part of this? This place even existing? The plane? The Greylands? The grove? The Bonewalker? Never mind all the mad shit that's going on back in the real world?

Jenna had no idea and no answer, and before she could even try, a vast shadow loomed through the windblown ash above the crossroads. *Giant monster coming down Wilmslow Road.* She laughed hysterically.

Can't run forever, babe; can't hide forever, either. Sooner or later, you've got to fight.

"How, exactly?" she muttered aloud.

To her left was a narrow terraced house with a mock-Tudor front and mullioned windows. A private residence, not a shop: an oddity here, but the door was ajar, so Jenna pushed it wide and scrambled through.

The ground shuddered from a massive approaching footstep. She slammed the door behind her, and a Yale lock clicked automatically. A door chain hung down above it; she almost reached for it, then snorted and turned away. At its current size, the Bonewalker would flick the door off its hinges with its middle finger, though it was more likely to peel the roof away like the lid of a biscuit tin.

Can't run, can't hide. Have to fight.

From outside came sounds of cracking stone, rending steel, shattering glass. Jenna ran through the house, kicking doors wide. In the front room: a sofa, armchairs, a TV and stereo system, shelves of LPs and CDs. The next one along was the same, except with bookshelves instead of music. Under the stairs, a small pantry stocked with tinned and dried foods. Behind the final door, at the end of the hallway, a breakfast room with dining table and fridge; beyond that, the kitchen.

Weapon. You need a weapon.

Cutlery clattered to the tiled floor as Jenna yanked drawers open, but even the deadliest-looking item on offer, a heavy meat cleaver, would be useless against the Bonewalker in its current form.

She grabbed it anyway in lieu of anything better, then sprinted back up the hall to the foot of the stairs. The building shuddered again. A picture fell off the wall and smashed; glasses and dishes rattled in the kitchen cupboards.

It'll keep looking, and it'll find you. And be honest with yourself, aren't you bored with hiding? Tired of running? Fight, while you still can.

Again, instinct guided her, this time upstairs. A weapon, a weapon, she needed a fucking weapon. She needed a gun. An earlier generation might have had an old service revolver lying around, but not anymore. A country farmhouse might have offered a twelve-bore, whatever good that'd have been.

Rose had a gun, and it didn't help her.

No, because she'd have needed something bigger, like an elephant gun. Or, if Jenna was wishing, why not a Kalashnikov? Might as well go all-out when hoping for the impossible.

She ran across the landing and kicked open the first door she found. It opened into a bedroom overlooking the street. The single bed was neatly made up, as if they'd been expecting guests.

Lying on the counterpane was an assault rifle.

"The fuck?" Jenna walked towards the bed, staring down at the weapon, not daring to blink in case it disappeared. But it didn't. Dull grey steel and varnished brown wood, a gun she'd seen in a hundred movies.

One Kalashnikov AK-47, babe. Ask, and ye shall receive.

Had she known that was its name? Probably. She'd read enough thrillers, seen enough action movies; occasionally she liked a romcom, but large quantities of cathartic violence were more to her taste.

It didn't matter: here a gun was, laid out before her. All that was missing was a little pink bow and some *Hello Kitty* wrapping paper.

As her hand closed around it, bright cold light flared through the windows.

Jenna threw herself backwards reflexively, landing on the floor and taking cover behind the bed. There was a splintering crash, the building convulsed and shuddered, and then the room was full of dust as the front of the house was torn away.

46.

Jenna looked up in time to see the Bonewalker's huge skeletal hand descending towards her, and scuttled frantically away from it. The Bonewalker dragged the bed out through the shattered wall, flung it aside, then reached into the bedroom again.

"Fight that, she says," Jenna muttered aloud. She wasn't frightened, though, not anymore: she was past that now. Admittedly, the assault rifle might have helped.

She braced the Kalashnikov against her hip, pulled back the bolt – she seemed to know exactly how to operate it, somehow – and pulled the trigger. The wooden stock slammed back against her hip, and the clamouring thunder of gunfire filled the bedroom.

The muzzle-flash was blinding; gunsmoke filled the room with its acrid, struck-match smell, forming a blue-grey haze that mingled with the dust from outside.

The Bonewalker roared again, but in annoyance rather than pain. No surprise, really: Rose had emptied a pistol into it at close range, and it had hardly broken step before tearing her in half.

It'd fuck its own plans into a cocked hat if it did that to you, babe. Can't breed if you're dead.

True, though as victories went, it wouldn't be much of one.

The Kalashnikov fell silent. *Empty.* With a woody creak and gristly crackle of joints, the Bonewalker crouched, till its burning eyes were level with the opened room.

TELL ME WHERE TELL ME WHERE TELL ME WHERE.

That thundering, incessant voice, even in her head, rattled her teeth; the numbing cold was like plunging into ice-water. Jenna stumbled, dropping the rifle; her heartbeat faltered, almost stopped. She dived sideways, into a corner, where a chest of drawers had fallen. It wasn't much of a shelter – virtually none at all – but it was the only kind available.

Weapon. Weapon. Weapon.

She'd had one. It hadn't worked.

The right kind. The right kind.

"Could've mentioned that before," Jenna muttered. Wood splintered and brickwork shattered as the ceiling was torn away. Chunks of rubble rained into the bedroom, one missing her head by inches. Limned against the grey sky, the Bonewalker bent towards her, its white-eyed glare flooding the room.

TELL ME WHERE TELL ME WHERE TELL ME WHERE.

Weapon. Weapon. Weapon.

Out of instinct, defiance, or both, Jenna scrabbled on the floor for something, anything to use against the Bonewalker, but only instinct could have guided her hand to the silver powder compact, shaped like a scallop shell, that sprang open as she caught hold of it.

An old powder puff fell out; in one half gleamed a small round mirror.

Useless, no kind of weapon at all. But instinct still made Jenna thrust it up towards the killing glare.

The white light streaming towards her seemed to spray out in all directions from the compact, less like light than a stream of water that'd hit the bowl of a spoon. A swirling rainbow pattern shimmered above her, a yard or two across: it seemed to act almost as an umbrella, because the corner she crouched in grew dimmer than the rest of the room. The rainbow effect brightened, then became searing, impossible to look at.

There was a brilliant flash and something slammed into Jenna's cupped hands; it reminded her of the AK slamming back against her hip, and drove her backwards so violently she felt the bedroom wall crack behind her.

The Bonewalker screamed – *screamed*, in agony and rage. The world turned white. A brief sensation of being flung, spinning, into space. Then nothing.

47.

Jenna reared back, flailing, and cried out; someone else yelped beside her. She thrashed away from them, then fell into space.

She cried out again, thinking she'd plummet forever, but no more than a fraction of a second later slammed into rough, worn carpet. She rolled, heaving for breath, and cannoned into something solid.

"Whoa! Look out, babe."

Hot liquid splashed her face. Jenna screamed.

"Babe. Jenna! Jenna. Jenn, it's okay, babe. It's okay. It's all right."

Hands on her, holding her. She tensed, blinking as her eyesight cleared. There were still gold and green afterimages on her vision from the Kalashnikov's muzzle-flash, but she was no longer in the Greylands. Holly was in front of her, hands on Jenna's shoulders. She flicked her head, tossing back the wing of dark hair so Jenna could see both gold-flecked eyes. "It's okay," said Holly. "It's okay."

Jenna wheezed for breath. To her right was a sofa. *I fell off that.* To her left, a coffee table, steam rising from beside a china mug on its surface, fluid dripping from the edge. *I rolled into that.* Her surroundings took shape around her, and she remembered where she was. The caravan, with Holly. Safe.

Sort of, anyway.

"It's okay, sweetheart. Babe, it's fine." Holly helped Jenna back to the sofa. "Bastards. Can't imagine the shit you've been through. But it's okay now."

"It's not. It's fucking not, Holly."

"It's gonna be. They're not getting hold of you again. I'll keep you safe."

That should have sounded ludicrous, coming from the chunky little figure beside her, but Holly had more than shown what she was capable of.

Even so, she didn't know about the Bonewalker, and Jenna couldn't even tell her about it without sounding utterly unhinged. Yet Holly *had* to be made aware. Jenna couldn't pretend that side of the battle wasn't real. Far less deal with it alone.

Except you just did.

"The fuck's that?" Holly said, then bent and picked something up off the floor. "Where'd that come from?"

"What is it?"

Holly held it out to her. Jenna stared at it for a frozen moment, then reached out and took it.

The silver powder compact was still open. At first Jenna thought the mirror had misted over, but it didn't wipe clean and had a strange, iridescent sheen. The reflecting glass had taken on the appearance of mother-of-pearl.

"That yours?" said Holly. "You bring it with you?"

"Yeah." Jenna clicked the compact shut on the second attempt. "I brought it with me."

48.

Sleep eluded Jenna for the rest of the night, but she was happy to avoid it. In the Greylands, the Bonewalker would find her. Holly had no such fears and lay snoring on the couch. Hard not to envy her that. She could afford to sleep. Jenna couldn't.

She made coffee, laced it with sugar and gulped it to stay awake, then began pacing up and down the caravan, stopping only to drink from the mug or put the kettle on again. She mustn't sit or lie down or even close her eyes.

But the constant pacing was tiring her, and the coffee would only keep her going so long. She should ask Holly if she had any speed. Although Holly probably wouldn't give her any, even if she had, as Jenna was still "recovering" from "all she'd been through".

Jenna hated that sort of phrasing. It made her sound like a victim, which she refused to be. Had always refused. Had always fought. Would barely have survived losing Mum, never mind everything that had followed, otherwise. Mum, Nan, their home, Dad. *Fuck you all for abandoning me.*

She shook her head. A silly thought. Childish. Another sign of fatigue: increased irritability, sluggish thinking.

Fuck.

She had to stay awake and find answers: had to know what to tell Holly, for a start. No, not *what* to tell her: *how*. She had, somehow to not only tell Holly about the Bonewalker and the Greylands, but *convince* her they were real.

Yeah, good luck with that.

Whitecliffe believed, and James had, but that wouldn't help; Holly just thought the pair of them were insane, and if Jenna tried to convince her of the truth, she'd most likely conclude Jenna had been so damaged by all she'd been subjected to that she'd come to share their lunacy.

And who could blame her? Jenna would have thought the same, if their roles had been reversed. It had taken Tallstone Hill, the visitation in the cellar at Cutty Wren Lodge and the overheard conversation between the Bonewalker and James – not to mention the spectacle of the creature itself tearing Rose in two before her very eyes – to convince her. After that, it hadn't been hard to believe in the Greylands.

But she couldn't produce the Bonewalker on demand; the closest thing to any kind of physical evidence Jenna had was the powder compact, and what kind of proof was *that*? She could have picked it up in any real-world charity shop; all it would prove, from Holly's point of view, was Jenna's self-delusion.

Maybe she didn't need to convince Holly. She'd begun to discover what she could do in the Greylands. And somehow, at the end, she was certain she'd hurt the Bonewalker. Maybe, just maybe, she could handle that side of things alone.

But to do that she needed a clear head; she had to be able to think, because however insane the situation seemed, however delusional her beliefs – to an outsider like Holly, at least – Whitecliffe's actions had a horrible rationality. There really was a way to live forever, after all: of course she'd try and use it, whatever the cost. Who wouldn't?

Well, you wouldn't, babe. Life's but a vale of tears and all that. And anyway, what about the price?

She'd learned to be hard over the years – no help for it when trying to hack out a place in the world on your own, and besides, she'd had plenty of pent-up anger and aggression in need of an outlet – but there was pushing your way to the front of the queue to build a career, and then there was devouring your children's souls to live a little longer.

Like you wanted kids anyway.

Not the point. Children, grandchildren, great-grandchildren: innocents who'd asked for no part of it all but who found themselves in the crosshairs through the accident of birth. How many generations of its own bloodline had the Bonewalker devoured? Maybe beyond a certain point the relationship was too distant to bother your conscience any longer.

If you had a conscience, you wouldn't do it in the first place.

But that was too simple an answer. There was deliberate cruelty and malice, infliction of suffering for its own sake, and then there were the things people did to stay alive. All too often there was no good or evil then, only necessity, and conscience commonly turned out to be an elastic thing. Most people could find a way to justify to themselves what they'd already decided to do. Besides, whenever you did some ugly but necessary thing, the first time was always the worst; soon enough it no longer stung. No doubt that held true for murder and cannibalism.

With a clear head, she was sure she could work it out. But for that she'd need rest. Sleep. The one thing she didn't dare grant herself.

How's that for Catch-22?

Jenna realised she'd stopped walking. Her legs throbbed and felt impossibly heavy, and she could barely keep her eyelids open. They drooped even as she stepped forward; she barked her shin on the coffee table and yelped in pain.

On the sofa, Holly stirred, mumbled, then subsided again. There wasn't much room there, but in a pinch Jenna reckoned the two of them could squeeze together. Holly would stir again, as she'd always done when Jenna climbed into bed, and slip her arms around her. Soft and warm, comforting and safe.

"No." Jenna shook her head. Holly stirred again, then once more settled. Jenna turned away from her. If Holly embraced her she'd be asleep in seconds.

A silver gleam caught Jenna's eye: the powder compact, which had ended up somehow on the kitchen counter. She gripped it tight and hard, letting the scalloped edges dig into her palm. The pain might keep her awake, and the thing itself would remind her what would happen if she slept.

Or had something else prompted her to pick it up? A kind of instinct? The kind that had guided her out of the wrecked aircraft, or into the house with the mullioned windows? Or, indeed, to the powder compact itself?

Jenna stumbled as she moved away from the counter, tripping over her own feet and almost going sprawling.

Nearly brained yourself on the stove there, babe.

She couldn't keep walking, physically couldn't. She had to sit down. Take a break. No, she mustn't. Daren't. But there was no choice.

The bedroom door was open. She could see the double bed, threadbare and creaky with several knackered springs, but right now, incredibly inviting. Jesus Christ, no. She'd be out like a light. But she had to rest, just for a moment.

She slumped into an armchair by the sofa. The ache in her legs seemed to bloom as she did, into a dull, monotonous throb. And her eyes were so heavy. She really couldn't keep them open much longer.

All right, then. She'd shut her eyes, just for a couple of minutes. Rest. Then get up again. Make another brew. Keep going somehow.

She let her eyelids close.

Only for a minute. Just a minute and then–

It was dark. Peaceful. She was sinking.

No. Oh shit, no–

Jenna opened her eyes.

49.

She was in the position she'd occupied just before waking, shoved back against the wall in a corner of the mock-Tudor house's bedroom, in that desolate, abandoned facsimile of Wilmslow Road. Back in the Greylands once more.

There was a bright light, but it wasn't painful or dazzling. Which was strange, because the cowled shadow that served as the Bonewalker's face hung barely ten feet above her.

The room was bathed in a cold white light that flung black shadows in all directions, but it was dimmed somehow. Jenna could look at it easily; even when she looked directly at the Bonewalker, its eyes, previously so painful to look at, were no brighter than the full moon on a clear night.

Similarly, she could hear its voice, a familiar refrain, but now so faint it was no more than a murmur: *tell me where tell me where tell me where.*

The air around Jenna shimmered, as if rippling. The effect extended for a short distance around her, and when Jenna looked down at her feet she seemed to be standing in a patch of greyish shadow. The rippling grew more pronounced closer to her body, and was at its fiercest around her right hand.

She held it up, and saw the shimmering was so intense around the object she held its outlines were almost unrecognisable. Not quite, though. She turned the compact this way and that, studying it, and was about to open it when the light around her dimmed further still.

The Bonewalker had straightened up; the great horned head swung to and fro, searchlight eyes sweeping the ruins. Finally, the creature stamped away, the devastated street shuddering to its footsteps. Fresh sounds of destruction erupted, rang, echoed and faded as it tore apart its surroundings, either in frustration or in its attempts to find her.

It can't see you while you've got the compact.

It seemed ridiculous, but she remembered the instinct that had prompted her to hold it up against the Bonewalker. Perhaps it had been the mirror: there was a certain strange logic to the idea that reflecting the Bonewalker's gaze back at it might have saved her.

She sprang the compact open. The mirror was still pearlescent: presumably an effect of the light from the Bonewalker's eyes. Perhaps it had somehow created a permanent blind spot where the Bonewalker was concerned.

A theory only, and not one Jenna was in any hurry to test. The shimmering had faded; the protection the compact had given her might already be spent.

The house groaned; the floor sagged underfoot. Probably best to get out of the building; even if there was no immediate threat from the Bonewalker, other kinds existed. Jenna shoved the compact deep into her jogpants pocket, ventured back out onto the landing and picked her way downstairs.

When the Bonewalker had torn away the bedroom's front wall, it had taken a substantial chunk from the ground floor too, including the front door, so it gaped open to the street. All to the good, as the damaged structure's creaking had grown downright alarming and Jenna could see how badly the floor above her had begun to sag.

When she slipped through the doorway, the replica of Wilmslow Road, formerly deserted with a handful of derelict buildings, now resembled a scene from an all-out war. The street was cratered where the Bonewalker had trodden, its weight fracturing the paving slabs and tarmac alike, and most of the buildings were now without roofs or frontage. Every car in sight was likewise wreckage: most had been trampled by the Bonewalker in its advance or retreat, but one had been embedded in the top floor of a ruined building and another torn in two. *Like Rose.*

Grey dust blanketed the entire scene. There'd been none here before, in this refuge she'd stumbled into through sheer blind luck–

No, babe. That voice, so much like Holly's, was impatient now. *Because you willed it.*

That made no sense.

As if in answer, the wind that swept the Greylands picked up; fresh clouds of ash billowed down the street.

See? Look what happens. You doubted before, didn't you, that you'd had anything to do with it. And soon as you did, the winds started blowing.

"You mean I could make it stop?" Jenna said aloud. "Because I'd really fucking like to."

Yes.

"How?"

Just do it.

"For fuck's sake." She hated answers like that, always had. Like saying *just stop being depressed.* Christ, if she could will things into being here, she had a shopping list of items. A flight of cruise missiles aimed at the Bonewalker's forest for a start.

Why not? But don't forget: it can do the same, and it's been here longer.

All right: assume for argument's sake she could, somehow, control her environment. On the surface, ludicrous, but there was no denying it: just as she'd told herself *there is, must,* will be *somewhere*, this place had appeared. And not just any place, but the first one she thought of whenever she needed a refuge.

See? You willed a refuge. And this appeared.

It could have been imagination or wishful thinking, but Jenna thought the wind had dropped. The ash no longer seemed so thick.

You can stop it altogether if you want. You just–

"Will it," Jenna snapped aloud. "I know. *How*, for fuck's sake?"

Just will it. Want it. Shut your eyes and picture it.

"Fine," she muttered. "Whatthefuckever."

She closed her eyes and began trying to picture the street in other, happier times. No dust. No wind. Clean pavements. Undamaged shopfronts. Kerbside trees in bloom, because it would be spring, her favourite time of year. There'd been a privet hedge outside the old police station: she imagined its leaves bright and glossy green. Birds twittering. The cars along the roadside all undamaged, paintwork gleaming.

The wind felt – less.

No wind, she thought. *No wind at all. I want a quiet warm day and the smell of spring blossom in the air instead of this fucking ash. And something to drink – nothing fancy, just some cool clear water – and–*

The wind was gone.

Jenna opened her eyes.

The street was clean and undamaged. She turned three hundred and sixty degrees; even the mock-Tudor house she'd been hiding in was restored to its pristine state, and the previously derelict buildings were whole as well.

And she could smell blossom on the air.

It was warm. Sunny. The trees dotted along the kerbside were indeed in bloom. A few doors down from Jenna was a little coffee shop she'd loved, but which had closed the year after Mum died.

Doesn't matter, babe. You wanted it, so here it is.

Directly across the street was an ornate wrought-iron fountain. A drinking fountain, complete with tin cups attached by chains. No such thing had ever existed in any Didsbury Jenna had known.

Again: doesn't matter.

"I wanted it," she said, realising, "so it's here."

Exactly.

Jenna crossed the street, looking both ways out of habit. The town was silent; no birds sang. She could only create *things*: nothing that lived. The trees looked alive, but maybe they only appeared that way: far easier to do that with a tree than with a bird, a dog, a person.

Water trickled from the fountain, bright and crystalline water. Jenna filled a cup and drank it off, then did it again.

Nice. But you don't want the Bonewalker seeing it, do you?

The cup slipped out of her hand. Of course: the Bonewalker only need glance in this direction, and it would know Jenna was here. And even if the compact hid her from it, her one real advantage was that she was learning to manipulate the Greylands. If the Bonewalker realised that, her advantage was gone.

Like I said, babe – sorry, but that fucker's been doing this a lot *longer than you.*

"All right, got it," she muttered. "But what *do* I do now?"

*You know what to do. Or un*do.

"Right. Course." She'd have to stop addressing the voice out loud. First sign of madness. Then again, she was surely long past first signs by now. "You could've just said that, though."

Closing her eyes, she pictured the scene she'd first observed: the cratered ground, shattered frontages, roofless buildings. The car torn in half like Rose; the one driven into a building like a knife.

Don't forget the dust. Let the wind have a good blow.

"Oh, joy to the fucking world." But Holly was right, or the voice which sounded so much like hers. How much of that voice was Holly, and how much Jenna?

Maybe fifty-fifty.

"Bullshit." Jenna was the one who knew about fighting back.

How would you know? Weren't exactly eager to hear all about me, were you?

Which was true. Holly might have spoken about her past, but Jenna had hardly taken any of it in. Jesus. She couldn't believe Holly hadn't just written her off as soon as she vanished.

Well, you've got some good qualities, babe. That thing you do with your tongue for a start.

Jenna laughed hysterically, but it quickly dissolved into choking and spluttering as a sudden gale rocked her back on her heels, blowing ash into her mouth.

Might've slightly overcompensated there.

"No shit." Jenna squinted through the grey haze, shielding her eyes and looking for shelter.

The ground shuddered underfoot, so violently she almost fell. Then again. An earthquake? But no, the tremors were steady and repetitive: one-two, one-two.

Footsteps.

The Bonewalker rose, bigger than ever, a hundred, two hundred feet above the ruins. Seemed to be its go-to response: when in doubt, make yourself bigger.

Freud would have a field day there, eh?

The Bonewalker's eyes swept back and forth across the street, and struck Jenna before she could even try to evade them, but as before, the air around her shimmered and rippled, and the creature's gaze swept on. The compact's protection, whatever it was, still worked. But Jenna had heard that thick, tarry voice, muffled though it was, and what it was saying now.

Where are you Holly Where are you Holly Where are you Holly

The light swept back and forth without finding what it sought, and finally the Bonewalker turned away, but Jenna could still hear it.

Where are you Holly Where are you Holly Where are you Holly

It knew, or guessed, she'd somehow found a way to hide from it. So now it had changed tack. It knew about Holly – if she'd been beneath its notice before, it had no doubt pieced things together through Whitecliffe. Jenna doubted the good doctor would have much trouble uncovering her rescuer's identity.

Which meant that if she'd still had any doubts about Holly's allegiance, she could dismiss them now; if Holly had been in league with the Bonewalker, it wouldn't need to search for her. It wouldn't even have needed to search for Jenna.

Where are you Holly Where are you Holly Where are you Holly

Jenna had faced the Bonewalker both in the real world and the Greylands: Holly would think the Bonewalker and the Greylands alike to be madness or fantasy. Holly was a babe in the woods here, defenceless. If the Bonewalker found Holly in the Greylands, and turned its gaze on her, it would know in seconds where she was in reality. And with her, Jenna.

Where are you Holly Where are you Holly Where are you Holly

Jenna opened her mouth and screamed Holly's name.

But she couldn't even hear herself.

50.

"Jenna! Jenn!"

Hands on her shoulders. She struggled.

"Sweetheart, it's me. Jenn? It's Holly."

Jenna blinked herself awake.

She was in the armchair, curled up in a near-foetal position, shaking. Holly's face was close to hers, wide eyes full of pity and concern.

Where are you Holly Where are you Holly. Jenna heard the echo of the Bonewalker's call, and shuddered involuntarily.

"Babe?"

"I'm okay. I'm okay."

She held onto Holly tightly, wondering what came next.

It was just before dawn, rain tapping and spotting on the caravan windows, but all Jenna wanted now was to be outside. Ironic after her ordeal in the woods, but she'd spent too long shut up in small rooms at someone else's whim.

Holly grumbled, but agreed after a great deal of badgering, pulling on her shoes and coat and throwing Jenna a spare anorak. They stepped out into the drizzle, tramped across the field and drove back into the town, then crossed the rolling expanse of grassy dunes to Harlech's sandy beach.

The four-mile strand was a dull tan colour, deserted in the grey wet morning; there wasn't even a dog walker in evidence.

The tide hissed and foamed as it retreated into Tremadog Bay. The air was fresh, with a salt tang. It took Jenna back to Dinas Oleu, before all this started, and she began to cry.

She kept walking, though, along the shoreline. Holly remained beside her, saying nothing and letting her hand brush against Jenna's as they walked, till finally Jenna clasped it. How could she not? Holly had risked herself for Jenna's sake, and in ways she wasn't even aware of.

She'd no idea what the Bonewalker could do to Holly if it found her in the Greylands; for all Jenna knew, it had no power there except over its descendants: the threat to Holly might only be a bluff. But Jenna didn't dare call it.

The wise thing to do – the best, if she truly cared for Holly – would be to leave. Strike off on her own, and draw the Bonewalker away. She'd be alone, but she was used to that. Might even be throwing away her one chance of being whole again, healing herself of the legacy of Tallstone Hill.

I love her, she realised. She knew it for a certainty now; she wouldn't have been willing to give up what she most wanted for anything less. She realised, too, that Holly had changed something in her, and that for the first time she could remember, it didn't bother Jenna that a lover had succeeded in doing so.

But she wasn't sure she could cope alone. Or how long she could do so for. And even if she could, Holly would still be a loose end as far as both Whitecliffe and the Bonewalker were concerned. One or the other would come for her. Or maybe even use her to blackmail Jenna, as she'd feared Whitecliffe had intended before.

She endangered Holly by staying; she endangered her by leaving.

They walked along the shore, then back again. Neither said anything; Holly knew Jenna well enough to wait till she was ready to speak. But as they walked the strand a third time, the other woman's pace shifted, and Jenna turned to see her pull an old flip-phone from her pocket.

"What you doing?"

"Burner phone. Never been used. Picked up a few before I went down to Stonebrook."

"Who you calling?"

"Not calling anyone on this. Checking the time, that's all." Holly flicked the phone shut. "But Len should be up by now."

"Who's he when he's at home?"

"Hopefully, our boat to Ireland, love." Holly drummed her fingers on the phone. "There's a phone box up in the town. I'll use that. Play it safe." She took both Jenna's hands in hers. "Come with if you want, or stay here." She smiled. "Bit of time to yourself, where you're not locked up somewhere."

Jenna felt her eyes fill up. "You know me so well," she grinned, but heard her voice crack.

"Meh." Holly kissed her on the lips. "See you in a bit."

Jenna watched the little round figure stumping determinedly across the beach and waited for her to look back, but she didn't; a fierce wind was coming in off the sea now, blowing rain and spume, and despite the dampness, streams of windblown sand snaked across the beach.

I love you. She should have said it just now, when she'd had the chance. She thought of Mum: you could never be sure when you'd last see someone.

No. Holly would be back. She would.

Jenna turned out to sea, shoving her hands into her anorak pockets, hunching her shoulders and trying to pull up the hood, but despite her best efforts the wind blew it back. Well, the spray would keep her awake, which could only be good. Sleep would take her to the Greylands. So she mustn't sleep. Neither of them could.

What? Ever? Good luck with that. You'll die or go mental.

Either sounded preferable to being "absorbed" by the Bonewalker. But she had to stop it coming at her through Holly.

You have to sleep sometime, and so do I. What happens then?

In truth, Jenna had no idea. She'd managed to manipulate the Greylands on the most basic level, created some form of protection, but there was no telling how long it would last, let alone whether it would withstand any kind of sustained assault. Nonetheless, she'd got away from the enemy, if only for now; she'd just have to hope she could continue to do so.

Jenna's hand slipped into her pocket and squeezed the compact. That might shield Holly while she slept, if Jenna could pass it to her somehow.

And then the Bonewalker finds you. How's that gonna help?

She could try and create another such object; she'd done it once, after all.

And if you fuck it up, it comes for you. Or Whitecliffe and her gerbils do. Either way, you're bollocksed, and what happens then?

If it saved Holly, if there was even a chance of that, she'd no choice but to try.

Jenna realised she was crying again.

Footsteps gritted behind her. "Jenn?" Holly looked up at her, gold-flecked eyes worried and wide. "Babe, what is it?"

There were many things Jenna could tell Holly that she'd never believe, but one she hopefully would. Jenna reached out, stroked Holly's cheek, and managed to smile. "I love you," she said.

Holly smiled back, and the light in her face and eyes was enough to drive everything else away, at least for the present. "I love you too," she said. "But you knew that, right?"

"I did," said Jenna. "I did."

The worst thing about love, the reason Jenna had avoided it so long, was the fear you could feel for someone else, the pain you exposed yourself to just by loving them. But there was nothing to be done about that now. So she held Holly tight as the grey waves mumbled in the distance, and the sky grew black with rain.

51.

As they started back across the beach the storm broke, lightning flashing out to sea and sheets of rain sweeping in on the wind. Holding their hoods against it, they ran for the road, laughing one moment, screaming the next as cold water sluiced down the backs of their necks or lashed them stingingly across the face. *Like a pair of schoolgirls*, Jenna thought.

The rain grew in force and built quickly to a hammering barrage. Despite her short legs, Holly pulled ahead and reached the car well ahead of Jenna. She drove back to the caravan park, and the pair of them were solidly drenched again as they slipped and stumbled back across the field to the caravan.

"Fucking hell." Holly slammed the door behind them before looking up at the ceiling.

"What's up?"

"Just checking for leaks." The rain on the caravan roof sounded like machine-gun fire. "Right, you. Get your kit off."

"What?"

"Clothes. Off."

"And I thought romance was dead."

"Ha ha." Holly peeled off her anorak. "Clothes off, and into the shower. *Now*, before you catch your death. Be a bit shit if you got this far just to cark it from pneumonia."

"And I thought you were after my body." Jenna sighed, undressing. "You really don't do a woman's self-esteem any good."

Holly blew a raspberry, but then followed it with a loud and protracted wolf-whistle as Jenna ran to the bathroom.

Jenna's teeth were chattering by the time she turned the shower on; even so, she only realised how cold she'd been once the warmth began seeping into her again under the hot spray.

Steam swirled thick around her. It took her back, for a moment, to Cutty Wren Lodge, and how the shower there had been the one place she could be sure of privacy. So she jumped at first when a pink-and-white blur moved outside the fogged-up cubicle glass, till the door opened and Holly squeezed into the shower with her. "Room for a little one?"

"Think I can fit you in." Holly's shape meant she had trouble manoeuvring in the confined space, but as she was pressed against Jenna it wasn't much of a hardship, other than her being startlingly cold at first.

"Clothes are in the wash." Holly ran her fingertips over Jenna's breasts, then down over her ribs to her hips, her boobs squashing pleasantly against Jenna's belly. "Want me to scrub your back?"

The spray from the shower had plastered Holly's hair down and she was looking up at Jenna, bringing out her face's heart-shaped bone structure. Jenna grinned and stroked her cheek, touching Holly's lips with a fingertip. "Go on then. Ow," she added as Holly nipped playfully at her finger.

Holly turned her around to face the cubicle wall, and the sponge worked its way down Jenna's back, then between her buttocks. Then Holly's fingertips replaced the sponge, moving between Jenna's thighs to cup her vulva from behind.

"Oh," said Jenna; it came out in a long soft breath. For obvious reasons, sex hadn't been on her agenda in some time. Despite her occasionally threatening to at Cutty Wren Lodge, masturbation had been impossible knowing the cameras were there, besides which the whole forced-birth scenario had been anything but conducive to the erotic. But now she was free of James for good, and of Whitecliffe for the time being at least.

And the Bonewalker?

Jenna drew in a breath, tensing up.

"Babe?" Holly put her free hand on Jenna's shoulder. "You okay?"

"Yeah. I'm good."

"Should I stop?"

"Don't you fucking dare."

She wouldn't think of those things now if she could help it: they were all outside, waiting, and still would be later. But they had no place here and now. Nothing did, not here, but Holly and her.

Holly's hand remained cupped between Jenna's thighs; still hesitant, she'd made no further move. Jenna pressed her hands against the cubicle wall and pushed back with her hips. After a moment, Holly gently eased a finger inside her.

"More," said Jenna over her shoulder, eyes closed.

Slowly and carefully, Holly slipped another finger in; her thumb probed between Jenna's buttocks, massaging gently. She kissed Jenna's back and shoulders; her free hand cupped each of Jenna's breasts in turn, fingertips lightly pinching the erect nipples before travelling down over her belly. Jenna tensed for a moment, remembering how she'd unconsciously stroked her own stomach while pregnant, as if her body was betraying her, trying to persuade her to accept motherhood.

"You okay?" Holly whispered again, standing on tiptoes to reach.

Jenna twisted round, arm briefly encircling Holly's neck, fingers tangling in her wet hair. "Yes," she breathed, and kissed her. Holly's tongue slipped into her mouth, touching hers, and her left hand moved south over Jenna's belly and pubic mound to the tip of her clit, rubbing it in slow, gentle circles.

Jenna broke the kiss to gasp as the first waves of tingly warmth passed through her. Holly kissed her shoulder and ran her tongue along her neck, her hands continuing to work away, then eased a third finger inside her, before slowly working her thumb into her ass. Jenna gave a little groan and pushed her hips back, spreading her arms out across the shower wall and resting her cheek against the cool tile.

The hot water streamed down, the air thick with steam, and time went away. She didn't know how long they were under the spray, or care: all that mattered was what Holly was doing to her and how it felt. She came very fast the first time, but Holly didn't stop, bringing her to climax again. Jenna bit the inside of her arm to muffle her cries, and Holly laughed softly behind her. She came, and the rest of the world went away.

"Think we're running out of water," Holly said at last, laughter still in her voice, and it was true that the spray was no longer as hot as before. Jenna fumbled for the shower controls and shut it off, but pressed herself back against Holly as the steam billowed thick around them.

"Don't stop," she begged, but Holly's fingers and thumb withdrew, leaving her empty. "Ooh, you bitch," she panted.

Holly laughed and gave her buttocks a light slap. "Ungrateful little madam."

Jenna wagged her bottom in what she hoped was a tempting manner, but it sadly wasn't enticing enough; Holly opened the cubicle door and let the steam billow out. "Come on," she said, handing Jenna a towel. "Let's move things to the bedroom, eh?"

Jenna let Holly lead her to the double bed. "'Bout time we made some use of it, I suppose."

"Test the suspension, eh?" Holly grinned and lay back, spreading herself out. "Come on, then, babe. My turn now."

Jenna climbed onto the bed and kissed her, kneeling between her outspread legs. She'd always thought of Holly's body as the opposite of hers: full and yielding where she was spare and hard; luxurious and sumptuous, where Jenna was pared-down and spartan. Right now it was like a feast to a starving woman: just to touch, kiss, caress and lick and fondle it was arousing in and of itself.

She cupped Holly's big, heavy breasts, stroked her round belly, then gently spread her knees further apart and nuzzled lower, kissing the insides of those soft, white thighs, working her way up and breathing in the almost-forgotten scent of her before lowering her head to gently kiss her sex. Holly groaned, deep in her throat.

"I'd forgotten how beautiful you are," Jenna whispered. "Don't suppose you bothered to pack any toys?"

"Knew I'd forgotten something."

"We'll make do."

At some point the rain stopped, but by the time they finally finished the downpour had resumed. They were also soaking wet again, but this time from sweat. Jenna thought of the poem she'd remembered on Dinas Oleu: *"Sweat sweetens it"*. Truer words never spoken.

She pulled the bedclothes tight around them and snuggled close to Holly, wishing for a moment she could sink into the other woman, climb inside her, the two of them becoming one.

This is love, then.

It wasn't so bad, she decided. At least as long as she didn't think about all the dangers waiting outside their little cocoon.

Holly snored, then blinked and focused blearily on Jenna, smiling foolishly, and Jenna realised the same torpor – lack of sleep, sheer stressed exhaustion and good old-fashioned post-coital afterglow – had settled on her. She dimly felt panic rising, but her eyes were closing all the same: even knowing how dangerous sleep was wouldn't stop her surrendering to it. Then she remembered something she'd glimpsed as they'd entered the bedroom and twisted round, focusing on the bedside table.

"Whassup?" said Holly.

"Nothing." Jenna fumbled for the powder compact. Back at the flat, that had always been their system; whatever you found in the other person's clothes when putting them in the wash went on their bedside table. A place for everything; everything in a place. And the compact had been in her jogpants. *I trained her well,* she thought and turned back towards Holly, stroking her face.

"Love you," Holly mumbled.

"Love you too," Jenna said again, marvelling at how easy it suddenly was to both say and mean. She clasped Holly's hands in hers, folding them around the powder compact.

"Whassis?"

"Present." Jenna kissed her forehead. Holly's eyes closed; Jenna closed hers too. *Is this enough? Please let it be enough.* But it all felt very distant now, almost academic: she was so tired. Holly's hands fastened tightly around hers, refusing to let go. The warm hands, small and soft, and the cold metal of the case, were the last sensations Jenna registered as she drifted off.

52.

Metal clattered on stone, and a voice said: "What the *fuck*?"

Someone bumped into Jenna. When she opened her eyes, she saw it was Holly, stumbling backwards and almost falling over. Jenna caught her arm. "Babe! It's okay."

That's supposed to be her line.

Dust blew through the ruins of Wilmslow Road. There was sheer panic on Holly's face, not least as she was nude. They both were: that was how they'd fallen asleep. "It's okay," she said. "Wait a second."

She shut her eyes, trying to picture what they needed.

"Jenna? What the fuck are you–"

"Quiet." She held up a hand, and her tone was urgent enough that Holly obeyed. An idea came to Jenna and she let it take shape in her head. *I will this. I will it. Make it happen.*

"Whoa, wait. The hell did that come from?"

Sounds like it worked.

Jenna opened her eyes. Holly was crouching in the billowing dust, arms covering herself, staring across the street at a shopfront that now stood, pristine and undamaged, among the ruins.

"Result," muttered Jenna, and as she did a familiar bellow echoed across the landscape. The air grew colder and the stench of sickness and decay filled it, making them both gag.

"Fuck," muttered Holly, and wheeled to face it, fists clenched – then froze, mouth falling open, as the billowing dust clouds

271

parted for a moment to reveal the Bonewalker looming in the distance, two hundred feet tall now if it was an inch and in all its skeletal glory, eyes aglow. "What? What?"

She was staring, transfixed, paralysed. Jenna grabbed her arm. "Holly. Holly!"

"Whuh?" Holly stared wild-eyed at her, then back down the street. "What the actual *fuck* is that?"

"Not now," said Jenna. "Out of the wind first, eh?"

She squeezed Holly's arm, which snapped the other woman out of her daze. Holly smiled shakily. "Yeah," she said at last. "Sounds like a plan."

They were heading towards the shop when Jenna remembered the clatter of metal she'd heard and turned back. "Jenn?" called Holly. "What–?"

"Get inside, hun. I'll be right with you."

A layer of dust had already built up over the road surface and more of it was blowing down the street. For a panicky moment she couldn't see the powder compact and thought it lost, but then a silver gleam caught her eye. She knelt, grubbing through the soft floury dust, then shook the ashes from the compact.

She jumped onto the pavement and sprinted to the door of the boutique, slamming it behind her.

"I thought this place was in town," said Holly in a dazed voice, meaning Manchester. "Northern Quarter, somewhere like that."

"It is," said Jenna. "But things are a bit more flexible here."

"No shit." Holly was white and shaking, and looked even smaller in the huge thick coat she'd bundled herself up in. Both the cold and the smell still lingered in the air.

The shop was a favourite of Holly's, dealing in Seventies retro gear and off-the-wall jewellery: pocket watches shaped like love-hearts, that kind of thing. Jenna had always found it a bit twee, but it had been the first place she could think of for shelter, safety, and clothing. And somewhere Holly might feel halfway safe.

Jenna pulled a similar heavy coat from a mannequin and donned it, then dragged Holly to the old-style chaise-longue at the back of the shop, beside display racks of clothes and boots. She sat Holly down and pressed both their hands around the compact. "Just to be on the safe side."

"Huh?"

"If we're holding this, it can't see us. More importantly, it can't find us."

"Are you on crack?" Holly stared around them. "Am *I* on crack?"

"No."

"It's shrooms, isn't it? You put something in my tea. Fuck's sake, Jenna, this is no time to get high–"

"Holl!" Despite herself, Jenna tried not to laugh. "Where would I have scored drugs lately?"

"The clinic, maybe." Holly paused. "Then again, maybe not shrooms–"

"Holly."

"Okay, but – what? Hang on, wait. I'm dreaming, right?"

"Not exactly." The walls trembled as the Bonewalker's footsteps approached. Holly shrank back, unable to suppress a whimper. Jenna pressed close to her; she dearly wanted to hug Holly close, but the two of them holding the compact was all that might possibly keep them safe.

"What is this?" Holly's eyes were huge and damp with unbelieving fright. "What?"

Jenna took a deep breath. She'd never looked forward to this moment, but at least now Holly was more likely to believe her. "Long story," she said. "But here we go."

She started with Mum's death. Dad had always called it her *disappearance*, refusing to admit Elaine was gone and never giving up hope she'd reappear one day to set things right, but Jenna had always known.

Holly already knew about the dreams; now Jenna told her how the cold and stench in them were the same as she'd experienced the night Mum died, about her encounters with the Bonewalker at the cottage, and its destruction of Rose. About Whitecliffe, and the Rite of Cronos. And finally, about the Greylands.

Unbelievable. Sheer madness. And yet here they were in the middle of it all. Holly stared about her as Jenna talked, occasionally reaching out to touch the chaise-longue's arm or feel the fabric of a hanging coat. Wanting to believe it was a dream, but finding her surroundings stubbornly real. And unable to wake.

Through it all the Bonewalker's roar rang through the dust like a foghorn, and the earth shivered at its tread, as if to hammer home the truth of it.

The winds continued to blow, much to Jenna's relief, as layers of ash accumulated on every flat surface they touched, including – most importantly – the front of the boutique. By the time she'd finished talking she couldn't see the street outside: the shopfront was near-opaque with dust, meaning if the Bonewalker came back this way, there'd be nothing to distinguish it from the other buildings on the ruined street.

The shop shuddered violently, dust falling from the ceiling; a brilliant cold light shone through the ash-encrusted windows, and Holly cried out. It was back here, looking again.

The cold deepened, the stench thickened, and the light spilled towards them. Holly tried to stand, but Jenna gripped her hands tight, keeping them wrapped around the compact, and shouted, "Stay close," over the Bonewalker's rumbling growl. Despite the dust-caked window, the light grew blinding, and the air around Jenna shimmered as before – and around Holly, too.

As before, the Bonewalker's voice was dulled to a thick faint murmur by the rippling air. But they could hear it nonetheless.

Where are you Holly Where are you Holly Where are you Holly

"The fuck?" Holly was shaking. "The *fuck*?"

Tell me where Tell me where Jenna tell me where Where are you Holly Where are you Holly Jenna tell me where

Holly was hyperventilating by now. Jenna wanted to pull her close but didn't dare move her hands from their current position. If either of them let go of the compact, the thing would find them instantly. She leant forward, resting her forehead against Holly's, whispering, "It's okay, it's okay, it's okay."

Finally the glow dimmed, and the Bonewalker roared and stamped. At least, Jenna assumed it must have. The boutique rocked, more dust cascading from the ceiling; the shop windows splintered but thankfully held and, more concerningly, the wall behind them cracked.

"Shit," Holly whispered.

The building shuddered and groaned. Jenna was tempted to will a repair to the damage, but compact or no compact, the Bonewalker would probably sense it if its surroundings were altered. She could only wait, eyeing the cracked ceiling nervously.

The glare faded and the creature's footsteps slowly rumbled away. Jenna relaxed her grip on Holly's hands, keeping hold of the compact as she wrapped her arms around Holly and pulled her close. This felt good in a way; it was good to be the protector instead, to be the strong one. More familiar ground. *She protects me; I protect her. An equal footing. Balance.* "It's okay, hun. It's okay."

"Okay?" Holly stared at her. "Okay? On what fucking planet is *that*–" she waved in the direction of the fractured windows "–in what fucking *universe* is *any* of this okay?"

A reasonable point, but Jenna couldn't hold back a burst of near-hysterical laughter in response. Holly glowered, then snorted, shook her head and gave a faint, reluctant chuckle.

"Yeah," she said at last. "S'pose you've got to laugh, haven't you?"

As if in answer, thunder roared.

Or rather the Bonewalker did. This was different from any other sound Jenna had heard it make before, and it boomed and rumbled on and on without end. It was so monstrously distorted it was barely recognizable, but at last Jenna's stomach hollowed as she realised what it was.

"Oh fuck," she said.

"What?" Holly was hyperventilating again. "Jenn, what?"

"It's laughing." And not the tarry rumble Jenna had heard in the cottage cellar, either; this was a booming, baying roar of triumph.

"I know *that*, but why?"

"I don't know. Can't be anything good."

Jenna felt Holly grip her arm; when she turned, Holly was staring at her, and Jenna realised she'd worked it out. And then Jenna did, too.

"It knows where we are," Holly said.

"But the compact..." Jenna broke off. "Whitecliffe. She's found us."

They stared at one another, and Holly said: "We need to wake up."

The laughter boomed on and on.

"How do we wake up?" Holly shouted.

"I don't know," Jenna shouted back.

And then the world turned white–

53.

–and Jenna rolled out of bed, landing unceremoniously on the floor. It knocked the wind out of her so she couldn't scream, but she could hear Holly letting out high-pitched whoops of panic.

Jenna clawed at the threadbare carpet, then the bed, pulling herself to her feet. She reached for Holly, who was clutching the bedclothes around herself, face white and drained, eyes and mouth gone huge. "Holl. Holl! It's me. It's me."

"Fuck," said Holly. "Fuck. Fuck. Fuck."

"We just did," said Jenna – a daft thing to say because they were in danger and there wasn't time for jokes; but the right thing to say too, because it made Holly laugh, however shakily, and broke the spell. "Get dressed," said Jenna. "I need clothes."

Holly pointed across the room, to the walk-in wardrobe on the far wall. "Brought some of your gear up. It's in there."

Jenna ran to it, grinning weakly when she saw her patched jeans and paint-spattered boots, her old leather jacket and Rammstein hoodie. She dressed quickly as Holly rooted through the wardrobe for clean clothes of her own. She felt scared, but energised too: she'd something to fight for now. She'd do whatever it took to keep that.

She stumbled into the front room, boots in hand; she put them on, foot braced on a chair to lace them, and peered through the window and the rain across the muddy field.

Holly came out of the bedroom, zipping her fleece. "Anything?"

"Can't see owt. Best get moving, though."

"Jenn?" Holly was still shaking. "Was that real? Are you sure?"

Jenna held up the compact. "This came from there. From the Greylands, I mean. So, yeah. Wish I wasn't."

"Okay." Holly took a deep breath, steadying herself. "I got hold of Len," she said. "Didn't get a chance to tell you before, between getting piss-wet through and all the bow-chicka-bow-wow afterwards–"

"You weren't complaining."

"True." Holly pulled her backpack on. "He can take us across today. He's in Barmouth, so not far."

"Barmouth." There was an aptness to that, somehow; the place they'd been on that last day before all this had invaded their lives. Along with Whitecliffe and the Greylands. And the Bonewalker, of course. Although it, really, had always been there.

"Yup. Won't be any time for sightseeing, though."

Jenna managed a laugh. "I can live with that."

"Cool. Anything else you need?"

Jenna shook her head. She'd always travelled light; besides, there'd been precious little of hers here to begin with. She was in clothes of her own again, and for the first time in a small eternity felt something like her old self once more.

Holly threw the caravan door wide and led the dash to the Land Rover. The engine was coughing into life even as Jenna pulled the passenger door shut behind her; as she scrabbled for her seatbelt Holly reversed hard, swinging the vehicle round to face the exit, mud splattering the windscreen and spraying out from under the wheels.

Holly turned the wipers on, then accelerated across the field, the 4x4 fishtailing as its tyres battled for a grip in the mud. Jenna fastened her seatbelt, then reached across to secure Holly's.

At the exit Holly spun the wheel left, and they tore down the lane towards the coast road. She spun the wheel right as they hit the road, and the Land Rover fishtailed once more.

"Jesus," said Jenna.

"Sorry." Holly shifted gears and eased up on the accelerator. "Slow and steady wins the race, eh, babe? No point drawing attention, right?"

She was smiling tightly, still shaking, as they went back through the town. Probably all she could do was to focus on the simple, mundane task of getting them to Barmouth right now, having been so suddenly yanked back into this world from the Greylands and the presence of the Bonewalker.

Where are you Holly Where are you Holly

Only it no longer had to ask, because it knew.

"Not for much longer," Jenna muttered.

"What?"

"Nothing. Nothing." Jenna reached out and squeezed Holly's hand. Holly gripped it tight. Jenna said nothing else.

The road took them inland for a while, through Pensarn, Llanbedr and Tal-y-Bont, then back to the coast. They drove past the thirteenth-century church overlooking the stony beach at Llanaber, and then they were entering Barmouth.

The town looked drab and washed-out in the overcast autumn drizzle. Dinas Oleu loomed over them to the left in dull green, grey and ochre, the purple heather and yellow gorse long gone.

"Where do we find him?" Jenna said.

"Huh?"

"Your mate Len."

"Up at his gaff. We'll sort things out there, then get to the boat." Holly took deep breaths. "It'll be okay," she said to herself. "He'll be fine."

As they drove past the quay, Jenna saw with dismay that half the boats were stranded on the sand because the tide was out, the estuary narrow and dotted with sandbanks. No chance of getting out till the tide was in. How long would that be? How many hours? Long enough for Whitecliffe and the Bonewalker to find them again?

She bit her lip, dug her nails into her palms. It was out of her hands; it was all down now to Holly and Len, who she didn't know and had never met. It was hard to give herself over to anyone like that, even Holly; to a stranger it was near-impossible.

No choice though.

She breathed out through her teeth, trying to force herself to stay calm. It had begun to rain again in earnest, dotting the windscreen; Holly switched on the wipers as she turned up Marine Parade.

Jenna tried to let the wipers' beating soothe her as they passed the tall stone B&Bs, heading north through the town. The sandy beach – a muddy brown in the autumn rain, rather than the gold it'd been in summer – gave way to broken grey rocks and wooden groynes.

Holly turned right. The houses now were plainer and smaller, more recent in construction. Most were pebble-dashed, with fronts like rough grey sandpaper.

Holly finally pulled up outside a plain semi-detached property and shut the engine off. "Here we go, babe. End of the rainbow."

She'd said that at the caravan park, too. But that had proved a refuge, at least at the time. She was still pale. "You okay?" Jenna said.

Holly managed a strained laugh. "Why would I not be?"

Jenna squeezed her hand again; once more, Holly squeezed back. "I'll be all right," she said. "Long as I don't think about it too much."

"Amen to that," said Jenna, then got out of the car and followed Holly up the drive. Holly pushed the doorbell; footsteps sounded in the hallway.

Behind them, a vehicle pulled up. Brakes squeaked. Doors slammed.

Her spine prickled.

Run.

But the door had already opened.

"Hello, Jenna," Whitecliffe said. She was still wearing her white coat, her hands thrust deep into its pockets. "Didn't think we'd forgotten you, did you?"

THE TEMPLAR OF GALILEE

A letter by Fuad Şinasi, an Ottoman officer, to his cousin in Bursa in 1869, describes a peculiar legend centring around "a certain hill near the village of Khirbat Karraza, overlooking the northern shores of Lake Tiberias".

Şinasi's letter is the only source in which the legend is found; the story may have been his own invention, or that of a local prankster. Nonetheless, it's an interesting and unusual tale.

For some years following the Fall of Ruad, and even after the Order's dissolution, a man in the armour of a Templar Knight was often seen roaming the hill. Eventually these reports reached the ears of an official of the Mamluk authorities called Ayyub, in the Hijri year 722 (roughly equivalent to 1322 CE).

"Ayyub was the kind of official all thinking men dread," Şinasi writes, "small-minded and petty, pedantic and intolerant. He harboured a particular hatred of Christians, and on hearing a Crusader lived openly among the faithful, vowed to root him out."

Ayyub made his way to Khirbat Karraza, where the villagers told him the Templar had haunted the hill for many years, but kept company with an evil spirit, who instructed him in the black arts; therefore the villagers had left him well alone, and advised Ayyub to do likewise.

"Of course," writes Şinasi, "he ignored them completely, and went out to the hill with several armed men to capture or slay the infidel. You will be unsurprised to learn that they never returned – at least, not alive, or whole. Their dismembered corpses were found outside the

village the following morning. The mysterious Templar was never seen again, but to this day the inhabitants of Khirbat Karraza avoid the hill, especially by night."

Lake Tiberias is one of the names by which the Sea of Galilee was known. The Bedouin village of Khirbat Karraza, which was ethnically cleansed by the Israeli Palmach in 1948, was built on the site of a far older settlement: a town known as Chorazin.

PART THREE:
The Children of Saturn

54.

Jenna turned, but Zoe and Angela were on the drive behind them, just out of arm's reach and both holding cattle-prods. On the street itself, a plain white van had pulled up alongside the Land Rover; Greasy Hair and Redbeard stood beside it.

All four orderlies sported the scars of their last encounter: Angela's eyes were still red, a purple bruise had flowered spectacularly along Zoe's jaw, and both Redbeard and Greasy Hair moved stiffly. None looked particularly good-humoured, and Jenna suspected they'd gladly embrace any chance to deliver some payback.

Still, she could hit Zoe or Angela with a good kick from this range, she reckoned. Knock them into the other companion, then try to tackle Whitecliffe–

"Jenn," said Holly.

She turned and saw Whitecliffe's right hand had come out of her pocket and now hovered at hip-level; in it was a small black automatic pistol. She pointed it, not at Jenna, but at Holly. "Walther PPK," she said cheerfully, "just like James Bond. Hardly a cannon, but I'm told it'll make quite a mess, so you'll behave yourself, Jenna, won't you?"

She remained very still, arms at her sides, as Zoe and Angela moved in close. She felt a cattle-prod dig into her back, saw Holly flinch as the same thing happened to her.

"I'm afraid your friend Leonard won't be joining us, Miss Finn," said Whitecliffe. "Someone made him an offer he couldn't refuse. A bit of stick and carrot: beer money for a week, or the mother of all beatings. He saw reason." She motioned towards the van. "Now, if you'd be so kind?"

She slipped her hand back into her pocket, but the barrel of the Walther pushed the fabric outwards, still angled towards Holly. Jenna turned, fumbling for Holly's hand, and the two of them went back up the drive, bracketed by Zoe and Angela. The front door shut behind them as Whitecliffe followed.

Greasy Hair got behind the wheel; everyone else got into the back of the van. Inside were bench seats, one of them with soft restraints for the wrists and ankles; Redbeard, grunting and wincing in pain, secured first Jenna and then Holly to it, while the others stood ready to intervene as necessary.

"Right, then," said Whitecliffe, rapping on the screen that hid the driver's cabin from them. "Home, James, and don't spare the horses."

The engine started, and the van managed a clumsy three-point turn, then rumbled back along the road.

"Well," Whitecliffe said, "you two really have caused me a good deal of inconvenience. Still, nothing that can't be fixed. Minor property damage and minor injuries to four employees–"

"I don't know about minor," growled Redbeard, glowering at Jenna.

"Nothing life-threatening, at least," said Whitecliffe, then smirked at Jenna. "As I'm sure you'll be sorry to hear."

"I'll try harder next time."

Whitecliffe laughed. "I do genuinely like you, Jenna."

"Didn't we agree it was Ms McKnight?"

"I apologise. You did express that preference, but I feel I know you rather well by now."

"So you know my choice, but you're ignoring it and doing what you want anyway? Yeah, that sounds like you."

"I suppose I walked into that one."

"And as for knowing me, piss off."

Whitecliffe sighed. "Swearing is a sign of a limited vocabulary, Jenna."

"It's always been my profound conviction that such an assertion is, *ipso facto*, a classic example of absolute fucking bullshit," said Jenna.

Holly gave her a wan half-smile, and Whitecliffe chuckled again. "Well, as far as knowing you goes, I believe I'm far closer than when we last spoke. I offered financial inducements to persuade you then. Not enough. You're very self-sufficient, aren't you? From having to make your way in the world alone. Privation's nothing new to you. And emotionally you've always been the same, haven't you? Doesn't take a genius to diagnose abandonment issues, fear of commitment and so on. All those short-term relationships. Always walking away when things got too entangling. Hm?" Whitecliffe looked at Holly. "And yet."

Holly didn't reply, shoulders hunched, eyes lowered. Whitecliffe studied her in silence for almost a minute, then returned her gaze to Jenna and smiled. "Do you know the saying 'give me a place to stand, and I will move the world'?"

"No."

"You disappoint me. Archimedes of Syracuse said it, over two thousand years ago. Remarkable man. Know anything about him?"

"Wasn't he the one who shouted *Eureka*?"

"Glad you retained some details. Yes, *Eureka* – meaning 'I've got it'. 'It' being the Archimedean Principle: the displacement of water. But there was more, much more. He invented Archimedes' Screw – *not* a sexual technique, before you make the obvious tiresome jokes, but a means of raising water from one level to another. And the basis for the modern propellor. He even, supposedly, built a heat-ray, using parabolic mirrors, to burn Roman ships attacking Syracuse – two thousand years ago, remember. A man of parts, as you see. But that particular quotation refers to Archimedes' work on levers."

"Levers," repeated Jenna.

"Archimedes didn't *invent* the lever, of course, but he was the first to prove the principle mathematically. Hence his quotation. Given a fixed point and something to lift with, you can move almost anything to where you want it to go. It's all a question of – well. Leverage."

Whitecliffe looked, again, at Holly.

"Fucking hell, Jenn," Holly managed at last. "Think she's trying to drop a hint?"

"Ah, it speaks," said Whitecliffe. "I should really be very cross with you, Ms Finn, but in fact I'm grateful. After some initial complications, you've actually made my job considerably easier. As I said, Jenna, I'd rather do this *with* your cooperation than without, but you will insist on always having your way, won't you? That matters to you more than almost anything else." This time her glance at Holly was so brief Jenna might have missed it had she blinked. "Almost."

"Fine," said Jenna. "You've made your point."

"Oh, good," said Whitecliffe. "So?"

Inevitable it would come to this, in the end; it'd always only been a matter of time before Whitecliffe worked out how to force Jenna's compliance. No guarantee, of course, that she'd keep her word, but at least she wasn't James: once she had what she wanted, she wouldn't need Jenna or Holly anymore, and was too well-connected to fear retribution.

She might just as easily decide to tie up any loose ends.

But Whitecliffe wanted to see herself as fair and rational, a healer, pro-choice. Much easier to do that if Jenna was paid off and released with documents proving her consent. Whitecliffe's version of events would be so convincing, with time she might believe it herself. Even Jenna might.

"Jenna?" said Whitecliffe, politely.

"Babe?" said Holly, in a tiny voice.

"Fine." There was enough give in the soft restraints that Jenna could reach out and take Holly's hand. "Whatever you want, as long as you let us go afterwards."

"Of course. And amply remunerated, as promised. There'll be forms for you to sign, of course."

"Of course."

"Cheer up, Jenna. Once we get through all this, you'll never have to worry about unplanned pregnancy again, and you'll be rich. Well, relatively." Whitecliffe beamed. "So glad we could reach an accommodation. Knew you'd be reasonable in the end."

Jenna turned away from Whitecliffe. Holly looked up at her. Those eyes. She never wanted to stop looking into those eyes. She leant forward, resting her forehead against Holly's, the tip of Holly's nose brushing hers; they stayed like that for the rest of the journey. Shutting out Whitecliffe, shutting out the world.

Gravel crunched under the van wheels, snapping Jenna out of her reverie. She sat up, blinking. Holly's hand slipped from hers.

"Home again, home again, jiggety-jig," said Whitecliffe. "Now, we're going to remove the restraints and let you walk to the clinic under your own steam. Escorted, of course. I'm trusting you to be sensible now."

Only the barest hint of a threat. That was all there needed to be.

The van ground to a halt, gravel crackling underneath. Greasy Hair stood up, painfully, and unlocked the van doors. Angela unfastened Holly's restraints, Zoe Jenna's. Redbeard hung back and watched, a hand in his pocket, no doubt waiting for the chance to whip out some unpleasant surprise, like a cattle-prod, or a baton of his own.

Whitecliffe motioned to the door. "After you. Guests first."

Jenna stood, stiff and awkward, then stepped out of the van onto the gravel forecourt in front of Stonebrook. Behind her the lawn she'd seen before gleamed in the moonlight, with the trees black bristling shadows at the perimeter. *Fucking trees again.* Jenna grimaced, turned away and helped Holly down.

"As you see, we like to keep things nice and private."
Whitecliffe stepped down and stretched. "Shall we?"

She marched round the front of the van; reluctantly, Jenna
and Holly followed, the orderlies trailing after them towards
Stonebrook.

It almost looked like an ordinary farmhouse from the
outside, with its whitewashed walls and warm-lit windows,
except for the fire escapes on either side of the building,
and one other detail: instead of a normal-sized front door, it
boasted a pair of heavy oak double doors that wouldn't have
looked out of place on a castle. Those were the only hint
at how extensively the interior had been remodelled to fit
Whitecliffe's needs.

The main doors led into a wide reception area with a desk
– unoccupied, of course, as the clinic wasn't officially open
yet – to one side. The reception area wasn't what Jenna
had expected, though; she'd thought it would be white and
antiseptic-looking, but instead it had been designed with an
old-fashioned, almost Victorian feel, with a marble floor and
oak-panelled walls. There was a marble bust on either side of
the staircase leading to the upper floors, and oil paintings on
the walls. The subjects were exclusively women, in settings
ranging from classical antiquity to the modern.

Whitecliffe indicated the busts. "The one on the left
represents Peseshet, lady overseer of female physicians in
Egypt's Old Kingdom, two and a half thousand years before
the supposed birth of Christ. Earliest woman in medicine in
recorded history. On the right, Ubartum of Garšana, female
physician from the Third Dynasty of Ur in Mesopotamia –
around 2075 BC." Whitecliffe's normal bluff demeanour
had disappeared: there was something close to reverence in
her voice. She motioned to the portraits, going left to right.
"Agemede of Elis, a physician from the twelfth century BC,
before the Trojan War. According to Homer, she knew the
healing powers of every plant on Earth. Agnodice of Athens,

fourth century BC. Had to disguise herself as a man to learn and practise medicine; when she was exposed as a woman, the Athenian women she'd treated defended her so fiercely the law was changed to allow women to practise medicine. Metrodora – a comparative latecomer, hailing from between the second and fourth century AD. Like the busts, these portraits are exercises in imagination. We've no idea what these women really looked like."

All the women in the portraits, Jenna noted, bore a striking resemblance to Whitecliffe herself.

"All we know of Metrodora," Whitecliffe droned on, warming to her theme, "is that she wrote *On the Diseases and Cures of Women* – the first female-authored medical text. Next we have Hildegard of Bingen…"

Jenna did her best to tune her out.

"…and, of course, Marie Stopes and Helen Brook," Whitecliffe finally concluded. "As ever, we stand on the shoulders of giants."

"Wonder what they'd make of you?" said Holly.

Whitecliffe glared, her mouth tightening; for once, a barb had hit home.

"Then again, wasn't Marie Stopes into eugenics?" Holly went on. "Wanted to sterilise mixed-race kids? Not exactly pro-choice there. She'd probably be well into all this–"

Whitecliffe wheeled on her, half-raising a hand, then lowered it with a brittle chuckle. "Point to you, Ms Finn," she said. "But we should move on to more important matters. This way, Jenna."

"Hey, wait a minute – get off, you–"

Jenna turned: Holly was being restrained by Redbeard and Greasy Hair. She stepped towards them, but Angela and Zoe gripped her upper arms. "Let's not be *silly*," said Whitecliffe. "No harm will come to Ms Finn, Jenna, if you're sensible. But my instruction only applied to you. This leg of the journey, I'm afraid, is yours and yours alone. And, Ms Finn," she added, as

Holly drew breath to cry out, "all either of you'll achieve by screaming or making any other kind of scene is to irritate me profoundly. Along with the ladies and gentlemen I've entrusted with your welfare." Whitecliffe indicated the orderlies.

"What happened to our agreement?" said Jenna, trying to gauge how quickly she could break free from Zoe and Angela. As if guessing her thoughts, they tightened their grip on her arms.

"My dear Jenna, I've done nothing to break it. Keep your side of the bargain, and neither of you will be harmed. But we need to prepare you for treatment, and I've no hesitation saying you're fit for it by now. The sooner it's done, the sooner you can both be on your way."

"So what's this?"

Whitecliffe sighed. "Jenna, I'm many things, but stupid isn't one of them. Both you and Miss Finn are intelligent and resourceful young women, and each of you is a thundering great headache in your own right. I'm not compounding the problem by letting you conspire together. You can see Ms Finn after we've begun treatment – for a time, under supervision. That arrangement will continue throughout your stay, until you're both released. All right?"

"And meanwhile, I'm a hostage for her good behaviour?" said Holly.

"As I said, intelligent," said Whitecliffe. "Now, shall we proceed?"

Redbeard and Greasy Hair began marching Holly up the stairs; Zoe and Angela steered Jenna towards a door on the right-hand side of the reception area.

"Love you," said Holly, as the orderlies hustled Jenna away.

"Love you too," Jenna called back.

She didn't look back. Her face was burning, her eyes filling up, and she couldn't have seen Holly's face and held herself together, not then.

55.

The door itself was solid oak, in keeping with the surrounding décor, but with a reader beside it, through which Whitecliffe swiped a card. A series of locks *clunk*ed. The door opened, and Whitecliffe motioned them through, into a white-walled vestibule with a uPVC door. This door had glass panels, reinforced by wire mesh.

"We like to present our newly arrived patients with a comfortable, olde-worlde sort of setting," Whitecliffe explained. "It seems to put them at their ease. But beyond this point, our only concern is clinical excellence, as you'll see."

She swiped her card at the second door, then led them through into a corridor. There was a door on either side, and a fire escape at the far end. "We've two rooms for patients on each floor. We also offer two *types* of patient accommodation. You experienced the comforts of the first on your initial stay." Whitecliffe swiped her card again, at a reader beside the first door. "Now you'll experience the second."

The room they pushed Jenna into was very different to the one she'd originally occupied. White and windowless, the only furnishing a bed, which, like every other surface in the room, was solidly padded.

"Necessary precaution, I'm afraid," said Whitecliffe. "Some people resort to desperate measures. I did tell you, you might recall, that we had facilities for difficult patients. For their own good, of course. Now, if you wouldn't mind undressing?"

Jenna minded considerably but had very little choice, with Angela and Zoe both present. She stripped, dropping the clothes on the floor in as untidy a pile as she could, refusing to be embarrassed or ashamed.

Not like you've ever been shy before.

True enough: she'd had an active love-life, plus a few stints as a life model for art classes. But in those instances she'd had a choice, unlike now. If it was the price of Holly's survival, then under those terms, and those alone, she'd do as they told her. But she didn't have to do so gracefully. So she stepped back, hands on hips and chin cocked, and presented herself to Whitecliffe and the rest. "See anything you like, girls?"

Zoe coughed and looked down; even Whitecliffe, Jenna noted with spiteful amusement, had turned pink. "Yes, Jenna, we can all see you're in splendid physical shape. Now, if you'd just put on this gown?"

A small victory, and while she hadn't been looking for an ego-boost, the "splendid physical shape" remark gave Jenna a welcome one nonetheless. She did her best not to smile too openly as she put on the gown. Angela gathered her clothes up, unlocked a compartment on the underside of the bed, and stuffed the clothes inside before relocking it and handing Whitecliffe the key.

"Ah, thank you. And if you'll just put your paw print on these?" Whitecliffe handed Jenna a clipboard with a white ballpoint pen attached to it by a chain. "Sign at the bottom of each sheet."

Jenna didn't bother reading the documents. No doubt she'd regret it later, but it wasn't as though she had any choice.

Being up the duff does not *agree with you.* Holly had been right about that, but neither did being so manipulable. Not that Holly was exactly a damsel in distress – but if (*when*, she told herself) they got out of here, Jenna was signing her up for some Muay Thai classes.

Didn't exactly keep you *out of trouble, did they?*

Eric might have thought differently, Jenna reminded herself.

"Splendid." Whitecliffe took the clipboard back. "You can go."

A bizarre statement under the circumstances, till Jenna realised she meant the orderlies. They filed out; the door clicked shut behind them.

Jenna looked around the featureless room. "Alone at last, eh?"

"I'd better point out that, as before, you're on TV." Whitecliffe indicated a camera in the ceiling corner. "Any aggressive move on your part will provoke an immediate response."

"I'm sure it will." Jenna grinned. "Will it be quick enough to help you, though?"

Whitecliffe took a small step back. "I thought we had an agreement, Jenna."

"We do," said Jenna, although she was already doubting the wisdom of having accepted it – however little choice she'd had – or the likelihood of Whitecliffe adhering to it.

"Because it won't just be you who bears the consequences of any untoward behaviour."

"Yeah, I got that."

"If you wish to be reunited with Ms Finn–"

"I said I *get* it, doc." Jenna was pleased to see Whitecliffe's face tighten at "doc". "Just joking."

"Were you? But I've admittedly been accused of lacking humour."

"You do surprise me."

Whitecliffe sighed. "I'll be along later to give you a brief physical. Eaten today?"

Jenna realised she hadn't; strangely she hadn't felt hungry before, despite the various calorie-burning activities she and Holly had engaged in, but now she was ravenous and her stomach growled. "No."

"I'll have something brought to you. And some bottled water. Got to keep hydrated. Don't do anything silly with it."

"Like what, masturbate?"

Whitecliffe rolled her eyes. "Your sense of humour can be a little tedious after a while."

"What can I tell you? I've got a one-track mind."

"A dirt track, it would seem."

"You sound just like my mum there. Careful about that, doc. Look what happened to her."

Jenna couldn't tell if the comparison amused Whitecliffe or unsettled her. "Pleasant as this banter is, I must leave you for the time being. Someone wishes to see you."

Jenna frowned. "Who?"

Whitecliffe gave her a small, cold smile. "I'll let them introduce themselves, I think. See you shortly, Jenna."

"Hey, hang on–" But Whitecliffe, having had the last word, swiped her card in the door lock and swept out. The door clunked behind her.

The room was very quiet. Soundproofed, no doubt. *In Stonebrook, no one can hear you scream.* The silence felt loud, somehow, and along with the glaring whiteness, seemed to press in on her. She'd heard of a room somewhere that was so soundproof you could hear nothing but your own breathing and heartbeat, that no one could bear to be in for more than a minute or two. She pulled her knees up to her chest and hugged them tightly.

White silence. The only break in the whiteness, apart from Jenna's own skin, was the black dot of the video camera lens: even the camera casing was white.

Sensory deprivation, like at the cottage. James had used a dark cellar, Whitecliffe a white, clinical room, but the purpose and intended result were the same: to break her down, erode her will to resist.

She might keep you here for as many weeks or months as this takes, babe. Till your brain melts and you're ready for the gibber academy.

The gibber academy: Jenna smiled, then realised that to anyone watching through the camera she'd look as if she were already starting to unravel. Besides, it wasn't a pleasant thought: her one guarantee of freedom was Whitecliffe's word.

There was nothing to do but wait, so, hugging her knees, she sat back against the wall and waited.

Someone wants to see you.

The soundproofing in the room – the cell, really; might as well call it what it was – cut off all sound from the corridor outside, so there were no approaching footsteps, just the abrupt *clunk* of the lock, gunshot-loud. Jenna started, nearly falling off the bed.

Redbeard came in with a chair, smirking at her. Jenna thought of Holly in his and Greasy's care and clenched her fists, but that only made him grin the wider. She was helpless and he knew it. *Let Holly be okay. Let them not have hurt her.* She'd not only hurt Redbeard, but humiliated him as well. He'd want revenge.

Redbeard set the chair down a short distance from the bed and went out. Whitecliffe stood in the doorway, beside a squat, broad-shouldered man about a head shorter than her. "Here she is." She motioned towards Jenna and smiled coldly. "Your visitor, Jenna. Do try to be polite."

The squat man crossed the threshold, and the door *clunk*ed shut behind him. He put his hands in his pockets and smiled, not speaking.

He was almost fascinatingly ugly, heavy-browed and bulbous-nosed with loose thick lips, snaggly yellow teeth and a prognathous jaw. He had tangled, slightly wavy brown hair, complete with sideburns, that framed jowly cheeks, a dewlapped chin and a low, sloping forehead, together with watery brown eyes. But his smile was amiable enough and, when he spoke, his voice was warm and pleasant.

"So," he said, "you're Jenna. May I sit?"

Jenna answered with a shrug; the visitor moved towards the chair. His clothes, she saw, were something of a mishmash: brown loafers on sockless feet, grey corduroy trousers and plain white t-shirt, a pinstripe suit jacket thrown over the top. None of them fit particularly well: the trousers and jacket were baggy, the t-shirt too tight. The first impression was of a homeless man wearing charity-shop cast-offs, but the clothes were clean and he seemed self-assured and confident to an almost unsettling degree.

He lowered himself into the chair, resting his hands on its arms with the air of a king assuming his throne, his heavy chin raised as he studied her. The performance grated on Jenna. She unclasped her knees and straightened her legs, trying to assume a more relaxed position.

"Well?" she said, after a few more long, uncomfortable seconds. "Do I pass inspection?"

The visitor laughed. "Oh, I love it," he said. "They told me you had – what did Dr Whitecliffe call it? – 'the attitude problem from Hell'. But I like it, I really do. It has a certain charm."

"I'm so glad," she said. "I live for the approval of complete strangers."

"It's a special kind of attitude, though," he said. "Not just petulance or ego. That's cheap. That's everywhere. Spoilt children, basically. Like James Frobisher. I'm sorry not to have intervened earlier with him; his treatment of you put your life at risk more than once, and all because of his wounded ego." He sighed. "I ought to have let Dr Whitecliffe take matters in hand from the first. I have had to eat a certain amount of humble pie there. She'd have done what was necessary quickly, efficiently, with a minimum of fuss or drama, and we'd all have what we wanted by now."

His English was perfect and with no accent she could identify, but here and there was an odd inflection on a vowel, a consonant pronounced a fraction harder or softer than necessary. English might not be his first language, but if so he'd learned it long ago, and spent a great deal of time getting it right. "Would we?" Jenna said.

"You'd have money. That always makes life better. Far too

much of my time's spent in ensuring my financial security for the foreseeable future. Spending one's immortality in a condition of poverty really isn't to be countenanced. But of course, you're different, aren't you, Jenna McKnight? You have *will*. Determination. A refusal to be broken. To yield. James Frobisher couldn't hold you, or the good doctor. You escaped each time."

"Had a little help the second time around."

"True. But what kind of person inspires such devotion? I doubt your little lover ever did anything so daring in her life, or would've if she hadn't met you."

"Wouldn't bet on it," Jenna said, feeling a need to leap to Holly's defence.

The visitor shrugged, dismissing the question. "Doesn't matter, anyway. Are you saying you wouldn't have broken out of here if she hadn't done it for you? No answer? I thought not."

The visitor gnawed a hangnail, then wiped his hand on the pinstripe jacket. "But what really impressed me was your conduct in the Greylands. That showed real skill. Natural talent. Most people couldn't have accomplished what you have with years of training…"

He trailed off, and seemed to hesitate. Then he smirked again. "If your ancestry wasn't already beyond dispute," he said, "that would've told me whose descendant you were."

"You're better-looking in person, I'll say that for you," Jenna said. "That isn't saying much, mind, but at least you don't have the same BO problem."

He laughed. "You really don't care, do you? Or pretend not to." The smile dimmed. "Except about Holly Finn, of course. Makes a nice change. Greed is most people's Achilles heel. Refreshing to find someone for whom it's actually love. I imagine that surprised you as much as it did everyone else."

Jenna didn't answer; he was uncomfortably close to the truth there, and she didn't want to concede the point.

Then change the subject, babe.

"So what do I call you?" she said.

The visitor leant back, drumming his fingers lightly on the chair arms. "I have to admit rather liking the name you came up with: the Bonewalker. It does have a certain ring. The real one isn't quite so evocative. But, for the record, it's Robert. Robert de Lavoie. *Sir* Robert, in fact, but I won't stand on my title. I know you don't set much store by those."

When she didn't speak, he frowned. "No questions?"

"Plenty," she said. "But I doubt you could answer them."

"Why not try me?"

"No point."

De Lavoie pursed his lips. Obviously not the reaction he'd expected. "I thought you'd want to meet me, at least. The real me, not the form I took in the Greylands."

"Not really," she said. "You know what really gets me about people like you?"

He looked amused. "There *are* no people like me, Jenna. Well, maybe one or two, but I doubt you've ever met them."

"I've met plenty," she said. "Seen a lot of you out in the world, or on the news. Even dated a few, worse luck. You think you're so fascinating and original and important, and you know what, you're fucking *boring*. Think every time you fart it's special."

"Is that so?" said de Lavoie.

"And you think it's everyone else who's boring, don't you? Only good for what you get out of them. Just take, take, take, then shit it out. And that's it. *All* you do. *Ever*. And then you bang on to anyone who can't get away from you fast enough about how fucking *amazing* you and your turds are."

He wasn't smiling anymore, and spoke more sharply. "Well, aren't you knowledgeable, after one-and-a-half score years on this earth?"

"That's the thing, you see," Jenna said. "It's not about how much time you've got. And you know what the funniest thing of all is?"

"Please, enlighten me." De Lavoie's irritation seemed to have dissipated, and his voice was an easy drawl once more.

"You don't get that, and you taught it me."

"Did I?" He was amused again, like an adult listening to a child explaining who's who at their doll's tea party.

Jenna leant forward. "I had this safe, comfy little life – private school, nice home, didn't want for anything. But then you killed Mum, and everything changed, pretty much overnight. Dad fell apart. We lost everything, and then I was all on my own. Had been even before Dad died really, state he was in, but I *knew*, by then, nothing was guaranteed. No point making plans. What mattered was today. Not wasting the time you've got. So yeah, thirty years, but I've used them."

"Really? A few drawings, and an awful lot of fornication? Is that really an achievement?"

Jenna remembered stopping on Dinas Oleu, sitting beside Holly and passing the bottled water back and forth, looking out to sea. *"I don't think that we should have to earn beauty / it's just that / sweat sweetens it."* The beauty and stillness, the peace of that moment. Feeling close to something essential. Seconds that lasted forever. "Moments," she said. "Little moments of beauty, connection, love…" She groped for the word. "Grace," she said at last. "And the sad thing is, you don't even know what I'm talking about."

She'd forced herself to maintain eye contact with de Lavoie throughout; a mocking smirk had been on his lips, but when she said "Grace" it fell away and she glimpsed something close to pain, before anger replaced it. Then all emotion vanished from his face, as if he'd wiped a blackboard clean. "You really do presume, Jenna. You've had thirty years, and how many of those were wasted as a baby, an infant, a child? How many of them were *real*? And you think you got more out of those that I have out of over seven hundred?"

"Seven hundred? Really?"

"So you *are* curious," said de Lavoie, smirking again. "Well, then, I'll tell you."

56.

"Know much about the Knights Templar?" de Lavoie said.

Jenna shrugged.

"All right: a quick history lesson. The Templars were a military Catholic order, founded in the twelfth century to protect pilgrims in the Holy Land and defend the kingdom of Jerusalem. They grew into one of the wealthiest and most powerful organizations in medieval Europe, before being accused of heresy, sodomy, devil-worship and any other nonsense the pope and the king of France could concoct between them, then slaughtered and suppressed, enabling their accusers to steal all they had. Oh, books could be written about the Templars, and of course many have been. Sadly, most of them are absolute rubbish. The important thing is that I was one of them, up until the year of Our Lord – well, your Lord, anyway, as I doubt He'd want much to do with me anymore, if He existed, but fortunately he doesn't."

"I'm gripped," said Jenna. "Is there a point to this?"

"Of course there is. The year, as I was saying, was 1302. Jerusalem had long since fallen, and Acre. The Templars had established a stronghold on Cyprus, but they still had one last toehold in the so-called Holy Land, a little rock called Ruad, off the coast of what's now called Syria. They used it as a staging area to launch raids on the coast – and eventually, they hoped, to invade the Holy Land again." De Lavoie sighed and shook his head. "Pipe dreams, really. That time was past. In 1302, the Mamluk Sultan

Al-Nasir Muhammad sent a fleet to take Ruad back, under the command of his viceroy, Sayf al-Din Salar. To cut a long story short, they won. I remember it well, Jenna; I was there."

He told her of the Beast of Chorazin, whose mummified remains became known as Baphomet, the so-called Idol of the Templars; how the reliquaries had been recaptured from the Mamluks, brought to Ruad and put into the care of Jean de Messins, to be transported to Cyprus. How the Mamluk attack and the siege of the island had prevented this, and how de Messins had died before the siege's end.

"Marshal de Quincy – our commander – had to appoint another custodian to take de Messins' place. At which point a young Templar knight called Robert de Lavoie–" he gestured modestly to himself "–enters the story."

"So this creature was a thing like you?" said Jenna.

"Jenna!" De Lavoie looked piqued; after so many centuries, he was probably used to having things his way. "You've spoiled my big reveal. Yes, it was immortal. And it offered me the same gift in exchange for its freedom."

"I was never great at maths, but the Templars were founded in the twelfth century, right?"

"Glad you've been paying attention."

"But this siege was two hundred years later, right? Don't you have to eat a descendant every thirteen?"

"The creature had entered a kind of… stasis. Like a coma, or more accurately, hibernation. It would resurface at intervals – usually at any change in circumstances that might give it a chance of escape. If you've no further questions, I'll tell you about that."

"Naughty me." Jenna slapped herself on the wrist. "Sorry, mush, on you go."

De Lavoie scowled; then an amused, reluctant smile briefly touched his lips. "None of the surviving brethren had anything like de Messins' knowledge of demonology, but that wasn't what de Quincy required. De Messins had made certain the remains were secure, so what was needed was someone thoroughly trustworthy who wasn't about to drop dead. I was chosen. I was the youngest sworn brother in the garrison. Despite the siege, I was still strong, fit and in good health, and de Quincy had no reason to doubt my faith."

"I'm guessing he should've."

De Lavoie sighed theatrically. "I'm afraid so. A Templar Knight's soul was meant to be as armoured by his unyielding faith as his body was by steel, so neither man nor demon could prevail over him. But my faith hadn't just weakened during the siege; it had collapsed altogether. I don't know why. It had seemed perfect before, and other men have come through worse with theirs intact. Heaven and Hell, God and the Devil were all just pretty stories; the reality was blood and meat and guts, and death the end of all. I was honestly terrified, convinced I'd wasted my life on foolishness, that the only life I'd ever know was now about to end. I couldn't tell my brother knights that, couldn't even bring myself to confess such appalling treason of the soul to our chaplain. Least of all could I admit it to the marshal. So I lied and told de Quincy my faith remained secure."

De Lavoie stood and stretched. "Unpleasant place, this. Sets the teeth on edge. Anyway, my duties regarding the remains were simple enough: I just had to pack the reliquaries safely in straw inside locked wooden chests, then ensure they reached Cyprus undamaged. There were seven of them in all; I put off handling the one containing the head till last, as it was a truly unlovely thing to behold. But eventually it had to be done, and so I went to pack it away in its straw. And I would have, without incident, except that was when it spoke to me."

"It spoke?" Jenna was interested in spite of herself.

"I told you, it was still alive – after a fashion. What was left of its eyes moved in their sockets – they made little noises, I remember, like twigs brushing over dry stone. And the lips moved and it spoke – whispered, really, having no lungs, but I heard it. It said: *De Dampierre will kill you all.*"

De Lavoie grunted again. "I dropped the case, and the glass shattered. I probably would have whatever it had said – the fact it spoke at all was the horror of it – but as I stood looking down at it, the import of its actual words sank in. Hugh de Dampierre, you see, was the knight negotiating promise of safe conduct with Salar. Like many of my brethren, I'd never had much faith in that to begin with, but we'd all been clinging to the hope it was genuine. And for me, at least, that sentence had dashed it.

"I went to put the head in its wooden chest, but it spoke again. *But you do not have to die*, it said. Then, last of all: *There is a way to live forever*."

Seconds of white silence ticked by.

"The Rite of Cronos," Jenna said. "Right?"

"Just so. I needed only to uncase the creature's fragments and place them together to restore it. In exchange, it would help me escape, and teach me its secret." De Lavoie sighed. "I'd like to tell you I agonised over the decision, but de Quincy had chosen his man badly. And Keret had chosen well."

"That was its name?"

A curt nod. "It – he, rather – was a man of limited ambition. Just wanted to rule his little hill at Chorazin. His territory, you see. Also, his descendants populated the surrounding area, so he had a vested interest in protecting his food supply."

"And he really kept his word?"

"Well, I'm here, aren't I? It was a different world, I suppose. Honour, the given word – they meant something then. To Keret, if not to Sayf al-Din Salar."

Nor to Robert de Lavoie, Jenna suspected – not anymore, if it ever had done. For all his protestations, she trusted his promises of safety even less than Whitecliffe's. But she could do nothing about that.

Or perhaps she could.

How do you reckon that?

She ignored the voice, and kept listening.

"Although his body didn't move," de Lavoie continued, "Keret had long ago learned to walk between the sacred silence and sleep, as he called it. The realm between dream and death."

"The Greylands?" said Jenna. "Right?"

"That's another word for them. Reality there's very – pliable – as you've discovered. With time you can bend it to your will, even make a home there. And from it, project a version of yourself back into the waking world. As I did by the river in Scotland, to save you."

"And to kill my mother," Jenna said, remembering Tallstone Hill.

De Lavoie shrugged. "I giveth and I taketh away."

"So, the Greylands–" Jenna began, but he cut her off.

"I shan't apologise for what I am, Jenna, or what I've done to survive. Why should I? When have you ever done so? We are what we are. We do what we must; we do what we *want*, and make whatever justifications are necessary after the fact, to others or ourselves. And consider how easily you could have become just another bovine suburban housewife. Instead you stand, independent, yourself alone and no one else. If anything, you should be grateful to me for setting you on that path."

"Grateful?" Jenna clenched her fists and made to get off the bed. De Lavoie stepped towards her, daring her to attack, all humour wiped from his face, the brown eyes emptied of emotion.

"Certainly," he said. "If nothing else, you should be grateful you don't have to die, or even have to worry about my coming for you in the future. Our arrangement today protects you from that. Think you can control yourself now?"

Reluctantly, Jenna subsided, and de Lavoie smiled pleasantly again. "Once I'd reassembled his parts, Keret projected a form similar to the one you call the Bonewalker, out into his lands around Chorazin, to seek out one of his descendants and absorb them. That was enough to restore part of his strength – enough, at least, to transport us both from Ruad to his mountain. He had to 'feed' again several times after that, to make up for lost time. But having done so, he was restored to his fullest strength, and my instruction began. That took several years. Out of I'm not sure what – sentiment, perhaps, or some vestige of conscience now long-dead – I still wore my Templar's armour, which I believe gave rise to a quaint little legend in the area. Especially after Keret and I had to deal with an annoying Mamluk official who insisted on poking his nose into our affairs... but I digress. Naturally, before I could perform the rite I had to sow my wild oats as far afield as possible, and amass enough worldly wealth to do so safely on my travels. Unlike Keret, I intended to see the world. Besides, it made more sense to spread my seed as widely as I could – I'd seen how quickly war could wipe out a bloodline."

"And you still underestimated it," Jenna pointed out.

"Mankind grows ever more inventive at destroying himself. Anyway, I fucked my way from the Levant to the Balkans, then across Europe to England, where I finally performed the Rite of Cronos and became immortal. The rest–" de Lavoie made a deep, theatrical bow "–is history."

He stood as if awaiting applause; when none came, he sat back down. "Still no questions for me, Jenna?"

"Maybe a couple."

"Well, ask away. This is your big chance. We shan't see one another again."

"You've been around for, what, seven hundred years now?"

"I was twenty-one years old when Ruad fell. Seven hundred and forty years."

"So what have you done with it?"

He frowned. "I'm not sure I understand."

"You've got forever, so what have you done with it? Have you been an artist, a philosopher? A poet? A scientist? What have you done?"

"Must I justify my existence with accomplishments? Where would that leave you, Jenna, with your scribbled drawings and sexual escapades? Or must we fall back on your so-called 'moments of grace'? I've seen empires rise and fall, seen the religion I once embraced dwindle and shrink, while I live in ease and comfort and slip away fast should danger even threaten. What else is there?"

"Apart from the danger of running out of descendants," she pointed out.

"Now remedied."

"Not yet."

His eyes narrowed. "It's about to be. I hope you're not contemplating anything *silly*, Jenna. Easy enough to put you under restraint until they're ready for you – which won't be long now. And besides, your precious little Holly would pay the price if you made anything go wrong."

"True."

De Lavoie smiled. "Anyway, it's been nice to meet you, Jenna McKnight. If there's nothing else–"

"Just one thing."

He sighed and sat back down. "Well?"

"What happens to you when the sun goes out?"

"What?"

"I mean, one day the sun's going to die. Right? All the stars will. The galaxy, the universe. The Heat Death, they call it. Nothing'll be left alive. No descendants, nothing. Just you alone in all that cold and silence, until your last thirteen years are up. And then it'll be over. It'll be cold and lonely, and you'll be all by yourself, and what do you think that'll be like? Did Keret ever tell you that, Robbie?"

De Lavoie looked disgusted. "Do *not* call me 'Robbie'."

"Did Keret ever tell you how immortals die?"

De Lavoie looked at her for a long time; finally he smiled, but there was something forced about it, and something in his eyes. She'd got to him there, left something that would fester and nag. Maybe not deeply or long, but she would, at least, have left some sort of mark. She remembered how the Bonewalker bellowed and roared, stamped and smashed around the Greylands in search of her, like a furious toddler denied some object of desire. A child afraid of the dark.

"That day," he said, "is far, far off, Jenna McKnight. So far off it's not worth considering. So I don't. And now I must be off. If it makes you feel any better, you never really had a chance. The Templars and Saracens combined couldn't kill Keret, and the wards and seals they used to bind him are long lost. You put up a good fight in the Greylands, but sooner or later I'd have found you there – and through that, found you in what you like to call the real world."

De Lavoie took his hand from his pocket and flicked the powder compact open. The light glinted on the pearlescent surface of the mirror. "I'll keep this, I think, in remembrance of you."

He smiled one last time, made an imperious gesture, and with a *clunk* the door swung open. Robert de Lavoie stepped through it, and it locked behind him, leaving Jenna alone in the white, silent room.

57.

Jenna's best friend at school had been Sarah Warne. Well, more of a frenemy, in retrospect. Often enough she'd turned on Jenna with bouts of vicious teasing, on her own or with other playground bullies; she'd always seen herself as the dominant partner in the friendship and found a dozen ways, subtle or otherwise, to put Jenna in her place.

After Tallstone Hill, everything had changed. Jenna came back to New Colwyn Girls' School different. Her musical tastes were already darker – Kate Nash had given way to Slipknot, Korn and Rammstein – and her dress sense soon changed with it, but even before it showed in her outward appearance, the other girls felt it.

It sparked a kind of mass hysteria: beyond the initial rote expressions of sympathy, the other girls came to regard her as a Jonah. At first they avoided Jenna – even Sarah, after the first week, having seen how the wind blew. But keeping their distance soon wasn't enough: they wanted her gone.

And so the stories started. Jenna McKnight was a weirdo; a devil-worshipper; schizophrenic; a raging lesbo who'd been caught fisting the gym mistress in the staff bogs. Jenna McKnight hung around parks at night looking for boys and sucked their dicks for a fiver. Jenna McKnight's mum had been an escort, murdered by a client. Some stories were petty, some so luridly disgusting they were ludicrous. Anything would do. In a way, their cruelty was its own justification, aiming as it did to brand Jenna as someone vile enough, at least in her accusers' narrow minds, to deserve it.

Jenna had experienced her share of bullying before, though nowhere near as bad as girls like Sunita Duggal, who'd left abruptly in the middle of the previous year having supposedly had a complete breakdown, or Joanna Melnyk, who'd tried to cut her wrists. But in the weeks and months following her return to NCGS, it reached an intensity she'd never known before. It was like pelting a scapegoat with stones, driving it out, away from the tribe; something atavistic they couldn't explain.

Sarah abandoning her as she did, by itself, was hurtful but comprehensible to Jenna; even, in time, forgivable. But Sarah went beyond that, first joining the ranks of Jenna's tormentors, before finally emerging as the cruellest of them all.

Maybe, as Jenna's former friend, she felt a greater need to distance herself. Jenna would never know for sure. What was beyond question was that having known Jenna better than the rest, Sarah had genuine confidences to betray, and could invent stories with far more credibility than others. And she did.

There's no bottom to human cruelty. Jenna learned that during the autumn and winter of 2007, and that the biggest lie told in schools was that bullying would not be tolerated. What they meant, of course – especially in a fee-paying school like NCGS – was any blatant physical sign of it. No black eyes or bloody noses, but the taunts whispered behind Jenna's back in the classroom, or in the library where she sought refuge during lunch breaks, went unpunished and unremarked.

Jenna tried to conceal the hurt, but could never hide it all, and like sharks scenting blood in the water they homed in on any sign of weakness, goading her to an outburst – for which, of course, Jenna was the one punished.

And the cruellest whispers came from Sarah Warne. It was Sarah who'd spread the rumour about Jenna being a lesbian (coincidentally nearer the truth than she'd realised), about Mum being a hooker, about Dad having molested Jenna; Sarah who'd claimed Jenna had once confessed to fucking a dog.

Jenna cried into her pillow at nights, then punched and punched it, imagining those smug hateful faces beneath her fists. But though she often felt as if her mind would snap like an overstretched rubber band, she could never quite bring herself to translate those fantasies into action. Not until Sarah's final story, the one that crossed the line.

As with anything else, the law of diminishing returns applied: once they'd accused her of prostitution, incest and bestiality, going back to *she's a lezzie* or *she's schizophrenic* was something of an anticlimax. They always had to think of something worse, and always did.

Jenna heard Sarah Warne's final contribution to the whisper game second-hand one lunchbreak, from a girl called Sonia Thorpe. Sonia was talking just a little too loud, as people do when they want you to overhear. Jenna remembered the ground falling away, *everything* falling away, and Sonia's voice echoing as though Jenna was at the bottom of a well.

"Tell you what really happened. She killed her mum. She did. Sarah Warne's dad knows one of the policemen who worked on the case. She went mental and did her mum in with an axe."

"Come off it, they wouldn't let her come back here."

"Calling us a liar, Maddy? Well, then. Telling you. That's what the coppers say. Just couldn't prove it. The Warship–" as Mrs Winship, the headmistress, was universally known by the girls "–didn't want her back, but her dad's wadded and said he'd pay for a new school gym–"

For a moment, Jenna was in the car again, cringing paralysed on the front seat as Mum screamed and the stench and cold washed over her. Then there was a blur, and her next memory was of Sonia Thorpe on the ground, Jenna's hand knotted whitely in her hair, and Jenna screaming, *"Fucking lying cunt, who said that, who fucking said that about me,"* into Sonia Thorpe's terrified, sobbing face. Of course, she'd already known, but a part of her hadn't wanted to believe Sarah had gone *there*, said *that*.

Jenna had stood, a hank of Sonia Thorpe's hair in her hand, blood on the roots, then let it drop and began walking towards the far end of the playground, near the tennis courts. Nothing felt real. It was like a dream.

But people got out of her way; they took one look and moved. Except for Sarah Warne and her new cronies, who didn't realise what'd happened at the far end of the playground, or why several teachers and prefects were coming across it after Jenna.

"What you want, weirdo?" one of them said.

"We supposed to be scared?"

"Fuck off, dog-shagger–" Helen Mutinda began and ended. The insult hadn't cut particularly deep, but she wouldn't get out of Jenna's way, so Jenna punched her in the stomach, hard as she could. It was easy, because it took Helen by surprise. Like the others, Helen Mutinda was so used to inflicting pain through whispers, anonymous notes and hateful scrawls on the classroom whiteboard that she'd forgotten there were other methods, simpler and more direct, and very easy to use as long as you didn't let the consequences scare you. And Jenna didn't. Not anymore.

The rules had changed: the other girls, scattering, realised that now. As did Sarah Warne, though far too late to save her.

It took three sixth-form girls and two teachers, including the Warship herself, to drag Jenna away, and six months and two operations before Sarah Warne returned to NCGS. Luckily her parents were rich enough to replace her front teeth, and ensure there were no visible scars.

Jenna was the one punished again, of course, not that she cared about being expelled. She didn't really care about anything by then, having made what she considered the philosophical discovery of the age: nothing mattered, not really. School and exams, after Tallstone Hill, were a pointless, boring game. When something could reach in and take away whatever you had at any given moment, why should you waste a second doing anything you didn't want to, or feeling anything you didn't want to feel? Don't like a situation? Walk away from it. And if the situation was in your head, then you got *out* of your head. You changed your thinking or stopped it altogether. And you put up barriers against other people, barriers like the steel of battleship plating. As Jenna had, till now. Till Holly.

Get drunk, get high, get fucked: it was all a means to an end. All that mattered was *Does it feel good or not?* One thing about your world falling apart: it made coming out a bit easier, in Jenna's case anyway. Tallstone Hill and its aftermath only heightened the absurdity of getting hung up over what your partner had between their legs, or what pronouns they preferred to use.

The rage she'd felt that day had made her capable of anything: it was useful to remember that now. But after Robert de Lavoie had left the room, Jenna had thought of Sarah Warne for another reason. However false a friend she'd proven to be, Sarah had taught Jenna one useful thing, before the summer Mum had died. She'd taught Jenna how to faint.

It was all about your breath, Sarah had told her; you either held it for long enough, or you hyperventilated. From what Jenna recollected, the breath-holding had always worked best for her. She didn't know long she'd be out once she'd fainted, or how long that would translate to in the Greylands, but if it worked, she could just do it again, and again.

She lay back on the bed. Hopefully, Whitecliffe would think she was resting.

What's de Lavoie gonna think, though?

That was the question, but she'd no choice. She'd realised something while de Lavoie had told her his story, or rather she'd realised *why* he was telling her: whether or not Whitecliffe intended to let her live, the Bonewalker couldn't. It had been a gut feeling at first, but as she'd sat brooding, it had become a certainty. Even if she accepted Whitecliffe's terms now, she might change her mind and come after him, driven by conscience, some vestige of maternal instinct or plain bloody-mindedness. And Robert de Lavoie hadn't survived nearly seven hundred and fifty years by turning his back on a potential threat, let alone giving it time to grow.

What threat?

He had to have some weak point. Had to.

Why? Because you want him to?

He had to have. Everything did.

Everything's supposed *to, babe. But everything's supposed to get old and die, and* he *doesn't, does he? So maybe there really isn't any way with him.*

No. He'd die without descendants to feed on, so there was at least one way, right there.

But what really impressed me, he'd said, *was your conduct in the Greylands. That showed real skill. Natural talent. Most people couldn't have accomplished what you have with years of training…*

And then de Lavoie had, very quickly, changed the subject, and had done so again later on when she'd tried to broach the topic a second time. He'd been happy to talk about everything else, but quick to skate around anything that shed too much light on the Greylands. Which meant he didn't want Jenna, with her "real skill" and "natural talent", to know more.

No doubt de Lavoie had both more experience and greater power, but it might not come down to a simple contest of strength. Victory didn't always go to the strongest and most practised; sometimes you just had to be good enough, in the right place, at the right time.

In any case, she'd nothing left to lose.

You'll get yourself killed, and that's if you're lucky.

Maybe, she almost said aloud, but stopped herself in time. *But fuck it. Now shut up, sweetheart.*

Besides, even if she died, she might buy Holly a chance. Self-sacrifice for a loved one, after having those steel barriers up for so long: maybe that was healing, of a kind.

Let's see if I can still do this.

Jenna rolled onto her side, shut her eyes, and held her breath.

58.

She gasped for air, then broke into a coughing fit as she inhaled fine dust. Her eyes were streaming from the coughing and the ash. When she wiped them, she was standing beside the chaise-longue at the back of the boutique, wearing the hospital gown, the coats she and Holly had worn crumpled at her feet.

First things first: Jenna strode to the shop counter. There was a display case, full of retro jewellery: rings, necklaces, lipstick and cigarette cases. And powder compacts. She went behind the counter and opened the case, fumbling for a flat gold compact and flicking it open. She tossed away the powder-puff, studying her reflection in the glass. *Jesus, I look rough.*

Think you've got a good excuse, babe. It's been that kind of day.

"Try that kind of fucking year," she muttered. Then again, this year had brought her Holly, too. Jenna shut the compact, then opened it again and closed her eyes. The last time, it had happened by chance; now she was trying to will it. She'd no idea whether it would work or not, or whether the attempt would alert the Bonewalker, if her return to the Greylands hadn't already.

She pictured what she wanted, *willed* it, and felt the object in her hand shift and change. Even so, it took long seconds before she dared look. When she did, a shaky laugh escaped her and she supported herself against the counter with her free hand, faint with relief.

The gold powder compact was gold no longer, but silver; no longer plain and flat but sculpted to resemble a scallop shell. And the mirror had turned to mother-of-pearl, smeared rainbows shimmering in it.

Jenna snapped the compact shut, stepped out from behind the counter and went through the shop, gathering supplies for what lay ahead.

Retro or not, the clothing in the boutique wasn't all for show: Jenna found heavy boots and thick socks, jeans and a linen shirt. Simple but practical. An old-fashioned leather flying helmet and pair of goggles were mounted on a mannequin's head; she donned both, tying a bandanna round the lower part of her face. The overall result was equal parts grotesque and comical, but she could live with that.

She stuffed the new compact into her jeans pocket. Finally, she selected an old, heavy walking stick and a knapsack, which she packed with a few other items she'd gathered before venturing outside.

Thankfully the door opened inwards and not outwards, or she might never have got out: ashes had piled almost knee-deep up against the shopfront, flooding into the boutique when she opened the door and billowing through the air.

Outside, the grey ash covered everything in layers. Many buildings had collapsed completely; the rest looked well on the way. The boutique was still in decent condition, but Jenna suspected it would follow quickly enough. To actually maintain a place here long-term must take something more, a constant effort of will. No wonder so many ruins, like the giant plane, littered the desert: dreams that had failed, that could not be sustained.

Unlike the Bonewalker's forest, which had stood for centuries and might stand centuries more.

And you really think you've got a chance?

"No fucking choice, Holl," Jenna said, and set off along the ruined street.

It took a while to get clear of the village, but the walking stick helped, as did the goggles and bandanna. So did knowing where she was headed.

The last buildings fell away from her; Wilmslow Road petered out and faded into the dust beyond. The Greylands stretched out before her, but Jenna knew them a little better now. She could see the plane in the distance: that would do as a marker, at least for now.

You've still no idea how to fight it.

No, that was true enough.

But Jenna thought she knew who might.

59.

She forgot her fears as she walked the Greylands again: the fear she'd snap awake, out of her faint; the fear the Bonewalker would discover her, the new compact proving to be useless; the fear that only death lay at her journey's end. Soon none of those things mattered: everything became about slogging across the monotonous plain of ash.

Still, it was far easier than her first journey across the desert. She was better equipped, able to see clearly and progress more easily. There was no storm, and no giant antlered figure roaming the ashes in search of her. At least, not yet.

The wrecked aeroplane, in all its vast ruined glory – now even more ruined than before – approached, split apart and broken, its pieces once more subsiding slowly into the grey desert. She rested beside it briefly, melancholy settling on her. Given time, perhaps she could have restored it to its original condition; it would have been an experience worth having, to fly aboard it and stand in that saloon, a drink in hand, watching the world pass through the floor-length window.

Then again, so would Mum still being alive, and Dad.

But who'd you be, babe, without all that? Would you really not want to be you?

A big question, but there were other, more pressing ones at hand. She'd never worked out how time passed in the Greylands, compared to the waking world. How long had she been unconscious at Stonebrook? How long would she remain so, if no one interfered? And how long would that give her here? Then there was the new compact, assuming it worked at all. If she brought it back with her on waking, they'd know what she'd been doing.

Leave it here then. You'll leave your clothes and gear behind when you wake, and when you put yourself under again, it'll be here waiting for you.

In theory, but only in theory. She couldn't even be sure she'd return to the Greylands next time she slept. The abilities de Lavoie had mentioned were still new and untried. The Bonewalker must have drawn her here in the beginning; for all she knew, he could stop her coming back.

That way madness lies, babe.

Well, madness lay in every direction just now, not least the one Jenna was taking, and she could no longer afford to hesitate or delay. She began walking again, leaving the plane behind, till a low dark hump appeared in the distance. As she grew closer, the ashy ground rose to a thickly wooded plateau; on one crumbling slope was the bare, dry streambed she'd first followed out of the Bonewalker's forest.

She'd stopped walking. Her hand had slipped into her jeans pocket, gripping the compact. The deep wind moaned; there was no other sound. No thundering footsteps. No roars. The forest looked peaceful and whole, though that didn't make it any more appealing a destination.

No choice, though.

Jenna gave the compact a last good-luck squeeze, wiped her damp hands on her jeans, and began following the dry streambed, fumbling for handholds in the ashy soil as it grew steeper.

She slipped and almost fell several times; on each occasion the urge to turn back was overwhelming, but she persevered. Gradually the ground levelled out and grew more solid underfoot, and she could smell damp earth and leaf mould. Water began trickling along the streambed again; it was the only sound in the woods. No birdsong, no animals in the undergrowth, and, most importantly, no whispers among the trees.

At last Jenna reached a familiar landmark: the big oak, leaning over the slab of rock that overhung the stream, loose roots dangling down. She halted, letting the water run around her ankles. The boots kept her feet dry, but she relished the coolness.

"Well?" she said. "Where are you?"

Only the stream's chuckle answered her.

"I know you're there," she said, but she was uncertain now. What might the Bonewalker have done to the voices, for helping her escape? Perhaps he'd silenced them forever, or made them suffer so much they were now afraid to speak.

Desperation made her angry, and anger made her bold. Jenna grabbed the hanging roots, hauling on them like ropes to climb out of the stream channel. Beyond the oak, she moved through the trees till she found a small clearing. As good a place as any, she decided, and stepped into its centre, looking about her.

"Well?" she said. "Come on. Talk to me." She knelt and spread her arms. "If there's a way, if anyone else knows, it's you. You can help finish this. Maybe you can even be free. So come and tell me how to kill him."

The only answers were the chuckle of the stream and the rustle of the breeze, and she almost despaired, certain she'd failed. But then she realised that the rustling wasn't just the wind, and it was growing louder. Jenna held her breath, waiting, and at last the voices of the dead, of the lost, devoured children of Saturn, were with her, and they told her what she needed to know.

60.

When she finally had it all, Jenna stood and began moving, slowly and quietly, through the trees.

She wanted to rush; at any moment she might be detected or shaken awake in her room at Stonebrook. At the same time, she was nearing the heart of the Bonewalker's domain: the place she needed to be, but also that of the greatest danger.

It hadn't been easy to get the information she'd wanted. Having succeeded in helping a victim escape, the voices hadn't been eager to enable what they saw as her suicide:

No, girl; Run, girl; It's the heart of his power, girl; Just go and be grateful you aren't us.

But she'd persisted, determined to continue, with their help or without. Still they'd tried:

You'll die, girl; Can't win, girl; Least of all here, girl; It's where he's strongest.

But, at last, once they'd recognised there was no dissuading her, they'd talked.

Reality there's very pliable, de Lavoie had told her, *as you've discovered. With time you can bend it to your will, even make a home there. And from it, project a version of yourself back into the waking world.*

A thin hope, a reed, but she had no other; so for her sake and Holly's, Jenna had followed it. She'd guessed a possible way and packed the knapsack accordingly, but if she'd guessed wrong–

325

No, girl; You guess truly, girl; This forest, girl; It's his home and heart.

"Tell me," she'd whispered. "Tell me."

Without this, girl; His home, girl; His anchor, girl; His power fails. The grove, girl; The heart, girl; Strike there, girl; Burn it and he dies.

"That's what I thought."

The little boutique Holly had so loved had also sold weed paraphernalia, along with lighters and, of course, lighter fuel, so there was a fully functional Zippo lighter in the left-hand pocket of Jenna's jeans, and a bottle of fluid in the knapsack. There was also a bundle of old t-shirts and bandannas, which she bound tightly around the handle of the walking stick.

She carried the stick in her right hand, the lighter fluid in her left, not using it to soak the head of her improvised torch yet. The Bonewalker, if present, might detect the acrid smell, and in any case, the fluid would evaporate quickly. Jenna prised the nozzle of the can open so she'd be ready when the moment came, then set off towards the grove.

She wormed her way through the thickening trees with ever-greater difficulty: the closer she came to the grove, the more tightly packed they were. *The heart, girl.* The heart of the Bonewalker's power. No, de Lavoie's: better to think of him by that name. As a flawed, fallible man who could be beaten, who could die.

But he's the Bonewalker, too. He's the monster. Don't forget that.

The trees had almost become a solid wall. She began to fear they'd sensed her coming and closed their ranks tighter to keep her out. But just as the barrier seemed impenetrable, she broke through, stumbling into the grove.

Jenna spun around, the unlit torch in hand, but the long narrow space between the trees was empty. Yes, this was the place she knew from so many nightmares: tapering to a point at one end, lost in darkness at the other.

But different now, too. She was still afraid – the weight of it was like a stone sewn into her gut – but it was only fear, not the vast, paralysing terror she normally associated with here.

Dead leaves crunched underfoot; old twigs snapped. How often had her bare feet sunk into this earth? Now she was dressed for battle, or at least in something more than underwear or a nightshirt. That gave her a little more courage, which she was glad of: part of her still wanted to run.

But that wasn't an option anymore.

A whiff of lighter fuel came from the open can. Her grip was warming the contents, turning some of the fluid to vapour.

Lighting-up time, babe.

Not yet. She'd need every second of heat and light from the torch when the time came. She'd have to wait until the last moment.

Okay, but if something happens unexpectedly…

The air became colder and damper as she neared the dark at the end of the grove, and the autumnal smell of mulching leaves was corrupted by the stink of the Bonewalker. But there was a stale, muted quality to it; it wasn't as thick or stifling as it would have been in the presence of the thing itself. It was just the smell it had left behind.

Which is great, but he could show up any time…

The soil and leaf-litter gave way to old, stained rock. Raw, unchiselled stone, dotted with dark stains. Some ancient place of sacrifice, where the first things to resemble men and women had made their offerings to forces they couldn't comprehend, only hope to appease. The rest was hidden beneath shadows thicker than any the trees could cast.

Now, Jenna. Come on. Now.

Yes; she'd delayed the final step too long. Jenna pointed the can's nozzle at the swaddled end of the walking stick and squeezed: clear fluid squirted out, soaking into the cloth. She turned the stick to and fro, till the end of the torch was dripping, the smell of naphtha blotted out all others and her head began to ache.

Quick, now, quick.

She dropped the half-empty can and took out the lighter, flicking back the cowling. On the second strike the flame caught, and she touched it to the wet material. Fire engulfed the end of the torch, bright and hot. Jenna crouched, retrieved the can, and pressed forward into the dark.

The torch illuminated a flat, uneven rock that had presumably served as an altar once. She squirted the remaining fuel over that and around the clearing, then lit it with the torch: fire raced across the floor of the grove, igniting the fallen leaves, then shot upwards, clutching at the trees above.

Bolder now, she dashed across the grove to another tree and thrust the torch at the lower branches. Sparks glowed, and there was smoke and small tongues of flame. But they just smouldered and guttered, and didn't spread.

Not enough, Jenna. Not in autumn, when the trees are damp.

A breeze blew through the grove: chill, rising to a gale, rank with spoilage and decay. There was laughter on it, too. The flames on the altar-stone dwindled and died, and the blackness swallowed it again. And then two pale eyes shone like lamps, the dark at the end of the grove welled up like ink in a wound and overflowed, the torch went out and the black flood swept Jenna away.

61.

Silly girl, he said. *Silly, silly little girl.*

Jenna was floating as if in a dense but breathable liquid. At first there was only blackness around her, but then light of a kind appeared: cold and silvery, gathering in a phosphorescent nimbus around the Bonewalker as it approached her. He was closer to normal human size than at any other time she'd encountered him.

He was chuckling. *Silly, silly little girl, coming here. What did you think you'd do?*

He reached for her with a clawlike hand. Jenna tried to pull away, but couldn't move: the paralysis from her old nightmares, that she thought she'd shaken off, had returned, leaving her immobile.

Stupid, stupid, stupid. You've really gone and fucked it now, babe.

What else could she have done? Jenna would have demanded of that internal voice if she could, but she was no more capable of speech than any other form of movement. Besides, anything the voice had to say ceased to be of interest a moment later, when the Bonewalker's yellowed talons, filthy with dirt, decay and old blood, stopped an inch from her eyes.

He could blind her with a gesture, peel off her face, and Jenna could do nothing to stop him. She knew that and so did he. The pale eyes shone in the black void beneath the cowl, and then he chuckled and the hand moved away, reaching for the walking-stick torch instead.

This? He was giggling, so hard he could barely speak. *You were going to fight me with* this? *Oh, Jenna, Jenna, Jenna. I mean, full marks for courage, but for judgement, for wisdom…*

It transferred the extinguished torch to its other hand, and the one that had brushed her face descended to her hip. She shrieked inwardly. He was going to violate her, as if he hadn't done enough one way or the other.

But the tip of the claw plucked the opening of her jeans pocket instead, there was a purr of ripping fabric, and the hand rose back into view holding the powder compact.

Clever, he said. *Clever, clever, clever Jenna. Or you thought you were. A good try, though, yes. Almost worked. It did* work, *out in the Greylands. Even in the forest. But not in the grove, no, no. Not here in my grove.*

He squeezed the compact, hard. The metal didn't buckle or splinter but crumbled like dried mud, the bright silver turning grey and lustreless, and then there was only ash, scattering on the nonexistent wind. He held the torch above her head, and that crumbled away too, as he intoned:

Here I'm master of reality. All things are to my will. Nothing exists unless I permit it. You can't even move *here, Jenna. You are what you always were: a means to an end, for me. To do with as I will.*

James, Whitecliffe and now de Lavoie: they were all the same, really, in the end.

Do you know what I'm going to do to you, Jenna? I'm going to hold you here, in the dark, so you can't wake and cause mischief – you've already caused plenty, after all, and will no doubt do so again, given the chance – until Dr Whitecliffe's finished her work. Months and months, Jenna, even years, till we've all the babies we need. We don't need you conscious for that. And then, Jenna – and now the curve of long sharp teeth gleamed in the shadows of the cowl *–* then I'll *absorb* you, as I did your mother. Consume you. Take you into myself. Not necessary, no. I don't need another such feast yet. I'd have been happy to let you die peacefully in your sleep once you'd served your purpose. No pain. But now, little girl, you've annoyed me.*

So you'll get what your mother got. And the process, by the way, is exquisitely *painful.*

Gloat, gloat, gloat. What a boring fucker; Jenna would have laughed, were she able. He seemed to sense that, somehow: the blackness around her seemed to darken by another shade, and he leant closer. *And with you in a coma, we won't need your precious little Holly anymore. Sadly she's no relation of mine, or I'd consume her in the same manner. You could be together forever that way, after a fashion. But as I can't, be glad: at least she'll have a quick death.*

Oh, the hate, the hate, the hate she felt for him now. All the years, all the fighting, and this was what she came down to, all she'd ever been. Not a person, just a pellet of food. *A means to an end,* as he'd said. If she could only break free, only find a way to strike back–

She heard his hateful chuckle again. *Nothing,* he said. *You can do nothing, Jenna. Accept it. I control everything here; nothing happens outside my will. You can control nothing now, Jenna. You own nothing. You* are *nothing.*

If she could only have made the torch light again, brought one flame to life in the darkness and kept it there – if she could have done that she could have hurt him, weakened him, maybe found a way to strike at his precious grove. But she couldn't, so to speculate was pointless: she controlled nothing, outside the prison of her own body.

And then she realised she might have one card left to play. For hadn't this whole business always been about who controlled that piece of flesh and bone – containing those all-important ovaries – that called itself Jenna McKnight? James had wanted it to incubate his child; Whitecliffe to provide children for de Lavoie; both of them to use it, in one way or another, to make themselves immortal. She hadn't mattered.

And yet she had.

She had refused, and she had resisted, fighting always to keep herself whole.

And if her mind was trapped inside her body, there might be one thing yet it could bend to its will.

No way. It can't work.

There were no other options; it was worth a try.

Even if it works, you'll die.

Then she'd die. She'd rather have lived, of course, especially as she felt she'd finally begun to crawl out from under the long shadow of Tallstone Hill, but the choice wasn't *whether* she died but *how*, and better this way than another. She'd die, gladly enough, if in doing so she avoided that final violation he threatened, and spared Holly. And if she destroyed Robert de Lavoie.

Because she might have annoyed him, but he'd *seriously* pissed her off too.

The Bonewalker went still, head cocked, as if sensing something awry.

Do it now, then, Jenna. Do it now.

And so Jenna McKnight thought, pictured, willed:

I will myself into fire.

And so it was.

Her flesh, her organs, her bones and the very marrow of them weren't consumed by flames; they *became* them, cell by cell, bright and searing. In the final instant of consciousness Jenna saw at last the face beneath the Bonewalker's cowl: a skull, half human and half that of some predatory reptile, with long hooked spines for teeth, jaws agape in a soundless scream and coated in a feculent slime of glistening decay.

But she saw it only for a moment, before that mask of slime dried and then caught fire in the sudden blistering heat. The Bonewalker's cowl flared up into flame and burned away too, and its hanging rags of rotten skin.

For a moment, it stood there, holding itself together against the fire that Jenna was becoming, like a man standing against a hurricane wind. And then abruptly, without warning or fanfare, the pale glow of its eyes went out. The Bonewalker was driven backwards, lifeless, and fell asunder, its bones flying apart and plummeting away into the darkness, burning as they went.

Jenna saw them fall, then wink out like dying stars. Was it done, then? Even now she could stop this; even now she could draw herself back together, will herself whole again, if the Bonewalker was gone for good. But she knew that was a false hope; the real substance of Robert de Lavoie was in the forest he'd created. If she spared it, he'd only rise from its soil in a moment, and all her effort would have been for nothing.

And so Jenna did nothing to stop the process she'd begun. And felt the last of herself unravelling into fire, a great howling ball of flame that exploded outwards with the fury of a nuclear bomb, devouring the dark at the end of the grove, and the grove – and forest – beyond.

62.

Holly Finn had never considered herself brave. Too often, before Jenna, she'd been quiet and withdrawn, except with those she knew well. Making new friends, let alone lovers, had never been easy. But when she'd met Jenna, it had been instant. Not just desire: an immediate sense of ease in Jenna's company, the ability to be open with her as Holly had never been before.

Jenna had changed her, even over the course of the month before the kidnapping. That said, had Holly been told on that camping trip to Wales that as well as assuming the role of detective to track her lover down she would assist a man's suicide, commit arson, help a mental patient escape custody and commit/become an accessory to various forms of GBH, she wouldn't have known whether to laugh out loud or run away from whoever had told her so on the grounds they were barking mad.

She'd no idea how she'd have handled the Greylands, or the Bonewalker, before meeting Jenna either. She was still struggling to accept what she'd seen, but it had been too prolonged and vivid to dismiss as the nightmare it had so resembled. She still felt as though she was suffering from mild vertigo, but suspected that the pre-Jenna version of her would still be rocking in a corner and whimpering.

The Bonewalker wasn't present here, at least, but even so, at this moment Holly felt more frightened and helpless than ever before. Here she was, locked up in a padded white room in Stonebrook, and for all she knew they'd never unlock the door again. They'd dispose of Jenna once they'd got what they wanted, and just leave Holly here. The room was soundproof, after all. No one would hear her scream. Thirst and hunger would take care of the problem, and in a few months they could come and hose out what was left. Or just panel over the door and pretend there'd never been a room here. Like walling someone up alive.

It would be, after all, no madder than anything else Holly had witnessed in the past few days.

She dry-washed her face, trying to rub away the fear and exhaustion, but they wouldn't go. The fear, especially: she felt tiny, helpless. Dwarfed by it all.

She was tempted to give in. Let things take their course. Trust Whitecliffe; after all, Holly tried to tell herself, she'd no reason not to let them go. A deal was a deal.

But she'd be safer not keeping it, wouldn't she? And then there's the Bonewalker.

They wouldn't leave her to starve. Someone would come back, either to bring food or water, or to kill her. It didn't matter. If they came, whatever reason they came for, she'd have to take the chance then and there. Fight. Steal an orderly's key-card. Get out and find Jenna. *I got her out once, I can do it again.*

But you weren't a prisoner too. And you had a plan. And pepper-spray, a baton (even if you didn't use it) and a getaway car, and a hole in the fence. And you knew where she was.

So? I'll think of something.

Or so Holly told herself. But she was still trying when the explosion went off.

There was a heavy brutal *THUD* that Holly felt rather than heard; the room, the whole building, juddered and lurched. Things broke and cracked overhead. Dust came from the ceiling. The lights flickered.

And the door *clunk*ed. Several times, in rapid succession.

Holly was already on her feet, the old nursing instincts screaming *emergency, emergency,* and ran to the door. By the time she reached it she'd remembered it was locked, but remembered the *clunk*ing sounds too. The lock made that noise both when it engaged and when it opened.

She grabbed the handle and pulled it: the door didn't open but shifted slightly, letting in screams, the shrilling of the fire alarm, and a smell of burning.

The lights flickered again; the lock *clunk*ed each time they did. *Clunk*ed when the power went out, *clunk*ed when it came back on. She pulled the handle again, and timed it right: the door swung open. Holly staggered back, losing her grip, and caught the door just before it could swing shut again.

She slipped into the corridor. People were shouting in panic; someone was screaming in pain. The smell of smoke was choking. Holly's eyes stung. She pulled her sweater up over her face: they hadn't taken her clothing as they weren't operating on her, and probably wouldn't have minded at all if she'd hanged herself with her belt or laces. One less problem to deal with.

When they'd been separated, Holly had seen Jenna being herded towards a doorway on the ground floor. She had a rough idea how Stonebrook was laid out; this side of the building was for patients, the other for staff. Two rooms on each floor; an ordinary room, and a secure one like this. In which case, Holly was fairly certain Jenna was directly beneath her.

Fairly.

Head down, she barrelled through the smoke, but faltered as another scream sounded – a howl, in fact.

She'd heard it before, and yet she hadn't. She'd heard that voice howl in the Greylands, in laughter or triumph, but never in agony and fear, till now.

Christ. The bloody thing is *here after all.*

The building shuddered again, the corridor tilting under her; she staggered towards the emergency exit at the end as blow after blow smashed into the structure.

Holly cannoned into the fire-door with painful, jarring force, as the building continued to shudder. The mesh-reinforced glass had cracked, but she could see the lawn and trees in the lights from the building, just before those lights went out for good.

The floor sagged further beneath Holly, then cracked open under her feet. She threw herself against the door, trying to force it open, coughing as she inhaled smoke.

Red emergency lighting came on, bathing the smoky corridor in a scarlet fog. Smoke caught at Holly's throat. *Move. No fucking time. Find Jenna. Get her out.* She threw herself against the door again, and this time it crashed open.

Coughing and choking, she staggered out onto the emergency staircase. The metal creaked and groaned; the stonework cracked. The stair wobbled and shook. It was coming loose. She could hear things cracking, breaking, tearing, burning, all around her. Looking down, she saw a body draped over the railing outside the first-floor emergency exit. It was Angela; her mouth hung open in shock and her eyes, glassy and dead, stared up at Holly.

The stair sagged. For a moment Holly thought it was about to topple and froze in place, clutching the rails. But it stabilised, for now at least, and so she climbed down as far as the first floor.

Something warm brushed Holly's arm. She looked down and realised she'd inadvertently touched Angela's face. She made a muffled, disgusted noise and moved around her, climbing down to the ground floor. She fumbled at the emergency door, but couldn't get it open.

There was a thick stench of smoke in the air. The crackle of flames. Stonebrook was on fire, and it was spreading. She had to find a way to get Jenna out.

Holly ran round towards the front of the building. The air was hot and full of smoke; a moment later, a huge section of the building's ground-floor façade burst open. Shattered masonry bounced and thudded across the lawn; Holly threw herself down. A body thudded into the grass. She couldn't tell who it was. The body was on fire.

It could be Jenna.

But the explosion had come from the other side of the building, the staff side. Jenna was on this side of it, so it couldn't be her.

Then a ball of fire rolled out onto the lawn.

That was how it looked at first, but then she saw limbs flailing in it, burning claws hacking and gouging divots from the turf as it rolled madly back and forth before rearing upright again. It wasn't as vast as it had been in the Greylands, but was still easily twice a man's height, and even ablaze from head to foot its outline was unmistakable.

Still howling, the Bonewalker charged across the lawn, its claws raking at the empty air, but the fire was relentless and showed no sign of going out; if anything, it was blazing ever brighter, as if determined to consume every trace of it.

Jenna's work. Holly had no idea how, but it had to be.

The burning shape slowed down, weaving, tottering. It seemed to be making for the trees at the end of the lawn, but its strength was ebbing. As Holly watched, it crashed to its knees, then pitched forward, sprawling. It still moved, but only feebly, and the flames continued gnawing at it.

Almost the entire front of the building's staff side had gone; the ground and part of the first floor had been smashed outwards by the Bonewalker's dying, convulsive rampage, and the upper part of the façade was falling apart. Fire roared out of the hole in the building. She couldn't hear anyone screaming now.

The front doors were gone. One hung off a single broken hinge; Holly couldn't see the others. Firelight flickered out of the doorway across the forecourt and black smoke boiled out. Shadows flickered in the firelight: movement. A moment later, Redbeard staggered out of the main entrance, or at least half of him did.

One side of him was the orderly Holly had come to know and heartily dislike; the other was a scorched, black-and-red thing that smouldered and stank of charred meat. He stared at Holly, but the single eye that remained in his face didn't see her. All it seemed capable of containing was the kind of agony Holly wouldn't have wished on anyone. Redbeard staggered forward, waving his unburnt arm, then halted and stiffly toppled over on the gravel forecourt. He rolled onto his back and coughed out smoke; then he was still.

Smoke poured out of the main doors. A fire of some sort was raging in there. She had to get inside, to Jenna, but she'd never get through that. Jenna was going to bake, or suffocate. Holly had to–

"You bitch," a woman screamed.

Holly spun around; only reasonable to assume the shout was directed at her, after all. Especially when she saw that it had come from Dr Whitecliffe, who was clinging to the building's shattered frontage.

One of Whitecliffe's spectacle lenses caught the firelight. The other was broken. Blood and soot marred her white coat and smeared her face, which was cut and scratched in a dozen places, and her scraped-back hair was disarrayed. But the biggest change was how her poise and composure had disintegrated. All the doctor's earlier urbanity was gone, as if the flames had burned it away.

"You bitch," Whitecliffe shouted again, and staggered towards Holly. Holly realised Whitecliffe was clutching the pistol she'd threatened her with earlier. She backed away, retreating round the corner and almost collapsing across the bottom of the listing fire escape. She broke free of it, tried to stumble further back as Whitecliffe rounded the corner and lurched, swaying, towards her. "You fucking bitch," the doctor said again. She sounded very calm now; almost matter-of-fact.

Holly looked for a hiding place or weapon without success, but Whitecliffe ignored her, turning instead to the fire-door, wrenching and pounding at it. "Jenna! Jenna, you fucking bitch!"

There was a *clunk* and Whitecliffe dragged the door open. Smoke drifted out, and she staggered through it into the corridor.

Of course. With the Bonewalker dead – and surely it had to be, or well on the way – Whitecliffe could whistle for her precious Rite of Cronos. *Sorry, doc. No immortality for you.* And whatever had happened to the Bonewalker, Whitecliffe had no doubt guessed, as Holly had, that it was somehow Jenna's doing.

And when nothing else was left, there was still revenge.

And Whitecliffe had the pistol. *Walther PPK. Just like James Bond.* How many bullets did it hold? Six? Seven? One would be enough.

"McKnight!" screamed Whitecliffe. "Jenna, you fucking bitch!" She staggered down the corridor, and began throwing her weight against a red-lit door.

Holly charged, head down. *Stay low, then if she shoots, she might miss.* If she could get close enough, she could tackle Whitecliffe. But they were still five or six feet apart when Whitecliffe got the door open and lurched through.

There was a fire extinguisher on the wall; Holly wrenched it loose, then hurled herself towards the door as it began swinging shut again. She caught it with her shoulder before it could close, and knocked it wide.

Whitecliffe was aiming the gun at the bed, but the bed was empty. She wiped her eyes, then turned and pointed the Walther down at the floor, where Jenna, Holly now saw, lay sprawled in a hospital gown.

Jenna didn't react to the threat; she was shuddering violently, as if in a fit, her eyes rolled up. Whitecliffe hesitated and moved forwards. Maybe the doctor in Whitecliffe was surfacing one last time; more likely, she just wanted to be sure Jenna knew who was killing her and why. It was, in any case, enough time for Holly to run forward and bring the fire extinguisher down in a two-handed blow on the crown of Whitecliffe's head.

Whitecliffe staggered and grabbed at the bed to steady herself. She swivelled round, blinking at Holly. Blood ran over her forehead, into her eyes. "No," she said, almost petulantly. "No, you can't. That's not fair."

She was still holding the gun. She might have used it, or might not, but Holly hit her with the extinguisher again before she could try, this time in the face. Whitecliffe stepped back against the end of the bedframe and slumped down into a sitting position, the pistol slipping from her hand. Holly brought the extinguisher down once more, with all her strength, and felt the skull collapse like wet clay. She turned aside and vomited, then stumbled over to Jenna.

Fire everywhere, consuming everything – de Lavoie, the grove, the forest. The ghosts in the trees screaming; for a second Jenna thought she'd got it wrong and they were suffering like de Lavoie. Then she realised the screams were of joy, and if there was any pain in them, it was that of someone seeing the light after an eternity in the dark.

She'd been surprised, vaguely, that she could comprehend that, or indeed anything else. Astonishing that she still possessed any scrap of consciousness at all; astonishing that it was taking so long for that very last remnant of who she was to either become fire, or to burn or melt away in it. But everything comes to an end, and she'd very nearly reached hers.

De Lavoie's screams had ended, and so had those of the ghosts. The forest and the grove – the Bonewalker's anchor in the Greylands, his immortality – had been destroyed. Therefore the Bonewalker, too, must finally be gone.

The very last, tiny spark of Jenna McKnight had been about to disappear, and then she'd thought *No*. He was gone at last, and she wasn't. So why should she die too?

Holly was waiting for her, and, with her, a future worth embracing.

And so that final trace of her had thought, pictured, willed: *I will myself whole again.*

Picturing herself, her body, her face, the hospital gown, whole and unwounded and unmarked.

And as she'd willed it, so had it been: there'd been a brief sensation of tumbling through darkness, a glimpse of a scorched ruin that might once have been a forest, and then she'd woken on the floor of her room, Holly kneeling over her, while Stonebrook burned around them.

"Babe? Babe!"

Holly saw Jenna's eyelids flicker. "Uh?"

"Babe? It's me."

Jenna blinked. "Holly."

"Yeah. C'mon, sweetheart. Let's get out of here before the sky falls in. Mind the puke."

Jenna laughed weakly. When they reached Whitecliffe's body Holly thought she'd either tripped or fallen, but instead Jenna knelt, took a key from the dead woman's pocket, and unlocked the compartment under the bed, where Holly saw her clothes had been stowed. She pulled her boots on, then straightened up, holding the Walther. "Just in case," she said thickly. Which, given how things had gone so far, seemed an entirely reasonable point.

They staggered out through the fire escape and onto the forecourt just in time; Holly's throat was raw, her head spinning from the smoke, and almost as soon as they got down the steps a deafening crash sounded from inside the main building.

Almost the entire staff side had collapsed, and alarming cracks came from the remainder. As they staggered across the lawn, there was a creaking sound and they looked back to see the fire escape finally come free of the wall and collapse like a deformed, skeletal tree.

Someone was crying. Holly saw it was Zoe, kneeling on the lawn, rocking to and fro. *Hell of a night, eh, love?* Not that Holly could feel much sympathy for her; she'd helped Whitecliffe in all this, after all. You got what you paid for. No one had forced Zoe. Or had they? It wouldn't be a surprise in this whole business.

Jenna flung off the hospital gown and began putting the rest of her clothes back on. There was another crash as more of Stonebrook collapsed into the fire; smoke and flame and sparks billowed into the night sky. When Holly turned away from the sight, she saw Jenna plodding tiredly across the lawn, the Walther hanging by her side, towards a spot near the trees where a fire had burned itself out but from which thick black clouds of smoke still billowed upwards.

She caught up with Jenna beside the blackened crater the Bonewalker had burned or burrowed into the lawn in its agony. At first all Holly saw inside the crater was scorched earth and blackened cinders, but then something moved amid the debris. A man tried to crawl up the inside of the crater, his clothes burnt to rags and half his face red and raw and weeping.

"Meet Robert de Lavoie," Jenna said, her voice a gravel croak. The man slid down the inside of the crater to the bottom and rolled onto his back, staring up at them.

"Is he...?" Holly began. "Is that him? I mean, it?"

"Yup."

Robert de Lavoie looked at Jenna with dazed, vacant eyes. Maybe he was in too much pain to understand what was going on, or maybe whatever she'd done to him had shattered his mind. Maybe, in his defeat, he simply no longer cared.

In any case, there were no last words from either of them.
Jenna raised the Walther and fired again and again. Four
bullets hit him in the torso; the last two hit de Lavoie in the
face, and dark wetness splattered up the smouldering ash slope
behind him. His head snapped back, a jolt running through the
body; then he slumped back down, as if deflating, and was still.

Behind them, Stonebrook burned.

"And now it's done," said Jenna.

She stood motionless and silent, the gun hanging at her
side. After a moment, Holly took her arm and led her away
into the night.

THE LAST CRUSADER

In the 1580s, Dr John Dee – adviser to Queen Elizabeth I, astronomer, mathematician, scientist, alchemist and occultist – travelled throughout Europe, gathering knowledge of occult symbols, rituals and practices.

Following his return to England, he was appointed Warden of Christ's College, Manchester – now Manchester Cathedral – and it was in the cathedral's archives that a fragment of manuscript was discovered, recording part of a conversation between Dee and a rabbi from the Great Synagogue of Prague, one of the scholars Dee had consulted during his European journey.

The conversation had turned to the topic of alchemy, and more specifically to one of its goals, the attainment of immortality. The rabbi related an obscure tradition, prevalent in the Levant, of a Templar Knight who had gained eternal life, though at a dreadful price.

The source of the rabbi's tale has never been determined. Some scholars believe it was as a parable, intended to warn Dee that some goals could only be attained at a price so high it made them worthless. Alchemy was a spiritual quest as much as anything else, after all, and to become so bound to the transient world of matter that one became a demon and a cannibal could only be a form of damnation.

By devouring his children, like the Roman god Saturn, and repeating this process in each successive generation, the Templar retained health, vitality and youth and was almost entirely immune to physical harm.

As long as any of his blood remained alive, death could never wholly claim him. Even if he were somehow slain, his dybbuk, *or spirit, could take possession of a surviving descendent and live again.*

(Note: This is the last of five partial documents recovered from a flash drive, believed to have been the property of Dr Margaret Whitecliffe. Found at the site of the Stonebrook Clinic Fire.)

GALLOWDANCE: DINAS OLEU, 2023

63.

Holly got them first to Birmingham, then home to Manchester. In the early hours of the morning after the fire she let them into her flat in Withington – empty the past couple of weeks – and they collapsed exhaustedly into bed. Holly was sure they'd be woken almost instantly by the police kicking in the door, but they slept without disturbance till the following afternoon.

Picking up the threads of their lives, in fact, proved far easier than she'd expected; they spent a few weeks waiting for the axe to fall before realising it wasn't going to. Presumably Whitecliffe had covered Jenna's trail so well that no one ever connected them to the disaster at Stonebrook. Zoe had either said nothing to the police, or made herself scarce before they arrived, not wanting her own role to come under scrutiny.

Certainly there was nothing to connect the explosion at Stonebrook with the tragic death of Sir James Frobisher in a hunting accident. An only child, he'd died without issue, so with his passing the baronetcy became extinct.

"Oh dear," said Holly when she read that. "How sad. Never mind."

She returned to nursing, Jenna to the life of a freelance artist, and the two of them moved in together. At first that was out of necessity, Jenna's flat no longer being available due to the whole non-payment-of-rent thing, but having got her things out of storage they pooled their resources and rented a small house in Tameside.

They were happy, or at least Holly thought they were. Jenna was far more open than before. The barrier between her and the rest of the world wasn't gone altogether; from time to time it would come up again, as solid as ever. Nonetheless, they carried on. Things got better. The old year became a new one. Winter became spring.

"This is the longest I've ever been with anyone," Jenna whispered to Holly, one still, warm April morning. "I'd stay with you forever if I could."

"You can," said Holly, but Jenna only smiled. Rather sadly, Holly thought.

And then it was May, and the days were warm again, the world in bloom. And Holly woke one morning to find the bed beside her empty, and a note bearing her name on the pillow.

"No," Holly heard herself say aloud. Her voice, croaky with sleep, sounded tiny and lost. *Not after all this. Not after everything.* But it wasn't just grief; it was fear, too. Because she already knew this wasn't a break-up letter. This was something worse.

Because she remembered the sadness in Jenna's smile when she'd said "forever". She wiped sleep and tears from her eyes, sat up in bed and fumbled for the note.

There'd been a shadow on Jenna all this time. Holly hadn't wanted to believe it, not after all they'd gone through. But she should have. Not wanting to believe, she'd ignored it, and now her bed was empty and there was this note:

Holl,

I love you. You've got to know that to begin with. I love you, and if that could've saved me it would have, so for fuck's sake don't blame yourself for this...

"No," Holly said again, reading. "No. No. No."

Then she was out of bed, throwing off the skeleton onesie she'd taken to wearing while the weather had still been cold (and because she had a bit of a thing for Phoebe Bridgers, which Jenna had teased her lovingly but unmercifully about) while rooting around for her clothes. So many things to find and put on; so much time wasted when every second was precious.

She ran downstairs. Outside, Jenna's hot-pink Aygo was gone, and the olive-green Jimny sat alone in the drive.

"Fuck," she shouted, then ran back upstairs for her car keys. And the note.

"I'll fucking kill her," Holly muttered as she drove. "I'll get her home in one piece, and then I'll fucking kill her."

She put a hand to her mouth, fighting a sob, as soon as she'd said it, tears misting her eyes. *Don't even joke about that. Don't even joke. And for Christ's sake don't fucking drive when you can't see.*

She turned off the main road and pulled in, crying helplessly, wiping her eyes. *Stop crying. Stop crying. Get yourself under control, Finn. You'll be no help to her otherwise.*

But she couldn't stop, just fucking couldn't; had to sit and sob as Jenna's life ticked away.

A year ago, Holly would have called the police and done all she could, then sat at home waiting, making mug after mug of tea she couldn't even taste while wishing for the phone to ring. But that had been another time and place: her view of the authorities and their competence (not to mention integrity) was more than a little jaundiced, and her faith in her own abilities far stronger than it'd been.

Should it be, though? I mean, yeah, you got her back that time, but look at her now.

She mustn't think like that. It wasn't over yet. Wasn't finished, wasn't lost, not until she knew she was too late–

And she wasn't thinking like that either.

Holly let the crying jag burn itself out; when it had, she wiped her eyes, then took out the note and read it again, beginning to end, parsing every line for clues, trying to reassure herself her first instinct had been correct.

But when you started second-guessing yourself you were done for, so in the end she crumpled up the note, threw it aside, and started the engine again.

But before she pulled out, she smoothed the crumpled note again, her hand pressing it flat against the passenger seat. Then she took out her phone, typing in the first address she remembered near the place she needed to go.

That she hoped she needed to go.

If she'd guessed right.

The address came up, and the postcode. She typed it into the satnav, muttering "Come on, come the fuck on" as it calculated her route, then put the car into gear and drove.

Two hours and fifty-odd minutes, the satnav said it would take.

We'll fucking see about that.

She had to battle through the weekday morning traffic till she reached the M56, wondering with each passing second how much of a head-start Jenna had, grimly aware of the delays already inflicted on her by traffic and her own panic, and that while neither of them were driving racing cars by any stretch of the imagination, Jenna's Aygo had a slightly higher top speed than the sturdy little Jimny. Holly had woken just after eight in the morning, but the whole bed had been warm from the May sunlight streaming through the curtains, so she'd no way of gauging how lately Jenna had vacated it.

Just before the Welsh border she passed the refinery at Stanlow, and hummed a few bars of the OMD song about the place. What'd Jenna called it? "A fairy palace for Goths." That'd been the night of the pregnancy test, lying in bed after they'd fought and made up. That had made Holly laugh.

She saw a road sign: *Croeso i Gymru. Welcome to Wales.* And then she was across the border, in another land.

The M56 became the A494 and she kept going, through Queensferry and across the Dee. The road dropped suddenly and steeply, and Holly felt her stomach seem to fall away. "Fuck me," Jenna had said on the journey there, "can we go back for my ovaries?"

The industrialised towns on the Clwyd border gave way to smaller, quieter settlements separated by long stretches of hills, moorland and woods. She'd had her work cut out on the drive up to distract Jenna from those, helping her stave off the panic attacks. Luckily Jenna had slept most of the way back.

Heather bloomed on the moors. Beautiful, but the beauty was tainted now, because of the journey and what waited at its end.

Not if you're in time, Holl.

She crossed the Dee again at Bala, where its long, winding course brought it to feed the lake. Brick and stone and pebble-dashed houses; shops, cafés and hotels. Leaving the town and driving alongside the lake she glimpsed a derelict side-road, its entrance almost completely overgrown, a rotted sign saying *Fferm Heol Capel* and a boarded-up, roofless farmhouse. Then the lake flashed by her on the other side of the road, a-glitter in the sun, and was gone.

Drws-y-Nant, Rhydymain. Bont Newydd: endless fields and hills and woodlands, and the pebbled beds of streams. Dolgellau, with its rows of stone houses and its market square, and then the road again. Across the Mawddach at Llanelltydd, and then onto the A495 to follow the river to the sea, past Pen-y-bryn and alongside the flood plains that surrounded the Mawddach as it widened to an estuary. Mud flats combed with creeks; rocky fields sloping up to the roadside, dotted with tree-topped knolls like the memories of islands.

Towards the sea, towards Barmouth, towards the mountain they'd walked on, the day before it started. Dinas Oleu: the Citadel of Light.

Fields and floodlands to the left. Steep woods to the right, giving way to stone cliffs netted with wire mesh against rockfalls. Then, in the distance, the jagged, saw-toothed line of the iron bridge across the estuary mouth between Barmouth and Morfa Mawddach. Nearly there. Nearly there.

But in time, or too late?

The Victorian Gothic hall called the Clock House, perched on a small headland overlooking the estuary, passed her on the left. "You used to be able to stay there," she remembered telling Jenna after checking the place out online, "but it cost a grand a night."

"When we win the lottery," Jenna had said, laughing. That laugh; that smile; that light in her eyes. Holly's own eyes prickled with tears and the road ahead of her blurred. *Christ.* She wiped them on her sleeve again, and just in time, too; the road past the Clock House was bordered by a sheer rockface to Holly's right, with a stone wall to her left the only thing between her and the estuary. The road veered sharply just ahead of her too; another second's distraction and she'd have ploughed clean through the wall and ended up in the water.

Don't start skriking now. Be just like you to wrap yourself round a tree like Marc fucking Bolan when you're nearly there.

Around the bend was the old harbour at Aberamffra; across the road from that, Orielton Woods, narrow and steep, climbed the hill.

Let me be right about this. Please God, let me be right. All of this, this whole journey, was guesswork based on the letter's final paragraph and the hope that Holly knew Jenna as well as she thought. If she didn't, Jenna was dead.

Might be already, Holl, depending how much of a head start she had.

But Holly's instinct hadn't been wrong; as she drove down Porkington Terrace (thinking, as she always did every time, how un-Welsh a name that seemed), just before she reached the bridge, she saw, to her right, the entrance to Panorama Road. Beside it was a parking area and a pair of garages – no doubt for residents only, but in one of the parking spaces was a Toyota Aygo in a very distinctive shade of hot pink.

Holly parked the Jimny in the entrance and jumped out, wobbling for a moment on legs that were unsteady after the long drive. The Aygo's bonnet was hot to the touch, but that could have been from the sun; again, there was no way to tell whether the engine was still warm, or cold. Couldn't Jenna have picked a miserable fucking day for this, at least?

But Holly knew Barmouth, and she knew Panorama Road. It was very steep and ran uphill, all the way to the Panorama Walk.

"Just up past the farm, then on through the woods. Takes us up to Panorama. You can see for miles. Up the coast, out to sea, inland–"

Huffing and puffing, Holly broke into a run.

64.

Holl,

I love you. You've got to know that to begin with. I love you, and if that could've saved me it would have, so for fuck's sake don't blame yourself for this. It really isn't you. It really is me.

I told you what happened in the grove. How I "won", or thought I had. I was happy to die if I killed that bastard, after all he'd done. But I came back. And that was for you, I admit it. Another split-second and I'd have let go altogether and been gone for good, but I realised I could pull back, so I thought why the fuck shouldn't I? I knew I'd beaten him: I could hear them all singing, all the souls, as they got away when the grove burned...

Fucking hell, I should stop there, shouldn't I? This letter would get me sectioned if anyone else read it. But it's not going to matter. They won't get the chance.

What matters is that I was wrong. I didn't beat him. I thought I had. I nearly did. If I hadn't been selfish and decided to live, I could've put an end to the fucker then and there. But I wanted to be with you. So I pulled back, and I came home.

And when I did, I brought him with me.

She'd known, somehow, when she'd woken for the last time at Stonebrook, she'd need the Walther. Even then, she'd known she wasn't done with Robert de Lavoie.

He'd still been alive when she'd reached him, but from his

empty, vacant eyes she'd known only his body remained, that his mind was quite gone. She'd made sure all the same.

That, she'd thought, was that, realising only later that while de Lavoie's body had been an empty, mindless shell, its immortality burned away like half its skin and the grove he'd reared in the Greylands, the essence of him remained. When Jenna had pulled back at the last second, before her own mind could wholly unravel, and drawn herself back together, when her spirit, soul, or whatever name she gave it had returned to her own body, the last vital spark of Robert de Lavoie had come with it, clinging like a tick.

He's in my head, and he's trying to push me out, Holly. At first it was just now and then, but the longer he's there, the stronger he's got, and now it's every night. Every time I close my eyes.

I know what he wants, obvs. A new body. He'll take me over. That's his plan. I don't know what'll happen to my mind or soul or whatever then. I don't know if I'll go out like a light, or if I'll be chucked out of my own body so I'm like a ghost, or if I'll be trapped inside it, just having to watch everything he does, forever.

Cos it will *be forever, if he gets his way: he'll use my body to get a new generation going, and then he'll perform the Rite of Cronos and be immortal again.*

But before he does all that, he'll do something else. He's going to kill you.

At first she'd thought they were just bad dreams. She'd be standing in ashes – a mixture of the soft grey powder of the Greylands and something blacker, grittier and coarser: smashed-up charcoal, burnt wood. The air had stunk of smoke and worse.

The first couple of dreams – on different nights, weeks apart, near the end of the previous year – had been nothing more or worse than that. She'd dismissed them as echoes and nightmares. But just over a month into the new year, she'd dreamt of it again. The beginning of February: the old feast day of Candlemas.

The dust had been greyer, with only the odd blackened smut and stump remaining, but a faint, rotten scent she recognised had permeated the fading odour of the smoke.

And then there'd been laughter, and water had poured up through the ground, swirling and icy and pulling at her ankles – filling the world, trying to drown her.

Thankfully, her instincts had been good: she'd turned and run till she reached ground still unaffected by it – the Greylands, she saw, had reclaimed all but the very heart of the Bonewalker's forest, the remnants of the grove itself. She'd willed a great high rock out of the dust, an island to serve as sanctuary.

She'd woken, then, and been safe for a while.

But a fortnight later, she'd dreamed again, and in it the waters rose to flood her island. She'd willed a boat into being then, and escaped across the now seemingly endless sea.

A fortnight after that, in early March, she was there again and now the sea was rougher, stormier, full of jagged rocks. She'd reshaped the boat into a larger vessel; in another fortnight, she'd had to shape that, in its turn, into a battleship. But the storms smashed her onto reefs and shoals, buckling the hull as fast as she could repair it. She'd woken as she'd begun to sink, gasping for breath, to find herself standing in her own kitchen. She'd been sleepwalking. She hadn't understood why. Not then.

It was only a week before the next dream came; finding herself on the bridge of her sinking battleship once more, she'd reshaped the vessel into a submarine and dived beneath the waves to avoid the storm. But in the next dream, less than a week later, something followed her down and attacked her there. She'd woken kneeling up in bed that time, looking down at Holly as she slept.

It was mid-April by then, and the next fortnight passed in safety. But on May Day Eve the dream returned: the seabed rose, forcing the submarine out of the water, stranded and helpless and trapped in the thick ooze that covered the ocean floor. The mud had hardened around it like cement, inexorably crushing the hull; she'd made her escape just in time, and that had been when she'd woken up – standing in the kitchen again, this time in front of the open knife drawer.

After that the dreams became more frequent: de Lavoie was getting stronger while she weakened, and more aggressive as his triumph approached. She never saw him, but could always feel him – his spite, his gloating, his mocking laughter. Winged monsters had chased Jenna across the plain of dried cracked mud; when she'd found a hiding place, other monsters had come burrowing up from beneath. It had taken all her wits to escape them, but she'd nearly been lost for good.

And then, three nights ago, she'd woken to find herself standing over Holly with a knife in her hand.

You and me, Holl, we're the only ones who know, and he won't have to worry about me much longer.

My arm was coming up, and I didn't think I could stop it, but I managed, in the end – just. Or maybe it wasn't me at all: he hasn't tried since then. Maybe he realised first things first. *He needs to take over properly, make sure he gets away with it. Last thing he wants is to end up in prison – locked away for years, till I'm all dried up and menopausal.*

I'm the only one who can stop him, Holl. You, with all your love – there's nothing you can do here, sweetheart. And I'm not risking your life too. I'm not. I'm the only one who can stop him, and I'm gonna lose, Holl. Not yet, but soon.

* * *

The dreams had returned each night since, and she'd woken this morning knowing the final outcome was no longer in doubt. It wasn't *if*, but *when*: de Lavoie had centuries of experience on his side, after all.

She'd hoped to have her cake and eat it, kill the beast without sacrificing herself in the process, but that wasn't to be. Her only triumph would be the Bonewalker's final extinction, and Holly's survival.

But Jenna found she could live – as it were – quite happily with that.

I didn't want to do this. I really didn't. But I've got to, and it's got to be now, or it'll be too late.

So I'm gonna go somewhere. Alone. I don't want you finding me afterwards. Or trying to stop me, because it's got to be this way, Holly. I'm sorry – I am so fucking sorry – but it's got to. But it'll be somewhere I'll think of you. Somewhere we should've gone together when we had the chance, before all this kicked off.

I love you, Holl. I love, love, fucking love you.

And I'd stay with you forever if I could.

But I can't.

Jenna x

Once she'd decided, she felt at ease: all that remained was the how, when and where. The *when* was simple enough: today, before she slept again. She puzzled over the *how* a little longer, briefly wishing she still had the Walther – now at the bottom of a Manchester canal after having been thoroughly wiped clean of fingerprints – but found her solution soon enough.

The *where* was knottier. Almost anywhere would have done, but she wanted to ensure Holly wasn't the one to find her.

Tough shit on the poor stranger who does though, eh?

In an ideal world she'd do it in some wilderness, so she'd disappear entirely and never be found, but Jenna wanted to die somewhere that at least offered her a memory of happiness. She considered Didsbury, but it was too close to home, there were too few places with the necessary privacy, and too few memories of it that included Holly.

In the end, though, she found her answer: the last place she'd known happiness before it had all begun. The last time she'd let her fears stop her.

Holly had said it was a beautiful place, with a view to marvel at. So be it. Jenna would see it before she died.

She went into her studio and packed everything she'd need. She carefully wrote her note, folded it and left it on Holly's pillow. And then, a few minutes after 7am, she'd tiptoed downstairs on stockinged feet, walking boots in hand, and softly, softly let herself out – deep sleeper though Holly was, it was better not to take the chance today – and got into her car.

Jenna drove sedately at first, not wanting to draw attention. The journey passed without incident until Bala, where sudden spasms set in in her hands as she exited the town; they kept stiffening on the wheel, then jerking, trying to wrench it round.

U-turn. He's trying to take me back home.

Jenna didn't want to believe it – didn't want to believe de Lavoie's influence could be that strong while she was awake – but shortly afterwards, grogginess set in. She greyed out for what seemed a second, then resurfaced to discover she'd been driving back the way she'd come for nearly fifteen minutes. She swerved the car around, so hard, and with such anger, that the Aygo had nearly fishtailed off the road into a ditch, then drove back to Bala.

She was shaking from shock, but also, she realised, hunger. She found a café and ordered a bacon roll; she mustn't delay unnecessarily, but it would be all too easy to go off the road again, the state she was in. If she crashed, death would be slow and painful. Or worse, she'd be knocked unconscious, and de Lavoie could take control for good.

And that she could not, would not, allow.

The condemned woman ate a hearty breakfast, eh?

Her eyelids kept drooping. She was tired, near exhausted from the past week's nightmares, which could only help de Lavoie. Jenna bought three espressos, downing each one fast, one after the other, then a latte with caramel syrup to drink in the car, and to dispel their bitter taste.

She was still shaky and frightened, but that wouldn't change anytime soon. There was no telling when Holly would wake, no telling how long Jenna had before Holly came after her. No telling whether she'd said too much in her letter, if Holly could guess where Jenna would go. Because however conclusive the arguments, however ineluctable the logic, Holly would never accept that Jenna had to die.

She got in the Aygo and drove, grinding her teeth from the caffeine rush.

At last she reached Barmouth, the May sunshine glittering on the blue estuary. Part of her ached to carry on into the town. One last drink on the Quayside. But even a brief delay might be all de Lavoie needed.

No time for that. No leisurely hikes across the hill. You want to do this, do it now and do it fast, by the shortest route.

The voice was right. Of course, it would've been righter still to point out that by that logic, everything she'd done this morning was madness, giving de Lavoie more rope to hang her with. But mad or not, it was one last defiant gesture to both the Bonewalker and brute necessity, and she'd make it. If she was to die, she was choosing the when, the where and the how.

And besides, it wasn't easy to kill yourself, however badly you needed to.

She reached Porkington Terrace and parked up, then took her knapsack from the passenger seat and, out of habit, locked the car behind her.

The sun was bright and hot in a clear blue sky. Gulls called. All else was still. Jenna started up the Panorama Road.

There was the farmhouse, there was the footpath, and there, beyond both, were the woods covering the shoulder of the hill.

She'd bought a bottle of water in Bala and stowed it in her pack. She'd drunk most of it, because she was sweating hard, the sun beating down on her scalp. She poured the last of the water over her head, feeling it soak her hair. *Don't go passing out from heat stroke, babe. That'd never do.*

A path led between two stone walls to a gate. Beyond it were the woods, the trees looming tall and green. She hesitated for a moment, but she wasn't afraid anymore. That, at least, was gone.

She walked to the gate and went through. The woods and their verdant smell enfolded her. There was another gate to her right and a path leading up through the trees, between shelves of mossy rock on her right and wooded slopes below to her left. The worn sign pointing to it read *PANORAMA*.

Jenna went through the second gate and followed the path, taking in the stillness and beauty of the place. Something else the Bonewalker had robbed her of, now returned, just before the end.

And then, at last, Panorama itself.

From the topmost point of the hillside, looming over the Mawddach Estuary, the view extended miles out to sea: on a clear morning, Holly had claimed, you could make out the long arm of the Llŷn Peninsula extending across the top of Cardigan Bay, and Anglesey off the end of it.

Today there was a thin haze along the horizon, so Jenna couldn't see if that was true, but she could still see far out to sea and down the coast as well. If she turned she would see the Mawddach winding inland, the creeks weaving through the green mudflats. Purple heather on the rolling hills, each side of the blue water. The bare rock and scrub grass that she stood on.

Its breadth and beauty struck the breath from her. This had been Holly's gift: spurned at the time, now belatedly accepted. And it was all Holly had said it would be.

Moments of grace, she'd told de Lavoie. She'd meant moments like this.

Down beside the Mawddach, cars moved along the A496 like little bright beetles. One of them might even be Holly.

Too late to do any good.

Jenna hoped so, anyway. But in any case, she'd already delayed far too long.

Back in the woods, she climbed over a low stone wall to descend the wooded slope below the path, just till she was out of plain sight. After that, it was a matter of finding the right tree. It didn't take her long to locate a tall oak with a thick branch just high enough off the ground and a fallen trunk lying beside it.

Best crack on, then.

Jenna unzipped her knapsack, took out the coil of rope and threw it over the branch. She let it drop to the ground, then wound one end around the bole and pulled to raise the noose to the correct height. The slipknot was already tied; Jenna stood on tiptoes on the fallen tree so her face was level with the noose, then got down and fastened the rope tight.

All ready, then?

She stood in silence, warm light dappling her face. The trees whispered.

"I don't want to go," she whispered back.

I know, babe.

Jenna breathed out. "Yeah," she said.

But she couldn't move. Then she found herself pivoting on her heel, facing back towards the path. Greyness flooded the edges of her vision, trying to encroach. She took a step up the slope, away from the noose. And then another.

No, she thought. The next time she said out aloud. "No. No. No!"

She threw the hardest punch she was capable of at the nearest tree to her. Something cracked in her left hand. White pain speared up her arm and she cried out, gasping; her eyes were full of tears and she couldn't move all her fingers, but when she turned back towards the fallen tree, there was no resistance. Her body was hers again.

How long for?

Jenna took one last deep breath, then released it. For a moment, she thought fear would paralyse her, but then she moved, stepping lightly up onto the fallen tree, reaching for the noose and fitting it – a little clumsily with her injured hand – around her neck.

"Sorry, Holl," she said. Bitterly inadequate, but the best she could do. And then she jumped as high as she could. Her weight pulled her back down groundward. The rope snapped taut, and the noose bit into her throat.

65.

Holly sagged against the low stone wall overlooking Orielton Woods, heaving for breath.

Easy. Walk, don't run. Can't help Jenna if you give yourself a cardiac.

She couldn't help Jenna if she arrived too late, either.

Assuming you're not already.

"Fuck off," she croaked.

She pushed herself away from the wall and carried on, but this time she walked. Her thighs ached and throbbed. She shambled on, wiping sweat from her eyes, till the farmhouse and the Panorama trail came into view.

Hope you're right, Holl. If not–

"Oh, fuck off," she said again.

Holly stumbled along the path. Sheep bleated nearby. She smelt crushed grass, heather, sheep shit. A spring trickled nearby. She went through the two gates and into the woods, plodding through the trees towards the summit. She walked faster now; the ground wasn't as steep. But her thighs still ached, and she was still too out of breath to shout Jenna's name.

She stopped, leaning on a low stone wall to get her breath back, silent, letting her breathing slow. If she hadn't, she wouldn't have heard it.

A creaking sound, rhythmic and slow. Of course, trees often creaked, especially in the wind. But there was no wind this morning. She'd wished for it more than once on her uphill climb, to cool her down as she'd burned and sweated.

Creak, creak–

Steady, rhythmic, back and forth. Like something swinging on–

On a rope.

"Oh fuck." Holly clambered over the wall and scrambled down the slope. As she did, she heard something else: a gagging, choking sound. And then she was in among the trees, and saw.

"You silly little girl," said de Lavoie. "Couldn't even break your neck."

Jenna didn't bother answering; she just hung in the air, above the trees, looking down at the swinging, twitching body as its hands gave a final spasm and then fell away from the noose.

"Choking," he said. "Slow and painful. As you deserve."

And yet she felt no pain, any more than him: she was outside it all, watching that final, bitter victory.

"It could all have been so much better," he snarled at her. "It didn't have to be like this. We could have both had what we wanted."

"Liar." She was aware de Lavoie was nearby, but struggled to perceive his form. She was only dimly aware of her own. She no longer had a body, after all: that was twisting on a rope below her. She had something instead now, but wasn't sure exactly what. To the extent she could perceive it, she did so in terms of arms, legs, head and eyes, but knew that wasn't the reality, just the closest terms of reference available. "You'd have killed Holly, and me. And you've had your time. Not just yours, either. How many people's time have you had? Well, it's all gone now."

De Lavoie snarled. She was beginning to make him out: a sort of swirling distortion, an amorphous airborne stain. At times it seemed about to become a face. One moment she almost saw the man who'd visited her at Stonebrook; the next, the Bonewalker – both the mass of shadows inside the cowl with its pale glowing eyes, and the reptilian skull she'd seen at the very end. "Centuries," he whispered. "I'd seen so many centuries. Knowledge. Memories."

"Nothing of worth," Jenna told him placidly, knowing it was true – although even if it wasn't, it gave him no rights over her life or body, or anyone else's.

De Lavoie snarled again. His form was dark and somehow toxic; the darkness was as much his rage as anything else, and she took grim satisfaction in it.

"You're done," she said. She realised she was drifting up away from him, and that washes of greyness were sweeping across the scene below, like windblown dust. The Greylands; the place between dream and death. She was passing through them, perhaps, on her way to whatever lay beyond. "Whatever else happens, I finished you."

"Oh?" he crooned suddenly; there was a new and suddenly triumphant note in his voice. "Are you quite sure?"

Jenna looked down through the blurring grey, and saw Holly run screaming towards the hanging corpse.

"No, no, no no no no no–"

Holly panted it like a breathless mantra, crashing through leaf-mould and undergrowth towards the tree. She could see the whole scene with pitiless clarity – the knapsack laid neatly at the foot of the tree, the rope so carefully fastened and tied, and the glimmer of the red-gold hair above the leather jacket. Jeans stained dark where the bladder had let go and maybe worse, and boots, one still twitching, swinging to and fro above the ground.

"You silly cow, you silly cow–" And then she was too busy scrambling up onto the fallen tree and clutching at the swinging legs to speak. She pulled the body against her, pushed up against its weight to slacken the rope around its neck.

She dug her Swiss Army knife out, fumbling awkwardly at its saw-toothed blade with the same hand clutching Jenna's legs. It took Holly so long she was sure she must be too late, but at last the blade opened and she began cutting at the rope, the blade working through it with maddening slowness.

De Lavoie was laughing and laughing as his substance poured, like a flood of effluence, back down through the air and the grey haze towards Jenna's body. Whatever was pulling Jenna away wasn't affecting him. "I'll fix it, I'll fix it," he was cackling. "Patch the body up, good as new."

Could he? No reason to suppose not. No wonder he was laughing; in Jenna trying to destroy him once and for all, de Lavoie had won – and thanks above all to the intervention of the person Jenna had done this to save. He'd take her body over, then kill Holly, make himself immortal again and–

No. No way. Not on my fucking watch.

She strained against the current that was trying to lift her beyond the Greylands. It pulled at her, trying to hold on, but somehow she broke free. She flailed for a moment, directionless, struggling to control her new form before the pull could resume. She was newly born into this shape, clumsy and unsteady, but at last she managed to direct herself downwards in a swooping dive to intercept de Lavoie, screaming, "Get away from her, you–"

Something smashed into her, flinging her aside, her vaporous, invisible form literally flying through the trees like smoke, and beyond them through the earth and down into the rock beneath. She might have hurtled away forever into the depths of the world – maybe beyond, into the empty vastness of space – had she not fought to arrest herself, battling the force behind the blow just as she'd resisted that other, gentler pull from above.

Halting herself at last, she propelled herself back towards the surface, towards the woods, back the way she'd come, towards de Lavoie.

The stain on the air that was his soul had gathered around the head of the hanging figure; Holly continued struggling to cut the rope, oblivious to the struggle taking place around her. Jenna cannoned into de Lavoie; the collision forced him away from the body. He struck at her and tried to envelop her; she tried to envelop him and struck at him in turn, and for a moment the two of them were one, like two clouds of mingled smoke.

It was brief, but equally appalling to them both. At the same time, Jenna couldn't allow him to escape her. She kicked and punched and tore at de Lavoie to drive him away: at least, those were the closest analogues she could think of to what she tried to do. But wherever she tried to strike him, he evaded or parried the blow, before retaliating each time with one that smashed into Jenna from a completely different angle. She was punched and kicked, choked and crushed, swung and wrenched, and through it all he laughed.

"You can't beat me here," shouted de Lavoie. "Silly girl. Silly, silly little girl. You wouldn't even know how."

A final blow shocked through her. She wasn't even sure what it was he'd done, but it had paralysed her and sent her tenuous substance spinning upwards, unable to resist as the current laid hold of her again.

Jenna rose upwards. Drifts of grey swept through her vision again, over the scene below, but not thickly enough to obscure the sight of de Lavoie, howling in triumph, as he descended to take possession of his prize.

The rope snapped. Jenna's body flopped forward, across Holly. Holly struggled to maintain her balance, but it was a lost cause, and the two of them crashed to the ground.

"Fuck, fuck, fuck." Holly was bruised but nothing more. *More padding to soak up the bumps: stick that up your jumper, Weight*

Watchers. But if Jenna had struck her head she could've cracked her skull, and then even if Holly had been in time, she might have failed after all.

But there was no sign of a head injury, so Holly concentrated on getting the noose from around Jenna's neck and checking the airway was clear, all the while whispering: "Don't be dead, babe, don't be dead." Feeling the throat for a pulse, feeling the heart for a beat, blowing into the open mouth. *Don't be dead, babe; don't be dead. Please, anything, only don't be dead.*

Then looking up, as she felt a darkening in the air.

The world below Jenna was dissolving in the grey haze, beginning to fade from view.

Until something stopped her. Not a blow: a gentle, cushioning softness that slowed her ascent to a standstill. And there was a voice – voices – saying – ***Easy, girl; You're safe, girl; We're here, girl; All will now be well.***

Other presences darted downwards, past Jenna. They were bright as angels, lithe as sharks, pitiless as both, and they fastened themselves onto what had been Robert de Lavoie.

And de Lavoie began to scream.

At first Jenna thought it was their faces: they were familiar ones, after all, those of the men, women and children he'd "absorbed" over the centuries. But no, it was more than that: they not only had hold of him but were bearing him upwards, into the hazy grey above. And there was real terror in his cries.

Between death and dream, between the sacred silence and sleep. That was what he'd called the Greylands. A boundary place between the realms of the living and the dead. Through which, sometimes, you could slip from one to the other. Especially if there were enough of you, with enough of a shared purpose. Like taking someone where he should have gone centuries before.

Jenna was being pressed downwards now. And still the voices whispered: *Now, girl; Rest, girl; Easy, girl; It's done now, truly. Our thanks, girl; You freed us, girl; Fought for us, girl; And won*.

They pressed Jenna down till something caught hold of her, a kind of gravity. She hurtled back towards the wooded slope, the body on the ground, the small kneeling figure that sobbed beside it. A sea of faces was above her, fading back into the Greylands' mist. Among them was one Jenna hadn't seen in fifteen years, since that night on Tallstone Hill. Her mother was looking down.

And Elaine McKnight was smiling.

A hoarse, wheezing gasp. Air sucked into lungs. Coughing, choking, retching. And then the limp body moved; the eyes flickered open, and focused on the face above her.

"Holl?" A hoarse, rough croak.

"Jenn?" A small voice, piping, barely daring to hope.

"Yeah." A weak smile. "Me. He's gone, sweetheart. He's fucking gone."

Jenna knew that beyond doubt. Her throat and hand throbbed, but the weight of de Lavoie's clinging presence was gone, and the difference was like that between night and day. She had a life again: however long or short, it would be hers alone. And Holly's, if Holly wanted that.

Jenna reached up and tried to touch Holly's face with her uninjured hand. Holly slapped her hand away, then gripped it tight, her free hand clenched into a fist, laughing and crying all at once. "Don't you ever, ever, *ever* fucking do that to me again," she said at last. "Don't you fucking ever."

"Don't worry." Jenna reached up again; this time Holly let her. *Forever after all, perhaps*, Jenna thought, stroking the soft skin of Holly's cheek; *forever and a day*. "I won't."

Needing only this moment, inside this skin.
Lisa Baird

ACKNOWLEDGMENTS

My wonderful wife, Cate Gardner, for listening to the original version of this beast and putting up with my weird obsessions. I love you, and you mean the world to me.

My agent Meg Davis, my editor Simon Spanton, publicity genius Caroline Lambe, Amy Portsmouth, Desola Coker and everyone else at Angry Robot.

My beta readers, led by the ever-reliable Emma Bunn. Lizzy Cooper, Rachel Verkade, Hannah Dennerly especially, for sharing their experiences as bi or queer women.

Rachel Verkade (again!,) Sammy HK Smith, Nicola Monaghan, Caroline Smyth and the wonderful Priya 'Poppins' Sharma, for medical and fertility-related advice.

Anything I've got right is thanks to the people named above. Any errors are mine alone.

Lisa Baird, for kind permission to quote from her poems. The opening and closing epigraphs come from 'The Guide Books Were Wrong' and 'These Hot Days' respectively; the lines Jenna recalls throughout the book are taken from 'Sweat Sweetens It.'

Ladytron, Doro Pesch and Venom, for the music.

Bloggers, vloggers, YouTubers and other reviewers: (takes deep breath) John Mauro at Grimdark Magazine, Lezlie Smith at the Nerdy Narrative, Tammy at Books, Bones and Buffy, Laura McMenemy at Terror Tree, Yvonne at The Coy Caterpillar, Sam Tyler at SFBook Reviews, Tony Jones at

Horror DNA, Matthew Cavanaugh (the mighty Womble!) at Runalong The Shelves, Lynn at Lynn's Book Blog, Alex at Spells and Spaceships, Elloise Hopkins at the British Fantasy Society, Eric Primm at Strange Horizons, David Niall Wilson, Andrew Wallace at Life in Sci-Fi, Liz Robinson at LoveReading, Dave at Espresso Coco, Lori at She Treads Softly, Paul Holmes at The Eloquent Page, Kam at Kam Reads and Recs, Alexis M. Collazzo at Neon Splatter, David Royce at Horror Reads, Tina at Sound and Fury Book Reviews and, of course, Lisa Tuttle at the Guardian. You guys are all amazing.

Anyone whose kindness, advice or help I have forgotten to acknowledge here.

And, of course, anyone who bought a copy of this or of The Hollows. Especially you.

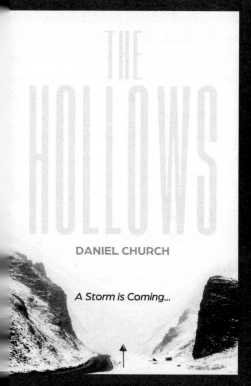

1.

White sky stretched from Wakeman's Edge, across the wedge-shaped valley of Thursdale, to Slapelow Hill. Drystone walls and bare black trees marked the blanket of snow; nothing broke the silence. The only signs of life were a police Land Rover parked halfway up the hill road, and a policewoman in a grey fur hat, peering over the crash barrier.

Ellie crouched and squinted down the slope. The man lay on one side, doubled up around the base of a tree in the beech coppice below. He wore a donkey jacket, jeans and Wellington boots, dusted by the snow that clogged his tangled hair and covered his upturned face.

The air was clear and sharp, the afternoon cold and still.

The two hikers who'd called it in were huddled together in the back of the Land Rover. Only idiots went blundering around the Peaks in this weather; at least stumbling over the corpse had stopped them from getting lost in the snow while Ellie and Tom Graham spent the night out looking for them. Or adding two more bodies to this year's total, because some idiot always thought he or she knew better – especially, for some reason, when it came to this part of the Peak District. It was usually hikers who came to grief, although a couple of years ago some amateur archaeologist looking for the ruins of Kirk Flockton had drowned in the marshes on Fendmoor Heath. Every year, it seemed, there was always at least one.

But a body was a body: somebody's husband, somebody's son. Someone, somewhere, would be missing the poor sod.

Hopefully. There was always the possibility that nobody was, a prospect so depressing Ellie never cared to contemplate it for long. Either way the body would be retrieved, but not just yet. Ellie had no intention of risking a Christmas in hospital by trying to shift the body single-handed. Tom was en route, with Milly Emmanuel; Milly would help her move the body and cast an eye over the scene besides.

Ellie tramped back over to her vehicle. She was a small, sturdy woman in her forties, her dark hair salted grey, and there were days where she felt every one of her years and every degree of cold. This was one of them.

In the Land Rover, the boy was crying, the girl hugging him. Ellie softened a little: they were kids, after all. Seventeen, maybe eighteen at the outside: Richard would be that old now, if he'd lived. Better she was called out for them because of this than because they were injured or dying.

Ellie opened the Land Rover's tailgate, making the kids start at the sudden sound. Knowing she'd be out for a while, she'd filled two flasks before setting off and stowed them in the back; she took them out and shut the tailgate, then opened the driver's door. "Hot chocolate?"

"Please," the girl said.

Ellie handed her a cup. "Careful," she added. "Hot." Which should have been obvious, but she'd learned long ago never to take the general public's intelligence for granted.

The girl cradled the cup and sipped. The boy, wiping his eyes, eyed it with some envy, so Ellie sighed, took the cup from the other flask and poured out a measure for him. "Let's go over it again," she said.

"We weren't going far," said the girl. "I just wanted to show Rick the Height."

Rick: an unwelcome jolt passed through Ellie at the name. Just coincidence, but still unpleasant, after the similarity in the boy's age. The moment passed, and Ellie was glad to see it gone; she leant against the doorframe and breathed out.

"Are you okay?" said the girl.

"Fine," grunted Ellie. The wind was blowing hard along the hill road and making a low, dull moan. She climbed into the front seat and shut the door. "So," she said, "the Height."

"Yeah. You know –" The girl gestured up the road.

"Yeah, I know where it is." Ellie tried not to sound snappish. "Where were you coming from?"

"Wakeman Farm," said the girl, now gesturing down the road.

"Grant and Sally Beck?" said Ellie, then remembered they had a girl away at university. "You're the daughter?"

"Kathleen Beck. Kate." The girl took the boy's arm. "Rick came up to stay. I wanted him to see it."

Ellie nodded. Maybe the girl, at least, wasn't as thick as she'd thought. Wakeman Farm was close by on Spear Bank, which ran from the bottom of the hill road across Thursdale to the Edge. Even that wasn't without risk in these conditions, but it wasn't as dangerous as a longer hike. "You tell your folks where you were going?"

Kate shrugged.

"You need to," Ellie said. "Main roads are gonna be cut off for the next couple of days, and there's more snow coming. You get caught out in it and get in trouble, right now there's exactly two coppers in the area." Or one, if she included Tom Graham.

The girl's story was simple enough. They'd stopped for a short rest, as the hill road was pretty steep; before setting off again, the boy had gone to the road's edge to study the view, and seen something lying in the snow.

"Took me a few seconds to realise what it was," said the boy, wiping his eyes again and giving Ellie a shy smile. "Sorry about that. Gave me a bit of a shock – never seen anyone dead before."

Town lad – a bit soft, maybe, but polite. Well-mannered. The kind you'd bring home to meet your parents.

"Happens sometimes round here," said Ellie at last. "You get used to it. What happened then?"

"Managed to get a signal," Kate said. "So we called it in."

"Lucky again," said Ellie. "Reception's a nightmare round here, specially when it's like this."

She had no idea what else to say, so she looked out through the windscreen. To her relief, an olive-green BMW X5 came round the hill road's bend and drove down towards them. Barsall Village had two full-time officers and one official vehicle, so at times like this Tom Graham's own 4X4 – a seven-seater SUV, no less, a proper Chelsea tractor – was pressed into service; a blue police light had been hurriedly mounted on the roof, but, as usual, he'd forgotten to switch it on.

The BMW halted beside Ellie's, and Tom got out. "All right, Ell. What have we got?"

Ellie trudged over and pointed. "Body, Sarge."

"Oh, yes." He scratched the back of his neck. "You did say."

He looked lost – as usual – so Ellie, once again, stepped in. "The young lady and gentleman over there found him. I thought if you took them back to the station and got their statements, Dr Emmanuel and I can retrieve the body."

"Oh. Yeah. Makes sense." Tom gave the kids an amiable if vacant smile, then frowned at Ellie, or more accurately the fur hat. "For God's sake, will you stop wearing that bloody thing on duty?"

"It keeps my head warm and the regulation cap doesn't. I like having ears."

"I wouldn't mind so much if you'd take *that* off it." He had a point, given that the hat was Soviet-era Red Army surplus, complete with a hammer-and-sickle-emblazoned red star badge Ellie had never trusted herself to remove without tearing a gaping hole. "Ernie Stasiolek's gonna think you're the bloody Stasi one of these days and take a pot at you."

"Ernie Stasiolek's Polish, Tom. The Stasi were East German."

"All right, clever clogs." Tom took a step towards the kids and called out. "This way, you two. Nice cup of tea when we get in, eh?"

He probably hadn't even noticed the cups they were already holding, but you could never have enough hot drinks on a day like this. The kids followed him back to the X5 as Milly Emmanuel climbed out of it, hidden under multiple layers of clothing culminating in a neon pink puffa jacket and matching ski-hat that rendered her almost globular. She waved to Ellie and waddled over as Tom managed a clumsy three-point turn before driving back up the hill road towards Barsall.

"Afternoon, Constable," she called.

"All right, Doc. Got enough layers on?"

"It's all right for you. My Dad was from Jamaica, remember? I'm not half fucking penguin like you are. So where's the patient?"

Ellie pointed. Milly peered over the crash barrier. "Think we might be a bit late to help."

"What would I do without you?"

"Many a true word."

"Oh, sod off."

"So what's the plan? Please tell me you can call someone in."

Ellie shook her head. "Phone and radio reception's up and down like a whore's drawers and the main roads are snowed up anyway."

Milly groaned. "Don't suppose we could just shovel a bit more snow over him and leave him till the spring?"

"I wish."

"Great. So, heavy lifting duty, then?"

"That and your medical expertise, Doc."

"I'm not a pathologist –"

"You're the closest I've got."

"Fair enough." Milly's breath billowed in the air. "But you'd better have some decent wine in for later."

"Do my best. Got some hot chocolate in the meantime, if you want it."

They got in the Land Rover and Ellie drove down to the bottom of the hill road. She cleared space in the back, spread a blanket out there, folded another over her arm and picked up a small black pack. She opened it and checked the contents – latex gloves, evidence baggies, a pair of small flashlights – then slung it over her shoulder and turned away. Ellie wasn't expecting to find any evidence of foul play – chances were a drunk had slipped and fallen on the path, and the cold had done the rest – but it was best to be prepared.

Milly had already climbed over the crash barrier and was waiting. Ellie climbed after her. Intermittent snow drifted down. Ahead of them a narrow footpath ran along the hillside, past the edge of the Harpers' land, towards the silent trees.

We are Angry Robot, your favourite independent, genre-fluid publisher, bringing you the very best in sci-fi, fantasy, horror and everything in between!

Check out our website at www.angryrobotbooks. com to see our entire catalogue.

Follow us on social media:
Twitter @angryrobotbooks
Instagram @angryrobotbooks
TikTok @angryrobotbooks

Sign up to our mailing list now: